SAVANNA

Operation Stargate

Herbert Grosshans

SAVANNA
Copyright © 2019 by Herbert Grosshans

ISBN: 978-1-68046-760-4

Melange Books, LLC
White Bear Lake, MN 55110
www.melange-books.com

Published in the United States of America.

Cover Design by Ashley Redbird Designs

OPERATION STARGATE NOVELS

Codename Salamander

Savanna

[1]

Jeremy John Sheppard stuffed his duffle bag into the overhead compartment and took his seat on the shuttle that would take him down to the surface of Savanna.

He was happy to see the long journey through space come to an end and to soon assume his new position on Outpost Alpha. One month cooped up in a transporter far from being a luxury liner, with a bunch of eager fortune hunters, scientists, and settlers looking for a new life on an alien planet, was one month too long.

"Hey, Sheppard," a familiar voice said beside him. "I just realized something. All this time on the ship you never told me about your plans on Savanna."

Sheppard turned his head to look at the short, stocky man who had taken the seat beside him, a man he had no particular wish to associate with. "What makes you think I would have told you?"

Daniels chuckled. "As always, the mystery man. Are you by any chance one of the convicted criminals they send to frontier planets to serve out their sentence doing hard labor?"

"Hardly." Sheppard had no intention telling the man details about his life. It was nobody's business, especially not Daniels'.

"Let me take a guess. You're, obviously, not a scientist. Neither are you a farmer, since you're traveling alone. You claim you're not a convict. That only leaves miner, fortune-hunter, scout, or Space Force. Or might you be a doctor?" He shook his head. "No. Not a doctor. You don't have the slim, cultured hands of a medical professional." He gave Sheppard an inquiring look. "Well? Am I close?"

Before Sheppard could respond, a voice over the speaker said, "Please, fasten your seatbelts. We'll be lifting off in a moment. The ride will be a bit rough. We've detected some turbulence in the upper atmosphere, but there is nothing to be worried about. This is just an advisory."

"This is so typical," Daniels commented. "Why does the government hire a private company to take settlers to an alien planet? It's all about profits. They don't invest any money in upgrading. This shuttle is an outdated version and shouldn't be used any longer. Turbulence in the atmosphere shouldn't even be an issue."

Sheppard was happy for the subject change. "Whatever gave you the idea that Earth's government actually cares about settlers? They are happy to get rid of a few people, and they don't give a crap to which planet they migrate or if they survive. Savanna is far from the regular trade routes and too close to Spider-controlled space. The Solar Union doesn't have much interest in colonizing the planet. The only ships coming here are the ships of the Trading Commission and the ones bringing new settlers."

"I know all about that. It's the abundance of blue diamonds that attracted the Trading Commission, never mind that Savanna is an ideal planet for humans to colonize."

Sheppard chuckled grimly. "Are you forgetting that Savanna is already occupied?"

"You mean the Cats?" Daniels grunted. "From what I understand, they are not numerous. This planet is sparsely populated. There is plenty of room for us humans."

"What about the reptilian humanoids living in the jungle? Don't they count? Or the desert-dwellers? Don't they have a right to live unmolested?"

"Sure, they do, but that's how the universe works, my friend. A superior species invades a region and, as their numbers grow, eliminating the weaker or less advanced species. If you know your history, you know how the Americas were colonized."

"I'm not ignorant of Earth's bloody history. Millions of indigenous people were murdered by the Spaniards, the English, and the French in the name of their king. What audacity. To land on the shores of a foreign land, plant a flag, and claim it in the name of a king or queen? What gave them the right? Sadly, nothing has changed to this day. Take Chrysalis, for instance. The inhabitants were wiped off the planet's surface, because they refused to buckle under and work in the mines for the humans."

"Bad example, Sheppard. They were murdering the colonists in their sleep. They burned down whole villages, killing all the humans in their homes. They destroyed crops and poisoned the water. We had no choice. It was either them or us."

"We could have left," Sheppard argued.

Daniels laughed. "Are you kidding? That planet was full of valuable resources Earth desperately needed." He gave Sheppard a sidelong glance. "What the hell are you? Some kind of priest or do-gooder?"

"I am neither." Sheppard sighed and leaned back into his seat. "I'm going to take a rest and calm my nerves. I know I'll need them when I get down there." He closed his eyes, ignoring Daniels, but there was no opportunity to relax.

The advisory had not misled them. They did get into turbulence, and the shuttle was rocked back and forth with sudden drops that made Sheppard question the ability of whoever sat in the pilot seat. Most likely it wasn't even a human pilot. The sounds of protest and subdued curses from the other passengers didn't help, either. A couple of children were crying, and their mothers tried to convince them there was nothing to worry about. One woman shouted that everyone was going to die, that God didn't approve of humans leaving their planet of birth to spread the evil that was humanity to other planets.

"Somebody should tell that stupid woman to shut up," Daniels cursed beside Sheppard, who was not going to argue that point.

The shaking stopped, and the rest of the flight was relatively calm. Sheppard wished for windows to see the landscape below them, but the walls of the shuttle were smooth and unbroken. He had no idea if it was day or night on this side of the planet.

"Did I tell you I'm an engineer?"

"More than once." Sheppard sighed. He was looking forward to being rid of the forever talking Daniels. From the beginning of the journey, the man had latched onto him like a magnet to a piece of metal, difficult to remove. He had to listen to Daniels' life story at least half a dozen times. To make it worse, it was a boring story.

"My specialty is bridges."

"I know that, too."

Daniels wasn't discouraged. "Did I ever mention that I designed a bridge on Backwater?"

"You might have. I'm sorry, I don't remember."

"Then let me refresh your memory. It is actually a funny story."

"I believe I remember it now. It that the one where the monkey-like natives were the first ones to cross the bridge?" Sheppard had no intention to listen to it again.

"That's the one. I just love telling it." Daniels chuckled. "Perhaps you would like to hear it again?"

Sheppard took a deep breath and exhaled slowly. "Perhaps another time, Daniels. Right now, is not a good time."

"Does that mean you and I will stay in touch?"

"We'll see. It's a big planet."

"Almost as big as Earth. Apparently, Savanna is not much different from Earth. I mean it's got seasons, and the weather is pretty much the same. Fewer oceans, which means more landmass, which is great." He chuckled. "Also, plenty of rivers where bridges are needed. I shall be busy."

"I wish you luck." Sheppard smiled thinly. "Remember, this is not Earth. Neither is it Backwater."

Again, he was saved by an announcement. "We are approaching Crystal City and will be landing in fifteen minutes. Please, make sure you're wearing your seatbelt. Good luck to everyone. It has been a pleasure to be of service."

"As if a computer experiences pleasure," Daniels said with contempt. "I'm looking forward to living in a society that is not run by computers. That's one of the reasons I left Earth and came to Savanna. Life will be more relaxed and basic here. That will be *my* pleasure."

"I hope you won't be disappointed. Life on a frontier world is not a picnic. It can be harsh and difficult," Sheppard commented.

"You've had experience?"

"I have." Sheppard didn't elaborate. The sudden complete silence and lack of vibration told him that the shuttle had landed. He unbuckled and waited for the announcement telling the passengers to disembark. A slight breeze in the air signalled that the outer doors had been opened. The announcement came a moment later. "Time to go," he said.

He waited for Daniels to get his personal luggage bag before getting his own, and then he followed the short man to the air-lock. The air entering the shuttle smelled fresh and crisp, and he was looking forward to breathing real air instead of the recycled air in the transporter for the past month.

Taking a deep breath, he climbed down the steps toward the alien soil of a new frontier world. It wasn't his first time on a new world, but this time it was different. He was not here of his own free choice.

Looking around the spaceport, he saw more than a dozen shuttles standing on the tarmac. Theirs had been the last one to leave. Some of the shuttles carried passengers, most of them new colonists looking for a better life. A number of shuttles carried only supplies and the belongings of the colonists.

Sheppard shouldered his large duffle bag, his only possession. Most of what he needed would be supplied.

He bumped into someone and mumbled, "Sorry." Then he realized it was Daniels.

"Hey," Daniels said. "I guess this is where we part ways."

"It seems that way." Sheppard wasn't sorry to see the last of the short, chatty man.

"I think I see my ride."

"Don't you have to go through immigration first?"

Daniels shook his head. "Not me. I have special status. I'm not really an immigrant."

"Neither am I." Sheppard looked and spotted a vehicle speeding toward them. Even from this distance it was clear it was military. Only the military and the Solar Trading Commission were allowed to possess modern weapons and equipment, which included transport vehicles. The small, armored bus stopped in front of the two men. One of the two troopers on board jumped out. He saluted sloppily and said, "Captain Sheppard?"

Sheppard nodded and stepped forward. "That would be me."

The trooper looked at a device in his hand, gave Sheppard one more look and turned his attention to Daniels. "Then you must be Major Daniels," he stated and saluted again.

Daniels waved it off with one hand and chuckled. "I guess I must be. Relax, trooper. Let's not get too formal."

Sheppard threw him an astonished look. "I thought you were an engineer?"

With a smile, Daniels said, "I am. I just forgot to mention that I'm an engineer with the Solar Union Space Navy. So, you're a Captain. Hmm. The mystery man has been unmasked. It seems we'll be seeing much more of each other in the future." He made a motion with his hand. "After you, Captain Sheppard."

Sheppard took his seat with some misgivings. Major Daniels! That meant Daniels was his superior.

2

"There he is," Kristie Collins said to her husband. She was the first one to spot the man they were looking for.

Dennis Collins followed his wife's pointing finger and saw a bearded man holding up a sign with the name Collins in bold letters on it. "Let's go," he said, grabbed his big backpack, and headed for the man who was going to take them to his ranch, according to their immigration papers. His wife, daughter, and two sons followed him at a slower pace.

The man watched them coming closer. His face was hidden in the shadow of his wide-brimmed hat, and his features were not clear, but Collins noted he was dark-skinned. He also took notice of the large holstered gun hanging from a wide belt on the man's right hip. The woman standing beside him was small and slim. She had her black hair tied behind her head.

"Nelson Haggard?" Collins gave the man a questioning look. He had expected him to look much older.

The man held out a hand. "The name's Herman Sanchez. Nelson couldn't make it. He's not in the best of health." He smiled, showing a gap of a couple of missing front teeth. "Old age does that to you. He asked me to pick up you folks. You must be Dennis Collins."

Collins nodded. "This is my wife, Kristie, my daughter, Lisa, my sons, Traverse and Randolph."

"Welcome to Savanna," Sanchez said and indicated the woman beside him. "My sister, Rosita."

"We are so happy to meet you, and we thank you for picking us up," Kristie said. "I don't know what we'd do if you didn't do this for us."

"Somebody else would'a helped you out," Sanchez said with a little chuckle. "We all help each other. It's the only way to survive." He became serious. "Savanna is not Paradise. I hope you know that."

"We've been briefed," Collins assured him. "We know what to expect."

"I don't believe you do. Our grandparents were briefed before they immigrated here," Sanchez said grimly. "They only show you the positive things, and those are painted in a bright light. Reality tends to be more somber."

"Don't let my brother discourage you," Rosita said. "Ever since Dolores died, he's been in this down mood."

Kristie looked at Sanchez. "Your wife?"

Sanchez nodded. "She died a year ago. She was thrown from her horse and broke her neck." He sniffed, took off his hat, and ran a hand across his head, disheveling his long, black hair even more.

"I'm sorry for your loss." Collins didn't know what else to say. He had never been good with consoling others. His years as a cop had hardened him to the misery of others, the only way to stay sane.

"She was a good woman." Sanchez shrugged. "That's life. She was third generation, just like us. Our parents and grandparents had it much harder than you will have it. You have the advantage of getting advice and help from an established community. I'm not trying to dampen the enthusiasm you must have, just preparing you for what you will face. Enough of that. It's time to introduce you to your new world."

"What about our things?"

"Everything needs to be inspected first before it's released. It'll be a few days. Don't worry. You won't need anything for now. You'll spend the night at our place and tomorrow I'll take you to your new home."

"Your place? Aren't the Haggards expecting us today?"

"The Haggard ranch is more than a day's travel from here. That's the other reason I'm picking up you folks."

Collins hesitated. "How will we know when we can get our things?"

"They'll send a courier. Nothing to worry about."

"I'm not quite sure about that," Collins mused. "They seem a little unorganized in immigrations. At first, they got our names mixed up with someone else. They thought I was Josh Gardner, a miner, and then they wanted to know where our four-year old son was. We only have these two and Lisa. I hope they don't get our stuff mixed up. I was hoping we wouldn't be left stranded here, because it took so long to be processed."

Sanchez chuckled. "Things move at a slower pace here than back on Earth, I'm sure. I didn't mind waiting. The most important thing is you're here now. Let's go."

They followed him to one of the wagons parked on the lot in front of the Immigration Building. Collins had not expected a luxury carriage, but it was still a bit of a shock to see what he could only describe as a large wooden wagon pulled by a couple of giant goat-like animals.

"You don't have any horses?"

"We have but only for riding. Goats are stronger and not as skittish," Sanchez explained. He opened the back of the wagon and pulled down a ladder. "We use this wagon normally for hauling taters. I gave it a good scrubbing and put in a couple of benches for you to sit on. I even brought a few pillows." He glanced at Rosita. "You'll have to thank my sister for suggesting the pillows. She thinks of those things. It won't be as comfortable as the modern vehicles you're used to, but you'll survive the trip. Go on, climb in."

If the Haggard's don't have one, one of the first things I will build is a carriage. This is a bit too primitive for me. He helped his wife climb the ladder.

She gave him a forced smile. "I'm all right," she whispered.

He waited until his daughter and sons sat on the benches and then he loaded up their suitcases. Once the suitcases were safely stowed away, he used the ladder to climb onto the wagon.

Sanchez and his sister took their places in the front, and with a loud "Ho" from Sanchez, the goats started moving.

Even with the pillows, the ride was extremely rough. The road they traveled on was just trampled dirt with ruts and holes, and the wagon bounced all over the place. It didn't matter. Inhaling deeply, he concentrated on the fresh air entering his lungs, relished in the feeling of joy as he realized that they had arrived. This was it, the beginning of a new life, the start of a new future.

Collins could see the city to the south. At least, he assumed it was south, judging by the position of the primary in the sky. A few clouds covered the blue sky, and he felt a tinge of homesickness, thinking of Earth, but only a tinge. Even though only a month had passed, it seemed forever since they boarded the huge starship that brought his family and the other settlers to Savanna.

According to the many presentations they had watched and listened to, Savanna's temperature and weather were nearly identical to Earth's. Even the vegetation wasn't so much different. Trees, shrubs, and a variety of grasses grew everywhere and flowers. The mountains in the distance glowed white, which indicated snow, and tall grass covered the flat land that stretched to all sides and was lost near the horizon. It was not unlike the prairies in the American West must have been centuries ago before much of the land on Earth was used for building large cities.

Of course, there'd be many things that would be different, like the animals and the indigenous people. He expected challenges, and he was prepared to face them.

He didn't regret making the decision to take his family to a frontier planet. Earth was overpopulated, the air and water polluted, and life on humanity's birthplace was difficult and with an uncertain future for the average citizen.

He was only forty-three years old and had, hopefully, many years left to make a life for himself and his family on this new planet. He needed to put his past behind him, forget about the violence, the dangers, and constant threats he and his family faced because of his profession. His children deserved a good life and a safe and secure future.

It was strange to see nothing but grass and trees along the way and no signs of civilization anywhere. He had to get used to this.

"It seems you'll be getting your first chance to meet members of the *Cats* in a moment," Sanchez said suddenly. He turned around in his seat and looked at Collins. "I want you folks to just sit quiet and say nothing. We don't want any misunderstandings that could lead to some kind of confrontation. We've got things under control, and things will go smoothly if you follow instructions. Understood?"

"Not really," Collins said with a glance at the shotgun Sanchez had lying beside him. Rosita held another one across her lap.

A sudden feeling of danger rushed down his spine and brought back unpleasant memories. His ears detected the screaming sound of some kind of beast, and when he looked to the east, he saw a small herd of animals with curved horns coming toward them. From the many vids they had watched he recognized them as alck. The indigenous people used them as riding animals, and then he could make out the riders sitting astride the broad backs of their black-coated steeds.

When he saw the long-bows, he wished he had a weapon, any kind of weapon, but preferably a laser.

A hand squeezing his arm in a painful grip. "I'm scared," Kristie whispered.

"According to what we were told, they are peaceful," he assured his wife, but looking at the band of natives coming closer, he did not feel convinced by his own words.

Traverse and Randolph didn't seem concerned. He received the impression they were curious and even a little bit excited to meet their first aliens. They had never before seen living members of an extra-terrestrial race.

His daughter, Lisa, put on a brave mask, but he could see the fear in her green eyes.

"Remember, don't make any sudden moves and keep your hands in plain sight," Sanchez warned.

The riders swarmed around the wagon.

Collins counted fourteen. He had seen pictures of them, but seeing them close in real life was not the same as watching three-dimensional images.

Their muscular upper torsos and legs were bare, with only a strip of animal skin around their loins and hips. They looked savage and intimidating. Fine fur covered the chest and face of the one closest. Sharp fangs gleamed white in his open mouth, and his golden eyes with their slit pupils lent him the ferocity of a feral predator as he stared at Collins.

Collins stared back but refrained from saying or doing anything, not even smile. It might be construed as a threatening gesture. They had not been briefed enough about the behavior and traditions of these natives.

They didn't wear any head coverings. A thick row of stiff bristles ran from the front of their head down to the nape of their neck.

The one confronting Collins turned his attention to Sanchez. "Human!" He spoke with a harsh voice. "You have not paid your tribute."

"We are just now beginning to put seeds into the ground," Sanchez said. "Come back at the end of summer for the early harvest. We'll have something ready for you."

"We will come." The native eyed Collins again. "You bring more humans to our world," he stated curtly.

Collins did not miss the threat in his words.

"They just arrived. They will be taking over the Haggard ranch. It will be a good thing for the Clan of the Valley-riders," Sanchez said calmly, but Collins saw his white knuckles where he gripped his shotgun.

"Too many humans already on the world of the Sun-people. Don't need more."

"This is a big world, Cloud-rider. There is enough room for all of us." Sanchez chuckled softly. "Humans are supplying you with many good things, and it's all free. All you have to do is come and get it. We expect nothing in return. How much better can it get?"

"Not free," the alien growled. "If not for us, humans would be fighting the tribes of the Mountain-Claws. They are not as peaceful as the Valley-riders. We protect."

He made a harsh sound and turned his mount around. Without another word, he rode off, followed by his companions.

Sanchez let out a loud sigh. "Welcome to the real world of Savanna. The one they don't tell you about."

"They certainly didn't. What's going on?"

"As you will find out soon enough, Savanna is not the ideal, peaceful world the government agencies on Earth are letting colonists believe. Far from it. The planet itself may be an ideal planet, but it's a different story with the indigenous population. Humans are not welcome here. We are invading their world, and more than a few are fighting back. It is a losing battle for them, even though they are not aware of it. They are brave and savage fighters, cunning and devious, but not devious enough. They'll be squeezed out and eventually either be absorbed into the world we are creating, or they will disappear. It will take time, but it will happen. It has happened on our own home world and many of the planets humans have or are colonizing. Let's face it, humans are an invasive species."

"I never thought of it that way," Lisa said.

Collins looked at his daughter. "Nobody thinks of it that way, sweetheart. We humans may think of ourselves as civilized, but that is only a disguise. Deep down, we are as savage as those natives we just met. If you knew the things I saw and had to do, you would have nightmares. Why do you think I quit my job and became a farmer? And why I brought my family to an alien planet?"

She shrugged. "We left a civilized world behind to exchange it for one that is wild and untamed. I hope I like it here."

"At least, it won't be as crowded," Traverse said. "We can deal with a bunch of naked savages." He looked at Sanchez. "Right, Mr. Sanchez?"

Sanchez nodded grimly. "We can. We are." He patted his shotgun. "Superior firepower helps against their bows and arrows, but don't let that fool you. They are experts with those bows and other primitive weapons they have. Unfortunately, there are some unscrupulous men among us humans who have no problem selling prohibited weapons and ammunition to the natives." He gave Collins a long, thoughtful look before he spoke again. "Life is not easy here, but we can make it, as long as we humans stick together. However, the natives are not the only ones who make life miserable. There are others who have an interest in Savanna."

"Are you talking about the Spiders?"

"Not so much the Spiders. They are here, but they haven't given us any problems—yet. It's the Snaar. They've been coming to Savanna and openly abduct young Cats. So far, they've left us alone, but it's only a matter of time. Someday, one of their shuttles will pay us a visit, and there is nothing we'll be able to do. They have the superior weapons, because of the stupid law the union enforces on us by restricting the types of weapons we can import."

"There is a reason for that law," Traverse injected. "We've learned about that at the information sessions. Every planet is classified according to the level of development the native population has achieved. Savanna's population is still primitive, and modern weapons are therefore prohibited. Should they be given those kinds of weapons, it would only cause unnecessary bloodshed."

Sanchez let out a barking laugh. "Unnecessary bloodshed?" He turned in his seat and looked at Traverse. "Don't be naïve, young man. You don't need advanced weaponry to kill people. Stones, clubs, and knives made from flint are all you need. The Snaar don't worry about using lasers and flash rifles. They have them and use them. Neither do any of the other alien races dropping in for a look-around."

"You have a shotgun. Isn't that considered a modern weapon?" Randolph commented.

"Sure, if you go back a thousand years. On Earth, it's considered an antique just like the six-shooter on my hip and the single-shot rifles we're allowed to possess."

"Better than a bow and arrow," Randolph insisted.

"I guess it is." Sanchez shrugged and wiped his forehead with the sleeve of his shirt. "As I said, we have many problems to deal with, and then there's the Trading Commission. It controls the trade on Savanna. Everything that happens goes through the Commission. It also handles and controls the money and the bank."

"You'll have to explain the monetary system," Collins said.

"You'll learn soon enough. For now, let's just get to our place and out of this heat."

"Good idea," his sister said beside him with a little chuckle. "Besides, my butt is beginning to hurt."

The wagon rolled on down the uneven road. Collins moved in his seat, his thoughts much more somber than at the beginning of their journey.

They crossed another road. In the distance, he could see a small forest and what appeared to be buildings. He was just about to ask Sanchez about the buildings when Sanchez turned around and said, "That's my daughter's place. She and my son-in-law, Josef Gardner, have an orchard. They're growing a variety of fruit trees. The land around here is quite fertile. Once you're settled, I will take you to meet them. You'll like Josef. He's an ambitious man."

"I'm looking forward to it," Collins said. *Right now, I wouldn't mind getting off this damn wagon. My backside is beginning to suffer from the beating it's receiving.* He didn't voice his desire, asking instead, "Is it still far to your ranch?"

"Another fifteen minutes and we'll be there," Sanchez assured him.

Collins happened to look has his daughter, who sat across from him. She gave him a crooked smile. "It's about time," she mouthed. "I'm getting sore."

He nodded. "Soon," he said. "It'll be over soon."

Sanchez had been close with his estimation. They turned into another side-road. It wasn't any better than the main road, but the thought that their ordeal was coming to an end made it bearable.

As they traveled toward the collection of structures, Collins watched a small herd of cattle grazing in the field. A couple of riders sitting on animals with thick, curved horns watched over them. In the field behind him, a group of workers picked something off the ground and deposited it into small baskets. One of the workers walked behind what appeared to be a large tiller drawn by a giant goat. They were too far away to make out what they were collecting.

"What are they harvesting at this time of year?"

"Parras. Edible roots. They are at their best when picked in the spring. Once they've been collected, we'll start seeding taters."

The ranch consisted of one large building, obviously the main house, a couple of slightly smaller buildings, one of them clearly a barn, and a number of small units. The yard looked well-maintained. Wagons of different designs and sizes stood in the yard, but no modern farm machinery. Everything looked primitive, and he was reminded again that Savanna was on the list of low-tech planets where modern equipment was not allowed.

When the wagon stopped, he rose and jumped to the ground. He waited for Traverse and Randolph do the same thing, and then he put the ladder against the back and helped his wife and daughter down.

All of them walked around on stiff legs and stretched.

"I thought we'd never get here." Kristie stomped her feet. "My legs are asleep," she complained.

"Sorry about the rough ride," Sanchez said behind them. He took off his hat and slapped it against his leg. "The road's dusty at this time of year. It hasn't rained for a while."

"I can just imagine the condition of the road after a rain," Collins commented.

"It gets kinda muddy," Sanchez agreed. He grinned. "I usually avoid traveling for a couple of days after a rain, but sometimes you got no choice. Then, all you can hope for is not to get stuck in the mud."

"Let's get you into the house," his sister said. "You folks must be hungry and thirsty."

"I admit I am," Kristie said. "And tired."

Grateful to get out of the sun, Collins and his family followed Rosita into the house. It was surprisingly cool inside. The layout was different from what he was used to on Earth. They had never lived in luxurious surroundings, and he was pleasantly surprised by the spaciousness of the place. He admired the massive timbers that supported the high ceiling and fireplace made from stones that dominated one wall. Everything was more primitive but functional. The furniture was made from real wood, obviously handcrafted and not molded out of plastic and steel in some factory.

"Don't stand there gawking." Rosita told them.

3

"WHAT DID YOU SAY YOU DID ON EARTH?" SANCHEZ CUT OFF A piece of meat and stuffed it into his mouth. Then he took a swig from a huge mug. Looking expectantly at Collins, he wiped the foam from his beard.

"Actually, I never said, but to satisfy your curiosity, I worked at a state-owned farm for the last couple of years, as did Kristie."

"Before that?"

Collins hesitated before he answered. "I was a law enforcement officer."

"Hm." Sanchez grunted and took another swig. "A good government job. Why did you quit?" He eyed Collins with one eye closed. "Or did you?"

"Believe me, I did. The job was taking its toll. You can only take so much violence before it gets to you. I wanted to leave before I lost my sanity and humanity."

"So, you became a farmer. Why?"

"That's easy," Kristie injected. "To learn about farming. We applied for immigration status when Dennis quit his job. We didn't care where they sent us. Any colony would do. It didn't matter which one, as long as we got off Earth."

"Why?"

She laughed. "You are full of questions, Mr. Sanchez. We figured that's what colonists do on a new planet. To work the soil, to grow your own vegetables, fruit, and other crops, like grain and corn. There is always demand for food." She lifted her shoulders. "To be honest, I don't really know. We thought it would be nice to own land and work it. What can be better than that?"

"Many things. Farming is hard work. Physically and mentally. You depend on the weather mostly. It can be a frustrating business. If you manage to have a good harvest, you need someone to buy the crops from you." His chuckle was not enthusiastic. "Here on Savanna, it's the Trades Commission that negotiates the price, and it always ends up their favor. You'll find out. By the way, call me Herman. Nobody calls me Mister Sanchez."

Kristie gave him a friendly smile. "You can call me Kristie."

"I'm Dennis." Collins looked around the table. "You have a large family, Herman."

Sanchez grinned, displaying the gap between his teeth. "Mine is small compared to some of the other farmers and ranchers. Without children, humans would not flourish here. My oldest, Daniella, is the one with the orchard we passed. The little one with the hair tied into a ponytail is Kalia. She's twelve, pretending to be grown already. Beside her, my sons Roberto and Ronaldo, twenty and seventeen in that order. Emilie is the one with the long hair, and the other one, the one with the large, green eyes is Maria. I have no idea where she gets the green eyes from."

Maria laughed. "You told me I inherited them from Great-grandmother Maria Moon. You named me after her."

"So, the story goes." Sanchez gave her a fond smile.

Collins pointed at the food on his plate. "I suppose, you grow these tubers?"

Sanchez nodded. "And others. These are genetically engineered taters. They grow well in Savanna's soil."

"I noticed on the way in that you also have a herd of cattle."

"Just a small herd. Enough for our own supply of milk and meat. That brings me to another subject. What do you know about raising cattle?"

Collins shrugged. "To be truthful—not much. Actually, nothing."

"You are aware that Haggard is a rancher. He raises cattle and horses."

"I know."

"How did you ever get chosen to take over his ranch? I mean, it's a sweet deal. Not many immigrants are that lucky."

"You may or may not know this, but on Earth there are no ranches. All the meat is grown in vats. The land is too valuable to waste on animals. We volunteered for this. We thought it might be exiting and interesting." He smiled. "I have no other skills besides being a cop, but Kristie and I are willing to learn. How hard can it be?"

"How hard indeed." Sanchez emptied his mug and put it down on the wooden surface of the table. His eyes studied Collins. "Are you sure ranching is the only reason you came to Savanna?"

"Of course. What other reason could I possibly have?"

"I wouldn't know. Many, I guess." He rose. "Not my business. Forget it. Perhaps the women can help Rosita with cleaning up the dishes." He looked at his daughters. "Emilie, Maria, go help your mother."

The girls got up. Kristie did the same and gave her own daughter a nod. "Come. You might as well help."

Lisa rose from her seat and followed the others into the kitchen.

Sanchez groped around in his pocket and pulled out a pipe. Then he stuffed some crumpled, dry leaves from a small leather bag into the pipe bowl. Using a light-stick, he lit the leaves and sucked on the pipe. Exhaling a plume of bluish smoke, he sighed and leaned back in his chair. The sweet aroma of whatever Sanchez smoked wafted into Collins' nose, and he unconsciously held his breath for a second.

Sanchez didn't seem to notice his distaste. "Nothing better than the gentle caress of tobacco smoke in your nose to calm your nerves," he said.

"I wouldn't know," Collins said, taking shallow breaths.

Sanchez squinted at him through the small cloud of smoke that surrounded him. "You don't smoke, I suppose."

"Nobody smokes on Earth. It's against the law. The air is already polluted, but, unfortunately, there are unscrupulous individuals everywhere who ignore the law. They don't smoke tobacco, though. It's forbidden to grow. If they can afford it, they'll smoke some kind of drug, but mostly they suck on smokeless artificial cigarettes."

"We don't have to worry about any pollution here on Savanna. The air is pure and sweet, most places anyway. Smoking here is permitted. It is quite popular with the indigenous population." He chuckled. "They grow some mean stuff."

"Is that another vice humans introduced to Savanna?"

"Hell, no. We humans adopted it from them, but nobody wants to smoke what they do. We're growing our own. Somebody, I don't know who, managed to bring real tobacco seeds to Savanna. That was about fifty years ago, and it was next to impossible to get your hands on tobacco, but now it's available everywhere. You should try it."

"No, thank you." Collins suppressed the urge to cough. "I like my lungs to stay clean."

"You sound like my sister. She doesn't approve of my filthy habit as she puts it." He took another puff and then laid his pipe into a clay dish. "I can see you're in distress, my friend. I won't torture you any longer." He cleared his throat and coughed. "You'll have to get used to many things. This is a frontier planet, and you may find people doing stuff that isn't done on Earth, prohibited even on the old home planet. You'll have to adapt if you want to make it here. You can't be timid or judgemental. Remember that."

"I will." Collins stretched and yawned. "I wouldn't mind catching up with my sleep. We didn't sleep much the last couple of days on the ship. Everyone was excited about our new home. We spent hours sitting in front of the display screen watching Savanna growing in size. It's a beautiful sight from space."

"I wouldn't know. Never been in space." Sanchez chuckled. "No reason to unless we wanted to move to another planet, and that won't happen. Once on Savanna, you'll never leave. This is our home and yours now, for better or worse. I hope you know that."

"I'm aware of that. Anything is better than life on Earth. You have no idea how crowded it is."

"No, I don't. I hate crowded places. That's one of the reasons I became a farmer, even though life out here can get lonely sometimes. Newcomers have a difficult time adjusting, and many wish they'd never come here." His gaze fell on Traverse and Randolph, who had been listening to the older men without saying anything. "You boys have been silent. Nothing to say?"

"Plenty," Traverse said with a little smile, "but our dad taught us to listen when older people talk. It's not polite to butt into their conversation."

"It seems your father raised you well. Not all young people are this well-behaved. How old are you anyway, son?"

"I'm nineteen, sir."

Sanchez laughed. "Sir? Nobody ever called me sir. You don't have to call me or anyone on Savanna sir. Besides, you're nineteen. That makes you an adult. Call me Herman. I forgot your name."

"It's Traverse, sir. Sorry, I mean Herman." He smiled. "I'm not used to calling an older man by his first name. It'll take me a while."

Sanchez looked at Randolph. "You're the youngest then. Let me guess. Sixteen?"

Randolph nodded. "That's correct. Turned sixteen a couple of months ago." He grinned. "We were still on Earth then. I'm Randolph, by the way."

"Nineteen and sixteen," Sanchez mused, nodding to himself. "Leave any girlfriends behind?"

Both boys shook their heads. "Nobody special," Traverse said.

"That'll make it easier. You should adapt quickly to the way things are here. It's more difficult for older people like your parents." He rose. "Let's see how the women are doing. Probably yapping their heads off. Rosita gets lonely sometimes, and she'll welcome having someone to talk to besides my daughters. She never got married. It's not easy to find a husband who wants to plant crops or raise cattle or horses. She says she doesn't mind having no husband." He laughed. "A brother who drives her crazy is enough for her. She enjoys working the fields."

They heard the women laughing. As the men walked into the kitchen, the women turned their heads to look at them.

"You're just in time to help us finish drying the dishes," Kristie said.

"Why? You women can't handle the task?" Sanchez smirked.

"She's kidding," his sister said with a laugh. "We're done." To Kristie, she said, "It was nice to talk to someone a little closer to my

21

age. These young girls can get a bit silly sometimes. It's time for them to find a good husband to make mature women out of them."

"*You're* not married," Emilie protested.

"I was never interested in a man. Besides, I'm a mature woman by nature. Didn't need a man to complicate my life."

"But it would be all right for us? Sometimes you just make no sense, Aunt Rosie." Emilie gave her a hug. "We love you, anyway."

"I love you, too." Rosita smiled. "I don't want you to end up a lonely woman when you grow old. I'm fortunate to have all of you to make my life bearable. You may not be that lucky." She turned her attention back to Kristie. "The Haggard Ranch is less than a day's ride from here. You're welcome to visit us anytime you feel like company. Life here away from the city can get lonely."

"I'm sure we'll be seeing a lot of each other in the future," Kristie said.

"Same offer goes for you, Dennis," Sanchez said. "Any advice I can give you, I'd be happy to help out."

"I appreciate that." Collins spoke to his wife. "You look tired. I think we should call it a day. We have a big day ahead of us tomorrow."

"I won't argue about that."

———

As tired as he was, sleep just wouldn't come. Too many things kept going through Collins' head, especially the band of natives they came across on the road. Their leader had accused Sanchez of not paying his tribute. What exactly did that mean? Why would Sanchez pay tribute to those savages? They had not talked about that incident at the dinner table. It hadn't seemed important to Collins, then. Who were those savages? How did they interact with the humans on Savanna?

What about the Trades Commission? Apparently, the Commission controlled everything on Savanna from setting prices to the money itself, including collecting taxes. As far as he knew, the Trades Commission was a private enterprise. What gave them the right to collect taxes? What had they not been told about how things were run on Savanna?

He got up and walked to the window. One moon hung in the night sky. Savanna had three moons, one large one and two smaller ones. He'd always been intrigued by the stars. When he was young, he wanted to become a trooper or maybe a scout. To be able to travel to distant star systems, walk on alien planets, meet alien races, and see strange animals had been one of his dreams. It hadn't worked out that way. Most people on Earth never got the chance to visit other planets. Even Earth's moon was out of reach. Only the well-to-do could afford to go there on vacations or, possibly, on business. Mars, the asteroids, or the moons of the larger planets were an impossible dream for the average citizen.

The only way to the stars for them was to emigrate. He had heard of fortune hunters and drifters who traveled to frontier worlds, but those were usually one-way tickets. Nobody ever returned from those planets. Once there, you were stuck for good.

He and his family had taken the big step. Here he was in a dream come true. It hadn't really sunk in yet that he was actually on an alien planet. It seemed unreal. Traveling on a wooden wagon drawn by a couple of giant goats was, of course, vastly different from things he had experienced on Earth, it was almost surreal. The environment looked virtually the same. The one percent variance in gravity was insignificant. The air smelled cleaner than on Earth, and the sky wasn't hazy. It would have been difficult to tell they had landed on an alien planet, except for one major difference, and that was the lack of people. Earth was overpopulated and to find a place as serene and empty of people was virtually impossible.

Of course, looking at the night-sky, the constellations were different from the ones seen on Earth, if the sky ever became clear, which didn't happen often. Only now did he become aware of the many stars visible. He had never seen this many and never with such clarity.

"It's beautiful, isn't it?"

Startled by the sound, he turned to see Kristie standing behind him. "Did I wake you?"

Her hand stole into his. "No. I couldn't sleep. When I didn't find you beside me, I sat up and saw your silhouette against the window. Can't sleep, either?"

He shook his head. "I keep thinking about those natives. They did not appear friendly, especially their leader."

"I know what you mean. He was frightening. Are you expecting problems?" she asked with a slight tremor in her voice and increase in the pressure of her hand.

"Just a feeling I have, but that may be because of my many years as a cop. You develop a certain sense for detecting danger. It's what saved my skin many times."

She shivered beside him. "You're scaring me, Dennis."

He put his arm around her shoulders. "I don't mean to. It's probably nothing. I'm just paranoid. I see danger where there usually is none. I'm sure they would have warned us during the many informative seminars back on Earth about possible threats from the indigenous population, should there be any. Besides, Herman doesn't seem to be concerned."

"Perhaps you should talk to him about it in the morning?" Kristie suggested. "Just for our peace-of-mind."

"Maybe I will, but I don't want to come across as a man suffering from anxieties who sees danger behind every rock. You know I'm not that kind of a man."

"I know you're not. If you want, I can ask."

"It'll be better coming from me. He's more likely to tell me the truth. If there should be some kind of problem, I'll be the one who has to deal with it." He planted a kiss on her forehead. "Let me do the worrying."

"Don't be silly. You know I can't let you carry all the responsibilities. We are in this together. Do you think we did the right thing coming here?"

"If we didn't, it's too late to have misgivings now, honey. We're stuck here for better or worse. We knew it wouldn't be paradise, and we expected problems. Just remember we are not the first colonists on Savanna. Those early settlers had to overcome nearly impossible odds. We can't even imagine the dangers and obstacles they faced. Compared to what they had to endure, it'll be a picnic for us. Now, let's go back to bed. Hopefully, we'll be able to sleep."

[4]

Sheppard was a bit apprehensive about meeting Colonel Wainwright, the commanding officer of Outpost Alpha.

The Colonel sat behind a wooden desk, appearing busy with some paperwork. He looked up when Sheppard walked in. "So, you're the new guy," he said.

Sheppard saluted, surprised when Wainwright just lifted his hand and put it down again. "Captain Sheppard reporting for duty, sir."

"Relax, Captain. We're not that formal here. Have a seat."

"Thank you, sir." Sheppard followed the invitation and waited for the Colonel to speak.

"Who did you piss off, Captain Sheppard?"

Surprised by the unexpected question, Sheppard asked, "What makes you think I pissed somebody off, sir?"

The Colonel chuckled. "Come on. We both know this assignment is a dead-end road. Only misfits and troublemakers end up on a planet like Savanna."

Sheppard smiled thinly. "If that's the case, I could ask you the same question, sir."

Wainwright stared a Sheppard for some time before he said, "You don't take orders well, do you, captain?"

"If they make sense, I have no problem following them, sir."

"A good trooper doesn't question an order, and he certainly doesn't get chummy with his superior."

"I apologize, sir. Didn't mean to. Won't happen again, sir." Sheppard tried to suppress his irritation. It looked like this old bird was going to make his life miserable. He groped in his pocket and took out a sealed envelope. "My personal files, Colonel. For your eyes only."

Wainwright took the envelope from him and ran a decoder across the opening. Removing the thin electronic strip, he laid it onto the screen on his desk. Studying the information it contained, he looked up and said, "You were a member of the Solar Union's Special Forces. Interesting. It seems you barely escaped being court-marshalled. You were accused of collaborating with the enemy, but the evidence didn't hold. What do you have to say about that?"

"They railroaded me, sir. It was a suicide mission from the beginning."

"It says you were the only one to escape alive." Wainwright leaned forward. "I'm curious. Enlighten me."

Sheppard sighed. "Nobody believed me during the trial. Nobody was even interested in hearing my side of the incident. Why should you?"

"Because I know what it's like to be shafted. Go on."

"We were sent to Stardust to capture a man known as The Saber. He was the head of a gang of notorious pirates. They were involved in smuggling weapons, drugs, humans—you name it, they did it. The mission was doomed from the beginning. It should have been easy, but we ran into an ambush when nobody should have known we were coming. All my men were killed, including the undercover agent who had infiltrated The Saber's organization. I managed to escape. I won't go into details how. I had good reason to believe that General Ortega, who ordered the mission, betrayed us. Agent Summers, who was killed during the raid, told me he had proof that General Ortega was on the payroll of Interstellar Sunburst Conglomerate, which is rumored to be controlled by one of the giant drug cartels. After reporting to Internal Affairs what Summers told me, I was arrested."

Wainwright stroked his thick mustache. "Interesting story, Sheppard, if true."

Sheppard glared. "I'm not asking you to believe it, sir, but that's what happened. They never gave me a chance to defend myself. The trial was rushed through, and here I am. Like it or not."

"So, you did piss somebody off, and they got rid of you. Just like I thought." Wainwright rose from his chair and walked to a cabinet. Taking out two glasses and a bottle filled with dark liquid, he asked, "I hope you drink, Captain Sheppard." Without waiting for an answer, he filled both glasses. Turning around, he offered one to Sheppard. "The finest brandy available on Savanna. Don't make me drink alone."

Surprised for the second time, Sheppard accepted the glass with some misgivings, not knowing what to make of the Colonel's gesture.

"I have a feeling you and I will get along just fine, Sheppard." He lifted his glass. "Here's to the bastards who are responsible for us being here on this forsaken dust ball. May they rot in the hell they planned for us." Emptying his glass, he put it down on the desk with a loud thud. "People like us, Sheppard, always get the dirty end of the stick. It doesn't matter how hard we try, those fuckers always manage to screw us in the end."

Perplexed at the Colonel's sudden outburst, Sheppard lifted his glass and sniffed the dark liquid.

"Don't inhale it, man. Drink it. This stuff isn't easy to come by, and it isn't cheap."

Shrugging, Sheppard downed his drink, not expecting much. He was no stranger to drinking brandy or any other hard liqueur and was pleasantly surprised. "I have to admit, this is excellent brandy." He gave the Colonel an inquiring look. "I'm at a loss here, Colonel Wainwright. First you give me the third degree, accuse me of trying to get chummy, and now you offer me brandy."

Wainwright actually grinned. "Relax, Sheppard. I was just trying to have a little fun, hoping to get a rise out of you, but you kept your cool. Let me give it to you straight. This outpost is nothing but a big joke. The sooner you realize that you've reached the end of your career, the sooner you'll stop trying to be a good soldier. I don't give a crap about any ambitions you may have. Forget them. This is it, man. You're not going anywhere. When you meet the rest of the losers, you will see what I mean."

"I don't really consider myself a loser, if you don't mind."

"None of us do, but the fact you and I, along with the rest of the troopers on this post, are here is proof enough." Wainwright chuckled cheerfully. "It's not that bad once you accept it. There is one positive thing, though. We live a nice, quiet life, out of danger. We never have to put our ass on the line." He leaned forward, his face serious. "This friend of yours, what's his name—Major Daniels? He's an enigma to me. What's his purpose here? He sure loves to talk."

"He isn't my friend. I met him on the ship. I didn't know he was in the military until we were picked up. He told me a lot of stories about his life, but I'm not sure if any of them are true. He claims he's an engineer. You are right, he is a chatterbox."

"He worries me. I looked at his file, the one he gave me, and according to his file, he is an engineer, if the records are correct. There is nothing special about him in his profile. I don't know why he is here."

"He wants to build bridges." Sheppard didn't see any harm in divulging that much information. Even though the Colonel acted jovial and friendly, it didn't cause him to let down his guard. It could all be an act. To what purpose wasn't clear. Perhaps he was just paranoid, but it never hurt to be careful.

Wainwright grinned again. "It's possible they sent him to the wrong planet. We have no plans to build bridges. If there were any plans, we wouldn't be involved, anyway."

"What is our role here, Colonel?"

"We're supposed to keep law and order on Savanna, but that is only a formality. The Solar Trading Commission runs things here. They have their own lawmen in Crystal City. Military Command has no interest in Savanna. It is not in a strategic location and too close to Spider-controlled space. Did you know that Savanna didn't have any military outpost until only about twenty years ago? The Trading Commission requested our presence. That is the only reason we set up an outpost in the first place. Since we are not important, Military Command doesn't waste valuable manpower on Savanna. That's where you and I and the other undesirable troopers come in. It's the perfect destination to get rid of us." He laughed. "In a way, this is our retirement paradise. Not the place you envisioned to spend your retirement years, right?"

"Not at all." Sheppard looked out of the window. There was an armoured tank and a few military trucks parked in the yard outside. "It can't be all that bleak. If this outpost were completely forgotten and useless, you wouldn't have been supplied with an armoured tank, for instance. How about weapons?"

"Those we have."

"Outdated stuff?"

"We have lasers, flamethrowers, flash rifles, rocket launchers. Things like that, but I'm positive those are not the latest in weaponry."

Sheppard nodded. "Still, sounds pretty modern to me. I wonder if Military Command knows more than they're telling."

"Come to think of it, there was a large shipment of weapons and other military equipment on the ship you arrived in. Not everything has been unloaded yet, but, apparently, it's being stored inside a warehouse in Crystal City. I received that information from one of my informers in Crystal City."

"Don't you find that peculiar? It seems to me trouble is brewing somewhere. I wonder if the arrival of Major Daniels has anything to do with that," Sheppard mused. "There has to be a good reason he is here. If it isn't for building bridges, what other reason could there be?"

"I can't even guess. It seems to me I'll have to keep an eye on him. I hope he won't upset things. Life's been quiet here."

"That may change." Sheppard didn't want to sound pessimistic, but somehow, he sensed something was off. "You mentioned the Solar Trading Commission. You said they are in control on Savanna? I'm not surprised. This is going back twenty years now. I was a cadet and part of a mission on Epsilon, a planet covered with giant mushrooms and populated by dinosaurs and other nasty critters. You think Savanna is the end of the road? You should have gone to Epsilon. Hell can't be any worse. It was a planet rich with precious stones and other minerals. Many fortune hunters tried their luck to make their fortune, but the Trading Commission controlled everything. They made certain nobody got rich, and nobody ever left that planet."

"That's pretty much the way things are here," Wainwright interrupted.

"I was temporarily under the command of a Master Scout by the name of Stonewall." Sheppard smiled when he saw Wainwright's expression. Scouts and troopers didn't play well together. "It's a long story I won't go into. He was as tough as they come, and when he had a run-in with High Commissioner Quintana, the CEO of the Trading Commission on Epsilon, he sure put that man in his place. I can still hear Quintana shouting threats. Stonewall wasn't intimidated. He had my respect. He would have made a great military officer."

"Scouts are a different breed of men. That's why they don't become military men." Wainwright stroked his mustache again, seemingly deep in thought. "You know, I've always tried to stay far away from politics, but the Trading Commission can be a pain in the rear-end. Those small-minded bureaucrats tried to get us involved in some of the disputes they have with the farmers and ranchers, but I've been denying their requests. Just because they supply us with food and other items we need to survive here, they seem to think we're here at their disposal. I've made it clear we are not. The Trading Commission is privately owned, but they act as if the company is an arm of the government. The problem is they get away with it, because their empire is vast and well-connected. Many high-placed government officials have an interest in the Trading Commission."

"A few years back, before I became a captain, I was part of a unit assigned to protect an arm of the Trading Commission on Jackpot. They had problems with the settlers. Some of them refused to pay the levies the Commission charged and threatened to take matters into their own hands. Their argument was exactly what you just said, that the Trading Commission is not the government. The CEO argued that the company invested huge amounts of money and time to establish a safe environment for the settlers. Apparently, the indigenous population was hostile and unwilling to accept the presence of the settlers. Only when the Commission made a pact with them, assuring that no settler would encroach on their territory, which happened to be the most fertile land in the region and was also rich on valuable minerals, the natives agreed to leave the settlers alone. However, they also demanded the settlers share livestock and part of the harvest with them."

Wainwright made a sound deep in his throat. "Sounds familiar. Same thing is happening here with the farmers and ranchers. They are not happy. We've had reports that bands of natives are harassing them, forcing them to pay some kind of tribute, and the Trading Commission is charging them exuberant rates to handle their goods." He spread his hands. "The sad thing is there is nothing we can do. We have no jurisdiction over the Trading Commission. They can do what they want."

"That doesn't seem right," Sheppard commented. "I have no love for anyone who takes advantage of people and a situation."

"That's probably one of the reasons you're here," Wainwright said with a grim chuckle. "You can't stay neutral, and you won't leave things alone when they go against your principles. I'm surprised you made it to the rank of captain."

"You're a colonel, sir, but you don't strike me as a man who got where you are by being ruthless and stepping on people."

Wainwright poured himself another glass of brandy. "Don't kid yourself. I've stepped on people, but mostly I followed orders and kept my opinions to myself. I've done things I'm not proud of in order to get ahead. It helped to know the right people, too, but just when you think you can trust someone and you let your guard down, you stumble, and sometimes you can't keep your balance and keep on stumbling. Trusting the wrong people gets you a one-way ticket to a place like Savanna." Wainwright smiled crookedly. "I don't need to tell you that, because, as you already stated, here you are. Welcome to Outpost Despair." Downing his drink, he stared at the empty glass. "When it really comes down to it, there is nobody in the universe you can trust," he murmured almost to himself.

———

ONLY ONE ROAD RAN FROM THE OUTPOST TO CRYSTAL CITY. IT was nothing more than dirt and not well maintained. Sheppard was happy to be safe inside an armored vehicle as they rolled across the rocky and pitted surface. He imagined the road would not be in a good condition after a heavy rainfall.

It didn't look like there'd be any rain soon, and he was grateful for that. Looking out of the window at the landscape and the sky, it was difficult to accept he was on an alien planet. Savanna was much like Earth, starting with the vegetation, the soil, the color of the sky, and even the gravity. Not all planets humans tried to colonize were this ideal. Some were outright unpleasant, and yet, humans attempted to tame them and make them livable.

Of course, there were penalties to be paid. Over the centuries that'd passed since humans finally joined the other spacefaring races, some of the planets refused to be made into the image the humans visualized. Instead of the planet changing, humans changed. Subjected to harmful radiation, humans adapted, genes mutated, and the results were not always desirable. He remembered spending time on Deadrock, aptly named for the number of settlers who died after one of the early colonization ships crashed on a planet never designed for humans. Most of them died during the first years, but some survived. They worked the land, they built homes, and they adapted. Their descendants changed inside and outside. When this lost colony was finally found, the humans living on it were barely recognizable as humans. They were more alien than some of the real alien races.

"You're awfully silent, Captain Sheppard." The trooper driving the vehicle broke into his thoughts. His chuckle sounded almost amused. "Still trying to figure out which mischievous devil chose you to join us on this planet of continuous fun and excitement?"

"Colonel. Wainwright called it Outpost Despair," Sheppard said.

One of the two troopers sitting behind Sheppard laughed. "That's one of the nicer names we call this outpost."

"From what I've seen this far, it isn't that bad," Sheppard said.

"You're right, it doesn't seem so bad, at first. After being here for as long as some of us have been, you will realize what seemed so nice is nothing but a variation of hell. The boredom drives you crazy, and the realization you're stuck here for good. No assignments, no promotions, no action. You'll get tired of seeing the same old faces every day and listening to the same old stories, because there are no new ones. A war could be raging out there, we'll never know. The only excitement we get is when someone new, like you, joins us."

"You could always resign and become a farmer," Sheppard suggested.

"If I would have wanted to dig around in the dirt, I would never have joined the military in the first place. Besides, it isn't as easy as it sounds to resign from the military. Have you ever read the fine print?

You'll have to undergo a partial mind-wipe to prevent you from spilling any military secrets, and you'll lose any privileges you may have, including your pension. I for one am not willing to do that."

"Neither am I." Sheppard turned around to look at the trooper. "By the way, I never caught your name."

"I'm Lieutenant Edward Fox, and this guy with the red hair beside me is Randall Foster, Sergeant Randall Foster, actually."

"I'm Jeremy." Sheppard shook Fox's hand.

"I'm Robert McCallum," the driver said with a little chuckle. "Just plain Trooper McCallum. No special rank. Never made it."

"Doesn't make any difference. Nobody gives a crap about rank here anymore. We're all on first-name-basis," Foster said. "Or last name, whichever you prefer."

"I have no problem with that," Sheppard said. "What's the assignment we're on, anyway?"

"Supply run." McCallum smirked.

"What are we getting?"

"You'll see. You're lucky you've been chosen. You must have made an impression on the Colonel. It usually takes him awhile to trust newcomers enough to make them part of an important assignment like this."

"I suppose I should feel honored. What's the story with Colonel Wainwright, anyway?"

"Nobody really knows. He has his own demons to fight, like most of us." McCallum glanced at Sheppard sideways. "Like you, Captain Sheppard."

When Sheppard said, "I have no demons to fight," all three men laughed.

"Of course not." Fox snickered behind him. "They sent you here for a little holiday. A long holiday, Captain Lilli-white."

Sheppard stayed silent. He didn't get angry, because he didn't sense any malice. They were only having a little fun at his expense. So far, he hadn't met many of the other troopers on the outpost, but if all of them were like these three, it wouldn't be too bad, and he could accept his situation. Only one thing he couldn't accept, the fact he may have to spend the rest of his career on Savanna. That would really be a form of hell.

The first houses of the city came into view. Most of them were single stories, constructed of wood, with brown tiles covering the roofs. Each house was located inside a small yard with shrubs and short trees surrounding the houses. The ground itself was covered with grass and even some flowers.

The packed dirt on the road had been replaced by cobblestones, which didn't make the ride any smoother. Wooden carts pulled by goat-like animals traveled the road. Most of the carts were filled with some kind of vegetable or fruit, but some of them with other items. A few closed carriages carried passengers.

"Quite primitive," he commented. "Are there no somewhat more modern transport vehicles around?"

"No. Savanna is considered a Class Five planet. Modern machinery is forbidden, as are advanced weapons of any kind. It's all done for the protection of the indigenous population," Fox explained.

"How about the military? I know we have lasers, for instance."

"Different story. After all, we still have to consider the Spiders and any other alien race that might try to gain a foothold on Savanna. Even if we're just a bunch of useless misfits, in the eyes of our illustrious leaders, the aliens don't know that. We do need the weapons to defend this outpost should the unexpected happen. To say the least, we are expendable, but we still have to put up a good fight."

"Anything ever happened?"

Fox shook his head. "Not as long as I've been here."

The vehicle slowed down and came to a halt. When Sheppard looked outside, they were parked in front of a long building.

"Our first stop," McCallum explained.

They all got out. McCallum opened the hatch to the storage in the back of the vehicle and pulled out a large bag. Throwing it across his broad shoulders, he headed for the entrance. The others followed him. When they entered the building, Sheppard guessed that it must be some kind of distribution center. The shelves were filled with boxes, some large and some small.

"Hey, Miguel," Fox called in a loud voice. "Get you lazy butt out here."

"Coming, coming," a voice answered from the back.

A short, skinny man came down one of the aisles. He walked

slowly, dragging his left leg. When he spotted the four men, he grumbled, "I should have known it was you. Always seem to be in a hurry." Then he grinned. "I hope you brought me some good stuff I can sell."

"Don't we always, old man?"

"Most of the time but not always. I've got your box in the back. You'll have to get it yourself. I'm getting to old to lug everything around."

"No trouble." Fox turned to Foster. "Randall, go and get it."

Foster nodded and walked away.

"What have you got for me?" The old man's face appeared eager.

Fox emptied the sack. Sheppard stared with misgivings at the things that spilled onto the floor. "A couple of laser-pistols with spare power-packs, one pair of binoculars, one receiver-bracelet with half a dozen seekers, and a state-of-the art direction finder. More than adequate for what you're giving us," Fox said.

"My supplier is getting greedy. He demands more gold nuggets every time, and it is getting more difficult to sell this stuff. One of the Trading Commission agents has been sniffing around."

"Don't tell me you can't handle him, Miguel. I'm sure you know someone who will take care of him for you if he gets too close to your affairs. Remember, we can't afford to get exposed."

Fox spoke casually, but his voice had a chill to it, making Sheppard wonder what he was getting himself involved in.

"It'll cost. You'll have to pay your share if it ever comes to that." Miguel gave Fox a sly look. "You troopers are in the business of removing undesirables. Why doesn't one of you do it? It would save a lot of grieve, and nobody else would know."

"We're not coldblooded killers, in spite what you might think. We do have to follow a code of honor," Fox explained. He turned to look at Foster who was coming back, carrying a big, wooden box.

"I could use some help here," Foster called. "This damn box is getting heavier with every step." He stopped walking and put the box onto the floor.

"I'll help him," Sheppard said and went to meet Foster. Grabbing one of the handles and lifting the box, he had to admit it was heavy and wondered what was inside but didn't ask.

'Let's go," Fox said. "We have much to do still." He held out a hand to the old man.

Miguel grabbed and shook it. "Pleasure doing business with you," he said with a toothless grin.

"Wish I could say the same thing about you," Fox replied. "I always get the feeling you're cheating us."

The old man put a thin hand over his heart. "I would never do that. Besides, the stuff you bring me doesn't belong to you in the first place. You're getting most of the benefits."

"I wish that were so." Fox sighed and turned to go.

Once back in the vehicle, Sheppard asked, "What's in the box?"

"Brandy," McCallum said. "Today it's brandy."

"Brandy? You mean you're trading all those weapons for brandy?"

"That's correct. It's for the Colonel."

Sheppard stared at him. "Are you saying Colonel Wainwright knows about this?"

Fox laughed. "Knows about this? We're operating on his orders. He needs to still his craving for alcohol."

"I don't understand."

"Well, you'll find out sooner or later. The Colonel is a drunk, an alcoholic."

"I can hardly believe that." Sheppard shook his head. "He gave me the impression of a man who has things under control. A man of integrity who was dealt a bad hand."

"He probably was that at one time, but ten years in this forsaken place take their toll. He doesn't have much to live for. Alcohol is the only consolation he has. Don't condemn him."

"He's a good man and well-liked by most of the men at the post," McCallum remarked. "We could do worse."

"He's an officer in the Solar Union Space Navy, a trooper who was taught discipline, damn it! What kind of example is he for the enlisted men if he can't control his urges?"

"I guess you still believe in all that crap they teach us, Captain Sheppard," Foster said from behind Sheppard. He made a rude sound. "A trooper of the union doesn't show his emotions, he has no desires other than serving the union, he follows orders without question, he shows respect for his superiors even if they are a bunch of assholes. I don't think I need to go on. Wait until you've been here long enough. You'll discover none of those principles matter anymore. Nobody here gives a damn about rules and the rest of the galaxy. We've been abandoned, forgotten. Military High Command doesn't care about us. Why should we?"

"Why? I'll tell you why. If not for High Command, then for yourself. To discard what you've been taught is throwing away everything you've believed in until now. You'll end up losing your dignity and your self-respect." Sheppard didn't know why he felt this sudden anger. "Then there is this other thing. Why would you remove modern weapons from the outpost and make them available to civilians, possibly criminals, when they are forbidden to be present on a Class Five planet? You're breaking a law that carries severe punishment."

All three men broke into laughter.

"I don't believe you understand the way things work here. First of all, where will you report this so-called crime? Colonel Wainwright? He's the one who endorses it. The Trading Commission? I don't think so. They have no jurisdiction over us. Even though there is a slight chance they could cause some trouble, we'd deal with it, should that happen. The mayor of Crystal City? He's powerless. Face it, my righteous friend, when they sent you here, you entered a wild frontier planet with no laws but the ones we make. We do whatever it takes to survive and make our lives worth living." Foster took a deep breath. "Enough of this, let's get to our next assignment and then have some fun."

[5]

SHEPPARD WAS NOT A MAN WHO WOULD SIT BACK AND SULK, BUT it was difficult for him to accept this new reality. He was used to a life of order and discipline, but his world had been turned upside down. This wasn't the first time. Never having been a stickler when it came to rules, even having bent a few when he deemed it necessary, he had, nevertheless, always followed the laws of the military as closely as possible. He was not that naïve to think all high-ranking officers were honest and upstanding citizens of the Solar Union. He knew better, but he tried to behave according to his rank and his own code of conduct. To stay honorable and stick to his moral beliefs was important to him. To be sent to a place like this outpost had been like being condemned to death or sentenced to a prison-colony. Savanna was not a prison planet, but from what he'd experienced this far, close to it.

He was bitter, disappointed and angry for having been falsely accused of treason.

Making friends had always been difficult for him. He was a loner and liked it that way.

"You ever been married, Sheppard?"

McCallum's unexpected question ripped him out of his contemplation.

"What?"

"Have you ever been married?"

Sheppard shook his head. "No. Never had the opportunity. I joined the SUSN when I was eighteen."

"Perhaps he doesn't like women," Foster suggested. "Do you prefer men to women, Sheppard?"

"No, I'm not so inclined."

Behind him, Fox chuckled. "Ever been with a woman?"

"If you must know—yes, I have. I have desires like every healthy male, but you should know that for us, the opportunity to meet a woman has always been something that happens not often. Why the interest in my love life?"

"Just trying to get to know you better. If you're going to be part of our team, we should know as much as possible about you. You might be a spy for all we know."

McCallum's remark caused Sheppard to chuckle. "Really? A spy? Now you've made me curious. What special secret are you hiding that would be important for High Command to send a spy to this…this planet the colonel called Outpost Despair?"

"Perhaps somebody reported what happens on the outpost to High Command," Fox suggested.

Sheppard laughed. "I don't believe High Command cares about petty theft enough to send an officer to investigate. There are more important things to worry about. Just before my trial came up, there was a skirmish between the colonists and the Spiders on Fortune. Settlers on Chrysalis were being raided by Sleevers, and the Crows were demanding humans leave Rainbow's End. I think those incidents are far more important than the trivial crimes you guys are committing. Unless you are exchanging gifts with the Mollard or any of the other Dragon races, you have nothing to worry about. I can assure you, I'm not a spy."

"If you are, you won't have to worry for long why fate sent you here." Fox grinned but his eyes were cold.

They drove on in silence. A few pedestrians hurried alongside the buildings and fewer wagons traveled on the road. Most houses looked the same, but some did not appear to be as well-kept.

"Not the best part of the city," he remarked.

"No, it isn't, but this is where the action we seek happens." Fox poked him in the ribs. "As I said before, you're lucky the colonel seems to have taken a liking to you. Not everyone gets to leave the post too often and mingle with the regular folks."

"I'm anxious to find out what makes this trip so special, aside from trading prohibited weapons for booze." Sheppard didn't hide his sarcasm.

McCallum turned the vehicle into a narrow side-street. After driving for a few more minutes, he parked behind a low, dark building. "We have arrived, gentlemen," he announced with a dramatic voice. "Now, we shall leave the safety of our cocoon and enter the gates of nirvana where great pleasures await us, but beware, for danger lurks in every dark corner."

"Oh, shut up, Robert." Foster laughed. "You'll scare the newest member of our band."

"Just giving him heads-up," McCallum said and grinned.

They climbed out of the vehicle.

"There are a couple more sacks in the storage box," Fox said to Sheppard. "Take one out and bring it with you." He headed for a door in the side of the building.

McCallum helped Sheppard to pull the sack out of the vehicle. He grabbed a second one and took off. The sack Sheppard carried was heavy, but he managed to drag it behind him. Stepping through the door, he found himself in a dark corridor. The air smelled stale and humid, laced with dubious unidentifiable odors. Walking behind McCallum, he felt anxious and apprehensive, wondering what exciting, new experience waited for him.

Muffled voices came from somewhere ahead, but before they reached the end of the corridor, Fox stopped and banged his fist against a door. A moment later, the door opened, and a man stuck out his head.

"We're bringing gifts," Fox said, grinning. "Let us in."

The man stepped aside to let them pass. The room they entered was cluttered with furniture and shelves. Sheppard counted four men sitting in chairs, each with a gun strapped to their belts. Behind a counter sat a corpulent man, bald but sprouting a bushy, gray beard.

His thick lips parted into a smile when he saw the group coming into the room.

"Fox," he said with a rusty voice. "I hope you brought some useful stuff."

"Everything I bring is useful," Fox countered. "Don't try to cheat me by belittling what I bring." He turned to Sheppard. "Empty the sack and show this bandit what we have."

The man closest to Sheppard got up from his chair and picked up one of the lasers Sheppard spilled onto the floor. He turned it around in his hands. "Does this toy work?"

"Watch where you point that thing," Fox snapped. "It's a weapon not some toy and don't touch any buttons."

"I'm not an idiot," the man growled, giving Fox an angry look.

"Then don't act like one." Fox turned to the man behind the desk. "You should teach your apes to show respect for dangerous weapons, Max."

"Give me that thing, Dan," Max said to the other man.

Dan handed him the laser with a shrug and obvious reluctance. "I figured I should have one of those."

"You'll kill yourself with it." The contempt in Fox's voice was evident. "Let me give you some advice. You never hold a gun, and that includes lasers, by the barrel. Neither do you point it at someone, unless you intend to shoot them." He looked at Max. "Where do you find these guys?"

Max lifted a beefy shoulder. "Dan is a good and loyal employee, but I admit, not the swiftest."

"Hey, I'm over here," Dan protested. "No need to insult me."

"No insult intended." Max got up and walked around the desk. "Let me have a look at the stuff." Nodding, he surveyed the weapons and the other items.

Sheppard counted five lasers, including five extra power cells, a number of electronic direction finders, a couple of wrist hologram projectors, and a few other items that didn't belong in civilian hands.

"What else did you bring?" Max opened the other sack to reveal a large metal box. "What's inside?"

"Let's open it." Fox smiled as he bent to run his fingers across a computer plate in the top of the box. A moment later, a side panel swung open to reveal what appeared to be the compressed figure of human.

Sheppard cursed Fox silently when he saw the figure.

One slim arm snaked out of the box and then the nude form of a woman unfolded and rose. Stretching her slender body, she turned her head slowly to scan her surroundings.

Sheppard couldn't help but hold his breath. The body of the woman was perfect and her face a vision out of a dream.

"She's beautiful," Dan whispered hoarsely.

"Don't even think about touching her," Max warned him, his voice almost hushed. "She's mine."

"She will be after you bond her to you." Fox handed Max a wrist band. "As long as you wear this, she will obey your commands."

Max slipped the narrow band around his wrist. "Now what?"

The bright blue eyes of the woman fixed on Max. Her voice was soft and seductive. "I am here to please you."

"She just arrived with the last shipment." Fox broke the spell that seemed to have gripped the men. "The latest model from what I understand. She can do anything a real woman can do, only much better." He grinned. "And she will never say no, claiming she's got a headache."

Max gave Fox a calculating look, asking, "How much is she going to cost me?"

"If I'd have to charge you what she's worth, you wouldn't be able to afford her." He made a sweeping gesture with his hand. "She's my gift to you, old friend, as long as you remember this favor."

"I won't forget," Max assured him. "There is one thing that bothers me, though. Since when does the military have sex-droids?"

Fox glanced at Sheppard before answering. "She's more than just a sex-droid. In reality, she is another advanced weapon in the military's arsenal against our enemies."

"A weapon against whom?"

"The Snaar, the Sleevers, or any other species roaming the space-ways looking for trouble." Fox chuckled cheerfully.

"Wait a minute. Are you saying this one is just a loan?"

"Don't worry. She's yours as long as you want her and as long as nobody in the military finds out about you having her in your possession." He looked at his companions. "Aside from us."

"I'm not sure if I want a secret weapon near me. Maybe she's going to kill me in my sleep. For all I know she may spy on me and my operation, reporting back to you." Max eyed Fox suspiciously.

Fox laughed. "Why don't you ask her if she will kill you?"

"All right." Max gave the android an apprehensive look. "Are you programmed to kill me?"

"My program forbids me to hurt a human being in any shape or form. I am here to please you." She smiled and touched his cheek. "Just tell me what you want me to do and I'll do it."

Max laughed. "Don't worry. I'll think of something." His eyes focused again on Fox. "Are there more like her?"

Fox nodded. "Forget about what you want to ask me. This is the only one I managed to procure. By the way, don't even try to find out what else she can do, besides satisfying your desires. Just treat her like a sex-toy and you'll be happy." He rubbed his hands. "Now to business. I expect you pay me the usual price. Even though I said the android is a gift, I believe you owe me and my associates something special tonight." He pointed at Sheppard. "This is a new member of my crew. His name is Sheppard. He will have to be initiated. Give him an experience he will remember, but first we'll sample some of your best stuff. On the house, obviously."

"Anything you want, Fox. Anything. I'll let my staff know you're here."

"Good." Fox turned to his companions. "Let's have some fun."

"You're a lucky guy, Sheppard." Foster clapped him on the shoulder as they left the room. "Not every trooper gets a chance to let off steam, especially since you're a newcomer to Outpost Alpha."

"I have no desire to let off steam," Sheppard said.

"Then look at it as a bonus in advance." Foster laughed. "Something to look back at fondly when you go stir-crazy. Don't be a stuffed shirt. Go and relax. Enjoy yourself."

They reached the end of the corridor and walked into a noisy room filled with smoke and people.

"The best place in Crystal City," McCallum said. "You guys go ahead. I've spotted someone." With that he headed for one of the tables.

"I'm thirsty," Fox announced. "Let's see what Max is offering us." He turned to Sheppard. "Go and explore the place. Order anything you want. It's on the house, remember."

Sheppard watched him walk toward the bar. He didn't see Foster anywhere. Shrugging, he looked around and found an empty chair at one of the tables. The two men sitting at the table looked up when he pulled the chair away to sit down.

"I hope you don't mind if I join you," he said. "Don't let me interrupt you in what you were doing. I just need to sit down somewhere."

One of the men, a short, skinny guy with a goatee, looked him up and down. "Haven't seen you around here. Where have you been hiding?"

"On a spaceship. Just arrived a few days ago. Still trying to get oriented."

"You're a miner? Treasure hunter? Farmer?"

Sheppard shook his head. "I'm a military man. I'm stationed at Outpost Alpha."

The other man grinned and held out a hand. "The name's David Reed, and this oversized ogre is Jerry Buchanan. We're miners."

Sheppard shook the offered hand. "Jeremy Sheppard. Actually, Captain Jeremy Sheppard."

Buchanan lifted his hand in a mock salute. "Happy to make your acquaintance, Captain Sheppard. What reason do you have to make this planet of endless opportunities and great riches your new home?"

Sheppard grimaced. "It's a long story, and I wouldn't want to bore you with it. Let's just say I followed the ancient tradition of the military. A trooper's duty is to obey and not to ask questions."

"That's why I never joined the military," Buchanan said. "I'm not good at following orders."

"What do you mine, if you don't mind me asking?"

"We're after blue diamonds, like most other miners."

"Been successful?"

"We've been sort of lucky." Reed shrugged. "The problem is the Trading Commission controls the diamond trade. They pay us a trifle of what they're worth. The only way to get ahead of the game is to do a little trading on the side, if you know what that means." He stopped talking when Buchanan growled something and shot him a warning glance.

"He's had too much to drink," Buchanan said. "Sometimes he tells stories."

"That's okay." Sheppard smiled. "If you're worried, I might be some kind of spy for the Trading Commission, I can assure you I'm not, and the military is not interested in the affairs of civilians."

"Then why is the military here in the first place?" Buchanan lifted a questioning eyebrow when he stared at Sheppard, but it seemed he didn't care to hear the answer. Raising his mug, he put it back onto the table. "Damn thing is already empty again."

"Mine, too." Reed waved to one of the serving girls. When she came to the table, Reed looked at Sheppard. "Let me buy you a drink."

Sheppard waved him off. "Thank you for the offer but let me treat you. I'm a guest of the owner and can order whatever I want." He turned to the girl. "Bring me what these two gentlemen are drinking and fill their mugs. Put it on my tab."

"A guest of the owner? Hm?" Buchanan gave Sheppard a thoughtful look. "Word on the street is that Max Smirkov has his fingers into all kinds of businesses, none of them legal. He's a dangerous man, and you don't want to cross him. What's your business with him?"

"I'm not in business with anyone, especially not with a guy who lives outside the law. I'm a Solar Union trooper. I'm supposed to uphold the law."

He said it but wondered if he was only trying to convince himself that he wasn't doing anything wrong. After all, it wasn't his fault that he was sitting in a tavern operated by a racketeer.

Buchanan shook his head. "You don't appear to be a stupid man, but you can't truly expect to be treated like a king by a man like Smirkov without giving anything back? What's your angle then?"

"No angle." Sheppard shrugged. "I came here with three other troopers on an errand I was never made aware of. They said I was a lucky guy to be here." He accepted the mug from the serving girl and sniffed the dark liquid. "What am I drinking?"

Reed laughed and took a swig from his newly filled mug. Putting it down with a satisfied sigh, he said, "Nothing beats a mug or two of good old-fashioned ale."

"Well, here's to you, Captain Sheppard." Buchanan lifted his mug. "Hope you don't get too deep into whatever you're involved in."

Sheppard didn't get a chance to comment. He turned his head when someone tapped him on the shoulder. Looking at the scantily dressed woman, he noticed with surprise that she wasn't human, humanoid but definitely not human.

"I'm told you're looking for female company." She spoke with a soft and seductive voice. Her breath smelled of alcohol and some sweet, heady fragrance he couldn't identify.

He was taken aback for a moment to find a non-human woman in this environment. "Who told you so?"

She held a finger against his lips. "Hush, don't ask questions. This is your lucky day. I'm Riinih, and I'm yours for the night. You're Jeremy Sheppard, right?"

"That's correct, but I never asked for female company. I just want to sit here and enjoy a drink with my new friends."

Her cat's eyes shimmered golden as she regarded him with a smile, displaying a pair of sharp fangs. "I'll be your friend. It will be much more fun. Have you ever been with a female of my kind?"

He shook his head. "I'm a newcomer to your planet. You are the first female of your people I've met."

She laughed softly. "Then you don't know the pleasure I can give you. We are different from human females." Her hand touched his neck. It felt hot. "Once you've tasted my body, you may never ever want to lie in the embrace of a human female again."

Somebody touched his arm. "She's telling the truth." He recognized Buchanan's rumbling voice. "Be careful. The Cats are not to be trusted. She could rip your throat out with those fangs."

"Don't believe your friend." Riinih laughed again. "I am harmless. All I want is to give you pleasure. Besides, my employer would not treat me kindly if I ever harmed one of his friends."

"You mean Max, don't you?"

She nodded.

"Are you his employee or his slave?"

Her eyes clouded over for a moment, but then she smiled. "Nobody owns me. I do this because I want to, and I'm good at what I do. Let me show you." She reached for his hand. "Come with me. I promise you will not regret it." Her smile seemed suddenly forced. "Please."

"Go with her," Reed said behind him. "Just watch yourself."

Sheppard rose from his seat, looking back with regret at his untouched mug.

Buchanan saw him looking and grinned. "Don't worry. It won't go to waste. I'm still thirsty."

Riinih pulled him through the crowd of people milling on the dancefloor. He followed her somewhat reluctantly and with some apprehension but also filled with curiosity. He had never had sex with a female of a non-human species and wondered how it would be with this Cat-woman.

She walked gracefully, her slim body moving seductively. Her black hair ran from the top of her head down her naked back to the swell of her round buttocks in a narrow band and the visible parts of her skin seemed to be covered with fine, light-colored fuzz.

They entered a narrow corridor and climbed a set of stairs into another corridor dotted with doors on either side. She stopped at one of the doors and opened it. "This is my room," she said and pulled him inside.

With only a narrow bed and a small closet in one corner, it was sparsely furnished. A basin with a water jug beside it stood on a low table near the bed. Closing the door, she stepped up to him and pulled his head down. Her lips were hot on his when she kissed him, and when she forced her tongue into his mouth, he again tasted the alcohol and the unknown substance.

Suddenly light-headed, he realized she must have transferred some kind of drug into his system when she kissed him. He closed his eyes to clear his head, but it didn't help. Opening them again, he saw her standing in front of him, her body swaying slowly back and forth. Looking at him with large, luminous eyes, she undressed. Coming closer, she removed his shirt and ran her hands over his upper body.

"You are muscular," she murmured in a husky voice and tugged on his pants. "Take them off."

He did what she asked with shaking hands. A cloud of desire had gripped his brain, and his body seemed on fire. When he was naked, he grabbed her and threw her onto the bed. Laughing, she pulled him on top of her. He fell between her opening thighs and moaned loudly when the inferno of her hot flesh engulfed him.

"I'D BETTER GET BACK TO MY FARM." SANCHEZ HELD OUT A HAND to old man Haggard. "The seeding is in full swing, and I've got a million things to do."

Haggard shook the younger man's hand. "You should visit once in a while, Herman. Take a little time off. You used to come around more often when Dolores was still alive. She was a good woman."

"She was, and I miss her, but she's gone." Sanchez wiped his hand across his mustache. "Life goes on, though. I'm lucky I've got Rosita. She pitches in and keeps me on my toes." He looked at Collins. "Hope things work out for you and this is what you want. Remember, there is no turning back."

Collins nodded. "I'm aware of that. Thanks for your hospitality and for bringing us here. I'm sure this is not the last time we will see each other. After all, we'll be neighbors from now on."

"I'm looking forward to seeing you and Kristie again. You take care now and keep those boys of yours out of trouble," Herman advised.

"They're old enough to know better."

Traverse and Randolph had walked to the corral where a number of horses were grazing. They had never seen live horses and neither had he. He looked at his daughter, who stood near her mother, next. Both of them were admiring the big house that would be their new home.

Lisa would have the roughest time of them all. She was eighteen years old and should be having fun, going dancing and to bars with her girlfriends, looking for a man to marry. He had taken that away from her.

"You're right. They seem to be level-headed. Well-behaved, but they need to be able to make their own decisions and be mature enough to fight if need be. This is still a frontier planet, even though humans have been here a couple of hundred years already. Things haven't changed much since the first settlers landed on Savanna. The Solar Union keeps us on a low-tech level for reasons we don't understand. Perhaps someday that will change."

He took off his wide-brimmed hat and slapped it against his pants. Squinting up at the sky, he said, "It'll be a hot day. We need some rain, but not until we get all the seeding done." He climbed back onto his wagon. Tipping his hat, he drove off.

Collins looked after him, thinking about what he'd said. Turning to the old man beside him, he said, "He seems like a descent man." He smiled before he added, "Loves to talk, though."

Nelson Haggard chuckled. "I've known Herman since he's a little boy. He was always a talker. His dad and I grew up together. He was a big man, not afraid of anything. A little wild sometimes. That six-shooter Herman is carrying? It was his dad's. Seen a lot of action in those days." He sighed. "We were good friends, Nicolas and me. I miss him and the good times we had."

"At least you have some good memories. Not everyone has them. Plenty of bad things happening on Earth and the colonies."

"Plenty of bad stuff happening here on Savanna, too. Let's go into the house." Haggard turned and limped away.

Collins followed him slowly, thinking about the future. Haggard and his wife appeared to be descent people, and things would turn out just fine. He felt positive.

———

"IF NOT FOR THIS DAMN BUSTED LEG OF MINE, I'D STILL BE IN good shape, despite my age." Haggard puffed angrily on his pipe and blew a cloud of blueish smoke into the air.

"I'm glad he mentioned his age," Angelica Haggard commented.

Short and a bit on the overweight side, she moved slowly when she walked, but otherwise she appeared feisty and full of spunk. "Let's be honest, working this ranch is too much for him and for me. He's seventy-five, and it's time he gives up this place. As for myself, I would have done it years ago. I'm not getting any younger, either, and this arthritis in my joints is not helping."

"I assume you have no children that could take over the ranch?" Kristie asked.

Angelica shook her head. "Our son died of the fever a decade ago. He was a fine boy." She dabbed her eyes delicately with a small handkerchief. Looking at Kristie, she said, "They made you aware of the conditions, I hope."

"They did. At least I hope we got it right. My family runs the ranch, and we will look after you for the rest of your lives. Eventually, the ranch will be ours. If things work out, of course."

"You got it." The old woman smiled. "Nelson and I don't need much anymore. We eat like birds."

"I won't be a burden," Haggard said. "I can still do some work. In fact, I insist you let me help out, and I hope, you'll ask for advice. I'm not a feeble old man, you know."

Collins chuckled. "I have a feeling I'll be bugging you constantly for advice. This is a big ranch, and I'm afraid my experience as a rancher is limited. On Earth, we don't have huge tracts of land like this, not to mention the large number of cattle you have. The fact is I've never ever seen cattle up close. There are no ranches where they raise cattle. They only exist in the protected animal reserves."

Haggard waved it off. "You'll learn, and you will have plenty of help. Rhe-annur, our foreman, is the best cattleman around, and his crew is loyal to him and to me. They may be Cats and a little wild sometimes, but they know how to handle the cattle. They will accept you as the new boss if I tell them to."

He rubbed his knobby nose. "Just remember, they will respond to you the way you treat them. Treat them fair and with respect, and they will respect you. They are not human and have their own code of honor. As strange as it sometimes seems to us, they are not stupid, like many humans assume."

51

"That band of Cats we met on our first day seemed hostile, especially their leader," Kristie said.

"Yes, unfortunately, not all of the Cats are friendly. Like in every society, there are outlaws and renegades." Haggard regarded Kristie silently before looking again at Collins. "I might as well fill you in, Collins. You will find out sooner or later. That group of Cats you've met is made up of a bunch of ruthless cutthroats. The Clan of Valley-riders, as they call their gang, have been harassing ranchers and farmers alike for years now."

"What do you mean by harassing?"

"Their leader calls himself Kiimzaan, which means Cloud-rider. He and his band come periodically and collect tribute."

"For what?"

Haggard chuckled grimly. "For providing us with protection."

"Protection from whom?"

"Apparently from the tribes of the Mountain-Claws. It's ironic, because we've never had any problems with them."

"Is there nothing that can be done about that? What about the military or the Trading Commission?"

Haggard laughed. "We can't expect any help from either. The military outpost is a joke. Nothing but misfits and cowards, and the Trading Commission is only interested in profits. They suck honest citizens like us dry."

Collins shook his head in disbelief. "It sounds to me like there are no laws to protect the settlers on Savanna."

"Don't kid yourself. There are plenty of laws, but none of them beneficial to us."

Collins looked at Haggard with a thoughtful expression. "I've noticed the natives carried bows and arrows. Surely, humans have more superior weapons than that?"

"Only the troopers and the lawmen of the Trading Commission are allowed to carry modern weapons like lasers. Regular citizens only get single-shot rifles, antique six-shooters, and shotguns. None of them worth a damn. You're lucky if you hit your target with the first shot and make no mistake—those natives are deadly accurate with their arrows."

"Oh, my," Angelica exclaimed, "I believe it's time for some tea and a piece of cake. I'll have to go and check up on Ernina." With that, she rose and hurried as fast as she could into the kitchen.

"She's a good woman, my Angie, and she never complains, but I know she's suffering with that arthritis. We're lucky to have Ernina. She's a great help, eager to learn." Haggard puffed on his pipe. Putting it down, he bent forward, his body racked by a sudden coughing spell.

Collins watched him with misgivings, hoping the old man would not make it a habit to pollute the air inside the house with his tobacco smoke. Eventually, they'd have to deal with that problem, if it ever became one. He remembered Sanchez suggesting he'd better get used to many new things on Savanna. Smoking might be one of them.

"Are you all right, Mr. Haggard?" Kristie asked, sounding concerned.

The old man seemed to be catching his breath. "I'll be fine," he wheezed. "It's the air at this time of year."

"I think it's the tobacco smoke," Kristie said. "I don't believe it's beneficial to your health."

"Now you sound like my wife. She never liked me smoking. I need it though. It relaxes me."

Kristie refrained from making a comment, but Collins said, "That's what Sanchez said. Apparently, he also needs it to relax him."

"You don't approve, Collins?"

"I believe in healthy living. You're inhaling a foreign substance. It'll kill you someday."

Haggard chuckled. "That sounds funny coming from a man who lived all his life breathing the polluted air of Earth."

"I can't argue with you there." Collins turned to look at the opening door. Angelica walked back into the room, followed by a young girl. He couldn't help but stare.

The girl wasn't human. She was tall and slim, with large blue eyes and pupils like the eyes of a feline. Her pointy ears were tipped with little tufts of hair. Noticing his scrutinizing look, she gave him a shy smile, exposing short fangs.

Angelica introduced the alien girl. "This is Ernina. She's baked us a cake. She's such a treasure. I don't know what I'd do without her. By the way, she's Rhe-annur's daughter. I believe Nelson already mentioned our foreman."

"He has."

"She's lovely," Kristie said in a hushed tone.

Collins had to agree. There was no denying the girl's beauty.

Angelica smiled. "You can tell her yourself. She understands and speaks Inglis."

"That's another thing we were never told during our information sessions. We had no idea humans interacted with the indigenous population." Kristie shook her head. "It seems there is a lot of information they neglected to give us."

Haggard laughed softly. "That's because if you knew the whole truth about this planet you may have decided to go somewhere else. This is not the paradise you most likely expected."

"There was nowhere else to go. They didn't give us another choice," Collins said. "Here we are, and we'll have to make the best of it. This is our new home—if we like it or not."

"You'll get used to it," Angelica assured him. "It's not that bad. Don't let Nelson scare you off."

"He doesn't. Sanchez already did that." Collins chuckled as if he had told a joke, but that small pit in his stomach had returned. He looked up at Ernina, who stood beside him, offering a piece of cake on a small plate. He took the plate from her hands. "Thank you. It looks delicious."

"It is delicious," the girl said with a little smile. She spoke softly, pronouncing each word clearly. He detected a slight accent, though.

When she turned away to walk over to Kristie, he noticed the split in her rough-spun dress to accommodate the strip of reddish-brown hair growing from her back.

Angelica saw him studying the girl. "She's like a daughter to us," she said. "She grew up in our house. Her mother died when she was just an infant, and when Rhe-annur brought her with him, we fell in love with her instantly. Since we only had one son, we adopted her."

"Legally?"

Angelica shook her head. "No. It's against the law, but that didn't stop us from taking her into our hearts. We love her like our own, law or no law."

"Do human men have…"

Kristie didn't finish the sentence, but Angelica obviously

understood what she meant. Collins had to smile, wondering why his wife would even think about that. He knew his wife. She wasn't exactly a prude, but, coming from a strict religious family, she did have her hang-ups when it came to sexual matters.

With a little chuckle, Angelica said, "Of course some men have sex with them. There are plenty of miners and treasure hunters out there without female company. Many of them will take a native female into their camp to live with them."

"Are you saying they take them as sex-slaves?"

"They are not slaves. The females go willingly. Apparently, there are more females than males among the Suumir, and many young females end up alone, without a mate or protection."

"These men marry them?"

"They live with them. The law does not allow marriage between different species, but nobody can forbid a man to live with a native female."

"I see. Are there ever any children from these unions?" Kristie seemed genuinely interested.

"Not often, but there are cases," Angelica admitted.

"What happens to these children? Are they considered human or native? Or what?"

"Sadly, these unfortunate children have a difficult time. They are considered neither human nor native. Most of the girls end up in brothels and the boys in the mines, or they join an outlaw gang." Angelica sighed. "Such a shame. Some of them might make good and productive citizens, but racism is alive and well on Savanna."

"Not just on Savanna," Collins said. "I've seen plenty of it on Earth." He kept watching Ernina. She had finished handing out the cake and was pouring tea into small cups. She appeared to be concentrating on the task, but he could tell she was listening to the conversation with great interest.

"One would think she'd prefer living with her own people," Kristie said.

"Why don't you ask her what she prefers," Angelica suggested with a little smile.

Before Kristie could put the question to Ernina, the girl said, "I am living with my people. They adopted me as their daughter, and I consider them my parents. I am happy here."

"What about your real father? Is he not your parent?"

"He is also one of my parents." She chuckled. "I have two fathers. I am lucky." She walked over to Haggard and planted a kiss on his cheek. She laughed when he wiped his cheek with a little grunt.

"You know I don't like this mushy stuff," he grumbled. "Save it for your future husband."

"Oh, Nelson, don't be such a grouch," Angelica said. "It wouldn't hurt you to be a little bit mushy with me sometimes. I'm not too old for affection." She looked at Kristie. "Don't let your husband get away with that. Always remind him of his husbandly duties, if you know what I mean."

"That works both ways," Collins said with a little smile. "Sometimes a wife needs to be reminded of her wifely duties."

"Oh, you." Kristie gave him that look she always used when she didn't approve of his remarks. "You can't complain."

Before anyone could say more, the door opened. Traverse, Randolph, and Lisa walked in. "Those are beautiful animals," Traverse announced. "One of them came over and let me touch it. When can I ride one?"

"You'll break your neck," Kristie said. "The only horse you ever rode was a wooden one when you were a kid. These are live animals and may be wild."

"I can learn. How hard can it be?"

"I could teach you."

Traverse turned to look at the open door that led into the kitchen. Collins didn't miss the surprise in his son's face when he saw the alien girl standing there.

"You're not human," Traverse blurted out.

Ernina shrugged and smiled. "No need to tell me that. I know."

"I'm sorry. I didn't mean to offend you. I'm just surprized to hear you speak Inglis."

"That happens when you live with human parents. Besides, I'm not unique. Many of my people speak the human language." She walked up to Traverse and looked into his face. "You have blue eyes, like me," she observed. "We have something in common."

"Your eyes are different. You have the eyes of a cat."

"That's why the first humans to meet my people called us Cats. The name stuck." She opened her mouth a little and touched one of her small fangs. "I'm surprised they didn't call us vampires."

"Why vampires?"

"Because…" She snapped forward with a sudden quick move, her mouth wide open. "I might want to drink you blood."

When he pulled away from her, his hands up in defense, she laughed.

"Don't play such foolish games, girl," Angelica chided her. "You're scaring the boy. That's not the way to start a friendship. You must realize, these are not visitors. They'll be staying here—for good."

"I wasn't scared," Traverse said. "She caught me by surprise." He gave Ernina a haughty look. "You may be alien, but you're still only a girl. Girls don't scare me."

"You could have fooled me." She smiled. "I'm sorry. I only teased you. You don't have to worry. I'm not a vampire." She became serious. "That's not saying vampires don't exist on Savanna. Many different life forms live in the forests and in the swamps. Humans have never heard of most of them and never seen any."

Randolph asked, "But you have?"

She shook her head. "No, I haven't, but sometimes, when I sit with my father and the cattle-hands, they tell stories, and I listen. Humans will never hear those stories."

"Ernina," Angelica chided her gently, "don't fill their heads with old legends and other horror stories they tell around a campfire. Give them time to adjust to their new home. They come from Earth, and the change is scary enough for them. Let's not add to their anxieties. There is plenty of time for your stories later." She smiled and added, "Much later."

"Perhaps they can tell me stories from Earth." Ernina looked at Lisa. "I'm Ernina, and I'm not human. Even though I was raised by humans, I'm still a Suumir. On the outside, anyway."

"I'm Lisa," she said with a little smile. "I'm human. At least I was the last time I looked into a mirror."

Ernina chuckled. "That's all right. It doesn't bother me, as long as you don't mind. We'll get along. You have red hair and spots in your face," she observed.

"They're called freckles. I have them on my arms also. I inherited the freckles and red hair from my dad."

"I like them. Have you moved into your room yet?"

Lisa shrugged. "Missis Haggard showed it to me, but except for my little suitcase I have nothing else to move in. All our stuff is still at the airport with immigration."

"Come, I'll show you my room. We can sit and talk for a while. Just you and me, two girls."

"Okay."

Collins watched the girls run up the stairs and was glad to see it. Even though the two girls were from different species, they may just become good friends. Lisa sure needed a friend.

His wife appeared to think along the same lines. "It seems they're hitting it off. I have a good feeling about it."

Angelica nodded in agreement. "Ernina is a good girl. How old is Lisa?"

"She'll be nineteen in four months." Kristie screwed up her face a little. "In Earth-months. We'll have to get used to a new calendar."

"It won't be too much different. The Savanna-year is only nineteen days longer, which means every month has exactly thirty-two days. Our day is actually a little shorter than a day on Earth." She smiled. "You'll never notice. Your body will adjust."

"Does a day still have twenty-four hours?" Randolph asked.

"Yes, it has."

"How can that work if the days are shorter?"

Angelica shrugged. "The scientific brains figured it all out. From what I understand, clocks and watches on Savanna have been designed to run a little faster. Any you brought from Earth are useless here." She chuckled. "Frame them and use them as decorations."

"Actually, they did tell us about that at the orientation meetings back on Earth," Collins informed them.

"I must have slept through that." Kristy laughed cheerfully.

"It appears so did I." Randolph joined his mother's laughter.

"I recall something about that," Traverse said. "We were

bombarded with a ton of information. It was impossible to remember everything."

"No need to break your heads over all that. We have plenty of clocks all over the place, which doesn't really matter, anyway. We get up when the sun rises and go to bed when it gets dark. We don't need no clocks for that." Haggard got out of his chair and limped over to the old cabinet in the corner. Opening one of the doors, he took out an object. Holding it up, he said, "I inherited this here clock from my parents. It's old but keeps the time as good as it did when I was young. Look at the workmanship. All hand-carved by one of the best clockmakers in Crystal City. He's dead now, but his son carries on with the tradition. He'll build you a clock you can pass on to your sons or your daughter." He chuckled and then bent over to cough.

"You should drink some water," Angelica suggested.

He waved it off with an impatient gesture. "Drinking water seems to fix everything with you, woman. I told you a million times, I don't drink water unless I'm thirsty." He shook his head, put the clock back in the cabinet, limped back to his chair and sank into it. "A glass of wine would be nice, though."

"Normally, I'd tell you to get it yourself," Angelica said, "but since we have guests, I'll go into the cellar and get a jug. I hope you'll remember the next time I ask you for a favor."

[7]

THE FIRST THING SHEPPARD SAW AFTER OPENING HIS EYES WAS A
ceiling above him. It didn't look clean. A coat of paint would help to
make it more pleasant to the eyes. He didn't know why he thought
that. Turning his head, he noticed a woman lying beside him. She had
her eyes closed and appeared to be sleeping.

Then he noticed she wasn't human.

His mind was sluggish, and he tried to put together the pieces of
memory creeping back into his conscious mind into something that
made sense. He didn't have a hangover, and he didn't remember
drinking much, but his head felt heavy. How long he'd slept he had no
idea. He didn't remember falling asleep.

The woman's name popped into his head.

Riinih. She belonged to the Cats, one of the indigenous races
native to Savanna, and he had spent what seemed like hours in her
arms and in her bed. The memory of the night flooded back with a
rush, and he sat up straight, immediately sorry when what felt like a
team of miners began hammering inside his head.

Holding his head, he looked down at the sleeping woman, and he
had to admit, her exotic look enhanced the beauty of her alien face.
The thin cover had slipped when he sat up and exposed her shapely,

full breasts. They didn't look any different from the breasts of a human woman.

Realizing, he was as naked as she, he looked around for his clothes. He spotted his pants, his shirt and his underwear in an untidy heap on the floor. The mattress creaked when he slipped from the bed, and he heard her moving behind him. Turning around, he saw her sitting up. Her cat's eyes were half-closed when she looked at him sleepily.

"You're up," she said with a lazy voice and yawned. Her thin fangs were clearly visible in her open mouth. Her arms reached for him. "Come back to bed," she purred. "You don't have to leave yet."

He pulled up his underwear and reached for his pants. "I'm afraid my allotted time is up." He gave her a crooked smile.

"I never gave you a time limit." She pushed the covers off with her feet and let her thighs fall open. "Doesn't this entice you?" Her smile was seductive and inviting.

He would have lied had he told her no, but he knew the smartest thing would be to get away as quickly as possible. The memory of the night was strong in his mind as was his desire for her. She had been right when she told him that females of her species were different from human women. He remembered her animalistic passion, her wildness as she abandoned any inhibitions she may have. The drug she fed him had, of course, played a factor in his response, but even without it her hot body would have reduced him to the savage, sex-crazed animal he became in her embrace.

"I'm all played-out," he said. "I wouldn't be of much use to you right now." He put on his shirt and tucked it into his pants. "Besides, my companions are probably waiting for me."

Her full lips formed a pout. "I was looking forward to spending more time with you. I don't always get to entertain a handsome man like you. Most of them are miners and treasure hunters looking for a night to satisfy their lust after spending time in the caves or mountains. They have no discipline and no finesse." She wrinkled her nose. "And they smell."

He chuckled. "I hope I smelled okay?"

She slipped from the bed and padded toward him on soft feet. Standing in front of him, she looked him in the face. "You were just another job for me, but I like you. You told me you were a newcomer to Savanna. You seem like a decent human man. Be careful. Not everything is as it seems on this planet. Don't trust everyone who acts nice and wants to be your friend." She pulled down his head and planted a quick kiss on his lips. "Choose your friends and associates wisely, human Sheppard. If you can. Some of us don't have a choice." Stepping back, she gave him a teasing smile and struck a sexy pose. "You're sure you won't change your mind?"

He shook his head and grinned. "I should be angry with you the way you seduced me. I know you drugged me to make me more pliable, but I'm not angry. It would not be the truth if I said I didn't enjoy last night. I enjoyed it so much, I want more of you. I have a craving for you, but I know it can't be. I can't afford to fall under your spell. You're of an alien species, and I'm an officer of the Solar Union, a human."

"Your loss." A shadow flickered across her pretty face, but then she smiled. "Perhaps another time. When you come back ask for me, but now I'd better get dressed also, since my naked body doesn't seem to have an effect on you."

"That's not true. Looking at you makes me desire you. You're one of the most beautiful and seductive women I've ever met. Tell me, why are you selling your body this way?"

"Because that's all I know how to do. I have no family back in my tribe. None that I know of, anyway. A prospector found me wandering in the desert when I was still a child. He took me in and raised me. He was a good man, but he died in a mining accident. His so-called friends abused me and finally sold me to Max."

"Now Max owns you?"

"He doesn't own me. I work for him, that's all. I'm free to go wherever and whenever I want, but where would I go? Max is my family now. This place is my home. I want for nothing, and he protects me. I can't ask for more."

"How about your freedom? I mean complete freedom that takes you anywhere you want to go."

She regarded him silently for a moment. The light falling through the window reflected in her golden eyes. "Are you free, Jeremy Sheppard?"

"As free as the union allows."

He knew she was right to question his situation. His body and soul belonged to the military. The day he became a trooper, he gave up his freedom. The Solar Union Space Navy owned him. That was the truth. Perhaps she should have asked is anyone really free?

"I think you should go now," she said. "I will guide you. You'll never find your way out of this building."

She took him down a set of stairs and along a dark corridor. He didn't remember if it was the same one they had come the night before. It wasn't, because she opened a door that led to the outside. When he stepped into the bright light, he said, "I have to find my companions."

"I can't help you with that," she said and closed the door.

Looking around, he could see it wasn't the black building they had entered but the one next to it. When he looked up, a connecting corridor between the two buildings was visible. He stood in a narrow back lane and wondered why she would let him out here. Not knowing which direction to take, he took a chance and tried the one to his right. Coming to the end of the lane, he knew he had taken the right one. Ahead of him lay the small parking lot where they had parked their vehicle the night before.

There was only one problem—the parking lot was empty. The vehicle was gone.

The bastards had left him behind.

What the hell was he supposed to do now? He had no local money and no knowledge of where he was.

The only one thing for him to do was to go back into the nightclub and hope somebody would be willing to help him. However, this time he would enter through the main entrance. The door was locked when he tried to open it, and when he banged his fist on the door, nobody answered. He had to face the fact that he was on his own with nobody to help.

The street was quiet, and no one was around. His watch told him it was still early in the morning. He could knock on doors, but somehow it didn't seem like a good idea. The houses on either side of the street were old and rundown. A few looked abandoned, judging by the broken windows and the open doors. This didn't appear to be the best part of the city.

He heard a clattering sound on the cobblestones. Around the corner came a carriage pulled by a horse. He'd seen horses before on other planets colonized by humans, but this was the first one he saw on Savanna. The only draft animals he'd seen this far were those giant goats.

When the carriage approached, he made a quick decision and stepped into its path. At first, it seemed as if the horse would trample him. He was ready to jump aside, but the horse stopped, snorting as it did.

The coachman on the seat glared at him. "Do you have a death wish?" he yelled.

"Not really," Sheppard answered. He moved to the side and looked up at the man. He was elderly with a nicely trimmed goatee and dressed in some kind of uniform. "I just wondered if you could be of help to me. I'm kind of lost."

"What are you doing in this part of the city?"

Sheppard grinned sheepishly. "I celebrated a little too much last night, and it looks as if my companions abandoned me."

"You should be more careful when picking your friends." The man studied him casually. "I assume you celebrated in that nightclub over there. What kind of business besides celebrating takes you to this seedy area?"

"I had no business with anybody. My companions took me along for the ride. They wanted me to get a taste of the nightlife in Crystal City."

"It seems you got more than just a little taste. This place is mostly frequented by miners, treasure hunters, and gamblers, and, of course, pleasure seekers. You don't look like a miner. Are you a gambler or just a guy out for some fun?"

Sheppard shook his head. "I'm neither. I come from the military outpost."

"A trooper? You must be a greenhorn if you accompanied your companions to this place. No upstanding trooper in his right mind would come here."

At that moment a woman struck her head out of the window. "What's the holdup, Justin?" Then she spied Sheppard. "Who are you?"

"I'm sorry for bothering you, ma'am. I'm Captain Jeremy Sheppard. Like I explained to your driver, I could use some help. I got myself lost and need transportation away from here. Back to the military outpost, if possible."

"You're not wearing a uniform. How do I know you are who you say you are?"

"I can show you my ID." He pulled back his sleeve and exposed his ID-band. Putting his fingertip on it, he activated a hologram of his head with his name in large letters above it. "Satisfied?"

She nodded with a little smile. "I've decided to help you. You can join my driver on the front seat."

"Thank you, ma'am. I appreciate it. As long as I get away from this place." He pulled himself up on the ladder and took the seat beside the driver.

"Don't call me ma'am," she called. "It makes me feel old. I'm Dr. Nicol Savon. I'm a psychiatrist. My husband is Dr. Clark Evington, the only qualified physician in Crystal City. All the others are quacks."

"I'll remember that when I need a doctor," he called back. Turning to the driver, he held out his hand. "Glad to make you acquaintance, Justin."

Justin shook his hand and chuckled. "Actually, it's not Justin. My real name is Clark."

"You're Dr. Evington?"

The man laughed. "The very same. My wife has a strange sense of humor. She likes to play games." He clucked his tongue, and the horse moved. "We'll take you to our clinic. From there I can call someone who will take you to your outpost. I'm afraid I can't spare the time. My patients are waiting."

"May I ask what are you doing in this part of the city at this hour?"

The doctor sighed. "I made a house-call. Normally I don't do that, but this was one of the VIP's of Crystal City, and I had no choice. You're lucky I took a shortcut to get home. My wife accompanied me as my medical assistant. Not only is she a psychiatrist, she is also a capable medical doctor."

"Is it true that you are the only physician in Crystal City?"

Evington chuckled again. "I'm one of only three surgeons, but there are a number of good doctors in this city. I could never handle all the cases by myself. A couple of doctors work out of the hospital where I perform my surgeries. My wife wasn't quite incorrect when she called some of the doctors in Crystal City quacks. Unfortunately, there is no shortage of so-called healers. They usually do more harm than good."

The horse neighed loudly and reared up, hoofs clawing the air when a figure grabbed the bridle. Evington cursed and pulled on the reins to calm the horse. Two more shapes strode into view. Men with scraggly beards, dressed in shabby clothes. They wore wide-brimmed hats and carried clubs.

Sheppard knew trouble had stepped into their path, and there was no way to avoid the confrontation. He wasn't afraid for himself, but the two civilians with him complicated things.

"Rogues!" Evington cursed under his breath. "Damn it. I forgot my gun at home."

"You should keep that horse under control. It almost got away from you," one the two men said with a grin.

"There was no problem until you blocked the road," Evington said sharply. "Now if you don't mind, I'll be on my way. I'm a doctor, and I have patients to take care of."

"He's a doctor." The man looked at his companion. "Do we have use for a doctor?"

The other one laughed. "Not yet, but who knows?" He shrugged. "Anything can happen."

During that time, the one who had grabbed the bridle moved closer to the carriage on Sheppard's side. "You look like a gentleman dressed in those fine clothes. How about climbing down from your high seat to allow me a good look at you. I don't like to crane my neck. It hurts."

"I'm quite comfortable where I sit," Sheppard said calmly.

The man smashed his club into the side of the carriage. "I guess I didn't make myself understood, unless you're hard of hearing. I want you to climb down. Right now!"

"Why don't you come up if you're so eager," Sheppard suggested.

The man climbed partially up the ladder and grabbed Sheppard's pant leg. When Sheppard heard a woman scream, he knew the time for action had arrived. He lashed out with his foot, hitting the man who had grabbed him in the shoulder. The man was forced to let go of the ladder and fell backward to the ground.

Sheppard didn't give him any time to recover. Jumping off the wagon, he brought the edge of his hand down in a chop to the man's neck as he tried to get up. He grabbed the club from his lifeless hands and moved around the front of the horse to confront a second assailant. Taken by surprise, the rogue didn't have a chance to bring up his own club in defense. Sheppard smashed his club against his unprotected head, not caring if he killed the man or not. His body had gone into attack mode, and all feelings of mercy had left him. Troopers of the Solar Union's Special Forces were trained to kill without remorse when attacked.

Moving to the other side of the horse, he met a third would-be robber, who held a long knife in his hand. He held it in front of him, moving it in an arc, proclaiming him as an amateur. No professional streetfighter would ever hold his knife-hand in such a clumsy way. Sheppard swept the knife out of his hand with one swing of his club. He kicked him in the chest with his booted foot. Following the kick, he moved in and broke his opponent's collarbone with one short chop. The man screamed and backed away, holding his useless arm with his good hand.

Sheppard looked at the fourth rogue, calculating his odds in disarming him without putting the woman in danger. "If you come any closer, I'll cut her throat!" the man shouted, holding her in front of him, a knife to her throat.

"Don't be stupid. If you kill her, you're dead. Put down your knife and let her go. You'll be free to walk away."

The man laughed. "It's not going to happen, because I'm not that stupid to believe you. She's my ticket away from here, and this is how it will go. The doctor will treat my companions, the ones you injured, and then you'll put them into the carriage. Then you and the doctor will take a walk. The bitch will come with us. Once we're out of sight, we'll let her go. Now, throw away that club and take a few steps backwards."

Sheppard threw the club to the side. It was a useless weapon anyway. "All right, you win, but you must promise not to hurt her."

He knew these men couldn't let them go. They would not free the woman. They'd probable rape her and then kill her. He looked up at Evington. "We don't have any choice, Doctor Evington. I suggest you come down and fix up these men."

Evington climbed down the ladder. "I'll have to get my bag. It's in the carriage."

The rogue made a motion with his head. "Get it and make it quick."

Evington looked at his wife and gave her an encouraging smile. "Don't be afraid. It'll be all right," he said with a low voice. He climbed up the carriage and got his medical bag. "There isn't much I can do for him." He pointed at the man with the broken collarbone. "All I can do is put his arm in a sling. He should go to the hospital for treatment."

"No hospital," the injured man said harshly. "Just fix me up and give me something for the pain." He threw an angry look at Sheppard. "It hurts like hell, you bastard. I should kill you for this."

Sheppard gave him a cold look. "You're lucky you're still alive. I could have as easily killed you. I don't like to be threatened with a knife."

"I was only going to scare you away. That's all."

"Never point a weapon at someone unless you plan to use it. Remember that," Sheppard advised him.

"Enough chatter," the man who held the woman hostage rasped. "Let's get this over with."

Evington finished putting the sling on the injured man's arm. He walked around the horse and bent down to check on the man who lay lifeless on the ground. Getting up again, he shook his head, looking at Sheppard. "He is beyond help. You smashed in his skull."

Sheppard shrugged. "It couldn't be helped. A club against a head will do that."

Just then the rogue, who had tried to pull Sheppard off the carriage, came into view. When he saw his companion on the ground, he cursed, rushed to his side and bent over him. Then he stared at Sheppard with a hateful look in his eyes. "You killed my brother. I promise you'll pay for this."

"You do something stupid and you'll join him. That's my

promise," Sheppard growled, anxious to get this whole thing over with. "Why don't you pick up your brother and put him into the carriage."

The man put his hands under his brother's arms and tried to pull him toward the carriage. He was only partially successful. "He's heavy. I need help. Where are Julian and Len? Did you kill them also?"

"They're alive, except they're busy threatening a helpless woman. Neither one can help you. I'm afraid you're on your own, because I'm not going to carry your brother."

The man cursed, let go of his brother, and walked around the horse. When he saw his companion with his arm in the sling, he said, "What the hell happened to you, Julian?"

Julian spit onto the ground. "He surprised me and broke my collar bone. What about you?"

"Never mind me. I'm okay." His gaze shifted to the fourth man. "You're the only one with a brain here, Len. You've done the right thing. Keep that bitch close. If she makes a wrong move, cut her throat." He bent to pick up Julian's discarded knife. Turning to Sheppard, he said, "I don't know who the hell you are and how you managed to overcome the three of us, but be assured, you won't get away unpunished. Now go and carry my brother to the carriage. The doctor can help you if you can't manage."

Sheppard knew he didn't have much choice but to follow the rogue's orders. It seemed he had missed his chance. Now he was faced with two men holding knives. He went to the dead man, grabbed his legs and dragged him toward the carriage.

"He's not a piece of meat, you fucking moron!" Josh shouted. "He's my brother, and you murdered him. The least you can do show him some respect. Ask the doctor to help you carry him."

Evington came over without being asked and picked up the dead man by the shoulders. Together he and Sheppard carried the corpse the rest of the way.

Len, who still held the knife against the woman's throat, backed away when Sheppard and Evington came closer, pulling her with him. She struggled in his grip but stopped when he pushed the knife a little deeper. When Sheppard looked at her, she mouthed the words "help me". Seeing the stark terror in her eyes, he knew he had to try his best to save her.

He and Evington laid the dead man onto the floor of the carriage and stepped back. Sheppard took a few steps away from the carriage to get some distance between him and the men.

"What do you want to do with them, Josh?" Julian asked, while cupping the elbow of his injured, useless arm. "I'm hurting bad. I want him punished."

"As do I. He needs to pay for killing Marcel," Josh said.

"You men attacked us. Your brother was killed in defense. There is no more need for bloodshed. You got what you want," Nicol Evington said. "You can just let us go," she pleaded.

"Let's get the hell out of here," Len said. "Should I cut her throat?"

"Not yet. Put her into the carriage. We'll have some fun with that bitch first, but there is no need to wait before I kill this bastard."

When Josh walked toward him with his knife ready to stab him, Sheppard knew he had only seconds to act. He observed Len remove the knife from the woman's throat. It was now or never. With a fluid movement he bent, pulled his knife from his boot and threw it, burying it in Len's right eye. He knew the man was dead the instant the blade destroyed his brain. Without waiting for Len's body to collapse, he rushed toward him and pulled his knife out of the dead man's eye socket. Swirling around, he faced Josh who stood staring at him, obviously not believing what just happened.

"Who the hell are you?"

"Obviously somebody you should not have messed with," Sheppard said with an icy voice. "I suggest you remove your dead brother from the carriage and disappear. If you insist, I will kill you, also. It doesn't matter to me."

"What makes you think you can kill me? I have a knife, and I know how to use it." Josh looked at him defiantly.

"Let's go." Julian pulled on Josh's arm. "I have no desire to die today."

"Smart man," Sheppard said. "You asked who I am? I'm a trained killer. I've faced adversaries more formidable than you and walked away. Take my advice, don't try to be a hero. You cannot win against somebody like me."

"He's right, Josh. You saw how easily he killed Len. He's not a normal man." He moved toward the carriage, and with his good arm, he pulled the body of Josh's brother out.

Reluctantly and with hateful eyes, Josh helped him carry the body to the side of the road where they laid him down.

"Don't forget your buddy, Len," Sheppard said. He looked at Nicol Evington. "I suggest you get into the carriage, Dr. Evington."

She nodded and followed his suggestion, closing the door behind her. Her husband climbed up the ladder and took his place on the seat. Sheppard walked to the other side and joined him.

"Let's move," he said. "I've had enough excitement for one day."

"You're not even out of breath." Evington snapped the reins to signal the horse to get going.

"I'm surprised about that myself. I'm a bit out of practice. It's been awhile since I saw action."

Evington glanced at him sideways. "You're not just an ordinary trooper, Captain Sheppard. I've dealt with military men from the outpost before, and I've never seen anyone like you. Some of them are drunks, some are drug addicts, and most of them are just a bunch of misfits. How do you fit in?"

"It's a long story and not worth telling. Let's just say I was wrongfully accused of a crime, court-marshalled and sentenced to a lifelong term to be served on this forsaken outpost."

"I won't pry. Just tell me this, what did you do in the military before you were sent here?"

"There's no harm in telling you. I was a member of an Elite group in the Solar Union's Special Forces." Sheppard stared into empty air, bitterness welling up inside him. He had dedicated his life to the military, prepared to serve the union and, if necessary, give his life protecting the citizens of the Solar Union, and his reward was fighting thugs in the streets of a backwater planet.

Evington nodded. "You're a dangerous man, Captain Sheppard. Remind me never to get on your bad side. By the way, thank you for saving my wife's and my life. Without you, we'd surely be dead now. Those men have no conscience and no respect for honest men. To them, life is cheap, and they have no qualms about taking it. We'll be in your debt forever. If you ever need anything, just ask. We'll try to help you any way we can."

"You're already helping me by rescuing me from getting lost in this city. All I need now is to get back to my outpost."

"You shall. As soon as we get back to our clinic, I'll put out the word on what we're looking for. We'll find someone who will take you home."

Sheppard chuckled. "If you could only find someone with a spaceship large and fast enough to take me back to Ceres where I was born, then I would truly be home. Perhaps, I should have become a miner like my father and my brother. My life would have been more peaceful." He sighed. "I've lived a violent life, Dr. Evington, and I've become a violent man. My only friends are other violent men."

"I'm not a violent man," Evington said softly. "I'll be your friend if you want me."

[8]

COLLINS WAS SURPRISED HOW QUICKLY BOTH OF HIS SONS HAD adjusted to life on a ranch. Both of them had been eager to ride the horses, and it hadn't taken them long to become excellent riders. Even Lisa conquered her initial fear of the big animals and learned how to ride. Of course, having Ernina as a teacher helped.

"I can't help but worry when they ride off by themselves." Kristie looked after the two girls as they disappeared among the trees.

"Don't worry so much. Ernina assured me that they never ride too far, and there are no dangerous animals in this area. The only potentially dangerous animals they ever encounter are the Ealas, and they are not known for ever attacking either a Suumir or a human."

Collins didn't feel quite as calm as he pretended to be in front of his wife. It wasn't animals he worried about. His concerns were the native outlaws that roamed the area, especially Kiimzaan and his band of cutthroats.

Thinking about that gang always upset him. He couldn't see paying extortion money to them for protection he apparently needed against an alleged threat from the mountain tribes. According to the old man Haggard, this racket had been going on for years now, and there was no way around it. He didn't see it that way. There had to be something that could be done. In the past three months, the band had come twice to collect. Each time they rode away with half a dozen steers and a couple of fine horses. The last time they took one of the breeding stallions. He knew, someday he would have to put a stop to it. He just didn't know how, not yet.

"I'm going in," Kristie said. "I've got a cake in the oven."

"I'll ride out to take some supplies to the men and see how the last batch of new foals is coming along," Collins told her. "A couple of them seemed a bit weak. I hope they survived. Rhe-annur assured me they'd be okay, and I trust his judgment. We're lucky to have him. I think he and the others have accepted me as the new boss."

Kristie smiled. "Giving each of them one of the indestructible knives you brought from Earth didn't hurt, either."

"A small price to pay for their loyalty."

"Those knives weren't exactly cheap."

"No, but we traded them in for a much bigger prize. This place is ours now, but we can't do it alone to keep it going. We need the help of the Cats. We need Rhe-annur and his men. They know this ranch, they are familiar with the horses, and they are great cattlemen. We couldn't do it without them." Collins gave Kristie a quick kiss. "I'll be back in time for supper."

"Don't be late. I'm making a roast and boiled taters. I also have some fresh vegetables from the garden."

"I'm looking forward to that."

He walked away, heading for the stable where the riding horses were kept. Before he reached it, the big door swung open, and Randolph came out, three horses in tow. Two were saddled, and the third one loaded with the supplies Collins was going to take to the camp.

"Where are you going with those horses?"

Randolph gave him a little smile. "I knew you were heading out today. I've decided to come with you. I hope you don't mind the company."

Collins chuckled. "Why should I mind if my son decides to spend the day with me? We aren't doing much of that these days. It'll be a pleasure to have you around."

"I thought perhaps you can teach me how to properly shoot this colt."

Collins looked at the gun hanging from a belt around Randolph's hip. "I don't think your mother would approve of you wearing a gun."

Randolph grinned sheepishly. "That's why I never told anyone that I've been secretly practicing. I'm pretty good with it, but I need those extra fine points only an expert like you can teach me."

"I knew that you boys have been practicing. Did you really think all that missing ammunition would go unnoticed?"

"You never said anything."

"No, I didn't. I think it's a good idea for you to learn how to handle a gun. I'm not crazy about it, but this isn't Earth. This new home of ours is not a friendly place, and you have to know how to defend yourself. You'll notice I said *defend yourself.* Never be the aggressor. It usually doesn't end well. Remember that as your first lesson." He swung himself onto his horse and waited for Randolph to do the same.

The cool north wind made him glad he wore the lined leather jacket. He noticed with satisfaction that Randolph also wore one. They headed south. Having the wind blowing from behind made it bearable.

"Mr. Haggard said it'll be a cold winter," Randolph said as he rode beside Collins.

"He told me the same thing." Collins smiled. His son was becoming a man. Living on the ranch seemed to be good for both the boys. In a way, they adapted to this new world much quicker than he and Kristie. They enjoyed the freedom of the vast land that surrounded them. The Haggard ranch was huge with a large tract of land. It would take them a couple of hours to reach the herd.

"How do you and Mom feel about Ernina?"

The question came unexpectedly. "How do we feel about her?" Collins gave Randolph a surprised look. "Why do you ask?"

Randolph shrugged. "Just curious."

"Since you ask, Mom and I both agree she's good for Lisa. Your sister is lonely. She's having a harder time adjusting than you and Traverse. She misses her friends back home."

"Does it bother you that Ernina isn't human?"

"Why should it bother us? Of course not. She's part of the Haggard family."

"Do human men ever marry Suumir women?"

"Some men, especially miners and hunters, will take a Suumir female into their camp to live with them, but nobody ever marries one. It's against the law. Why this interest?"

"I think Traverse is smitten with Ernina, but don't tell him I told you, please. I just thought you should know. I personally think it isn't right."

Collins took a moment to let it sink in before he answered. "It's not a question of right or wrong. It's all about common sense. Even though Ernina was raised as a human girl, it doesn't make her human. She is still a member of an alien species, different from humans. There are many things to consider. Genetics, for instance. Will they be able to produce children? From what I've heard, it is possible, but those children will never be accepted by the humans. Neither will the Suumir accept them. They will always be outsiders."

"I understand, and I agree with you, but what if they decide not to have children?"

"Your mother would be devastated. I'm hoping to have some grandchildren someday, too. We live on through our children and grandchildren. Without them, the Collins name would die out on this planet." He gave Randolph an almost apologizing smile. "I'm counting on you to carry on our name. Once you're old enough, though. Let's not rush it."

"First, I have to find the right girl. Perhaps I should say a girl. I haven't met too many."

"I know. That's a problem. After the fall, all the farmers and ranchers in the area get together for a celebration. I'm sure there'll be a few eligible girls there, but you still have plenty of time. You're only sixteen, for heaven's sake."

"You can't start early enough." Randolph smirked. "Remember, not a word to Traverse, okay?"

"I'll have to tell your mother, but don't worry. I won't mention your name. She needs to know about it. It's better if I tell her before she finds out herself. I'll just say that I saw Traverse and Ernina kissing."

"I hate to be the bearer of bad news, but I'm afraid they've done more than that." Randolph shrugged. "At least that's what Traverse admitted to me."

Collins lifted a hand. "Spare me the details. That's not something I want to discuss with my sixteen-year-old son. I was hoping things hadn't progressed that far. That may complicate it a bit."

"Sorry, Dad, I didn't mean to upset you."

"I'm not as upset as your mother is going to be."

They rode on in silence. He was not happy finding out his oldest son was having sex with an alien girl. He couldn't even blame Traverse. He was nineteen years old. His hormones were working overtime, and the only and obviously available girl around was not human. Collins had to admit Ernina was a beautiful girl by any standards. Her exotic looks made her even more attractive and desirable to a young man in his prime. Not only to a young man. Collins could not deny he felt the pheromones Ernina exuded when she was around.

However, it was not a welcoming situation. He knew how Kristie would feel about it. She had nothing against Ernina, but she may find it difficult to accept the alien girl as her daughter-in-law. He pushed it out of his thoughts. There was nothing he could do about it at the moment. He had other pressing matters to take care of.

The land had changed around them. The prairie-like countryside had been replaced by a dry stretch of land where nothing grew but some variety of cacti, but it was only a small area. As soon as they topped the hill they were climbing, they'd reach the river and a lush valley. That's where they would find the herd and the men watching over it.

Sometimes, he couldn't believe that all this land belonged to him. Technically, the Haggard's still owned it, but eventually it would be his. This ranch was one of the largest tracts of privately-owned land around. The Haggard family was among the oldest families on Savanna and one of the first to lay claim to the land. Since there had been no natives anywhere near this area, nobody disputed their claim. The Suumir tribes that lived near the Haggard territory now were the result of an expansion movement that occurred nearly fifty years after human colonists arrived.

Old man Haggard was a living encyclopedia when it came to the history of Savanna. He didn't mind sharing his knowledge, and Collins didn't mind listening. He had always been interested in the history of humanity on Earth and knowing details about the colonization of Savanna was something he was willing and eager to learn.

They reached the summit of the hill, and Collins stopped his horse for a moment to admire the breathtaking sight that lay ahead of them. He could never get enough of looking at the river and the productive land on each side. The valley was fertile with lush grass that sustained the big herd without difficulty. The river was not deep here and the current gentle. The herders had erected tents beside the river near a grove of trees in a permanent camp. There was even a small log cabin which they used when the weather turned nasty, but most of the time they preferred sleeping in their tents.

The majority of cattle were grazing on this side of the river, but he also saw a couple of small herds on the other side. Only two of the herders were over there to make certain none of the animals strolled away. He counted six riders sitting on their steeds, watching the rest of the vast herd.

Looking at the camp, he saw one horse and one alck tied to trees near the cabin. It meant Rhe-annur and one of the herders were at the camp, most likely the cook. Rhe-annur was the only one who rode a horse. All of the others preferred the native horned alck. They were bigger and stronger than horses, but they also had a much nastier temperament.

"It's beautiful," Randolph said beside him. "I wonder if there are fish in the river."

"I'm sure there are. Perhaps we should take one day and do nothing but fish." Collins smiled and looked at his son. "How do you feel about that?"

"That would be great." Randolph sighed. "I know it'll never happen. There is always something else you need to do."

"I know. Maybe next year, once we have things under control and learned everything we need to know to run this place. This is all new to us and a bit overwhelming, but we'll get there."

He gave his horse a gently nudge, and they proceeded to the camp.

When they came closer, the door to the cabin opened, and a big, muscular native stepped outside. His upper body was bare, but he wore leather pants. Even from this distance, it was evident he was tall, but the stiff bristles on his head made him appear even taller. Collins knew that Rhe-annur was nearly a head taller than he, and Collins was five feet eleven inches.

Rhe-annur watched Collins and Randolph come closer. He lifted a hand in greeting and closed one fist. "I was hoping you'd come today, Boss Collins," he said when Collins slid from his horse.

"Why? Any special reason aside from the supplies I brought?"

"I suspect Kiimzaan and his band will pay us a visit today. My men reported a couple of his followers near the herd yesterday. One of these days he won't ask for anything. He'll just take what he wants."

"That'll be the day we'll kill that insolent bastard," Randolph said fiercely.

Collins didn't miss the disapproval in Rhe-annur's blue cat's eyes. "That would be unwise. Killing Kiimzaan will only bring the wrath of his people on us. We'd need an army and better weapons to defend ourselves."

Randolph patted the colt on his hips. "We have superior weapons."

Rhe-annur smiled, exposing his fangs. "You'd be lucky just to hit his alck with that thing. Besides, you'd be riddled with arrows before you can even draw your weapon." He turned to Collins. "We should soon get ready to move part of the herd back to the ranch where we can choose the animals we want to take to the market."

Collins nodded. "That was something I wanted to discuss with you. I'm not quite sure yet what the procedure is. I will need your input and advice."

"I will gladly help, Boss Collins. Did you want to inspect the horses first?"

"I wouldn't mind. How are the two foals?"

"They are coming along and appear healthy. We also have some new additions to the herd. One of the mares delivered twin foals, and they are doing fine. They'll grow into a couple of strong stallions to produce many fine horses for you."

"That's good news, especially since Kiimzaan helped himself to one of our best breeders the last time. We can't let that happen again." Collins sniffed the air. "What is the cook making for dinner? It smells good."

"Elgorke." Rhe-annur's teeth gleamed white in the bright sun as he smiled broadly. "You should give it a try again."

"No, thank you. Last time I got an upset stomach from eating it." Collins shook himself as he remembered. Elgorke was a typical dish favored by the Suumir. It was a stew made from lizard meat, mixed with a certain type of fungi and the leaves of a water plant.

"I'll tell the cook to prepare a couple of gills for you. We caught them this morning." He went back into the cabin and came out a few moments later. "They'll be ready when we return." He went to get his horse and swung himself onto its saddleless, broad back.

They rode along the river toward a low mountain ridge. The grass grew sparse and turned brown as they left the vicinity of the river, and the vegetation changed again to the cacti-like plants.

Had Collins not known what lay ahead, he would have wondered why they were heading for the mountains, especially since the landscape looked bleak and uninviting, but as they neared the mountain range, they came to a narrow gap between two high cliffs. The gap widened and then they rode into another lush valley. It was protected by mountains on all sides and only accessible through the gap they just passed through. A narrow river, which came down as a waterfall from the mountains, wound its way through the valley, providing water for the grass and the trees, and the horses that grazed along the river.

There was no need for a large group of men to guard the herd. The two Suumir-males, who sat in the shade of a tree beside a large tent, were adequate to make certain none of the horses escaped. They had only one way to go and that was through the gap.

When the two herders saw Collins and his companions approaching, they got up and watched the three riders come closer.

A large bird on a stick broiling over a fire appeared more inviting than the Elgorke the cook back at the camp was preparing. One of the Suumir saw Collin checking out the bird and said something in his native language. Not all of the Suumir-males working for the Haggard-ranch spoke Inglis.

"What's he saying?" Collins looked at Rhe-annur.

"He says he'd be honored to share the gral with you and your son when it's ready to eat."

Turning his attention back to the other Suumir, Collins lifted his left hand and made a fist with only his little finger up and touched his chin. It meant thank you in the native sign language.

"We won't stay that long. Besides, there isn't enough meat on that bird for all of us," he told Rhe-annur. "Tell him that."

Rhe-annur relayed the message. The other Suumir nodded and made a little bow toward Collins, showing his respect for his boss. He said something again in Suumir.

Rhe-annur spoke to him in his native language before turning to Collins. "He wants you to have a look at the foal that was born this morning. It has a white coat with only a patch of black on its forehead. He's quite excited about it. As you are aware, completely white horses are rare in our herd. We'll have to make certain Kiimzaan does not find out about it."

"That won't be an easy task. Perhaps, once the foal is old enough, we'll take it with us to the ranch and keep it close."

The mares that had given birth to new foals were kept in a corral, away from the main herd to give them a chance to bond with their offspring and to protect the foals and the mothers from predators.

The white foal was still a little wobbly on its long legs but seemed strong enough to follow its mother around. The mare was quite protective of its offspring and moved between the foal and the four intruders, snorting a warning not to come too close.

"She's a wild one with plenty of spunk," Randolph commented. "I noticed the foal is also a female. Perhaps we can start a new strain."

"If she passes on her genes to a stallion that would be wonderful. A completely white stallion would be a great asset in our herd," Collins mused.

"It would also arouse the interest of Kiimzaan." Rhe-annur dampened their enthusiasm a little.

"We would deal with that if it ever came about. Let's have a look at the other foals. I'm interested in their progress." Collins wandered over to the spot where a couple of mares stood in the shade of a few trees, their foals near them. There was a trough carved out of a tree filled with water that was pumped out of the ground by a windmill. The first time he had seen the contraption, he marvelled at the primitive way to supply water but also at the ingenuity of it.

Back at the ranch, they got their water from an artesian well that emptied itself into a creek near the main building. It provided them with fresh, cold water summer and winter.

None of the ranches and farmhouses had electricity. Homes were heated with wood. The cooking was done on wood stoves. Candles and oil lamps provided light when it got dark. It took him and his family quite some time to adjust to living under such primitive conditions, but humans are adaptable, and they adjusted.

One of the foals seemed intrigued by the newcomers and trotted closer, eyeing Collins and Randolph with suspicion but also with curiosity. Randolph reached out slowly to touch the narrow forehead. "You're an inquisitive little feller, aren't you?"

The foal rubbed its head against his hand. Randolph laughed happily. "I have a feeling you and I may someday be good friends." He looked at Collins. "We should take this one with us and train him, Dad."

"He's still too young. Once he's a little older, perhaps."

"We should head back," Rhe-annur suggested. "If Kiimzaan shows up I want to be in the camp."

Collins nodded. "Everything seems to be in order here. I agree with you. I want to be there also." He looked toward the herd by the river. "We'll take a couple of horses with me. I'm sure he'll be asking for at least one. That's all we'll be offering. He's already got one of our breeder stallions. Also, I don't want to give him more than three cows. We can't afford to give him more than that. He's been getting greedy and more demanding. I want to make it clear to him that what we give him is enough for what we get in return, which is nothing."

"I cannot argue that, but he will not be happy. Kiimzaan is dangerous and unpredictable. You have to be careful, Boss Collins."

"I realize that, but there comes a time when we have to stand up to the ones who take advantage of us. If we don't, they'll own us and control our lives. That is something I'm not going to let happen. Kiimzaan is no fool. He knows if he pushes too hard, the ranchers and farmers will eventually take a stand, and then there is our military post. They have superior weapons and can wipe out Kiimzaan's gang in a short time." Collins didn't add that according to what Haggard told him, the settlers couldn't expect much help from the military, but he didn't have to tell Rhe-annur that.

When they arrived back in camp, the herders had already finished with lunch, but as promised, the cook had prepared two gills for them. "There is more than enough here," Collins told Rhe-annur. "Come and share a meal with us. I don't feel like eating alone."

"You have your son for company," Rhe-annur pointed out.

"Yes, but I'd appreciate it if you joined us." He smiled. "Randolph eats with us every day, but to share a meal with you is a special privilege."

"Thank you, Boss Collins. I will accept your invitation, but you must allow me to offer a small piece of the meat to the many-armed Sky-gods."

"Gladly."

They ate in silence. Collins respected the custom of the Suumir not to have loud conversations when they consumed their food.

While they ate, he became aware of faint drumming sounds, evidence of many hoofed animals running across hard ground. The sounds grew louder as he listened. Kiimzaan and his band of raiders were near. At the same moment he thought this, Rhe-annur said, "Kiimzaan is on the other side of the hill. He's close."

Collins nodded and rose, adjusting his gun belt. He didn't anticipate any trouble, but with Kiimzaan one never knew. It was a good idea to be ready for anything. He looked toward the hill, and it wasn't long before the first riders appeared at the top. Kiimzaan rode in front of the others. There was no mistaking his imposing figure. The males of the Suumir were, on the whole, large and tall, but Kiimzaan was taller and bigger than most Suumir Collins had met.

He did a quick headcount as the riders came closer and estimated there were at least twenty raiders in the group. Too large a group to take on should things go sour. It wasn't the first time he wished he had a laser or at least one of the old-fashioned rapid-fire handguns. He cursed the restrictive rules the governments of the Solar Union and the Trading Commission imposed on the settlers. What use was it to be a member of an advanced race when you couldn't take advantage of the superior weapons technological advanced races possessed?

Kiimzaan reined in his steed in front of Collins, making it rear up on its hind legs. The alck pawed the air for a moment and issued a defying scream. With its painted horns, it looked as vicious as Kiimzaan. If the gang leader wanted to make an impression with his show, he succeeded. Collins had to admit, the Suumir outlaw was a formidable adversary.

Collins smile grimly. That's why Kiimzaan would be the first to die should trouble arise.

Kiimzaan read Collins' smile the wrong way. "This is the first time you greet me with a smile, Human Collins."

"There is always a first time, Cloud-rider." He took advantage of the outlaw's apparent good mood.

"I am glad to see you happy, Collins. It will make it easier for both of us. I need six food animals and three horses today." Kiimzaan fastened his gaze on Collins' and Randolph's horses. "I also want that one." He pointed at Randolph's horse.

"I don't think so," Randolph said with a loud, belligerent voice. "That's my horse. It is not up for negotiation."

Kiimzaan's golden cat's eyes focused on Randolph with a bemused expression. "The cub is showing teeth he wished he had. I don't believe you understand the way things are, youngling. I take what I want."

Randolph touched the gun hanging from his hip. "Not today. You come onto our property uninvited. You steal our cattle and our horses, and you want more and more. If you think that this will continue forever, you are mistaken. If need be, we will defend what is ours."

Kiimzaan's cat's eyes became tiny slits, but only for a quick moment. His lips pulled into a wide grin, giving him the appearance of a predator ready to pounce on its prey. His attention switched to Collins. "I will overlook this insolent cub's threat, because he is still young and stupid, but now I want both of your horses in addition to the six food animals."

Collins shifted his weight from one foot to the other, weighing his chances of survival should he draw his gun or how many of the raiders he would be able to kill before he collapsed under a hail of arrows. He had only six bullets. He couldn't count on Randolph or Rhe-annur. Randolph might kill one or even two, and Rhe-annur could possibly kill one of the raiders with a thrown knife. That still left too many of them alive to take revenge.

He clenched his jaws and forced himself to relax, even smile. "You have to forgive my son. Like you said, he is still young, but that horse is his favorite. He has made a special spirit-bond with it. You would not want to anger the gods by breaking that bond. The same goes for me and my horse. Once a bond is made, it is for life. If you forcefully separate a human from his bond-mate, you condemn the animal to eternal suffering, and the bond-breaker will die in a horrible way."

The outlaw leader looked perplexed. "I did not know humans practice spirit-bonding. I will honor your custom by not taking your horses, but I still request six food animals and three horses."

"That is another thing we need to discuss. We cannot sustain our existence giving you that many cows and horses. Our herd will be depleted. If you insist on taking many animals every time you come, I will be forced to give up ranching. That would be bad for my family and for you. I will give you two fine horses and three fat cows today. The same goes for next time. I believe it is a good deal for what you give in return." He wanted to add which is nothing but refrained from doing so. No need to antagonize Kiimzaan more.

"Your herd has many animals," Kiimzaan said.

"The ranch takes much gold to keep running. The only way I get gold is by trading my cows and horses at the market. The Trading Commission gives us little gold, and it takes many animals to get the amount of gold we need. I have no control over that. If you keep taking too many of my cows and horses, you'll ruin me. That is the truth."

Kiimzaan seemed to mull it over. Finally, he nodded and said, "I will take what you offer."

"Good." Collins held out his hand. "Let's shake on it. It is an old human custom to shake hands. It creates a bond of goodwill and trust between men."

Collins didn't expect it and was surprised when Kiimzaan bent and took the offered hand.

"I am familiar with that custom," the outlaw said.

[9]

DIRTY AND PHYSICALLY DEMANDING, WORKING IN A MINE WASN'T for weaklings or men who put too much emphasis on cleanliness. Most of the treasure seekers who went down into the underground tunnels expecting to get rich quickly didn't last long enough to make it happen. Even the ones that didn't give up were not guaranteed success.

Jerry Buchanan sat on one of the big boulders that some violent event in the past had haphazardly scattered across the tunnel floor. He watched as his partner, David Reed, tried to remove a large blue diamond from a stalactite with his small laser, careful not to damage the precious crystal.

Blue diamonds were not a rarity, not on Savanna, but they were worth a fortune in the rest of the galaxy. What angered Buchanan was the fact that the Trading Commission practically stole them from the miners. If they could get the diamonds off planet and get paid what they were worth, they would be rich in a short time, but the Trading Commission controlled everything that happened on Savanna, including the diamond trade.

"Take a break, Reed," Buchanan called. "That diamond isn't going anywhere."

"I'm anxious to see how clear it is. I think I struck it lucky this time."

Buchanan laughed, but it wasn't a happy laugh. "You mean the Trading Commission struck it lucky."

"No, I mean I did. I'm not going to sell this one to the Trading Commission."

"Did you find some other trader who will give you a fair deal?"

"If you must know, I have. Remember the last time we were in Crystal City? You may even remember that hot girl I spent a few pleasurable hours with. Well, she told me about a man who has dealings with Spacers that don't ask too many questions. They pay top price for blue diamonds and other precious stones. I will give her this diamond on consignment."

Buchanan shook his head in disbelief. "You're naiver than I thought. You don't really trust a girl you shagged, do you?"

Reed turned to stare at Buchanan. "You know for a big man you must have a really tiny brain. There seems to be no room in it to allow for a little trust in your fellow human beings. Not everyone is out to cheat you. There are actually still some descent, trustworthy people out there. Riimi is one of them. She's honest and open. We didn't just *shag*, as you so crudely put it. We had a long conversation about many things. She's quite educated and knowledgeable. The reason she works in that nightclub is to make some extra money to buy a little house. Besides, I'm not the only one she deals with. She showed me a box filled with diamonds other miners have entrusted her with."

"That is the reason you trust her? It only tells me there are other fools like you. Unbelievable."

"Watch who you're calling a fool, you big ogre. Remember when you made a deal with that so-called officer from the freighter Starstream? The one who promised you a berth on same freighter for a couple of your most precious blue diamonds? Remember that? Do you also remember how that turned out?"

"Thanks for bringing that up," Buchanan growled. "That's one incident in my life I'm trying hard to forget."

"Who's the fool now? Instead of spending the rest of your life lying on a white beach on a paradise-like planet the way you imagined, you're still living most of the time in these dark tunnels searching for the illusive perfect blue diamond."

"That's the reason I don't trust anyone anymore. You should do the same. A smart man learns not only from his mistakes but also from the mistakes other people make. You're my friend, and I don't want to see you get hurt. That's all."

"I'm touched by your concern." Reed put his hand over his heart. "By the way, are you going to sit there all day and watch me or are you going to do some work?"

Buchanan sighed. "Sometimes I get into this downer mood. Today is one of those days where I ask myself why the hell I ever came to this backwater planet to fulfill a lifelong dream of becoming rich. Let's face it, we're stuck on this friggen planet for the rest of our lives, condemned to live in damp tunnels below ground, like goddam rats, digging for treasures to make the Trading Commission become richer and more powerful."

"Where else would you have gone? The Trading Commission is on every planet that's being colonized. They have the monopoly. That's just the way things are, and there is nothing you can do to change that. Accept it and make the best of it." The little man went back to his diamond.

Buchanan groped in his pocket and took out the three stones he found in the morning. They were of a good size and should fetch a descent price, even at the artificially low price the Commission paid. If there was only a way to find a different buyer, but he knew it was useless to lose sleep over it. There was no other company in the Solar Union with the resources to even think about starting an enterprise on another planet, not in the early stages of its development. That and the fact that the commission would never allow a competitor setting up shop anywhere on the planets they controlled.

The Trading Commission built the first roads and the first homes in every new existing settlement. It provided building materials, tools, and machines. It even financed the first settlers, just to get things going. None of it was done for free. The stockholders of the commission demanded a return for their investment. Many people assumed the Trading Commission was just another arm of the Solar Government, but Buchanan knew that was far from the truth. The commission was an enterprise, a vast private company. Many of its executives were members of the government, which made the company a powerful entity.

He returned the diamonds to his pocket and rose from his place on the boulder. No sense to sit and brood. Nothing would come out of it. He had heard rumors that some miners had secret dealings with sailors from incoming ships, but those were only rumors. Nobody knew for sure. If any of the miners he associated with were aware of it, they kept their mouths shut. The Trading Commission had spies everywhere, and the peacekeepers of the commission were ruthless and merciless. They were the law, and nobody ever investigated the disappearance of a miner or treasure hunter or even wondered about it. Everyone knew that those professions were not without hazards.

Buchanan adjusted his headlamp. They were available from the Trading Commission. Without those lamps, none of the miners could work in the dark tunnels. The Commission provided them at a fair price. The energy-cells that powered the lamps lasted for a long time, and the light they emitted was as bright as the mini-suns some of the miners used to light up their workplace. Buchanan preferred the headlamps. They gave him light where he needed it without him worrying about shadows.

In some way, miners had an advantage on Savanna, even though every miner was required to register with the commission and buy a licence that needed to be renewed every year. They were allowed gadgets the settlers were not permitted to possess, like direction finders, seismic instruments to search for hidden caves, and other advanced tools. The special lasers the miners used to extract the diamonds from the minerals encasing them were also supplied by the Trading Commission. These items were strictly controlled by the Trading Commission and were only available from the commission. Only licenced miners were able to buy them.

Thinking about the commission made his thoughts drift to one of his friends. "Hey, Reed, have you talked with Gardiner lately? He's got himself that new gadget. You know the one that finds hidden caves with soundwaves? I wonder how that is working out for him."

"I talked to him last night back at camp. He hinted he may be onto something. He never said what. You know how secretive he always is."

"I know, but I'll bet anything he's looking for a cave behind these tunnels walls."

"I wouldn't be surprised." Reed lifted his head and listened to something. "Did you hear that?"

"I didn't hear anything, but it's no secret my hearing isn't the best anymore. Too many explosions without ear protection, that's what. What is it you think you heard?"

"A dull sound, like an explosion. It came from ahead."

Buchanan put a hand behind one ear and listened. "I hear nothing. Perhaps it was just a ghost. According to the Cats these subterranean tunnels are supposed to be haunted."

Reed made a rude sound. "Superstitions. I don't believe in ghosts or evil spirits. It seems humans are not the only ones who believe in the supernatural. I don't. No, this was definitely an explosion."

"Maybe Gardiner found his hidden cave."

"As long as he didn't blow himself up. He's one of the most accident-prone guys I ever met."

Buchanan laughed. "He's also got two left feet. Did you ever see him walk? No wonder he trips over everything." Buchanan stopped talking and listened. "That was definitely an explosion. You were right. It came from that direction, and that's where Gardiner and Kohud are working a spot."

Both of them listened for a while but everything stayed silent.

Buchanan shrugged and unclipped the UVL-Emitter from his belt. Sliding it slowly across the wall, he looked for telltales of certain minerals that would signal the presence of diamonds. It was a tedious job and required patience.

In his estimate, a couple of hours had passed since they heard the explosion, before he became aware of the sound of boots approaching fast. Then he saw two lights coming closer. It could only be Gardiner and Kohud. They were the only miners who had gone in that direction. He wondered why they were already returning. It could only mean they found something big.

"Maybe they hit the mother-lode," Reed voiced Buchanan's thoughts.

"Either that or one of them got injured." Buchanan hoped he was wrong. Miners couldn't afford to get injured. Most of them were loners and being unable to work could mean a death sentence. Unless they had been lucky enough to save up for such an eventuality and had the foresight to get a Suumir female to live with them, there was nobody to look after them. Suumir females, if treated fairly, were loyal companions.

Gardiner was the first one to arrive. He stopped and took a few deep breaths before he blurted out, "We discovered evidence of an ancient civilization."

"How can you tell it's ancient?" Reed sounded skeptical.

"Because everything is covered with a thick layer of dust. It hasn't been disturbed for centuries, and nothing like that should exist on Savanna."

"What exactly did you discover?" Buchanan was curious, even though he felt the way Reed sounded.

"We located a cavern behind one of the tunnel walls and blasted a hole through the wall. It was barely a couple of feet thick at that point. The air blowing out of that hole was icy cold. Kohud and I crawled through the hole and discovered a large cavern. One of the walls was covered with small and large screens with levers and buttons below those screens. Everything looked unfamiliar. One thing was clear to us right away."

He didn't pause as Kohud joined them.

"None of the indigenous races on Savanna are capable of building something like that, but what really convinced us that we had stumbled on ancient, alien technology was the fact that as we went closer to those screens, we felt some kind of pulling in our heads. It almost made us dizzy. That's when we split."

"You're sure you didn't image it?" Reed grinned. "I've heard you tell stories before."

"It's true," Kohud told them. "I felt the same thing. It was a strong magnetic field that made our instruments behave crazy."

Buchanan looked at his partner. "You want to check it out, Reed?"

Reed shook his head. "It's a long walk back there, and I don't feel like a long walk. We have nearly an hour to get back to camp."

"That's precisely why I don't want to go back there today," Gardiner said. "Maybe never."

"If what you say is true, you should report it. This sounds like military business. They'll send a few troopers to check it out," Buchanan said. "It could be dangerous."

"That's what I was thinking." Gardiner put down his backpack and sat on it. "Getting old. Can't run anymore like I used to. I should have looked for a closer spot to find my diamonds."

"Have you been lucky, at least?"

"Nothing to shout about. It was Arnold's idea to look for a cavern, something not yet found by anyone else." He chuckled. "Well, we found something like that, but not what we hoped to find."

"I wouldn't check it off yet." Buchanan had a thought. "If you want, the four of us could all go there tomorrow and have another look. There might be a fortune in electronic equipment, especially if it's some ancient technology. Once you get the military involved, they'll confiscate everything, and you may lose a great opportunity. I think we should examine everything a little closer before we report it."

"That's not a bad idea," Reed said. "I'd be willing to sacrifice some of my time to check it out."

"It's a dumb idea." Gardiner shook his head vehemently. "I'm not going back there. You didn't experience what Arnold and I did. My head still feels funny, and my legs are wobbly."

"That's because you ran for half an hour. My legs would be wobbly, too." Reed looked at Kohud. "How about you?"

"I agree with Terry. My head feels strange, also. There is something about that place that is eerie. Maybe it's haunted."

Reed laughed. "Now you sound like Buchanan. He believes in ghosts."

"Don't be stupid. I never said I believed in ghosts. All I said was that these tunnels are supposed to be haunted."

"That's like saying you believe in ghosts." Reed chuckled merrily.

Buchanan made a dismissing motion with his hand. He wasn't going to get into a useless argument with the little man. Reed enjoyed needling him, and sometimes he just had to ignore it. "Listen, Gardiner. If you want to report this to the military, I can give you the name of a trooper I know."

"Yeah? That would be nice. I didn't know you were chummy with a trooper."

"He's not chummy with anyone," Reed interrupted. "Last time we were in the city, we met a guy who claimed to be a trooper." He glanced at Buchanan. "What was the guy's name?"

"I was just about to tell Gardiner that, but you had to interrupt and put in your seven credits, which are worth nothing. The trooper's name is Sheppard. I believe he said he was a captain. I thought he and I made some kind of connection." He stared at Reed. "But you wouldn't notice those things."

"You can't notice things that aren't there."

"It was there. I make friends easily. Something you can't claim. You turn people away with your constant wisecracks. People don't like that."

"You two bicker like an old married couple." Gardiner shook his head in apparent disgust. "I think it's important to report that cavern to the military. They have the equipment to check out everything. I'm not going to mess with stuff I don't understand. Captain Sheppard. I can remember that name. Tomorrow morning I'll ride to Outpost Alpha. I need to get back to the city anyway to pick up some supplies." He glanced at his partner. "I hope you'll come with me. I hate to ride alone. One never knows what comes across the road."

"I'll go with you," Buchanan said. "They may not let you into the outpost, because Sheppard doesn't know you. I've been wanting to pay Outpost Alpha a visit for a long time. This would be a good opportunity, especially since I have a connection there."

Reed coughed loudly, but Buchanan ignored him. He looked at his watch. "Time to quit. We need to get ready for tomorrow."

———

"CAPTAIN SHEPPARD. I BELIEVE YOU'VE BEEN AVOIDING ME. We've been here over three months now and barely talked with each other. Is that how you treat old friends?"

Sheppard gave Major Daniels a cool look. "We're acquaintances from the ship. You can't call that being old friends or even becoming friends. Besides, I didn't want to disturb you since you've probably been busy drawing up plans for the bridges you want to build. Also, I've been occupied with my own stuff."

Daniels let out a short laugh. "You know as well as I that there won't be any bridges erected for quite some time on this planet. For that to happen, I'd need a full team of architects, engineers, and planners, in addition to modern construction machines, which aren't allowed on Savanna."

"If not building bridges, what is your purpose in being here, Major Daniels?"

"Let's say I'm here as an observer and researcher."

"In other words, a spy. Who are you spying on? Colonel Wainwright?" Sheppard chuckled. "Me?"

"Hardly. If I were a spy, there'd already be a team of MPs here to throw your friends Lieutenant Fox, Sergeant Foster, and McCullum into the brig. Perhaps even you."

"You have been spying."

"I make it a point to familiarize myself with my surroundings. I study the people I associate with, and I want to know what everyone is involved in. I'm not only an engineer, I'm also a trained psychologist." His smile showed no humor. "Don't worry. I'm not after your or your friends' hides, even though what they're doing is criminal. They're stealing military property, which makes them thieves. They're selling forbidden weapons to people who are not supposed to have them. I also know that Colonel Wainwright is turning a blind eye to their activities. They're doing it with his blessing to secure the brandy he keeps in his liqueur cabinet to feed his addiction."

"I'm sure you're also aware of the fact that none of the troopers, including Colonel Wainwright, are here voluntarily. To be stationed on this outpost is like a prison sentence. The men are bored and in despair. Is it any wonder they turn to activities that are not quite lawful? By the way, they're not my friends."

"I guess you're referring to the time when they abandoned you in Crystal City." Daniels chuckled. "I guess a man might develop certain negative feelings toward the ones who did that to him."

"You know about that also?"

Daniels smirked. "Nothing gets by me, Captain Sheppard. I'm aware of everything that's happening on Outpost Alpha."

"I assume you're keeping notes?" Sheppard didn't hide his sarcasm.

"In my head. Only in my head. I have nothing to gain by reporting what goes on here."

"Why are you here?"

"You'll find that out at the appropriate time. I've been watching you, Sheppard. You're not like the others here. Most of them are misfits, and a few of them shouldn't be in the military at all. We can't just eliminate them physically, so they were sent here, a place where they can't do any harm. You see, before I came here, I pulled the files on everyone on this post. I know the history of every trooper. I know why they are here. Your file was the only one I didn't see." He stabbed a finger at Sheppard. "It makes me curious. Let me ask you the same question. What is your reason for being here?"

Sheppard gave Daniels a level stare. "Colonel Wainwright has my file. Why don't you ask him? Perhaps he will let you read it."

"Still the mystery man, eh, Sheppard?" Daniels laughed jovially. "Tell you what. When the time comes when I need to put together a team, I want you on it." He looked down at his coffee cup. "How time flies. My coffee got cold. I wonder if there is still some hot coffee in that machine. If you'll excuse me, I'll see if I can still get a cup." He got up and walked away.

Sheppard looked after him, shaking his head. For some reason, he didn't care for the major. He couldn't put his finger on it, but there was something about the man he didn't like. He looked at his own cup. Pushing it away, he forgot about getting another cup. He was ready to get up, when one of the troopers approached him.

"Captain Sheppard, there is someone at the gate asking for you."

Sheppard looked up in surprise. "Who is it?"

"He says his name is Buchanan."

"Buchanan?" I don't know..." He suddenly remembered. Buchanan was the big miner he met in that nightclub months ago. "Did he say what he wants?"

"He says he has something of great importance to report to the military, but he will only talk to you. He doesn't trust anyone else."

"Do I need permission to talk to the man?"

The trooper shrugged. "I guess Colonel Wainwright should be notified."

"No need to get the colonel involved." Sheppard glanced at Daniels who had come back with his cup of coffee. "I can give you permission. Remember, I'm a major."

"I assume you want to be present at my meeting with this man?"

"I insist. After all, isn't he a civilian? I didn't know you were in communication with civilians?"

"I'm not. He's a miner. I met him that particular night in the nightclub. We talked, that's all. There is nothing going on between him and me. I didn't spill any military secrets, if that's what you're worried about."

Daniels lifted both hands. "Wow, Captain Sheppard. Don't shunt into defensive mode. If this miner has something important to report, I want to hear it. Let's go and meet him."

Sheppard was not overly excited about having Daniels present, but there was nothing he could do about it. Major Daniels was his superior and had the right to be there.

When they arrived, another man was at the gate with Buchanan. Both men were covered with dust, and they looked tired. "This is my friend Terry Gardiner. He's a miner, like me. He's actually the one who made the discovery we want to report." He looked at Daniels then back at Sheppard. "Is it all right to talk in front of this trooper?"

Sheppard had to smile. "This is Major Daniels. He has clearance to hear whatever you want to tell me."

"We've been on the road for a long time. We're tired, and our horses are exhausted. We've been pushing them. Is there any way we can come in, water our horses, and get something to eat and drink for ourselves?"

"I have no objections if Major Daniels doesn't." Sheppard looked at Daniels.

"I guess it's safe to let a couple civilians onto a military outpost," Daniels said. "As long as they're under surveillance while they are here."

"We're not going to invade you." Buchanan chuckled. "I promise we won't eat all of your food, either." He grinned. "Or drink all your ale."

Daniels told the guard by the gate to open it and let the two men in. He also told him to arrange for someone to come and take their horses to a watering trough.

"Let's go into the mess hall. I'm sure we can get you something to eat."

"We appreciate that." Buchanan looked around. "I've always been curious what Outpost Alpha looked like from the inside. Kind of bleak, if you ask me."

"It's no luxury resort, that's for sure." Sheppard walked beside the big miner. "Good to see you again. I hope you found more diamonds."

"We did okay."

Once they were seated at one of the tables, Daniels said, "Okay, what's so important that made you take this long trek from the city just to talk to Captain Sheppard?"

"If you don't mind, major, we'd feel more comfortable to make the report to Captain Sheppard."

"Fine by me. I'll just sit here and listen, but may I remind you Captain Sheppard is a member of the military and whatever you tell him he is obliged to report to his superior." He smiled. "Fortunately, we don't have to go through too many channels. I'm his superior. Go ahead."

Daniels leaned back in his seat, arms crossed in front of him, giving the impression of a relaxed man, but Sheppard knew he was anything but relaxed. He was like a starved predator, waiting for some morsel to still his hunger. Sheppard had the distinct feeling Daniels would be more interested in what the miners had to report than him.

With an uneasy look at Daniels, Buchanan said, "I'll let my friend, Terry tell you all about it. Like I said, he's the one who made the discovery. I actually never saw it."

The other man nodded. He seemed nervous, almost reluctant to talk. "I guess I should state my name and occupation to make this official. My name is Terry Gardiner, and I'm a miner of blue diamonds. My partner, Arnold Kohud, and I discovered a cave behind the walls of the underground tunnel we were working. After blasting a hole in the wall, we entered the cavern on the other side. There we found electronic stuff, huge screens with buttons and levers. It looked unfamiliar and appeared ancient. Everything was covered with a thick blanket of dust."

"Tell him about the funny feeling you and Arnold got," Buchanan suggested.

Daniels bent forward, an eager expression on his face. "At what point did you get a funny feeling?"

Gardiner glanced at him. "When we got closer to those screens, I felt kind of queasy in my stomach, and some force seemed to be pulling inside my head. It's hard to explain."

"Anything else you noticed that seemed strange?"

"It was freezing cold in that cavern."

Daniels blew air across his pursed lips. "Have you told anyone about your discovery?"

Gardiner shook his head. "Nobody."

"You two and your partner Kohud are the only ones who know about this?"

"Reed knows about it."

"Who's Reed?"

"He's my partner," Buchanan explained. "But, as I mentioned before, Reed and I never went inside the cave."

"Just you four then?"

"That's correct."

Daniels looked at Sheppard. "I want you to put together a team of men you trust. You should be able to find at least half a dozen troopers in this cursed place who are competent and capable of following orders and can keep their mouths shut. I want to check out this cave as soon as possible. Make sure everyone is armed. We'll take one of the tanks for protection."

"Are we starting a war?" Sheppard couldn't help being sarcastic. All they were going to do was look at some ancient machinery. He didn't see any need to go in armed to the teeth, unless Daniels expected to confront an army of alien ghosts.

Daniels pulled his brows into a frown. "You surprise me, Captain Sheppard. You of all people should know you don't go into enemy territory without being prepared."

"Enemy territory? Did I miss something here?"

"It is obvious you have no idea what these men discovered."

Sheppard shrugged. "Remnants of machinery left over by either an ancient indigenous race or a forgotten installation built by one of the alien races, like the Spiders, or perhaps one of the dragon races. That's all Mr. Gardiner found—dead machines."

Daniels' smile seemed full of pity. "I cannot go into details in front of these two civilians, but I assure you, they've made an awesome discovery, something that may have far reaching consequences. I will brief you at the appropriate time." He turned his attention back to the two miners. "Clearly, it's too late for you to ride back to the city. You will stay here until we're ready to leave and then you will accompany us to the site."

"Thank you. I was hoping we'd be allowed to spend at least a night. We're both tired from the long ride, and the horses are in no better shape. We'll all be rested tomorrow morning. Any chance we can get something to eat and drink? I'm thirsty and starving." Buchanan gave Daniels a hopeful look.

"Captain Sheppard will see to it that you're well taken care of." Daniels rose. "Sheppard, I will notify Colonel Wainwright about our plan. You look after these two men and get that team ready. I want to leave the day after tomorrow. We will also need supplies to set up a temporary base. Make sure we have tents and enough food to last at least for a couple of weeks."

"One day to do all that may not be enough?" Sheppard protested.

"That's all you've got. We'll leave o-seven-hundred hours sharp in two days."

"Yes, sir." Sheppard saluted and watched the stocky major walk away.

"Not an easy man to get along with, is he?" Buchanan shook his head. "This military life would not be for me. I'd rather be a free man and toil like a mole underground than jumping to attention every time an officer walks by. Is he always this uptight?"

Sheppard shrugged. "I don't socialize with him. I have no idea what he's usually like."

"Do you have any ale or wine on this outpost?" Buchanan bent forward and gave Sheppard an eager look. "I could sure use a mug of cold ale right now."

"I'm afraid alcohol is a luxury we don't get here on the outpost," Sheppard said. "And the food isn't gourmet style, either, but it sustains us. That's important." He paused for a moment before he said, "Outpost Alpha isn't like any other military outpost, so don't judge the men and the way things are done here. Of course, this is probably the only military post you've ever visited. You have no means of comparing it to another one, but believe me, normally on an outpost you'll find disciplined and dedicated troopers, efficient fighting machines who are proud to serve the Solar Union." He sighed. "I'm afraid not here. There are reasons for that, but I won't get into details. Suffice to say, the men on Outpost Alpha have little reason to love the union, but that doesn't make them criminals or men to be shunned. They're still human beings who deserve better than wasting their lives here on this dead-end outpost."

Both miners sat silent, giving the impression of being embarrassed by Sheppard's outburst. Finally, Buchanan said, "If you hate this place so much, why don't you quit and become a miner or whatever?"

"I never said I hated this place. I was talking about the other troopers." Sheppard stopped talking, then he chuckled. "Hell, who am I kidding? You're right, I'm one of these men. I apologize for getting carried away. It's not really any of your concern. I'm sure you have your own problems." He rose. "I believe I can arrange for someone to bring you that mug of ale. As far as food goes, it's almost suppertime. The troopers will arrive soon. Sit tight where you are. I'll make sure you get something to eat. Now you must excuse me. I'll have to put my team together and get everything ready for the excursion to the caves."

He felt elated. It seemed the boredom was going to be interrupted by some action, at least for a little while. He was looking forward to the coming days.

[10]

THE TWO TRUCKS TRAVELED IN RELATIVE SILENCE, EXCEPT FOR
the occasional squeaking of the springs as the tires rolled over the
uneven dirt-packed road.

"Had I been aware this outpost only has old-fashioned vehicles
like this antique model that still rides on tires, I would have insisted
on getting vehicles that float on an aircushion," Major Daniels
complained. "My back is already getting sore."

"We're lucky we don't have to use buggies and horses or the giant
goats the farmers are using," Sheppard commented with a little grin.
"That would have really given your back a good workout."

"It's torture, not a workout. I can live without that," Daniels
retorted.

The driver told them, "Before I was transferred to Outpost Alpha,
I was stationed on Silver, a small planet in the Epsilon Eridani system.
We hardly used ground vehicles, only traveled in sliders. They get you
to your destination much faster. The ground vehicles we used were
controlled by AIs and voice-command. They didn't have steering
wheels."

"Well, Trooper Benson, this isn't Silver. This is Savanna, a Class
Five planet, where modern vehicles, especially airborne ones, are
prohibited," Sheppard explained.

"I'm fully aware of that, captain, but damn it, we are the military. Shouldn't we have modern weapons and vehicles? How can we defend ourselves if we're attacked by a bunch of Mollard or Snaar? They have no qualms bringing modern weapons to this planet."

"That may all change, trooper, depending on what we discover today," Daniels said.

"What will we discover?"

The Major gave the trooper a hard look. "You'll find out soon enough. In the meantime, don't ask too many questions. Concentrate on the road and keep on driving."

"Yes, sir, sir."

Sheppard couldn't suppress a smile when Benson took one hand off the stirring wheel and saluted. He knew damn well that Benson mocked the major.

If Daniels noticed, he didn't react. All he said was, "Keep both hands on the wheel and try to miss some of the bumps."

"Yes, sir, Major Daniels. I'll keep my hands on the wheel."

It still took them nearly six hours to get to the small mining town. They couldn't travel fast. The road they drove on wasn't a real road. It consisted of packed dirt created by the wooden wheels of farmer's and miner's carts. Most miners used horses to get around. They used carts only when they brought supplies from the city. The road was dotted with holes and cracks, deep enough for a vehicle to break an axle.

Mining town was possibly not the correct description for the collection of small log houses, huts, and tents. Village would probably be the better name, but the miners called it their town.

Most miners and treasure hunters didn't want to travel constantly to the city, but they needed a base camp where they could rest and be in contact with likeminded individuals. They could even purchase basic supplies from some entrepreneurs who saw an opportunity to make a living without the difficult and often fruitless task of searching for treasures. A few miners started setting up semi-permanent structures alongside one of the rivers and others joined them. Over time, a small town had been created.

When they reached the first building, Daniels ordered Benson to stop the truck.

A crude sign at the outskirts of the town read, Welcome to

Goodluck. On top of a pole beside it perched the bleached skull of an unlucky adventurer.

"Somebody had a grisly sense of humor," Daniels said, shaking his head in obvious disgust. "Whoever that poor fellow was, he deserved to be buried with his head."

"I don't believe that man cares. He's dead," Buchanan, who sat in the back, commented. "For all we know it could be the skull of a woman."

"Some miners say the ghost of whoever this person was is walking the street of Goodluck at night when both of the two moons are full," Gardiner said.

"Don't tell me you believe in ghosts?" Daniels turned his head to look at the miner.

"I do. Even the Cats have stories about the dead haunting them."

"He sees things sometimes," Buchanan said with a chuckle. "Things that aren't really there."

"He does?" Daniels spoke sharply. "I hope he didn't see things when he discovered those ruins. I'd hate to have taken this trip to chase some ghostly sighting of some lunatic who hears voices and sees things."

"I'm not a lunatic. I know what I saw. Kohud is my witness." Gardiner spoke loudly. "There were screens and other alien stuff."

"There better be."

"We're here now." Sheppard tried to smooth things over. "It'll only be a matter of time until we can confirm what Mr. Gardiner discovered. Let's not get all excited over nothing."

"It's not nothing if the report turns out to be false." Daniels snapped and turned to Buchanan. "Do we have to drive through town?"

"Yes, the entrance to the tunnel into the mountains is straight ahead."

Daniels calmed down and asked, "How far is it to the entrance of the caves from here?"

"This one is about thirty minutes on horseback," Buchanan said.

"Obviously, we won't be using horses. We'll cover the distance in less time. Let's keep moving, Trooper Benson. I'm anxious to get there."

As the trucks and tank rumbled through the small settlement, a few curious miners stepped out of their homes and onto the street, obviously wondering why the military paid them a visit, unless news of Gardiner's discovery had already spread through the community. According to Buchanan, they had told nobody else, but Sheppard knew human nature. Most people couldn't keep a secret. They needed to tell someone.

They reached the foot of the mountains twenty minutes later. A gaping hole in the sheer cliff left no doubt that this was an entrance to the underground tunnels and caverns. From the carpet of rocks on the ground it was also obvious that somebody had blasted part of the mountain away to expose the tunnel.

"That hole is big enough for the truck to drive in," Major Daniels mused.

"I wouldn't advise it, unless you want to get wedged in from both sides," Buchanan warned. "You'll only get about fifty yards into the tunnel before it narrows."

"Any other openings leading to the tunnels?"

"Of course, there are. At least a dozen we know of, but only this one leads to the cavern you want."

Daniels sighed. "I guess we'll walk. How far is it until we get to that cavern?"

"We should be able to make it in under a couple of hours, depending how fast we walk."

"A long walk." Daniels ran his hand over his balding head. "Add two hours coming back. I'm not sure if I'm up to it. Damn!"

"We don't have to walk, Major," Sheppard informed him. "We've got a couple of air sleds in the trailer the tank has been pulling."

"Two air sleds? I must say, Sheppard, you don't disappoint me. What made you load up those air sleds?"

Sheppard smiled smugly. "It's no big deal. I knew we'd be entering tunnels and would have to use something other than a truck to get to our destination. Maybe I didn't relish the thought of walking long distances inside a dark tunnel."

"Good thinking. Let's get those sleds out and loaded up. Four of you troopers have to stay behind and guard the trucks and tank. I don't feel like coming back to find our transportation gone."

The sleds were long and narrow, able to carry six passengers, including the driver. Behind the seats was room for equipment. Daniels and the two civilians took one sled, with Trooper Benson behind the controls and two troopers in the last seat. Sheppard and five troopers rode in the second sled. Sergeant Brian Cahill and three troopers stayed behind.

"You'll be in charge, Cahill. I hope I can count on you not falling asleep while we're gone," Daniels said with a grim smile.

"I've never fallen asleep while on duty, major, sir." Cahill drew himself erect and stared the major in the face. "I and the other troopers will watch over the trucks and the tank as if they were our personal property."

"I also want to see the tents erected when we return."

"Will do, major."

"Good. Then let's proceed."

As soon as they entered the tunnel, lights in front of the sleds turned on to illuminate the dark interior. The crystals in the walls magnified the rays, and it was almost like driving in daylight.

The ground was dotted with rocks, some of them large enough to cause damage, but the sleds floated high enough above the ground to avoid them. They still had to travel at slow speed, in case they ran into larger objects. The tunnel wasn't straight. It wound its way into the mountain like the tunnel of a mole. A slight decline indicated they were dropping deeper underground. A couple of times, they took a side tunnel after passing by quite a few. It was clear that one could easily get lost in this maze.

It took a little over one hour to reach the hole in the wall that was the new entrance to the cavern. Sheppard waited until Daniels and the others left their sled, before he climbed out. The five troopers with him followed his example.

Daniels peered through the hole, but it was dark in the cave. "Perhaps you should take the lead," he told Gardiner.

The miner nodded, adjusted his headlamp and stepped through the hole.

"Follow him with weapons ready," the Major ordered Benson and another trooper.

The trooper standing beside Sheppard snickered. "Is he expecting to be attacked by a bunch of ghosts?" he murmured under his breath.

"Keep your thoughts to yourself, Wolansky," Sheppard warned him in a low voice, watching as Daniels climbed through the hole. Buchanan was close behind him.

"Let's go," Sheppard said. Before he followed the others, he turned to the troopers with him. "Don't shrug this off like some kind of useless exercise. Stay alert and be prepared for any eventuality. I've lost men because they were careless and nonchalant. Remember, this is unknown territory. Anything can happen."

He loosened his laser in its holster and stepped across the low piece of rock at the bottom of the hole.

Daniels and the others stood near the center of the cave. Gardiner had correctly described the contents. There were large and small screens on one wall and buttons and levers below them. Something else Sheppard noticed—it was cold in the cave. As he stepped closer to the wall of screens, he felt a strange sensation in his head. He could only describe it as a feather caressing his forehead, a kind of gentle electric current running through his brain.

"Do you feel it?" Gardiner spoke in a hushed voice as if scared he might awaken some sleeping monster.

"I feel it," Daniels said. He sounded excited. "This is more than I hoped for."

"It seems you know more about this than any of us," Sheppard said. "What is this place?"

Daniels turned to look at Gardiner and Buchanan. "What I'm about to disclose is not meant for civilian ears. Even though you have made this discovery, it's not in your best interest to know what you've found. I advise you not to talk to anyone about this place. If anyone ever asks you what you found in this cavern, you tell them old, unimportant ruins. I want you to swear an oath that you will never mention to anyone what you saw here. There will be dire consequences if you break your oath. Am I understood?"

"I know what you're saying, but I discovered this cavern, and I wasn't obliged to report it to the military. I did, because I thought it was important. Shouldn't I be rewarded some kind of finder's fee?" Gardiner gave Daniels an expectant but also defiant look.

"A finder's fee? You can count yourself lucky if we don't arrest you for trespassing on military property." Daniels spoke sharply.

"This isn't military property."

"It is now."

"It wasn't when we found it."

"That is of no consequence. Right now, you are standing on property that belongs to the military." Daniels' eyes focused on Trooper Benson. "Please escort the two civilians back into the tunnel."

Gardiner let out a strangled laugh. "This is ridiculous. I will report this to the Trading Commission."

"You do that, and you'll never see daylight again. I will have you thrown into the darkest pit we can find and throw away the key. Take him away." Daniels' voice was unfriendly and hard.

Shephard realized that the major had shed the mantle of the mild-mannered chatterbox he'd portrayed until then. He was like a completely different person.

Gardiner struggled in the trooper's grip, while Buchanan walked quietly behind the two.

"Was that necessary?" Sheppard asked once they were gone.

The coldness in Daniels' voice was still there when he focused his attention on Sheppard. "I suggest you never question my authority, Captain Sheppard. I decide when something is necessary."

Sheppard spread his hands. "If you say so. Now, are we privileged to an explanation or are we also not qualified to know?"

"Normally, you wouldn't be, but these are special circumstances. Before I tell you, I want everyone else to clear this cavern." He waited until all the other troopers had left and said, "What we have here is a star-portal." Daniels paused to let it sink in.

"A star-portal?" Sheppard echoed. "Are you talking about those mysterious doorways an ancient race was supposed to possess to travel instantly between star systems? I thought they were just legends. We don't even know if such a race ever existed."

"It existed and so did the gates. This is one of them."

"It's dead."

"Not dead, only inactive. Do you feel that pulling inside your head?"

"Some kind of magnetic force inside this cavern, I suppose."

"Not just some kind of magnetic force. It's the sleeping but beating heart of the portal. It is alive and waiting to be awakened." Daniels closed his eyes and stood like a man transfixed by a religious experience.

Sheppard refused to accept what Daniels told him. It didn't seem real and Sheppard was a man who dealt with realities not dreams. "This place has to be thousands of years old. Everything is covered with inches of dust that must clog all the instruments and delicate mechanisms of every piece of machinery. How can anything still be functioning after such a long time?"

"Not thousands of years but millions, Captain Sheppard. We know very little about that ancient race, but one thing we know is that they possessed knowledge and technological advances we can't even imagine. The theory is that the portals operate outside the known dimensions, sort of outside time as we understand it. We are just beginning to decipher a fraction of the principles on which the portals operate. I'm going to give you information known to only a few privileged politicians and high-ranking military officers and, of course, the scientists involved in the project. We have discovered an active star-portal on Salamander. A whole crew of brilliant scientists is studying it, and they have unlocked much critical data."

"Are you telling me we are in possession of a working star-portal?"

"That's what I'm telling you."

Sheppard wasn't quite sure if he could believe him. The knowledge that the military was in possession of an active star-portal was a little too much to swallow. "Why hasn't anyone heard of it?"

"Because all work is done in secrecy. Whoever controls the star-portals controls the power in the galaxy."

"Are humans the only ones who know about that portal?"

"Unfortunately, not. The Spiders, the Accilla, the Anorians, and a score of other races are also aware of it. That's why it is of utmost importance to keep the discovery of this portal a secret."

"I'm curious. Where did you gain this knowledge about the star-portals, especially the one on Salamander, if only a few privileged individuals are kept in the loop? Is there something you haven't told me about yourself? You're only an engineer who builds bridges, at least that's what you told me. Perhaps you're rank in the military is much higher than major."

Daniels smiled. "You got me there, Captain Sheppard. I'm an engineer, but I don't build bridges. My specialty is computers and spatial sciences. The only reason I'm kept *in the loop* as you put it, is the fact that I'm a genius and probably also because of my rank in the military, the rank of colonel, but I don't make a big deal out of it."

Sheppard nodded grimly. "I've suspected that you were not quite truthful about your person, Colonel Daniels. I'm wondering, why are you telling me about all of this if everything is such a secret? Even though the troopers don't know about the star-portal, they've seen this cavern and what it contains."

"I'm telling you out of necessity. I assume I can trust you not to broadcast what this really is. I'm not worried about the troopers telling anyone about the ruins. If they do, it doesn't really matter. Besides, who would they tell? Other troopers? They're all stuck here on Savanna, the same as you, but I believe you have much greater potential than ending your career here on this backwater planet. I have faith in you, and I hope you will become a great asset to my team."

"Your team?"

"The one that is waiting for my orders in Crystal City. The men in that team arrived on the same ship as you and I. They were ordered to stay in the background until they were needed."

"Who are these men?"

"Scientists and experts in the computer sciences. Men and women with brilliant minds and a few military people. Specialists."

"I'm at a loss here. What was the reason for you to bring a special team to Savanna? To what purpose?"

"To unlock the secret of a star-portal that was supposed to exist on Savanna. It was a longshot, but as it turns out our information was correct. Don't ask me how we got it. I won't tell you." Daniels smiled again. "You're not totally in the loop yet, captain. By the way, I hope I can count on your discretion and not discuss this portal with anyone, especially not with a member of the scouts."

"I don't know any scouts on Savanna, but I'm curious. Why would you worry about the scouts?"

"Because it was Master Scout Terrex Stonewall and his team that managed to unlock the key to get the portal on Salamander to work. Most of it is still hush-hush, but I know from reliable resources that they actually used the portal to travel to the other side of the galaxy. If they get wind of this portal, they'll be all over it. This Stonewall has powerful connections."

"You can sleep without worrying about me spilling this secret to any scouts, because, as I said, I don't know any."

"I take nothing for granted. You may just make the acquaintance of a scout. The universe works like that."

"What's our next move?"

"We'll secure this place by limiting access to the tunnel. No civilians will be allowed near it. We'll install an electric fence with a gate that will be locked at all times. Then we'll build a small fortress, a military base, to house the men and women on my team. They can't possibly travel back and forth to Crystal City every day. They need to be close to their workplace. Who knows, over time this small settlement will grow into a thriving community, an important city on Savanna. It will become a hub for travelers to Savanna and to other destinations among the stars. It may even become the capital city of this planet." He stopped. "I'm getting ahead of myself. It's only a dream for now, but if we're successful in cracking the code of this star-portal, Savanna will become the next Earth. Conditions are perfect."

"Aren't you forgetting that this planet is already occupied? What about the indigenous population?"

Daniels shrugged. "They will have to adapt. They don't have much choice. Either they'll be assimilated into the fold of the human empire or they will perish. That's just the way progress works. The ones who hold the power control and dictate the future." He held up a hand to stop Sheppard from making a comment. "You may remember we had this conversation when we were sitting in the shuttle. I know what you want to say, so don't waste your breath. There's nothing you or I can do to prevent it from happening, unless the universe has other plans."

"One can only hope."

Sheppard knew Daniels was right, but the future was not written in stone. Things didn't always turn out as planned or predicted. There were too many unknown factors to mess up most plans. The star-portal may never give up its secrets. It had lain inactive for millions of years and may stay that way for another million.

"There isn't anything we can do for now," Daniels said. "We'll seal off the entrance until we begin work here. I've seen what I was hoping to see." He looked around the cavern one more time and rubbed his hands. "This is an epic moment for me. I'm more than elated. This could be a monumental step for humanity and the beginning of a new era for humans in space. It will put us on equal footing with the Spiders and the other older denizens of the galaxy."

[11]

COLLINS SQUINTED AT THE RISING SUN AND THE CLOUDLESS SKY. It promised to be another pleasant day, not as hot as the week before. Fall was nearly coming to end, and the nights were already getting cooler. It was time to separate the cattle destined to go to the market from the rest of the herd.

"Are you planning to ride out today, Dad?"

He turned to watch his daughter approach him. It warmed his heart to see her in a good mood. She and her brothers had adapted to life on a ranch, on an alien planet, much more readily than he and Kristie. Dressed in tight pants and a leather jacket and wearing a wide-brimmed hat, she was obviously ready to go someplace.

"Yes, I am, sweetheart. You're alone today?"

"I am. Ernina plans to help Aunt Angelica in the garden. She feels guilty for neglecting her, and she wants to spend a bit of time with her."

Collins smiled. "Are you telling me you want to keep your old man company?"

Lisa nodded and giggled. "Is that so obvious?"

"Not at all, especially since you're wearing your riding outfit." Collins laughed. "To answer your question, yes, I'll be riding out. I want to check up on the herd and thought I might get some fishing done at the lake after. Get my thoughts together and do a little introspection."

The faint shadow of a cloud crossed her face, and she seemed disappointed. "Well, then I don't want to distract you. I'll find something else to do."

He stepped up to her and touched her cheek. "You never distract me. I'll gladly have you accompany me. We don't spend enough time together as it is, and I'm looking forward to it. We should pack lunch and have a picnic."

She clapped her hands together like a little child. "That sounds great. We haven't had a picnic since…" She screwed up her face. "I can't remember when."

"Neither can I. Probably a long time ago." He looked past Lisa to see Randolph coming out of the house. "There is Randolph. I see he's ready to leave. By the way, he's also coming with us."

"I didn't know. Nobody ever tells me anything." She pulled her eyebrows together in a mock frown.

"Because you were never really interested in coming along. That's why."

"I am now. I want to spend the whole day with you." She told her brother as he joined them, "And with you, Randolph. It'll be fun. I'll go and make a few sandwiches." She rushed away.

Randolph looked after her. "I'm surprised to see her wanting to come with us. She usually rides out with Ernina. They have their favorite place. Is Ernina coming along also?"

"No, she wants to spend time with her mom."

"Really?" Randolph smirked. "I saw her with Traverse early this morning."

"Don't read too much into that. It doesn't mean anything." Collins wasn't sure about that, but he was willing to believe Lisa told him the truth about Ernina. Of course, she could be spending part of the day with her mother and the rest with Traverse.

Perhaps that wasn't what bothered him. What disturbed him was that Traverse tried to keep his involvement with Ernina a secret. He was not blind to the fact that Traverse and Ernina were sexually involved. There was nothing he and Kristie could do about that.

When he brought up the subject with Haggard, the old man just smiled. "They're old enough to know what they're doing. I see no problem with it, and neither should you."

That's all he said, and that was the end of the subject for him.

Angelica had been delighted. "She's a good girl. Traverse could do worse. There aren't many eligible girls his age around here. I mean nice girls. The fact that Ernina is not human shouldn't be an obstacle. She'll make him a good and loyal wife. Remember, this is not Earth. You'll have to open your mind to new things."

At first, Kristie had been appalled, but she seemed to mellow to the idea that their son was in love with an indigenous girl. Collins wasn't sure what his feelings were. He liked Ernina well enough, but she was of an alien species. He'd hoped for his sons to marry human girls and someday to have human grandchildren.

He pushed the negative thoughts out of his mind. After all, everything was purely speculation. It wasn't easy, but he promised himself to deal with it when he came home. It may be time to confront Traverse and ask him about his plans with Ernina.

"Go and fetch the horses," he told Randolph. "I'll go back into the house and fill a bladder with cold wine from the cellar for myself." He smirked a little. "Not for you, young man. You'll have to wait a couple more years."

"I'm sixteen, Dad. Besides, who would know if I drink wine, or smoke, or take drugs? There are no morality police on this planet."

"I would know, son. Your mother would know. Just because this seems to be a lawless planet, doesn't mean we can forget about morals and do what we want to do. That's what sets us apart from the animals. It's called being civilized. We create rules, and we obey them. We know what's right or wrong. Neither do we act on our impulses and go crazy. Drinking alcohol in excess, smoking, and taking drugs are not healthy things to do. As your father, it's my duty to protect you from harm. Once you're an adult, I hope you're smart enough to realize what we taught you were not exercises to punish you but to give you a good start for the rest of your life. Hopefully, someday you will teach your children the same lessons."

Randolph's face was somber. "I appreciate all the things you and Mom are teaching us, and I take them to heart." He smiled. "Don't worry. There is no danger I'll ever drink that awful stuff Uncle Nelson is brewing in the basement. I'd rather drink logus-berry-juice."

Collins shook himself. "You like that juice?"

Randolph laughed. "I didn't say I like it, but I'd prefer it to Uncle Nelson's brew any day."

"I don't mind that awful stuff. I'll go and get some of it." Collins grinned at his son. "It's that or nothing."

They were on their way an hour later. All three were in good spirits, especially Collins. It wasn't everyday he was lucky enough to have two of his children with him for the whole day.

It took them nearly two hours to reach the camp. Collins was happy to find that the men had already begun to separate the cattle intended for slaughter. The herd needed to be culled for the winter to conserve feed. In the spring, new calves would be born to increase the herd again.

Lisa had been to the camp only once before. "I've never realized how large our herd is," she commented. "It must be difficult to keep them together all the time."

"It is, but we have a good team. The Cats are at home in this environment. They are good with animals, and they love this job." Collins slid off his horse. "I'm going to talk with Rhe-annur. We won't be staying long, but it may be a good idea to stretch your legs a bit and get the kinks out of your muscles."

He walked stiff-legged to the cabin. Rhe-annur wasn't inside.

"Rhe-annur with cattle," the cook told him. He pointed to the large herd down by the river.

"I'll have to ride down there," he told Randolph and Lisa. "You can come if you like."

"No, we'll stay here." Lisa smiled. "I don't really like the smell of all those cows."

"If you ever marry a rancher, you'll have to get used to that smell," Randolph teased her.

"No, I don't have to. Maybe I'll marry a vegetable farmer or maybe a lawyer and live in the city."

Randolph chuckled. "You'll never be happy living in a stinking city again, not after breathing the fresh air in the country."

Lisa wrinkled her nose. "I don't exactly call this fresh air, little brother."

"I'm four inches taller than you, *little* sister."

"I'm older. That gives me the right to call you little, brother."

"Okay, stay here," Collins said with a tiny smile. "Behave and don't argue too much while I'm gone. I'm planning to have a peaceful afternoon."

ALMOST AN HOUR PASSED BEFORE THEY RODE OFF AGAIN. Collins was satisfied with his inspection. He considered himself lucky to have a good team of herders. Not all ranchers employed natives, and some of them even criticized the ones who did, but he had his doubts about finding better herders among the humans. The Cats were loyal and never complained. Of course, he had taken old man Haggard's advice and treated them fairly, aside from paying them well.

They arrived at their destination shortly before noon. When they left the narrow trail leading through the small forest that surrounded the pristine lake he knew was hidden there, Lisa let out a surprised cry of delight. "This is beautiful, Dad. How come you never took me to this place?"

"Because you never gave me an opportunity." He sighed. "And because I never found the time to come here myself, but I promised Randolph to take him fishing one day." He looked at his son. "This is the day."

"I'm glad you kept your promise, Dad. To be honest, I had my doubts." Randolph gazed up at the cloudless sky. "Look, a flock of ganders. According to the Cats, they bring good luck. I have a feeling it will be a successful day." He laughed. "I consider myself the luckiest man alive today."

"You mean *boy*, the luckiest *boy*, and that may not be true, either. I'll be catching more and bigger fish than you." Lisa joined in his laughter. "Come, I'll race you to the edge of the lake."

With that she kicked her horse and took off. Randolph followed her, letting out a series of loud yells. Collins rode his horse slowly down the slight slope, relishing the warm feeling of happiness that engulfed him.

116

The surface of the lake was calm and smooth like a mirror. Tall reeds grew along the shore, promising hiding places for fish. Lush grasses, dotted with colorful wild flowers and short shrubs, surrounded the lake. The flock of ganders landed in the lake on the far side. They trumpeted loudly as they settled on the water.

Collins took it all in and said a silent prayer of thanks to whatever god was willing to listen. On Earth, pristine places like this didn't exist anymore. They disappeared long time ago. The home planet was overcrowded and noisy, the air and the water polluted beyond recovery.

Sliding off his horse, he removed the saddle to give the animal a rest. Randolph did the same, while Lisa walked down to the water to put her foot into it. She looked back at her father. "It's warm. Is it safe to go swimming in the lake?"

"I don't see why not. According to Uncle Nelson, there are no dangerous animals living in the lake. Did you bring a bathing suit?"

"No, I didn't, but if you and Randolph look away, I can go swimming in the nude."

Collins laughed. "I see no problem with that, even though I've seen you without clothes many times. Remember, I'm your father."

"You saw me when I was little. I'm a grown woman now." She glanced at Randolph. "Close your eyes, brother, or turn around. I'm going swimming."

"I'll get our fishing gear ready," Randolph said. "While you waste time swimming, I'm going to catch a fish."

Collins heard a loud splash and knew she was in the water. Turning around, he saw only her head above the surface. "How is it?" he called.

"Wonderful. You should try it. Too bad we don't have a lake like this closer to the house. I'd go swimming every day."

"Just don't go out too far," Collins warned her. "You're not a powerful swimmer. Swimming in a supervised pool with a crowd of other people is not the same as being alone in a big lake."

"I'll be careful. Don't worry."

"Did you bring the worms?" Randolph inquired.

"Of course. They're in a small wooden box in one of my

saddlebags. Watch you don't spill the soil. Did you find the fishing gear?"

"I did. Aren't the hooks kind of big?"

"Uncle Nelson gave them to me. He said that's what he's been using and, according to him, they do catch fish."

Collins rummaged in the saddlebag and pulled out the piece of wood with the string wrapped around it. He had to agree with Randolph. The hook looked bigger here than at home. Shrugging, he walked over to where Randolph sat, holding a big, fat worm in one hand and the hook in the other.

"Well, string it on."

"How?"

"Uncle Nelson showed me. You push the worm onto the hook. Like so." He proceeded to shove the hook into the worm. It wasn't as easy as it had looked when Haggard had demonstrated it.

"It looks messy." Randolph shook himself a little. "Won't it kill the worm?"

"Probably, but that's how it's done apparently." He grinned. "I've got mine on. It seems I'll be the first one to catch a fish."

He left Randolph sitting with his hook and worm. Let him figure it out. He was old enough. He headed for a spot free of reeds. Unwinding a length of string, he threw the hook into the water. He had never done anything like this before. It was supposed to be exiting and relaxing at the same time.

Lisa swam toward him, obviously ready to come back on land.

"Watch out," he said. "You don't want to step on my hook."

She headed for the reeds and rose out of the water. The reeds hid part of her nude body, but he could still see most of her. She had her mother's figure, slim and well-formed. Back on Earth, she had been part of a team of swimmers, an activity that kept her body tuned and strong. She had always been proud of her figure and had not been shy to display it. Here on Savanna, her beauty was wasted. There wasn't even a young man around to appreciate and enjoy it. He hoped she didn't resent him and Kristie for bringing her to this forsaken, backwater planet.

His thoughts were interrupted when he felt a strong tug on his line. Surprised, he almost let go of the stick in his hands. "I have a fish," he called out, excitement gripping him. Winding the line back onto his stick, he slowly pulled whatever he had caught onto shore.

It turned out to be large fish, and he managed to land it.

Lisa came running to see what he had caught. "Look at those beautiful colors," she said. "Are you going to keep it?"

"Silly question. Of course. We'll fry this one over a fire and have it for supper." He looked up to see she was still naked. "Perhaps you should put on your clothes," he suggested. "It doesn't bother me. I'm your father, but Randolph, even though he's your brother...you know what I mean?"

"Sorry, Dad. I just got excited when I heard you had a fish. I've never seen anyone catch a fish before."

"That's okay, sweetheart. I'm just as excited. This is the first fish I ever caught."

"I got one, too!" Randolph yelled. "It's a big one. I think I need help to pull it out."

"Don't lose it." Collins moved as quickly as he could to help his son. Grabbing one end of the handle, he and Randolph pulled on the string. "Forget about winding the string on the handle. Let's just pull this monster on land."

"I'll help you." Lisa took hold of the string and pulled with the men.

Slowly, they made progress. The fish thrashed in the water, trying to get free of the hook, but finally it flopped in the grass.

"Look at that large mouth. Those teeth look sharp," Lisa said.

"I wouldn't put my fingers into that mouth," Collins cautioned. "This is one big, boy."

"Maybe it's a girl." Lisa giggled.

Collins glanced at her. "You're still not dressed."

"Okay, okay, I'll get dressed."

Collins bent down to grab the fish. "I'll hold it and you pull out the hook."

He just managed to get a good grip onto the slippery, squirming body, when Lisa screamed. He turned to look for her, when he saw something that caused a cold chill to run down his spine.

A group of natives rode out of the forest. He recognized the first rider. Kiimzaan.

Collins rose, touching the butt of the gun in its holster hanging from his hip. He didn't have a good feeling about this.

The natives came closer. He estimated at least a dozen riders in the group.

Kiimzaan grinned broadly when he slid off his steed. He strode toward Collins with an arrogant gait. "We visited your camp and helped ourselves to a few of your fat cows. Winter is coming, and I have to feed my people."

"What do you mean you helped yourself to a few of my cows?"

"Exactly what I said. The traitors that work for you tried to stop us, but we convinced them to step aside if they wanted to live. Unfortunately, we had to kill one of them to make a point."

"I hope you are lying about killing one of my men," Collins said, clenching his jaw until it hurt.

"I never lie." The outlaw leader chuckled. "He tried to be a hero."

"I will kill you for that if it's true." Collins tried to stay calm. He knew, the moment he went for his gun, he'd be pierced by a dozen arrows.

Kiimzaan spread his arms. "How about now? It would be easy. As you can see, I am defenseless."

"There are a dozen arrows aimed at me. You are not defenseless, even if you don't carry your bow right now but don't feel so smug. An opportunity will come. I can wait."

Kiimzaan looked past Collins. "Your daughter's body is ripe and ready. I think I will taste her passion."

"You touch her, and you're a dead man, even if it costs me my life. You and I won't be the only ones who die, either. I will take some of your followers with me. Are you willing to risk that?"

"I am." Kiimzaan sprang from a standing position. He took Collins by surprise. Before he could react, the outlaw was on him. Collins fell backward when the heavy body of Kiimzaan smashed into him. Both men ended up on the ground with Collins on the bottom and Kiimzaan on top of him.

The outlaw smashed his fist against Collins' head, leaving him momentarily disoriented. Collins struggled to dislodge the big native, but to no avail. He got one arm free and clawed at his opponent's face. Laughing, the outlaw leader hit him again. Collins' head filled with buzzing sounds, and he knew this was a fight he couldn't win.

"Lisa, hide in the lake." He'd wanted to shout, but it came out as only a croak. He turned his head but saw with dismay that two of the outlaws were holding his daughter. Heaving up with one last surge of strength, he managed to push off the big native. Crawling away, he struggled to his feet and stood swaying. Fumbling for his Colt, he discovered his holster empty.

"Are you looking for this?" Kiimzaan held up the Colt with a teasing gesture.

At that moment, a loud explosive sound behind him made Collins turn to find Randolph with his gun in his hand. From the corner of his vision, he saw one of the outlaws topple from his alck. Before Randolph could fire another shot, an arrow pierced his right, upper arm. Randolph cried out in pain and dropped his weapon.

"That was a big mistake," Kiimzaan roared and crossed the distance between him and Randolph with two long strides. Standing in front of Randolph, the native glared at him. "How dare you kill a Valley-rider? You will be punished for that."

"I'd kill you all if I could, you bloody barbarian," Randolph shouted. With his left hand, he groped for his knife and pulled it free. Then he stabbed Kiimzaan with a vicious thrust.

The outlaw let out a surprised bellow. He twisted the knife out of Randolph's hand and stepped back. Looking down at the blood seeping from the stab wound in his side, he snarled, "You stupid human. I would have let you live, but not now." In a savage arc, he whipped the knife across Randolph's throat.

Collins screamed when he saw the blood spurting from his son's severed artery and lunged himself at the big outlaw. He never made it. One of the riders moved forward and his alck collided with Collins. The force of the collision threw him down. Before he could recover, two Cats pinned him to the ground. He lay dazed in their grip. As if from far away he heard a woman sobbing loudly and knew it was Lisa.

Kiimzaan stepped into his view. "You humans believe you own this world. You are wrong. It belongs to us, and someday we will take it back. With all your superior weapons you still cannot defeat us. How easily I overpowered you and how easily I killed your son. This weapon of yours did not save you." He leveled the gun at Collins. "I could kill you with your own weapon right now, but I want you to suffer." He spoke a few words in his native language to the two Cats holding Collins down and gave orders to some of the riders.

They laughed as if he had told them a joke. A couple of them jumped off their steeds and walked to the forest. They came back after a while, carrying a few short stakes. Using rocks, they hammered the stakes into the ground. With short pieces of ropes, they tied Collins' hands and feet to the stakes.

"Pray to whatever gods you humans pray to for one of the predators to appear soon to give you a quick death by ripping out your throat. If the carrion eaters find you first, death will release you only after you've suffered unbearable pain while they rip you apart piece by piece. Here is a little taste of what you can expect." He sneered and with one vicious kick, he smashed his foot into Collins' groin.

Collins screamed and gave in to the darkness that took it all away.

[12]

"THEY SHOULD HAVE BEEN HOME A LONG TIME AGO." KRISTIE stared at the old clock standing in the corner, a worried look on her face. "This is not like your father at all. I know something terrible has happened."

"You always think the worst, Mom. They're probably having such a good time and decided to stay longer."

Travers tried to sound calm, but deep down he was almost as worried as his mother. He glanced at Ernina. She was the reason he had not gone with his father. He didn't regret it. Ernina had spent a few hours with Aunt Angelica, but most of the day she had been with him. Glancing at his mother, he felt guilty keeping his relationship with Ernina a secret. His parents had a right to know that he was in love with an alien girl, but he worried they may not approve.

Ernina gave him a knowing smile. His loins fluttered, and his heart beat a little faster every time he looked at her. She was a wild, untamed animal when they made love, surrendering to him with unbridled abandonment. He knew he was addicted to her passion. She was a drug he never wanted to give up.

"I don't even know where they went." His mother broke into his thoughts. "If I knew I'd go looking for them."

"You know you can't go out there by yourself, not at night anyway.

You'd get lost." He chuckled. "You'd even get lost during the day. There is a lot of prairie out there, and some of the forest is so thick you would never find your way back out again. Have you ever been to the feeding grounds?"

"Once and it was a gruelling ride. Horses and I don't really seem to get along. I'd be more comfortable in a coach." She sighed. "Or a vehicle that rides on air, like the ones back on Earth. I miss those. I don't know why we have to live in such primitive conditions on this planet. Or why we can't at least have communication devices. I could be in contact with your dad when he was away from the house."

She looked again at the clock. Traverse made a decision. "I'll go and talk to Uncle Nelson. He knows where they went. I'll ride out and look for them. Two of the moons are out tonight, and they're full. It will be bright enough to see where we're going."

"I don't want you to get lost now. Don't go alone. Take a couple of the men with you."

"I will, Mom."

Traverse went into the room they called the library. He knew the old man would be sitting in there, smoking his pipe. He wasn't allowed to smoke anywhere else in the house. Aunt Angelica was strict about that.

Haggard sat in his big chair. In the flickering light of the oil lamps decorating the walls, his craggy face looked like it had been carved out of an old piece of bark. The pipe seemed to be part of his face. A cloud of smoke surrounded his head like a fog.

"Sorry to disturb you, Uncle Nelson, but we need your help."

The old man took the pipe out of his mouth. "Ah, it's you, young Traverse. Don't see much of you these days. What can I do for you?"

"Mom is worried about my dad. He should be home by now, and she fears something may have happened to him. Lisa and Randolph are with him. They went on a fishing trip. Mom says you know where that lake is."

Haggard chuckled. "I know it very well. I spent many happy hours on that lake. It's secluded and not easy to find. A good place to contemplate life."

"Perhaps you can give me directions to get there. Mom wants me to go looking for them."

"It's dark out there. You'll never find it in the dark, even if I give you directions."

"I'll ask a couple of the men to come with me. Please, Uncle Nelson, give me the information," Traverse pleaded. "I need to go. I'm worried, too."

The old man got up from his chair. "I'll come with you. I'm the only one who can find it in the dark. It wouldn't be the first time I traveled home from there in the middle of the night."

"Are you sure you can handle the trip?"

"I'm not so old that I can't ride anymore. Besides, it'll do these old bones good to get out there. I noticed that two of the moons are up, and it's a clear night. We should have no trouble finding our way." He gave a little laugh. "I'll probably find the place blindfolded. At least, my horse should."

Traverse gave a sigh of relief. He had secretly hoped that the old man would offer to accompany him.

"Go and find a couple of the men. At this time of night, it's best to travel in a larger group. We do have a few predators around that hunt during the night. Make sure you take a gun along. You know how to handle one, don't you?"

Traverse nodded. "I do."

"Good. Now go. I'll meet you by the stables. Get my horse ready while you're at it."

WHEN TRAVERSE ASKED FOR A COUPLE OF VOLUNTEERS AMONG the ranch-hands in the bunkhouse, they all volunteered, but he took only two.

"I don't believe we have to take an army," he told them, smiling, "but I appreciate that you are all concerned about my father's welfare."

They left thirty minutes later.

The two moons provided enough light for them to travel with ease. Traverse had never ridden in the direction Haggard was taking them. They had to ride around one forest. Apparently, it was too thick with overgrown vegetation to even attempt to ride through it. After that, they rode across a small desert and then through a narrow mountain ridge. Beyond that, came another forest where they took a narrow trail that wound its way through the tall trees.

The trail ended in a narrow strip of grassy area that surrounded a calm lake.

At first, they didn't see anyone, but then Traverse spotted a figure lying near the water. His heart beat faster as he spurred his horse to cross the distance between the forest and the figure on the ground. He knew it was his father. Even before he reached him, he saw the stakes in the ground and the ropes around his father's ankles and wrists. With an anguished cry, he jumped from his horse and rushed to his father's side.

"Traverse," Collins croaked. "You came."

Falling to his knees, Traverse cried out, "Dad, what happened? Where are Randolph and Lisa?"

"They took Lisa, and Randolph..." Collins swallowed hard. "Down by the lake." His voice came out in choked whisper.

One of the ranch-hands knelt down beside Collins and cut his bonds. Collins sat up and tried to get to his feet, but clutching his belly, he groaned loudly.

"You're in pain. Let me help you." Traverse put one arm around his father and helped him to stand. "Where is Randolph?" he asked again.

Leaning on Traverse, Collins walked toward the water. When Traverse saw the body of Randolph lying in the grass, he let go of his father and ran to the spot where Randolph lay. Sinking to his knees, he touched his brother's still body and called, "Randolph."

He saw the gaping wound in Randolph's throat and the crusted blood and realized his brother was dead. "No!" he cried out, his voice breaking. Getting to his feet, he stood with his hands curled into fists. "No! This can't be real! Not Randolph! Not my brother!" He turned to stare at his father. "How could this happen? Why would anyone kill Randolph? Who did this?"

"Kiimzaan." His father spoke with a toneless, dead voice that sent a chill down Traverse's spine. "He also took Lisa."

"Oh, my God, Dad." Traverse couldn't stop shaking. "What are we going to do?"

When he looked at his father, he saw something he had never seen in his eyes. He saw coldness that made him shiver. They were not the eyes of a rational man, and he feared for his father's sanity.

"I am going to kill him," Collins said with a voice that matched his eyes. "I will kill him and wipe his whole gang from the face of this cursed planet."

Old man Haggard spoke gently beside Traverse. "Let us take you home."

"They took the horses," one of the ranch-hands said. "I will bring the body of your son."

"You can ride my horse," Traverse said. "I can walk."

"I'm afraid we'll have to ride double. I don't know if I can stay on the horse by myself."

Any other time Traverse would have laughed at his father's remark, but not then.

The ride home seemed to take forever. They rode in silence. Nobody was in the mood to talk. Travers knew, eventually, his father would tell him what exactly went down, but he needed time.

Traverse felt empty inside. He still couldn't accept that his younger brother was dead and Lisa gone. To lose two siblings on one day was more than anyone could handle. He worried how his mother would take the news. This day had started so wonderfully and for a few hours he had lived in a world of happiness he wished would never end. Everything had come crushing down. Instead of remembering this day as one of the happiest in his life, he would want to never remember it at all. He wished this day had never happened.

─────

COLLINS HAD BARELY SPOKEN TO ANYONE. HE DIDN'T KNOW what to say. His soul felt empty and numb. Randolph was dead, and Lisa was gone, suffering a fate he didn't even want to think about. They buried Randolph four days later in a small graveyard not far from the house where family members of the Haggards rested in their graves. Simple, wooden crosses marked the graves with the names of the deceased, birthdates, and when they'd passed away.

One of the ranch-hands asked if he could make the cross and do the inscription. "Just write the letters and numbers down for me," he said. "I can copy them."

Randolph had been well-liked by all the Cats. They loved his spirit, his enthusiasm, and the interest he had shown in the history and ways of the Suumir.

Except for Kristie, the Collins family had never been religious, and Kristie wanted to have someone hold a spiritual sermon. Haggard told them about Reverend Jacob Oleski, the pastor in a small church not far from the Haggard Ranch. "He's been trying for years to convert me to his cause," Haggard said. "He'll be happy to do the service for you. However, it may come with a price tag. He'll want you to visit his church come Sunday and hopefully, many Sundays after that."

"I don't care. All I want is for my son's soul to rest in peace. He's met a violent death at the hands of that savage. He deserves a proper funeral." Kristie hadn't stopped crying since the night they brought Randolph's body home.

The day after the funeral, Collins went into the storage shed, where he had stowed away the large trunk with the double bottom. He removed the false floor and stared at the items he had smuggled into Savanna. He took out the body suit and unfolded it. It looked thin and flimsy, but it was made from materials not even a bullet from a colt could penetrate. An arrow would bounce off it like a rubber ball. After taking off his pants and shirt, he slipped into the suit, and it molded against his body. He put on his pants and shirt again.

He removed the case with the sniper rifle that fired shock pellets. When the pellets hit their target, they entered the body and exploded inside, leaving massive damage behind, destroying living tissue and organs beyond repair. Anyone shot with one of those rifles couldn't be revived.

Collins didn't remember how he came into possession of the rifle and suit. He just knew he had it. Along with the rifle, he also packed other special equipment into a leather bag, none of it legal on Savanna. He didn't care. Nothing would stand in his way to avenge the death of his son and to get back his daughter. He couldn't do that with the primitive weapons allowed on this planet.

Strapping a laser pistol around his waist, he slipped on a backpack filled with survival gear and some rations and was ready to ride out.

Rhe-annur was already waiting for him. He sat on his horse with a somber expression on his alien face. Traverse and Kristie stood beside him, watching Collins stride toward them. Kristie knew what he was going to do, and she had not objected. She didn't even question his possession of the rifle and suit. He might never come back, but that was the chance they both were willing to take, as long as he punished the murderer of their son.

She clung to him for a long moment. Her tears had stopped flowing, and she looked at him with large, dry eyes. "Come back safely, bring back our daughter, and kill that son-of-a-bitch who did this to us," she whispered fiercely.

He nodded, hugged Traverse, and held his hand. "You take care of your mother, Traverse. You'll be the head of the family until I come back. If I don't come back, you all know what to do."

Traverse smiled grimly. "I don't know if we can count on the military to come and protect us from Kiimzaan's gang of outlaws, but I'll plead our case."

"I hope it won't come to that." Collins patted the case that held his sniper rifle. "This will guarantee my victory, and my body armor will protect me from their arrows."

"What about Rhe-annur? He'll be vulnerable."

"I have this for him." He held up a vest. Handing it to the big Suumir, he said, "Put this on when we get to the camp of our enemy. It won't stop a bullet, but it will stop an arrow." He also gave him a laser pistol. "Leave your colt behind and put this into your holster. I'll teach you how to use it while we ride."

Rhe-annur took the vest and stuffed it into his saddlebag. He removed his colt from its holster but put it also into the saddlebag. "Just in case," he said. "Thank you, Boss-Collins. We should ride."

Collins put the bag with his special equipment into one of the saddlebags on his own horse, and he gave his wife another kiss. "I'll be back. I promise."

Mounting his horse, he rode away without looking back. He knew Rhe-annur was right behind him. They rode all day and spent the night in the protection of a grove of trees, lying on the hard ground. In the morning, they ate dry rations and drank water from their canteens before they rode on.

"We should get to their village shortly after noon," Rhe-annur said.

"You are sure we'll find Kiimzaan there?"

Rhe-annur nodded. "Quite sure. He accompanied his gang to take the cattle he stole from you to their settlement, of that I'm certain. His people need to stock up for the winter." He stayed silent, his blue cat's eyes regarding Collins for a moment. "I don't believe he will harm your daughter, Boss-Collins. He will want to sell her as a slave. A human female is worth a lot of gold."

"I hope we won't be too late. If she's gone, he won't enjoy his gold for long," Collins said between clenched teeth, trying to convince himself not to give in to despair. Lisa would be there. She had to be. Fate would not be so cruel and take away two of his children. Of course, as far as Kiimzaan's fate was concerned, he would kill him either way. Kiimzaan forfeited his life when he murdered Randolph.

RHE-ANNUR HAD BEEN CORRECT WITH HIS ESTIMATION. THE SUN stood at its highest point in the sky when they saw the first houses of the Suumir village. The village was situated near a small lake. Round houses with walls made from a mixture of clay and straw and roofs covered with reeds were strung along the dusty street. Collins had never seen a Suumir settlement and was a bit surprised to realize the Suumir weren't much different from the humans in the way they lived.

"How many people do you think live in this village?"

"I can't say for sure, but from the number of houses I estimate at least six hundred," Rhe-annur speculated.

"Do Suumir families have many children?"

Rhe-annur shrugged. "Four or five is about the average per family. Some may have more and some less."

"On Earth, we are limited to three children per couple, and the government family services frown on even that many. They would like to see the limit at one. You see, our home planet is over-populated. That's why the government encourages families to move to other planets."

"That is the reason humans came to our world?"

"That's right. Too many people are crowded into big cities with tall buildings and narrow streets. People are suffocating."

"I don't understand. If there is a limit on the amount of children you can have, how did Earth become overcrowded?"

"Limits were not always in place. For thousands of years humans were breeding like the rodents that plaque our stables. Families had ten and more children. In many cases, the poorest families and the ones living in drought-stricken areas of our planet had the most children. Many died of starvation, because their parents could not feed them or give them proper shelter."

"It seems to me humans are not as smart as they pretend to be. Why have children if you can't take care of them?"

Collins chuckled grimly. "We are no smarter than the Suumir, even if we are technologically further advanced."

"Humans do have magical things, like for instance this vest I am wearing. You say it will stop an arrow?"

"Arrows and more. We are practically invincible." Collins more so than Rhe-annur. While the Suumir wore only a vest, Collins' whole body was protected by his full-body suit.

They rode slowly down the street. Many young children were playing games that only children understand, running and chasing each other. They played in the street and in the grassy area behind the houses. He also saw adults and older children sitting in front of their doors. They were watching him and Rhe-annur with curious and surprised expressions. It was only a matter of time until one or more of them would block their way and challenge their presence in the Suumir village.

Collins did some quick calculation. According to what Rhe-annur told him, they might encounter up to two-hundred able-bodied males. Not all of the males living in this village would be around. Some might me out hunting or fishing, but there was still the chance a formidable number of males would object to having a human coming into their village.

He wasn't worried. He was ready to kill anyone who tried to attack him. This village was populated by members of an outlaw gang that terrorized the human settlers. It was time somebody took a stand against them and put an end to their terror.

Kiimzaan was at the top of the list.

As expected, a couple of Suumir, who had been attending a small herd of alck, stopped what they were doing and strode into the street. Both carried bows with nocked arrows.

Collins and Rhe-annur halted their horses in front of them. Collins recognized them as members of Kiimzaan's riders, and he knew he would kill them.

One of them pointed at Collins and said something in his native tongue, to which his companion laughed.

Without taking his eyes off them, he asked Rhe-annur, "What strikes them as funny?"

"He said for a supposedly dead man you look amazingly alive, but they'll change that after they had some fun with you."

"Tell them to start praying to their god, because I will kill them both."

Rhe-annur repeated it to the two valley-riders. They stared at Collins with an expression of utter amazement. Then they both broke out laughing. Lifting their bows, they released their arrows.

Had Collins not worn his special suit under his clothing, the arrows would have pierced his chest. It gave him great satisfaction in seeing the expression on their alien faces freeze when the arrows bounced harmlessly off him. He didn't even feel the impact.

Without giving them another warning, he drew his laser and shot them where they stood. He felt no remorse. There was no pity inside him. They deserved to die, and they would not be the only ones to die today.

The scene had drawn a small crowd of onlookers. Shouting in surprise as the two valley-riders collapsed to the dirt, a few of them moved forward to confront Collins and Rhe-annur. They stood with their bows ready and knives drawn, glaring at Collins with open hostility.

Again, Collins recognized a number of them as belonging to Kiimzaan's gang. He had a good memory for faces, even if they belonged to an alien race. The one closest to Collins spat out a string of loud words. Collins didn't need an interpreter to know he was angry.

Without being asked, Rhe-annur translated. "He wants to know why you murdered two of their best hunters without good cause. He also wants you to explain your reason for coming here."

"My reason is quite simple. I'm going to kill the ones who rode with Kiimzaan who murdered my son. Also tell him, I want Kiimzaan to meet me in the street so I can kill him. Tell him that."

One of the outlaws Collins recognized yelled something after Rhe-annur conveyed what Collins had said. Collins waited for Rhe-annur to translate.

"I put the arrow into your son's arm, and I will put one through yours, you stupid, insolent human. When Kiimzaan comes, he will slit your throat the way he did your son's."

Collins was not in the mood to play a game of words. Without another comment, he burnt a hole into the outlaw's forehead. "Where is Kiimzaan?" he shouted. "Where is my daughter?"

This time an older Suumir stepped forward. Spreading both his arms, he spoke to Rhe-annur, who listened to the old native without interrupting him.

"I am one of the elders of this village," Rhe-annur translated. "We want no trouble with the humans. Tell the human Kiimzaan does not listen to the elders. He does what he wants. We have no control over him. He has taken the human girl with him to the City of Stones."

Collins knew what he feared had become reality. "Ask him where exactly Kiimzaan took her."

When asked, the elder shrugged.

"He doesn't know."

More males had joined the group. Not all saw what had happened. One big Suumir pushed the elder aside and glared at Collins, his cat's eyes tiny slits. "You human. Stupid. Come to Suumir village," he said in halting, broken Inglis. "Kill you." With that, he drew his knife and advanced toward Collins.

"If anyone is stupid, it's you," Collins said and shot him.

Angry shouts erupted from the new group. They shot their bows, but all arrows bounced off Collins without doing any damage. He looked into their faces and recognized each one of them.

Methodically and without compunction he shot them. As they fell, wails from female throats erupted in the watching crowd. He didn't care. When they lay dead, he said, "They were all guilty of murdering my son. From now on, every Suumir who tries to steal our cattle or threatens to harm a human will be killed. There will be no more tribute paid to anyone. I'm going to ask one more time, where did Kiimzaan take my daughter?"

One of the females pointed at a young male who stood separate from the rest. "He knows. He is Kiimzaan's brother."

No sooner had Rhe-annur translated the female's words than the young male turned and ran toward a small herd of alck grazing nearby. Swinging himself on the back of one of them, he dug his heels into the animal's soft flanks. With a loud cry, he spurred the alck into taking off at top speed.

Collins lifted his rifle and found the rider in his sights. Instead of aiming at the rider, he aimed at the alck. Squeezing the trigger, he fired one, single shot. The animal collapsed under its rider. "Go get him," Collins told Rhe-annur.

The young Suumir tried to limp away, but Rhe-annur caught up with him quickly. He brought him back to Collins.

"You will take us to your brother," Collins told him. "If you refuse, I will kill you right now."

"You will kill me anyway," the young Suumir said in fluent Inglis.

Somewhat surprised, Collins said, "I've never seen you riding with Kiimzaan, which means I have no reason to kill you, as long as you don't give me one by refusing to help us find him. If you do what I say, you have my word, I won't harm you. Do you understand?"

"I understand, but you will kill my brother."

"Your brother has stolen my property." Collins spoke calmly, as if reciting a shopping list with an icy feeling inside him that wouldn't go away. "He has murdered my son and one of my men. He left me to die tied to stakes driven into the ground. He kidnapped my daughter, and now he wants to sell her into slavery. Kiimzaan is evil and does not deserve to live another day. I came to kill him, and nothing will change my mind."

"You killed all these men in cold blood." The young male made a sweeping motion with his arm. "You are no better than Kiimzaan."

"They were members of his gang. They were thieves, and they stole what belonged to me. They did nothing to stop Kiimzaan from murdering my son. You are his brother. I have in mind to kill you where you stand."

He gazed at the dead males lying in front of him. He should feel remorse, but there was only one feeling left inside him. The only thing he felt was anger. He blamed Kiimzaan for putting him in this position. He thought he left the violence behind when he left Earth, but it angered him how easily he had slipped to a level he didn't remember ever having experienced. He didn't know who he was anymore, and it frightened him.

"Kiimzaan may be my brother, but I am not like him. I do not share his desire for power and control. I do not believe in violence and taking what is not mine." He drew himself erect. "I am Rhaam, son of Rhaamzowl, who was once the leader of this village."

"Well, Rhaam, son of Rhaamzowl, here is the deal. If you take us to the City of Stones and to your brother's hideout, you will be free to go back to your people. Betray me and I will kill you."

"I understand. I will need an alck to ride. The City of Stones is not close. I cannot run the whole distance."

"I wouldn't expect you to. Go and get yourself an alck, but if you entertain any ideas, like trying to run away or getting a weapon, forget that. I will hunt you down and kill you, along with anyone who is foolish enough to help you. Understood?"

Rhaam nodded. His golden cat's eyes were veiled, but Collins knew he needed to be on guard. This young Suumir would betray him the first chance he got.

He walked over to the herd of alck and picked one of them. Swinging himself onto its broad back, he came back to Collins. "I am ready."

Collins looked around the silent crowd of Suumir. He fastened his gaze on the elder who had spoken before. "Tell your people not to follow me. Anyone attempting to harm us will be killed." He lifted his rifle. "This weapon finds its target no matter how far away my enemy is. As you already witnessed, no arrow can hurt me or my companion."

Rhe-annur translated his words. The old Suumir nodded solemnly.

"We will heed your warning. You have done enough damage to our people already." His cat's eyes flashed with suppressed anger. "You are no better than the one you are hunting. The ones you killed in cold blood did not deserve to die. It was Kiimzaan who killed your son, not them."

Rhe-annur translated the words as the elder spoke them.

"Tell him they were guilty by association. My son is dead, and my daughter is missing. I am in no mood to explain myself, and I will kill anyone who stands in my way. Tell him that." Collins spoke loudly, not hiding his anger.

Collins never looked back as they left the village, with Rhaam in the lead. He was confident none would try to stop them. As the elder said, he'd done enough damage to this village. He closed his ears and mind to the wailing cries of the females and children he robbed of their mates, brothers, sons, and fathers.

[13]

THEY RODE IN SILENCE MOST OF THE DAY. AS EVENING DREW
nearer, they searched for a safe spot to spend the night. According to
Rhe-annur, this part of the country was populated by dangerous
carnivores. The most dangerous one was the droocor. From his
description, Collins gathered they were closely related to the extinct
sabretooth tigers of Earth. He had seen hologram productions
featuring those ferocious beasts, and he had no desire to meet
something like that in real life.

The landscape had changed since they left the village of the
Suumir. Low, rolling hills dotted with shrubs and stands of trees had
replaced the flat land with an occasional collection of sheer cliffs rising
out of the ground without any rhyme or reason. Some of the cliffs
were crowned with gnarled, stunted trees. There was no easy way to
climb to the top of any of those cliffs, unless one was equipped with
climbing gears. Of course, they had no reason to climb them,
although, thinking of the animals Rhe-annur had described, Collins
wished they were able to make their camp on top of one of them.

When he shared his thoughts with Rhe-annur, the big Suumir
chuckled. "You may not be as safe as you believe, because you would
be vulnerable to an attack by a racc."

"What's a racc?"

"A huge flying reptile with a beak full of sharp teeth and more ferocious than a droocor."

"Good thing we don't have to worry about climbing one of those cliffs." Collins chuckled. "What is your suggestion then?"

"If we could find a cave that would be perfect." Rhe-annur scanned the cliffs ahead of them. "It doesn't even have to be deep."

"If you permit me to make a suggestion?"

Collins looked at Rhaam. "What do you suggest?"

"I am quite familiar with this part of the land. If we travel still a little further, we'll find the ruins of a village that was abandoned many cycles ago. Many of the houses are still usable. We will find protection in one of those."

"What do you think, Rhe-annur? Can we trust his information?"

The big Suumir shrugged. "His safety is at stake, also. I would say trust him. If he's leading us into a trap, I will kill him myself."

"Good. Let's ride on."

As Rhaam had said, the ancient village was not large. Most of the former dwellings consisted only of broken walls, but a few of them did still have all four walls intact. All were open to the sky. The roofs had collapsed and rotted away a long time ago. They managed to find a dwelling that was suitable.

"We need to get water," Collins said.

"I'll go back to the creek we just passed. The water should be pure and drinkable." Rhe-annur took both water-skins and walked away.

Collins put a question to Rhaam. "How long until we get to the City of Stones?"

"If we leave early, we should be there before the morning ends."

"Tell me, where did you learn to speak our language?"

"Kiimzaan and I were raised by humans."

Surprised by this revelation, Collins stared at the young Suumir. "What happened to your real parents?"

"My mother was killed by a droocor shortly after I was born, and my father drowned when he fell into turbulent waters of one of the rivers in the mountains. Because nobody wanted us in the village, the elders sold us as slaves in the big human city."

"Are you saying the humans who raised you, bought you as slaves?"

"They did. It is not uncommon."

"There is something I don't understand. You said they raised you. Do you by any chance hate humans because they mistreated you?"

"We were beaten constantly if we didn't behave according to what our owners expected of us. They made us work hard and many long hours." Rhaam did not hide the bitterness in his voice.

"I assume you finally escaped and went back to your village?"

"Kiimzaan killed our master one day after we were beaten again. We took what we needed to survive, including two horses. Then we rode away." Rhaam gave Collins a defiant look. "We only did what we had to do."

Collins nodded solemnly. "I can't even blame you. You got a rotten deal. Slavery is an ugly thing. Nobody should be owned by anyone." His expression hardened. "I can understand Kiimzaan's hatred for us humans, but he went too far when he murdered my son and abducted my daughter. We never harmed him. He was the one who came and demanded we give him our cattle and our horses, which we did. I will still kill him."

"I do not condone what my brother did, but he cared for our people in the village. He provided everyone with food."

Collins laughed sourly. "Yes, with my cattle. We work hard to keep them alive, but your brother took them from us without giving us anything in return. Your brother is a thief and a murderer."

Before Rhaam could comment, Rhe-annur came back with the filled water-skins. He also had stuffed his pockets with a number of large cucumber-like fruit. "I picked these from the trees that grow along the river. They will provide us with nourishment."

"Are you sure they're safe to eat? They have prickly skin."

"The skin may be prickly, but the inside is sweet and soft." He handed a couple to Collins and gave one to Rhaam. Taking his knife, he sliced off the hard skin and bit into the exposed, white pulp inside.

Collins watched him with misgivings. He had never seen these cucumbers and wasn't sure if he should eat them. Perhaps they were safe to eat for the indigenous population but not for humans. Even though their metabolism seemed to be the same, there might be some local fruit and vegetables poisonous to humans.

Rhaam peeled the skin from his fruit. "They are safe for humans," he assured Collins.

Collins was still cautious, but he was hungry and needed to eat something. After taking his first bite, he had to admit, the fruit tasted quite delicious.

It was getting dark outside, and they got ready to go to sleep.

"One of us has to stay awake and watch the horses," Rhe-annur said. "I will take the first watch." He looked at Rhaam. "I do not trust you. We must tie you up."

"I'll take care of it," Collins said. He searched inside his special-equipment bag and pulled out two bands of some soft material. "Put these around your ankles," he instructed Rhaam.

"What will they do?" Rhaam seemed reluctant.

"Nothing harmful. They will prevent you from coming too close to me and Rhe-annur and, also, from sneaking away during the night." He handed an object to Rhe-annur. "Put this into your pocket. It will sound an alarm if Rhaam comes within a few feet near you."

It was getting dark quickly, and Collins removed another device from his bag, a headlamp. He switched it on and illuminated the interior of the dwelling. "I'll put my sleeping bag in that corner. You, Rhaam, will sleep over there. Sorry, I don't have a sleeping bag for you."

"He can use mine," Rhe-annur said. He gave Collins an apologetic look. "To make the transition easier when you take my watch, Boss-Collins, I will sleep in yours."

Collins smiled. "That's quite alright. It's a good plan. I'm going to crawl into mine and hope to sleep until you wake me."

IT SEEMED HE HAD BARELY FALLEN ASLEEP WHEN RHE-ANNUR shook him. He opened his eyes and found it was bright enough to make out the form of his foreman leaning over him. The light from the two moons overhead illuminated the room enough to take away much of the darkness.

"It's your turn, Boss-Collins."

Collins crawled out of his sleeping bag and, rubbing his eyes, he went to take his place in front of the building. It was still dark outside, but once his eyes adjusted, the night didn't seem so threatening anymore.

Looking up at the night-sky, he remembered the first night on Savanna. He and Kristie had looked at the alien constellations in wonder and many misgivings, pondering how their life would turn out on this new world that would be their home from then on. Had they made the right decision to come here? A sudden lump in his throat made him question it. Randolph was dead as a direct result of bringing him to this planet. He would still be alive had they stayed on Earth.

And Lisa? She would be happy with her many friends instead of having been kidnapped to be sold as a slave with no future.

Anger welled up inside him. He would find her and take her back to his family, after he killed the man who did that to her.

A rumbling sound from close by made him sit up straight and stare into the darkness between the trees. He realized he had drifted into a light slumber. A low growl even closer caused him to reach for his rifle. With one hand he switched on his headlamp and cursed loudly when he saw the crouching animal about fifty feet in front of him.

A droocor. There was no mistaking the long teeth protruding from its upper jaw. Rhe-annur had given him a good description of this predator, and it was even larger than he imagined.

When the beam from Collins' headlamp bathed the animal with its bright light, the droocor flattened itself to the ground. With a terrifying roar it sprang, covering half the distance separating it from Collins in one mighty leap.

What saved him from being torn apart by the predator's huge claws were his quick reflexes and automatic reaction. Without conscious thought, he brought up his rifle and squeezed the trigger in one smooth move. The pellet entered the gaping mouth of the animal and exploded on impact inside the throat, destroying the brain and surrounding tissue. The roar was cut off, and the massive body of the droocor crashed to the ground. The body shuddered, its thick limbs thrashed, and then it lay still.

Collins let out his breath, his heart still beating fast. That had been close. He chided himself for being so careless.

Behind him, Rhe-annur appeared in the doorway with a drawn

laser pistol. When he saw the furry body of the droocor lying so close to Collins, he grunted.

Collins rose from his sitting position. "I didn't think they were this big," he said and went to inspect the carcass.

Rhe-annur followed him and looked down at the dead animal. Blood was seeping from its open maw. "They are not easy to kill, Boss-Collins. You are a good shot with that weapon."

"Anyone with a steady hand and good eye can do what I did." He downplayed what happened but wondered a little where he had gained such proficiency. He didn't remember ever using a rifle like that in his career as a law enforcement officer. He had been a detective, not a member of an assault team. He dismissed the thoughts and looked at his watch. "Sorry I woke you. Go back to sleep. You still have a couple of hours until you need to get up."

"I am not tired anymore. Let me take over the remainder of the watch and you sleep some more."

Collins nodded. "Normally, I would argue with you, but I'm really tired. I will accept your offer. Thank you, Rhe-annur. You are a good friend." He handed him the rifle. "Just in case this one's mate shows up."

He didn't think he'd fall asleep again, but he did. Plagued by disturbing dreams, his sleep was not peaceful. When Rhe-annur woke him, he was still groggy. He realized the events of the previous day and the anger and grief that had gripped him for days were finally taking their toll. A man can go on only so long with all that bottled up inside him without suffering some kind of consequences.

He went down to the creek to wash up and felt better after that. He knew this would be the day of reckoning, and he needed to have his wits about him. Today was the day he would kill Kiimzaan. The thought gave his adrenalin a boost. He would finally get his revenge and, hopefully, rescue Lisa from a terrible fate.

Back at their temporary camp, he removed the electronic shackles from Rhaam's ankles. "If you want to clean up you can accompany Rhe-annur down to the creek," he told him. He was almost apologetic when he added, "We'll have to keep watching you. Forget about privacy."

Withdrawn, Rhaam went with Rhe-annur without any comments.

Collins shared some of his rations with Rhaam. The young Suumir gave him a grateful look but stayed silent.

The morning air was crisp when they got underway, and a cool wind blew from the east. As the day progressed, it became warmer. However, the wind didn't die down.

They arrived in the City of Stones shortly before noon, just as Rhaam had predicted. It surprised Collins to see a city not unlike cities on Earth must have been a thousand years ago, except the houses of the Suumir were constructed from rough stones and clay. They were clustered close together with barely enough room for a person to squeeze between them. The streets were narrow and dirt-packed. After a rain, they'd turn into rivers of mud.

"We can't take our horses into the city," Rhe-annur said. "There is a stable over there where we can leave them. It will be expensive, but the owner can be trusted. They'll be safe until we need them again."

After some haggling with the stable owner, Rhe-annur handed him a few pieces of gold. Collins put the leather bag with his special equipment into the backpack and hung it over his shoulder. The stable owner gave him the impression of being shifty and, despite Rhe-annur's assurance, Collin didn't trust him.

As expected, the streets were crowded with people, not all of the Suumir race. He saw people of different cultures, dressed in strange clothes. They passed a group of tall, thin figures wearing long robes and hoods. He couldn't see their faces inside the hoods, but the occasional flash of light reflected from shiny eyes was enough of a clue for him to assume they were not even remotely related to the Suumir.

"What are those?" he asked Rhe-annur.

"Kiirikora. Desert-dwellers. They come to trade and to cause trouble." He chuckled. "Best to stay away from them. They are fierce fighters and deadly with their blowguns. Also, easily angered."

"I'll remember that." Collins smiled grimly. "Of course, I don't think there are many right now with tempers easier to explode than mine." On edge, his nerves raw were from not knowing what he could expect when he finally caught up with Kiimzaan.

The air in the city was pregnant with various odors, not all of them pleasant. Spices and cooking-odors blended with the smell of decay and waste.

Even though many different groups walked on the street, Collins did receive curious looks. He knew it was because he was human and, obviously, not a native of Savanna.

"We will have to buy a robe for you to hide your human identity," Rhe-annur suggested. "Humans are not popular with most of the indigenous people. Tolerated but not loved. We don't want to create a scene."

They found a shop that sold clothing. After slipping into a robe, Collins had to admit he felt more at ease.

"Now it's time to earn your freedom," he told Rhaam. "Where do you think we can find your brother?"

"He will most likely be at the slave-market."

"The slave-market?"

"That's where the slave-traders buy their slaves. It's an open market, and anyone wanting to buy or sell a slave can do it there," Rhaam said matter-of-factly as if it were nothing unusual.

"Where is this market?"

"If we stay on this road, it will lead us to it. You will know when we get there."

They walked no more than thirty minutes to find the market. A fenced-in spot in the center of an open area, holding a number of naked individuals was not easily missed. Aside from Suumir's prisoners inside the fence, Collins also saw dwarfs and giants, and people with skins that glittered in the light and with eyes that rivaled polished emeralds. They looked vaguely humanoid, but their scaly faces were animalistic and feral.

A number of carts with cages made from wooden poles surrounded the fence. Inside the cages, cowered more captives, some looking scared and some angry. What intrigued him most were the hooded figures standing by the carts and by the gate keeping the slaves penned inside the fence. A few of them had their hoods thrown back, revealing bald heads. Their faces were covered with grotesque masks.

"Slave traders," Rhe-annur answered his unspoken question.

"They don't appear to be Suumir."

"Nobody knows where they come from and what they are. Their faces are always hidden behind their masks. We call them Sky-demons."

"Why?"

"Because they have been observed to load the slaves into metal carts which rise into the air and disappear in the clouds."

"In other words, they are not native to Savanna, but I don't believe they are humans. That complicates things. I cannot let them have my daughter. If she gets taken off-planet, I will never see her again. I'm quite ignorant when it comes to all the alien races in space, and I don't know which ones have a habit of wearing those horrible looking masks."

Collins perused the crowd milling around the fence but did not see Kiimzaan or Lisa. "It seems your brother is not here," he said to Rhaam.

"If your daughter isn't inside the enclosure or any of the wagons, he hasn't been here. He will come. This is the only place where he will be able to sell her."

"We are not in a strategic position here," Collins speculated. "I would like to be higher up to give me a better chance to oversee everything. Where we are now, Kiimzaan may spot us before we see him."

"We should try to get into one of the houses," Rhe-annur suggested. Looking around, he pointed at a two-story house not far away. "That would be the perfect location."

"How are we going to get in? We can't just barge in, and I will not force my way into that house." The last thing Collins wanted was to draw attention to their presence. Breaking into a house would not end well.

"I will go and find out who lives in there and talk to them. It may cost you a few gold nuggets, but it will be worth it." He exposed his teeth in a smile. "I haven't met anyone yet who is immune to gold." He walked away, heading for the building.

Collins kept watching the crowd and the slave pen. Three Suumir males dragged a third one toward the gate. His arms were bound behind his back, and he had a rope around his neck. The group stopped in front of one of the slave traders, obviously discussing terms. It seemed they came to an agreement. The slave-trader poured something into the hands of one of the three Suumir males, grabbed the rope, and pulled the captive to the gate. Opening it, he shoved him into the pen.

Rhe-annur came back a short time later with a smile. "We're good to go. The upper suite belongs to an old couple. They were happy to take the gold I offered, and we can have the place to ourselves for the day."

"That's good news. We couldn't hope for more." Collins looked at Rhaam. "I hope you're right with your prediction that your brother will come. The sooner we get this over with the sooner you'll be free to go, but until then you'll stay our prisoner. If you try to warn Kiimzaan or run away, I will shoot you. I hope it doesn't come to that. I have no quarrel with you."

"I wish you would change your mind about killing Kiimzaan, but I can see it in your eyes your mind is made up. I cannot even blame you. I would not want my daughter sold as a slave."

"You have a daughter?"

Rhaam nodded. "She is still small."

"Where is she?"

"With her mother. My mate."

"You have a mate and a child. Then you have even more motivation to stay alive. Let's go."

They had to climb a set of stairs attached to the side of the building. At the top was a weathered, wooden door. Collins had, of course, never been inside a Suumir dwelling and didn't know what to expect.

The floor of the room they entered was covered with shabby, old furs. Pillows were strewn across the floor, but there was no furniture. The next room was, obviously, the kitchen. It was small. A metal cook stove stood in one corner with clay pots and pans along with a few crude plates and cups on a shelve beside it. A pile of wood and some cubes of dried peat moss were stacked in the other corner. A basin and an urn filled with water sat on a small table.

The wooden shutters on the window were closed. Collins walked over and opened them. He was pleased with the location. They couldn't have found a better place.

He removed his sniper-rifle from its case and leaned it against the wall beside the window, ready to be used when needed.

There was plenty of activity going on below them. The slavers began loading prisoners into the carts. A few of the carts left, pulled by those giant goats. Just when Collins began to think Kiimzaan wasn't going to show, he spotted the big Suumir outlaw coming down one of the side-streets. His heart beat faster when he saw Lisa with him. Seeing the rope around her neck only fuelled his desire to kill the murderer of his son.

"When I tell you to go you run and get Lisa," he told Rhe-annur, who stood beside him, watching. Grabbing his rifle, Collins got into position. He cleared his mind and pushed away any other thoughts. Nothing else was important. The only thing to do was to bring down his quarry.

The big outlaw had reached the gate and began talking to one of the slave-traders.

Collins put the crosshairs on Kiimzaan's forehead.

The result was almost anticlimactic when he squeezed the trigger, even though one drawback to the sniper rifle it wasn't as silent as a laser. The small explosion that propelled the pellet on its way seemed loud in the confines of the room. When Kiimzaan collapsed, he said, "Now! Go!"

He turned around and watched Rhe-annur rush away. Then he became aware of something that didn't seem right. Rhaam was not there anymore. He must have fled when he and Rhe-annur were looking out of the window.

At first, he chided himself for being careless, but then he shrugged. It didn't matter anymore. Kiimzaan was dead. His mission was accomplished. Now it was just a matter of getting Lisa, and they would be on their way.

When he turned back to look out of the window, Lisa struggled in the grip of two slavers. They were pulling her toward one of the wagons. Collins brought up his rifle again. Finding one of the slavers in his sights, he dropped him. Without letting go of Lisa, the other one turned and looked directly at Collins. He groped for something under his robe.

Collins shot him in the head, right through his ugly mask.

Unfortunately, the demise of the two slavers had drawn the attention of their companions. He knew he had been spotted. The slavers scattered and ran toward the house Collins was hiding in. He knew he couldn't stay and wait for Rhe-annur, but then he heard the muffled sounds of footsteps in the next room and wondered why Rhe-annur was coming back so soon. Something must have gone wrong. Taking another look out of the window, he didn't see Lisa anymore and hoped she was with Rhe-annur after all.

Expecting his foreman, he didn't react as fast as he normally would have when one of the slavers came into the room. He had removed his mask and held a tube against his lips. Fleetingly, Collins noticed the small ears and the flat nose and then something struck his throat, like the sting of a wasp. Drawing his laser, he shot his attacker in the forehead.

When he touched his throat, he encountered something stuck in his neck. Pulling it out, he looked at the small dart in his hand and realized he had been shot with a blowgun. He counted himself fortunate the dart had not hit him in the eye.

He became aware of someone else walking across the furs and waited, his laser drawn. This time it was Rhe-annur. He looked down at the unmoving form on the floor. "Looks like they found us," he commented. "We must leave. They are everywhere."

"Where is Lisa?"

Rhe-annur's face was grave when he said, "I couldn't find her. She was gone. I'm sorry, Boss-Collins. I saw this slaver and another one running up the stairs. I shot one but this one got into the house. I thought you may need my help. Are you all right?"

"I'm fine. He shot me with a dart, that's all." Collins bent and picked it up from the floor where he had dropped it.

"May I see that?" Rhe-annur took the dart from Collins and sniffed it. "This dart is poisoned. The Kiirikora use blowguns, but this one isn't a desert-dweller's dart. The poison may be different from what the Kiirikora use." He looked at Collins with concern. "We must get away now. They will send more, and we cannot fight them all."

"What about Lisa?" A wave of nausea rushed through him. "We can't leave her."

"We will find her, but we need to be alive for that. The first thing we need to do is get the poison out of your body, or you will die. You will be no good to Lisa when you're dead."

"All right." A second attack of nausea made him stagger. Even though a cloud seemed to settle over his mind, he had enough sense to put his rifle into its case and grab it.

Rhe-annur steadied him as they climbed down the stairs. He pulled the hood of his robe over his head and was glad Rhe-annur had the foresight to suggest a robe when they came to the city. They would not be recognizable from the back. His first instinct was to run, but Rhe-annur held him back. "We must not appear to be in a hurry."

Collins agreed. His mind was sluggish, and he found it challenging to form any logical thoughts. Rhe-annur pulled him into a break between two houses. They emerged on the other side and found themselves on another street, much narrower than the one they left. It reminded him of the back alleys in the big cities of Earth.

They increased their speed, but he found putting one foot in front of the other difficult. "I don't know if I can make it much further." His words came out slurred.

"You need medical help." Rhe-annur stopped in front of one of the houses and banged against the door. When it opened, an elderly Suumir-male stepped out. Rhe-annur pointed at Collins and said something in the Suumir language. The male nodded and opened the door to let Collins and Rhe-annur enter. The older one spoke to a younger male in the room, and the young one got up and left.

"Sit here, Boss-Collins. He went to get a healer."

With a grateful, almost incoherent thank you Collins sank to his knees. He became aware of the rifle case in his hand and put it down beside him but kept it close, afraid someone might take it away from him.

It seemed an eternity, in which he drifted in and out of consciousness, before the door opened, and the young male came back. An elderly male, dressed in a red cloak, entered behind him. He looked at Collins and said in Inglis, "So you're the one who caused that incident in the slave-market. I hear you killed a number of the slavers."

Collins tried to grin, but it was too much of an effort. "I tried to rescue my daughter," he said and was surprised when the words didn't come out of his mouth in a jumble.

"I'm told you were shot with a poisoned dart from a blowgun. Let me have a look at that wound." With that he pushed back Collins' hood. He let out a small whistle. "It looks nasty. That wasn't caused by the poison the Kiirikora use. This is something completely different. Do you still have the dart to allow us to analyze the poison?"

Before Collins could answer, Rhe-annur took the dart out of his pocket and handed it to the healer, who wrapped it in a small piece of cloth and put it into one of his pockets. "I can't do it here. We'll have to take you to our facility." He looked at Rhe-annur. "Can he walk?"

Rhe-annur shook his head. "He is quite weak."

"Then you must accompany him. It is not far from here."

Rhe-annur helped Collins to his feet and supported him as they left the house. Collin felt himself slipping into darkness but tried desperately to stay alert. When he became aware of his surroundings again, he lay in a bed.

[14]

THERE WAS SOMETHING STRANGE ABOUT THE ROOM HE LAY IN. IT didn't look like one that should exist in a dwelling built by Suumir. The ceiling and the walls were too smooth. He didn't see any oil lamps on the walls, nor did he see a window, yet the room was brightly lit. As much as he searched, he couldn't find the source of the light. It seemed to originate from the ceiling and the walls. Everything in the room looked sterile. It didn't take much guessing to know he was in a hospital room—but where?

When he moved his arm, he felt resistance. Looking down, he saw a tube running from it to a metal stand on which hung a bottle with some clear liquid inside. The tube was attached to the bottle. He was being fed intravenously. The Suumir didn't have the knowledge and equipment for that. Neither did they have electronic equipment to measure his heartbeat and other functions of his body, but that's exactly what he saw beside his bed.

Where was he?

Hearing a noise, he turned his head to look at the opening door. The woman walking in was human. She wore a white outfit and carried a tray with a cup and a plate of food.

She smiled when she saw him sitting up. "How are you feeling, Mr. Collins?"

He stared at her, wondering if this was a dream or if he had died and this was someplace in the afterlife, not that he ever believed in such a thing. "Where am I?"

"You're in our small hospital."

"Hospital? Where is this hospital? Who are you?"

"I'll explain everything in a moment. I'm Dr. Eguarii. I see you seem to be doing well. I brought you a cup of tea and something to eat." She gave a little laugh. "You can't beat real food. I bet you're hungry for something solid in your belly."

He shook his head. This was just too weird. "Are you real or am I hallucinating?"

She laughed again. "I'm as real as you. By the way, we thought you might feel more comfortable if I took on human form."

He lifted a hand. "Hold on, now. You're losing me. Can we start from the beginning? I have a million questions."

She cocked her head a little. "Okay. Go ahead. Ask."

"I remember being taken somewhere by a Suumir healer. I thought I was dying, but here I am, feeling well, lying in a comfortable hospital bed. What am I missing?"

She put the tray onto a table against one wall and came to sit on the bed. "You remember being hit by a poisoned dart?"

He nodded.

"We analyzed the poison and discovered it was not manufactured on Savanna. It's a poison popular with the Snaar. It's silent and efficient, in addition to being a perfect weapon to be used on low-tech planets, such as Savanna."

"I've heard the name Snaar mentioned, but who actually are the Snaar?"

"You don't know? Don't all humans know the major spacefaring species?"

"I'm from Earth. Most people on Earth know little about what is going on in space. We know we are not alone in the universe. We know about some of the other races, but I'm afraid, except for the name, I don't know anything about the Snaar."

"The Snaar are a terrible race. They are basically slave-traders. If they can't buy slaves, they will kidnap their victims and sell them on planets where slavery is legal."

"That sounds awful. I didn't know such things existed. What did you mean when you said you took on human form? Aren't you human?"

She smiled. "I'm a member of the Accilla race. Our true form is, well, let's say different from yours. You may even find us repulsive. We are shapeshifters, which means we can take on any form we wish."

"I have a feeling there are a few things I'm missing here. Before my family and I came to Savanna, the officials in immigrations showed us holograms of this planet, including information about conditions and other important facts we needed to know, but we were never told about other races residing here. Why would they keep that a secret?"

"Our presence here is not common knowledge. We like to stay in the background."

"Why are you telling me? Aren't you afraid I will tell others? Am I your prisoner?"

She shook her head. "Of course not. Accilla and humans are not enemies. If you report what took place here, it will change nothing, but we would prefer you don't talk about it. Your leaders probably suspect we are here. They're just not sharing that information with the general population. We're not the only ones with outposts on Savanna. The Kraach and the Anorians also have a post hidden somewhere on this planet."

Collins wiped his forehead. "This is a lot to digest. By the way, where is my companion?"

"The big Suumir who brought you? He didn't want to stay. He said he had to go and search for a missing girl. Apparently, she may have been kidnapped by the Snaar."

"My daughter. That's my daughter. Her name is Lisa. I failed her." Collins balled his hands into fists. "If what you told me is true and she was captured by those Snaar, she will face a terrible fate. I must leave here and find her." He tried to remove the tube from his arm.

The woman stopped him. "You are still weak. We've neutralized the poison and repaired some of the damage it did to your organs, but you need at least a couple more days to get your strength back and to get rid of the last remnants of the poison. I'm sure your companion will find her."

He fell back when the room spun a little around him and a feeling of weakness came over him.

She touched his arm. "Sit up slowly, drink your tea, and eat some food. It will help stabilize your metabolism. Tomorrow, you'll be feeling much better, Mr. Collins."

"How do you know my name?"

Her laugh was almost apologetic. "You must forgive me. I took a little peek into your mind, but only a little. We know humans don't like to share their inner thoughts."

"I don't understand."

"We are telepaths, which means we can read thoughts. Be assured, I'm not reading you mind now. We don't believe in invading the personal space of others, not without permission."

He let out a strangled laugh. "It seems there is much I don't know. All this new information you gave me is enough to blow anyone's mind. Shapeshifters, telepaths, Snaar, the Kraach. What else haven't you told me?"

"That this facility is underground. Another reason you can't just get up and leave."

"In other words, I'm your prisoner."

"Oh, no, Mr. Collins. There is no reason to hold you. Like I said, we are not enemies. Once you are healed, we will help you get back to your ranch."

"It seems you know everything about me."

"Not everything, I'm sure," she said with a little smile. Getting up, she smoothed out her outfit. "I'll leave you now. Make sure you eat something. I'll be back later to check up on you again." Before she closed the door, she turned around and gave him an encouraging smile. "Don't worry. We'll have you back on your feet in no time."

It was difficult for Collins to imagine she wasn't anything but a human woman, an attractive human woman. She was blond with deep blue eyes, reminding him of Kristie. Thinking of his wife, he felt anxious to get back home. She must be going out of her mind with worries, wondering if he was still alive and if he had been successful in rescuing Lisa. What would he tell her if Rhe-annur didn't find her?

As a former law enforcement officer, he had been privileged to information the general public never heard about, but he realized that the Earth government kept its citizens in the dark when it came to the denizens of outer space. Everyone knew humans weren't the only spacefaring species in the galaxy, but knowledge about the kinds of aliens that populated the galaxy was kept from the masses for reasons unknown.

He had never heard of the Snaar or the Accilla. The woman had mentioned Kraach and Anorians. Who were they? He promised himself to become more interested in what went on beyond this planet. It seemed humans did not have the monopoly on violence.

WHEN HE AWOKE AGAIN, A MAN WAS STANDING BESIDE HIS BED. He introduced himself. "I'm Doctor Inamiir. I'm the one who found the antidote to the poison in your system. You were lucky to get here in time. Had it been otherwise, you would have died a painful death. The Snaar are a terrible race. They enjoy inflicting pain on others."

Collins found he could sit without becoming dizzy. "Thank you for your help, Doctor Inamiir." He gave the man a closer look. "You appear human, but are you?"

Inamiir shook his head. "Like my colleague, I am Accilla. I'm afraid you are the only human on our outpost."

"Your outpost? How many of your people are on Savanna?"

Inamiir smiled. "That is privileged information, Mr. Collins. A fair number is all I can tell you."

"What about the Kraach and the Anorians?"

"The Anorians have a base on the other side of this planet, but the Kraach, well, they're another subject. Are you at all familiar with the political situation in this part of the galaxy?"

Collins spread his hands. "Nothing, I'm afraid."

"Dr. Eguarii told me about your...ah...ignorance. It seems your government is even more paranoid than ours. Best to keep the general public from gaining too much knowledge. It's the only way to keep a populace under control."

"I'm beginning to wonder what else our government kept from us. We were certainly left ignorant about many things on Savanna."

"Savanna. That's what you humans call this planet. We call it

Gateway to the Stars. I won't burden you with repeating it in my native language." He chuckled. "You won't be able to pronounce it."

"Why Gateway to the Stars?"

"Because of the star-portals. I can see from your expression that's another piece of information you don't have."

"I don't. Are those star-portals the reason everyone is showing such interest in Savanna?"

"Your guess is correct. This planet is near Kraach-controlled space. They are aware of some of the portals, but they don't know how to activate them. There is a reason why the Kraach allow us to set up outposts on this planet. They are hoping we crack the code that unlocks the portals."

"What exactly are they?"

"The portals are ancient. They were created by a race that disappeared a long time ago, long before most of the other races in this galaxy reached a high level of intelligence. They did not travel in spaceships the way we do. They used a network of portals to travel from one star-system to another. Travel was instant. The secret of the portals died with that ancient race, but the portals are not dead. We have knowledge of at least one that has been activated. It works on a limited basis. That portal is on Salamander."

"I don't know that planet and, obviously, nothing about that particular portal or any other portal."

"It is not common knowledge. Only certain governments know and a handful of scientists. The portal on Salamander is in human hands, but our government has an agreement that we, along with Anorian and Kraach scientists, can use and study it."

Thoughtful Collins said, "It is obvious to me you are not just a doctor, if indeed you are one."

Inamiir smiled. "You are right. I'm not a medical doctor. I'm a research scientist and a mathematician, among other positions."

"Why are you telling me all of this? I'm just a simple rancher not a scientist. What would I do with this knowledge of portals and the presence of other races on Savanna?"

"When you came to us, you were in possession of an advanced rifle, a laser pistol, and some other electronic gadgets a simple farmer would not carry, should not carry. You wore a suit that made you practically invincible." He smiled. "Not completely, as you found out. You can still be wounded, even killed, by a simple dart. As far as we know, the weapons you have are not allowed on this planet. We find it mystifying that you managed to bring in such weapons. You were not always a rancher, were you, Mr. Collins?"

"No, I wasn't. On Earth, I was in law enforcement."

"A soldier?"

"Not a soldier, a police officer."

"Why did you come to this planet to become a rancher?"

Collins chuckled. "You are not the first one to ask me that question. Tired of all the violence I witnessed, I decided to leave it all behind and start a new life on another planet, as a farmer. I was looking forward to a peaceful life."

"Are you certain that's what happened?"

Collins gave him a puzzled stare. "I don't understand the question."

"Isn't it possible that your memory is playing tricks with your mind?"

"What are you implying?"

"That someone implanted a false memory. What you think you remember isn't the truth."

"What you're suggesting is absurd. My wife can back me up."

"Someone may have tampered with her memory, also."

"What about my children?"

Inamiir nodded solemnly. "They would have been conditioned."

"Why would you even suggest something like that?"

"I assume Dr. Eguarii told you about our ability to read minds. I'm not saying we snooped around in your mind, but we needed to find out more about your identity. That's how we discovered that your name is Dennis Collins. You have a wife by the name of Kristie and two sons. Their names are Traverse and Randolph. Your daughter's name is Lisa. You came to this planet in the spring of this year and became a rancher. At first, there was no indication that this information isn't correct, but when we probed a little deeper, we encountered a strong barrier we could not penetrate without causing damage to your mind. That made us wonder. Why would a simple farmer have such a powerful barrier in his memory? What is it supposed to conceal? What are you hiding, Mr. Collins?"

Collins couldn't help but laugh. "If there is this barrier in my memory to suppress something in my past, how would I know what it's supposed to hide? I can assure you, I'm a former law enforcement officer from the Metropolis Denverado on Earth. My memories of that are quite clear."

Inamiir smiled. "So, you believe, Mr. Collins. Can you recall any details about that part of your life? A situation, for instance, that sticks in your mind, details of what happened and the names of people, places?"

"Not at the moment. My memories are somewhat vague. I purposely suppressed those memories. After I quit the Force, I went to see a psychiatrist to help me with that."

"A psychiatrist. A professional to manipulate your mind. I find that interesting. Was that your own decision to see this person or did somebody suggest it?"

"It was entirely my own idea. I wanted to forget the violence I had lived with for so many years."

"Of course, it could also have been planted into your mind."

"Somehow I can't believe that."

"How about your wife and your children? Did they also see a professional?"

Collins shrugged. "I'm not sure. If they did, I don't recall."

"Don't you find that peculiar?"

"It never entered my mind. Before you asked me this question, I wasn't aware of that."

Inamiir stayed silent for a moment and gazed at Collins. "We've decided you don't pose a threat to us and our outpost, and we have no cause to snoop around in your mind any further. There must be a good reason why you or someone else is trying to hide your past from you. It is up to you, not us, to pursue this matter. However, it may not be in your best interest to uncover the information buried deep in your mind."

"Somehow, it seems surreal to imagine my memory is not my own, that it may possibly belong to someone else. I admit, details of my past are sketchy, but I don't believe it to be so unusual. Most people remember only snippets of things they experienced in their life. I remember the apartment we lived in, my neighbors, and my precinct. I remember the name of my captain and my last partner. Those memories appear to be real. If I have a memory block, it's supposed to hide something else."

The alien smiled. "Whatever it is, it lies in the past and is probably best forgotten. I wouldn't worry about it. Maybe I was wrong to even bring it to your attention. It doesn't serve any purpose. I apologize. For now, I want you to concentrate on getting your strength back. Get some rest and forget what I told you. Someone will look in on you later and bring you something to eat."

He walked out of the door. Collins stared at the closed door. How could he relax? Who the hell was he? How could he ignore what Inamiir told him? A million questions popped into his mind. He didn't even know where to begin looking for answers that lay on another planet hundreds of lightyears away.

He lay back, closed his eyes, and thought about what he knew about himself and his family. Nothing seemed out of place. There was nothing there indicating what he remembered may be a lie. That brought up another question. Could he trust the Accilla? He knew nothing about them. They might be messing with his mind. After all, they had their own agenda on this planet, and it may not be favorable to humans.

He decided to put it out of his mind and deal with it when he was healed and back home. Did it really matter if his memory had been altered? They were on another planet living a new life. Whatever happened in the past didn't really matter anymore.

His thoughts drifted to Lisa. The Accilla female, Dr. Eguarii, told him that Rhe-annur went to search for her. He trusted him to try his best to find Lisa. As long as those masked aliens hadn't kidnapped her and taken her onto their slave ship, he may have a good chance to rescue her. He tried not to think of the possibility that she may be in the clutches of the Snaar.

[15]

"You are fit enough to travel, Mr. Collins. You may experience the odd moment of weakness, but otherwise you're in good health." Dr. Eguarii put away her instruments. "Even that should go away in a couple of weeks. I'd say you're a lucky man. Had you not found us, you'd be dead now. The poison that dart injected into your system is a wicked one."

Collins nodded. "I'm grateful for your help. How can I repay your kindness?"

The Accilla woman shrugged, making it difficult for Collins to imagine she wasn't human. Her gestures and manner of speaking didn't betray her true nature. He still didn't know what she looked like in her true form.

"You don't owe us anything. We only did what any civilized being would have done. We are a peaceful race, and we try to get along with all the other races inhabiting this galaxy. Not always an easy thing to do, but there is a certain affinity we share, especially with humans. All we ask is that you don't broadcast your stay with us. Perhaps someday we will meet again, and you can return the favor. Anything can happen. The gods of fate play games only they understand. They brought you to us, didn't they?" She gave him an enigmatic smile when he raised his eyebrows. "That's right. We also believe in gods.

They may have different names than human gods, but they are the same."

"I'm not really much of a believer," he said.

"That's okay. As long as the gods believe in you." She turned and looked at the two men coming through the opening door. They were dressed in some kind of uniform. Broad belts circled their narrow waists from which hung what could only be weapons. Both men appeared human, but at closer examination Collins noticed their glittering metallic skin and eyes that looked like shards of diamonds. The ears on the side of their bald heads were elongated ending in sharp tips. These two did not look friendly.

He shuddered when he looked into their cold eyes and expressionless faces.

Dr. Eguarii saw his surprised look. "We take on many different forms," she explained. "These are members of our military forces. They will accompany you to a place from which you will be able to get home." She put a hand on his arm. "Don't be daunted by their appearance. No harm will come to you while you are our guest."

"I feel like a prisoner escorted to his execution."

She chuckled softly. "If we wanted to execute you, we would have done it already."

"That is true. I'm glad you didn't." He smiled. "Where will they take me?"

"They will accompany you to one of our ranches. Our people there will take care of you." She held out a hand. "Good bye, Dennis Collins. May the gods be with you and guard you on your journey."

He shook her hand, again surprised by her action. It was difficult to image she wasn't human. "Thank you again, Dr. Eguarii. Perhaps we'll meet again. I hope you'll find what it is you're searching for on Savanna." He turned to the two soldiers. "I'm ready."

They nodded and walked out of the room. He followed them with some misgivings. His years as a cop had taught him to be careful and always be on guard. He shouldered his backpack and carried the case holding his rifle in his left hand. Somehow, he had not expected to have it returned to him.

After walking through a number of corridors, they came to a door that led into a place that looked like a garage. A number of oval shaped vehicles were parked on one side. Before they boarded one of the vehicles a man came out of another door and approached them. "I'm Captain Ogalli. I will accompany you. I hope you don't mind."

"Would it matter if I did?" Collins gave him a polite smile and climbed into the vehicle. It wasn't large. There was only room for four passengers, including the driver. Collins sat in the back seat with his pack between his legs and his rifle beside him. Captain Ogalli joined him.

They left the garage and entered a tunnel. He knew they were underground, but the lights in front of the vehicle lit up the darkness. The vehicle skimmed silently across the tunnel floor. As the walls sped by, Collins wondered about their safety at the speed they traveled but decided not to worry. Obviously, this wasn't the first time the Accilla used this tunnel.

He looked at his timepiece and noted the time. It was still early morning.

"Are you coming with me to the ranch? Will you be my new companion from now on?" Collins asked the captain in an attempt to break the silence.

Ogalli actually laughed. "You don't have to worry about that. I'll be leaving you before we get to the ranch. I'm on my way to work. We can take a short break, and I can show you around a little if you're interested."

"It depends what you'll be showing me."

"A star-portal."

Collins was surprised. "I assume you know who I am?"

"I know who you are, Mr. Collins. Everyone on the post knows."

"Then I'm more than a little baffled. I thought you wanted to keep the existence of the portal a secret. Why then would you want to show this portal to me, a human?"

"There are certain developments taking place. Your knowledge of our portal may be important in the future, important to you and other interested parties."

"I was told to keep silent about my stay with your people. To keep it a secret. I'm not sure I want to learn more about you, especially the star-portals. Too much knowledge can be dangerous."

"Knowledge can also protect you." Ogalli chuckled. "If I come across like some kind of mystic, let me assure you I'm not. I'm actually an engineer. I'm one of the people trying to decipher the secret of the portals, but we haven't made much headway, yet."

The vehicle slowed down, and they entered a large cavern.

"We've arrived," Ogalli said. "Come, stretch your legs and come with me. The vehicle will wait for you here."

Collins followed the captain as they headed for one of the tunnels. They didn't walk far, before they came to a wall made from metal with a door in it. On the other side was another smaller cavern. One wall was covered with large screens and what looked like computer consoles under them. There were levers, and buttons, and smaller screens everywhere.

Collins took a few deep breaths when he saw the slug-like creatures standing in front of the screens.

Ogalli noticed his surprise and laughed softly. "You've never seen members of my species in their true form?"

Collins shook his head. "I haven't. Sorry, if I look a little rattled."

"Don't be sorry. It's only natural. The first time I saw a human I was also shocked."

"I notice some of the screens are glowing. I also find it a bit cool in this room."

Ogalli nodded. "You are correct. It tells us that the portal is not dead. As you get closer to the screens, you'll discover a strange pulling in your head. It's another indication that this room is filled with energy."

"How can there still be energy? This portal must be very old."

"It is, but nobody knows how old. We can only guess. The ancient race that left it behind was gone long time before even the Kraach discovered space travel, and the Kraach are the oldest race in this galaxy that we know about."

Collins rubbed his forehead. "I just realized how much information is kept from the majority of people living on Earth. Before this, I never knew the portals existed. I didn't know about your species and your ability to alter your appearance."

With a smile, Ogalli said, "We've known about humans for millennia. Members of the Accilla have lived among humans for almost that long. They were the vampires and werewolves in your legends."

"Are they teaching that to your children in school?" Collins grinned.

"Not really. You may be interested, though, to know I lived on Earth for a number of years, which means I know a lot about human history."

"I guess that's something else I learned today. Another thing our government is keeping from us."

"It's not something we advertise to your government," Ogalli said with a soft chuckle.

"You are telling me."

"You're not on Earth anymore. This is a different planet with different conditions that are changing constantly. There is no harm in telling you after all the things you've learned about us already."

"What will happen if you can get this portal to work?"

Ogalli looked thoughtful as he answered. "It will give us an edge over other races. Even if only for a short time, it will help us to protect our interests in this galaxy."

"Dr. Inamiir told me about a portal discovered and made operable on a planet called Salamander. Why hasn't anyone heard about that?"

"Believe me, we know about it, but the military keeps it from the general populace on Earth and on other planets. It's a political game the military and the governments are playing. There's a lot at stake here. Whoever controls the portal gains the potential to control the galaxy. I have a feeling major changes are coming, and it's important that the changes are positive, that they bring peace between the different species populating this galaxy, not lead to conflict. Good will toward each other begins with individuals. Remember that, Dennis Collins. You and I are not enemies."

"I harbor no ill will toward your people." Collins held out a hand. "I'm in your debt. Without your help, I'd be dead now. I will never forget that."

Ogalli made a sweeping motion with his arm. "Here lies the past, but also the future of the denizens of our galaxy. May it be a peaceful one."

"I agree."

"I'm glad we met, Mr. Collins. It's time for you to carry on with your journey. I trust you will find your way to the vehicle?"

Collins nodded. "I will."

With a last look at the giant, slug-like Accilla by the screens, he left the room and walked back across the cavern to where the vehicle stood. He climbed back in and nodded to the two soldiers still sitting in their seats. Collins took one more look out of the window before the vehicle took off. This had been an educational trip. He wondered what other surprises lay ahead.

He tried to engage his companions in conversation, but they kept silent. Shrugging, he relaxed and leaned back in his seat. When the vehicle finally slowed down and stopped, he automatically checked his timepiece and found they had traveled for nearly two hours since leaving the cavern with the gate.

One of his escorts indicated for him to get out of the vehicle. He did, and before he realized it, they sped away. A light in the ceiling of the tunnel illuminated a small area. Looking around, he located a door in the wall. Opening it, he found himself in a small room with a set of stairs leading up. The only choice was to climb them. At the top of the stairs, he encountered another door. Cautiously walking through it, he peered into the semi-darkness. Recognizing primitive tools and small wooden carts cluttering the room, he knew he had emerged inside a storage shed.

A dusty window allowed enough light into the small shed to let him see a wooden door. He opened it and went outside. It was near noon, and the sun stood high in the clear sky. Blinking against the bright light, he saw a cluster of farm buildings. Shrugging, he headed for the main building, not knowing what to expect but hoping to receive a friendly welcome.

Before he reached the entrance, the door opened, and a man dressed in coveralls stepped onto the porch. Tall and well-built, his face tanned from spending time under the alien sun. He appeared to be middle-aged. Slowly, he walked down the wooden stairs and waited.

Watching Collins coming closer, the man smiled. "You must be the human who got shot with a poisonous dart by the Snaar."

Collins returned the smile. "I am that human. I assume you're not human."

The man nodded. "Guilty. My true appearance differs from what you see, but I'm pretty much used to this form." He chuckled. "Been walking around looking like this for a long time."

"Why?"

"Out of necessity. We'd like to keep our presence here a secret."

"Perhaps you've made a mistake revealing yourself to me."

"You were someone who needed help. We gave it to you. My colleagues made that decision, knowing it might be a mistake, but we count on your discretion."

"You have it." Collins held out a hand. "I'm Dennis Collins."

The man nodded and shook his hand. "I know. I've been informed about you." He made a motion with his head. "Come into the house and accept our hospitality. My wife has prepared a lunch."

The woman standing by the woodstove in the kitchen greeted Collins with a bright smile. "Welcome to our humble home. I hope you like what I cooked for you. Sit down at the table." She wiped her hands on the apron she wore around her slim hips and turned to the man. "Alfred, get a jug of juice from the cellar. I'm sure our guest is thirsty."

"Alfred?" Collins gave the man a surprised look.

The man grinned. "If we already look and act like humans, we might as well have human names. Don't you agree?"

"Seems logical." Collins didn't know what else to say. He took a seat at the table and watched the woman by the stove. She looked to be middle-aged, but since that wasn't her true form, she might be quite young or really old. How could anyone tell?

Slim and tall, with pleasant features, she could almost be called beautiful, in human terms. He wondered if she was considered beautiful from the standpoint of an Accilla male.

She turned and smiled. "Thank you for the compliment. A woman likes to hear that once-in-awhile."

Startled, he said, "I didn't say anything."

She put her hand over her mouth. "I'm sorry. I forgot humans can't read minds. We don't associate much with humans."

"That's okay. I have nothing to hide, nothing I'm aware of, anyway. You're not the first of your people to snoop around in my mind."

"I apologize. I'll stay out of your mind." She turned to Alfred who came back into the kitchen, carrying a large mug. "Mr. Collins thinks I'm beautiful. Do you think I'm beautiful?"

"Of course, I do"

"Even in my native form?"

"Why would you ask me that?"

"Because you never tell me."

Alfred shook his head and looked at Collins. "I think females are all alike. It doesn't matter what species they belong to. Does your wife ask you to tell her she's beautiful?"

Collins chuckled. "All the time. Let me ask you a question? Are you two married or do your customs differ from ours?"

"Our customs may be a somewhat different, but Helen is my mate. She's quite a bit younger than I am, and not my first. However, she's the one I appreciate most. We have much in common."

Helen laughed. "I guess that's the only compliment I'll get from you. Now, let's eat."

Collins found he was actually quite hungry, and the stew Helen had made tasted good. The juice she served him was sweet, with a pleasant tangy flavor. He didn't ask what kind of meat he was eating. Sometimes it's best not to know. Nobody spoke much while they ate.

When Collins was finished, he leaned back in his chair. "That was delicious. Is this what Accilla eat or did you make it because of me?"

Helen seemed genuinely happy in her reply. "If you ask is meat part of our diet, the answer is yes. We also eat vegetables and fruit. Our digestive systems are compatible, and it doesn't matter in what form we consume our food. We do enjoy a good meal the same as you. Accilla and humans may not look alike on the outside, but inside we are not much different from each other. I'm glad you enjoyed it."

"I was told you will take me to a place from where I can get home."

"That's correct," Alfred said. "We'll leave tomorrow morning."

"May I ask where you will take me?"

"To the military base. From there you can get back to your home."

"I'm not aware of a military base in this part of Savanna. The only one I know of is Outpost Alpha, the one near Crystal City, but that is far to the north."

"This one is not established yet. Your military is in the process of setting it up."

"Why would they do that?"

"Because of the newly discovered portal."

Surprised, he asked, "A portal? How do you know about it? I don't believe our military would broadcast such a discovery."

The Accilla chuckled. "We have our sources. There is a small mining town near an entrance to the underground tunnels by the mountains south of here, and your military never showed an interest in it, until now. When we noticed a sudden flurry of activity going on near that mining town, it aroused our interest."

"I can only guess how you became aware of that activity, but I'm curious."

"If you think we have watchers among humans, you are correct."

"You mean spies."

"I wouldn't exactly call them spies. We are not trying to pry in your affairs or affect your ways. They don't interest us much, but we have to guard ourselves against possible dangers or even attacks."

"From humans? I was under the impression humans and Accilla are not enemies?"

"True. We aren't, but there are factions on both sides who think differently. We take nothing for granted. Better to err on the side of caution than be taken by surprise."

"I can't agree more. I suppose I was lucky to run into a group of friendly Accilla." Reaching for his mug, he took a long swig and put the mug back onto the table with a satisfied grunt. "By the way, this juice is quite refreshing. How do you keep it so cold in the cellar? I haven't had a really cold drink since we left the ship."

"We have a cooling unit in the cellar." Alfred smiled. "We are not bound by human laws that forbid us to own modern equipment, even though on the surface it looks that way. This house and what you see inside and outside is only a cover. Below ground, we have all the amenities that make living comfortable. We don't believe in suffering needlessly."

Collins sighed. "I wish our government would think that way.

They are afraid that the native population will be corrupted if we introduce more advanced gadgets. It only works to a point. From what I've observed, they already have rifles and other weapons not allowed on Savanna."

"The native population has been exposed to advanced weaponry and knowledge they wouldn't have discovered for centuries were it not for the alien races that have taken up residence on their planet. The Kraach have tried to keep them unaware of their presence, but other races don't feel they have any obligation to let the natives of this or any other planet develop at their own, natural pace. Especially you humans are guilty of changing their way of life. The damage has been done and cannot be reversed. Sooner or later human governments will allow more and more modern weapons, modern equipment, and other items. It is inevitable. Major changes will happen with the discovery of the portal."

"By the humans, you mean? How can you be sure that your assumption is correct? Perhaps, it is something else our military is interested in."

Alfred shook his head. "We are quite certain it's a portal. The human outpost is—how should I put it—not your usual outpost. The troopers stationed there are, to be blunt, misfits and nonconformists. Since they do not represent the image the human military wants to project, they ended up here on this until now unimportant planet where they can't do any harm. We've been monitoring the latest immigrants from Earth, especially the arrival of new military personnel, and we have noticed a different breed of troopers. They were not sent to Outpost Alpha but are residing in Crystal City. That gave us cause to be concerned. Why would Earth suddenly send those troopers? And the unusual presence of your military near the mining town gave us enough clues. Earth would not waste valuable resources unless it had a good reason. What better reason than the discovery of a portal?"

"I guess it makes sense. I'm not a military man, and I'm trying to stay out of politics. Right now, my only interest is the welfare of my family and my ranch." He stared into his mug. "I haven't done a good job with that. My youngest son is dead, and my daughter has been kidnapped."

"We were not informed of that." Helen gave him an intense look. "What happened?"

"My son was murdered by one of the indigenous people, and my daughter may be on a slave ship bound for some unknown planet," he said, bitterly.

"The Snaar. That's how you ended up getting shot with one of their darts. You tried to free your daughter. I understand. What about the one who murdered your son?"

"He's dead. I shot him." His voice sounded savage in his own ears.

"At least you got your revenge." Alfred seemed genuinely sympathetic. "Obviously, you were unsuccessful in rescuing your daughter. Before you were shot by one of the Snaar, did you kill any of them?"

"I did. The one who put that dart into my neck and a couple more."

"They will not forget that. The Snaar will hunt you down, and they are relentless. Be on guard."

"How will they know I killed three of theirs?"

"Did the ones you shot wear a mask?"

Collins nodded. "The last one did. I shot him in the forehead, right through that ugly mask."

"They record everything they do with the built-in cameras in their masks. His companions will recognize you from that recording." Alfred's human face wore a grim expression. "I'm sorry to say you're a marked man."

"That may be so, but how will they know where I live?"

"It won't be difficult to find that out. They can extract the information from your daughter. If not from her, they will take another human hostage and use them to find out from immigration where you reside. The Snaar are resourceful and ruthless."

Collins shrugged. "I'll deal with them should they find me. I'm not exactly helpless." His gaze flickered to the case that held his sniper rifle. It was still standing near the entrance.

Alfred didn't miss the movement of his eyes. "We know about that weapon you carry. It should not be on this planet, according to your own laws. Neither should the suit you wear underneath your outer clothing. Not even your military has weapons and outfits like that.

Those are specialized equipment. How did you manage to smuggle them from Earth?"

With another shrug and a tight smile, Collins said, "I hid them under a false bottom in one of our traveling trunks. It seems our immigration department isn't overly concerned. Why do you ask? I didn't break any of your laws."

"No, you didn't. We don't care. I'm merely curious. Just don't let them fall into the wrong hands. That's when we might get apprehensive. We don't need the natives running around armed with lasers. When you humans introduced them to guns that fire bullets, enough damage was done."

"Don't worry. I won't broadcast my possession of those weapons. The less people know about them, the better. I'll have to be careful not to alert our authorities, either."

"That's probably a good idea."

"There is another thing I'm curious about. What do you actually do on this ranch? Or is it a farm? Are you raising livestock? Growing vegetables or grains? I haven't seen any workers."

"We breed and keep sheep."

"Sheep?"

Alfred smiled at Collins' reaction. "That's right. Sheep are easy to keep. All they eat is grass, which grows in abundance around here. Neither do we need many workers to watch over them. The ones who work for us on a steady basis are with the sheep right now. When we need more helpers, we hire them. The indigenous people are eager to earn some money, and they are reliable."

"What are you doing with the sheep?"

"We eat them. Sheep meat is quite popular with our people. Mostly, though, we raise them for the wool. The natives buy the wool from us. We even have dealings with humans."

"We also drink the blood of the sheep." Helen said, casually.

Collins shook himself. "I prefer other liquids. Do you drink their blood while performing some kind of ritual?"

"No ritual. Blood is part of our natural diet." She chuckled. "We are vampires by nature. I assume that's another piece of information you're not aware of?"

"No, I'm not. Are all Accilla vampires?"

She nodded.

"I hope you don't intend to drink my blood as payment for your hospitality." He meant it as a joke, but somewhere deep inside him welled up a slight feeling of distaste. Fleeting images of bloodthirsty creatures of the night with long fangs sucking the blood from unsuspecting victims appeared in front of his mind's eyes.

"We were hoping to take a little sip from your veins for desert," Alfred said with a gravelly voice.

Helen smiled, and Alfred laughed when he saw Collins' expression. "I'm kidding. Our primitive ancestors drank the blood from intelligent beings. We don't, not anymore."

"Captain Ogalli mentioned that members of your kind have been on Earth for millennia. I didn't quite understand what he meant by vampires. Now I do. Since your species is not only vampiric, but also has the ability to shapeshift, it only stands to reason that they are the origin for the legends about vampires and other creatures of the night."

"It's probable, but you humans have a fertile imagination and much of those stories could be just that—stories. Besides, we are not the only vampires. There are others out there, many of them ruthless, without compassion for living, intelligent beings. We are not like that." He rose from his seat. "If you're interested, I can show you around our ranch."

"I would love that."

[16]

HELEN GAVE COLLINS A HUG. "HAVE A SAFE JOURNEY AND GOOD fortune," she said with a warm smile. She handed him a small canteen. "Here, take this. It'll be a dusty road."

He fastened the canteen to his gun belt. "I thank you for your hospitality, Helen, or whatever your real name is." Looking into her human eyes, he had difficulty imagining she wasn't human but some giant, nearly formless slug.

"In this body, I'm Helen." She chuckled softly. "I've gotten so used to it, I'm thinking of myself as Helen."

"It's a good name." He slung his pack over his shoulder and grabbed the rifle case. "I'm ready," he said to Alfred.

"Good. Let's go then."

The wagon standing in front of one of the barns wasn't much different from the one Herman Sanchez used when he picked up Collins and his family from the spaceport. Even the two draft animals were of the same species.

He threw his stuff into the back and climbed onto the front seat. "How long until we get to our destination?"

"About five of your hours."

Collins gave the animals a thoughtful glance. "Too bad you don't have horses. I would have preferred spending those five hours on the back of a horse. We might even have been able to shorten the time."

"I find a wagon more practical. Besides, we don't have horses. Akilades are easier to care for."

"Akilades? That's what you call these animals? We've named them alck."

"We use the name the natives gave them." Alfred shrugged. "It really makes no difference. It's just a name."

"I raise horses," Collins said. "If you'll visit me at my ranch, I'll make you a gift by letting you have a couple of horses." He chuckled. "Without bragging, I raise the finest horses in the area."

"I may just take you up on that offer. Nobody raises horses around here." Alfred snapped the thin leash of his whip across the back of one of the animals. As the wagon began rolling, he looked into the sky. "It'll be another hot day, but at least it won't rain. We could use a little moisture for the grass, though. It's been a dry fall."

They didn't follow a road. Their journey led them across grass-covered meadows. Once they traveled through a small, dense forest.

"Who owns this forest?" Collins wondered.

"Nobody. Not even the indigenous people use it. The land here is wild and unfriendly, populated only by the many different species of animals, and they are not sociable."

"Sounds like a hunter's paradise."

"It is, if you enjoy chasing and killing animals. We Accilla are not hunters."

"But you drink the blood of animals."

Alfred nodded. "From living animals."

"Didn't you tell me you eat the meat of the sheep you raise?"

"We do, but the sheep are raised for food. They've never known the freedom of running wild through meadows and forests. When we kill them, we do it quickly? They don't suffer. A hunted animal may get only wounded by the hunter and may cause it to die a painful death. That's not our way."

Collins shrugged. "On Earth, nobody hunts anymore. The wild animals on Earth live in animal sanctuaries, and there are not many of them. I'm not much of a hunter." He smirked. "Not of animals, anyway. My quarry was of a different kind."

"I don't understand."

"I hunted men. Criminals. I used to be in law enforcement." He didn't believe it was necessary to tell Albert that his memories of the past may have been compromised. There was no proof of that.

"Is that why you have one of those advanced weapons in your possession?"

Collins shrugged. "I don't really know." That was the truth. He couldn't remember buying that rifle and all the other weapons he had. The only thing he knew he'd smuggled them to Savanna. He had no idea why.

Albert didn't pursue the subject, and Collins didn't mind. He sat brooding on the hard bench, his thoughts far away. There were suddenly doubts in his mind about his true identity. Who was he, and why was he on this alien planet?

Looking at his wristwatch, he realized they'd been traveling for over three hours. The alien sun had climbed higher toward its zenith and was a blazing ball in the clear sky. His dry throat reminded him to drink some water. He unclipped the canteen from his belt and took a few sips.

"You're awake," Alfred said.

"Did I fall asleep?"

Alfred chuckled. "I could have sucked the blood from your veins, and you would never have known."

Collins lifted a hand in an involuntary defensive gesture and touched his neck.

"Just a joke." Alfred laughed. "Like I told you, we don't do that anymore." He reached for his own canteen. "We do need our liquids just like you." After drinking, he sighed. "Even though this planet has moderate temperatures and for the most time is hospitable, sometimes I long for my home planet. I miss to be able to walk around in my own body, to bathe in the many warm ponds and lakes, not to have to pretend I'm something other than what I really am. To be with my own kind all the time. That is what I dream about."

"Why don't you go back home, then?"

"That's a valid question, but difficult to answer. Even though I'm not a scientist, I have useful skills. I'm good with animals, but I'm also an engineer and a builder, and I'm needed here. My place is here with my mate. She also needs me. What about you? Do you miss Earth?"

"Of course, I do, but I've made a home here, and I'm not as homesick as I imagined I might be. I have my family..." He paused as reality set in. "Unfortunately, things have changed. My son is dead, and my daughter missing. This might not have happened had I stayed on Earth."

"You can't blame yourself for that. Nobody can predict and choose future events. It was your son's destiny to die on an alien planet. There is no guarantee he would have lived on Earth. As far as your daughter goes, her destiny is still unsure. Things may still turn out all right." He pulled on the reins to stop the animals. "It's near noon. We should stop for a while and have something to eat. This is a good place. There is shade over there under those trees. Besides, I need to stretch my legs."

"I won't argue."

COLLINS CLIMBED FROM THE WAGON AND WALKED AROUND ON stiff legs. Sitting for such a long time on that hard bench gave him a backache.

Alfred grabbed a small box from the wagon and took it over to the trees. "Come, sit down. It's cooler here. Helen made us some sandwiches."

Collins declined the invitation to sit down and ate his sandwich standing up. "I can't believe how similar your species is to mine," he commented.

Alfred nodded. "If you study the different races occupying this galaxy, you will notice something peculiar. No matter their outer appearance, inside most are quite similar. Our ancestors started out primitive, unable to think in abstract concepts, but as they evolved, their brains grew larger, and their thought processes become more complex. They invented and discovered new things, and they begin to build and create, until they eventually left their birth planet to explore space and other planets. The majority of races evolve along the same lines. Of course, there are always exceptions. Some species will develop into something completely foreign to us. The reason we are so much like humans is because when we take on the human shape, we start to think and behave like humans. However, if we masquerade as members of the Kraach, for instance, we will become much like them."

"In other words, you lose your identity."

"We never lose that, but it gets pushed aside to make room for a new one. It is purely a survival trait. The longer we are in a different form, the more we become like the species we are mimicking. That's why it is important we have a base where we can change back into our native form."

"Has it ever happened that some forget what they are and never change back?"

"I have no recollection of that ever happening, but that doesn't mean it's impossible or has never happened." Alfred rose from his sitting position. "I guess we should move on."

According to Collins' estimation, not more than an hour passed until they saw a number of small buildings. After that, it didn't take long to get to the town. A crude welcome sign proclaimed it was Goodluck. He didn't miss a bleached skull displayed on a pole and wondered what it meant.

Most of the buildings were made from rough materials. The trees they used for the walls still had bark on them, and the roofs were covered with dried grass and reeds. There were even a few tents. Nearer the river, Collins saw buildings that appeared to be more solid.

Alfred stopped the wagon. "This is as far as I go. I cannot waste too much time. I want to get back home before it gets too dark."

"I understand." Collins looked around but didn't see anything that indicated the presence of military people. "I assumed you were going to take me to a military base."

"One that hasn't been established yet, but it's there. According to our information, it'll be near the foot of the mountain. Perhaps you can hitch a ride with one of the miners to get there. I'm sorry, but I need to get back."

Collins held out a hand. "No need to apologize. You've done more for me than I hoped Thank you so much for your help. When I said come and visit me at my ranch, I meant it." He smiled. "I'd like to get an opportunity to pay you back for your kindness."

"Who knows, I may just pay you a visit in the near future. A couple of horses might be an asset at our ranch." Alfred's expression became serious. "Remember my warning about the Snaar. Don't take it lightly. They will search and find you. Keep that weapon of yours near you at all times. You may need it." He took his hand and shook it. "May fortune be with you, my human friend."

Collins nodded. Then he climbed from the wagon. Taking his possessions, he stepped away and watched the Accilla turn the wagon around. He waved when Alfred looked back. "Give my best to Helen," he called but wasn't sure Alfred heard him.

Searching the buildings on each side of the dusty road, he saw a couple of men sitting in front of a nearby hut. They had been watching him. He walked in their direction. When he got close to them, he noticed their shabby appearance and stopped walking. "Good afternoon, gentlemen. I wonder if you can help me."

One of them got up and strolled toward him. "Depends what you're looking for."

"A ride to the mountain."

The man gave him a toothless smile. His scraggly beard made him look old, but Collins didn't think he was as old as he appeared. "Are you looking for treasure?"

Collins shook his head. "No, just for a ride."

"You must be a newcomer. Do you believe you'll find diamonds and other rocks once you get to the mountain?"

"No. I don't believe it's that easy, but, like I said, all I need is a ride. I can pay for it."

"You've got coins? Gold? Silver?"

"I've got gold."

The man turned back and called to his friend. "Hey, Tanner, he says he's got gold." He looked at Collins with a calculating expression. "How much you got?"

The second man got up and slowly came closer. He was taller than the guy Collin was talking to, with more bulk to his body. He didn't have a beard, but the stubble covering his face lent him an unpleasant appearance. An ugly scar ran from his cheekbone down to his jaw. "You've got gold? Show it to me."

"I don't think so, unless you can take me there." Collins took a step backward, suddenly wary. "Listen, I was told there are military people there. I need to get to them. Is my information correct?"

"It is. Why do you need to find them? Are you a trooper? You don't look like one. I say, you're a treasure seeker, trying to confuse us."

Shaking his head, Collin said, "I'm not a treasure seeker. I'm just a simple rancher, and I want to get home. That's all. Can you take me to the military post or not?"

Tanner chuckled. "Unfortunately not, considering I got no horse or any other transportation, but I'd be interested in some of your gold."

"Sorry, friend, if you can't help me, we're both out of luck. Perhaps you can point me in the right direction. I'll walk." Collins casually touched the holster of his laser pistol. He had not missed the other man circling around and positioning himself slightly behind him.

"It's a long walk, especially loaded down as you are with a backpack and that shiny suitcase of yours. What's in it?"

Collins shrugged. "Just some gear."

"Looks like some kind of rifle case to me."

"No rifle. A musical instrument, if you really must know."

"I thought you said you're a rancher. Now you're a musician? I don't believe that." He looked at his partner. "Do you believe that, Slim?"

"Not in a million lightyears."

"It doesn't matter what you believe." Collins said coldly, getting impatient. That icy feeling he experienced when he killed the valley riders came over him again. Even though he had no quarrel with these two men, he wasn't sure if he could keep from harming or even killing them, should they decide to rob him.

The sound of hoofs made all three of them turn to look at the two riders coming from the direction of the mountains. Collins let out a sigh of relief. Hopefully an encounter that might have turned violent could be avoided.

"It seems this is your lucky day," Tanner said.

"Perhaps it is yours," Collins growled.

The riders stopped their horses. One of the riders was tall and gaunt. The other one was big and bulky. Both men wore wide-brimmed hats. They carried rifles across their laps.

"Problems?" The big one looked at Collins and then at the two other men.

"Not anymore, I hope." Collins glanced at Tanner. "I was just discussing with these two fine gentlemen if they could help me get to the military base near the mountains."

"Fine gentlemen?" The big man snorted and spit into the sand. "Count yourself lucky we came along in time to save you from these two fine gentlemen. A little later and we may have stumbled over a corpse."

"Now, wait a minute," Slim protested. "We're no murderers. We just wanted him to share some of his gold with us. Can't blame a man from trying."

"One of these days you'll find yourself swinging from a rope," the second rider said. His gaze shifted back to Collins. "You were saying you want to get to the military base?"

Collins nodded. "That's correct. I was told the base is near the entrance to the tunnels."

"There are military people at that place all right, but there really isn't a base." The big one spit into the sand again. "Those military guys arrived here a few days ago and erected a few tents near one of the main entrances to the mountain tunnels. They went into the mountain, but we have no idea what it's all about. Apparently, they closed one of the tunnels. That's all I know. Something funny is going on, because we haven't seen Gardiner and Buchanan for these last few days. Reed and Kohud have also disappeared."

"Who are they?"

"Miners like us. They left without telling anyone where they headed. We assumed to Crystal City, but nobody's seen them there. Reed and Kohud were picked up the other day by a couple of troopers. We haven't seen them since. Like I said, there's something funny about that." He eyed Collins. "What business do you have with the military?"

"I'd like to hitch a ride home with them."

"I don't understand. How'd you get here in the first place?"

Collins sighed. "It's a long story. I had some business in the City of Stones."

"That's a long way from here. Did you have business with the Suumir?"

"I went there to kill one of them," Collins said bluntly.

"Were you successful?"

"I was, but I lost my horse. A friendly rancher brought me here."

The man shook his head. "I'll bet there is more to that story than you tell. Who are you, anyway?"

"Nobody special. Just a rancher who wants to get home."

"You got a name?"

"Collins, Dennis Collins."

"I'm Professor Andreas Kopke. I'm an archeologist." He smiled. "Turned treasure hunter. My partner here, the silent one, is Dr. Sleaman. He's a geologist."

"What made you change your profession?"

"You can't survive as an archeologist on Savanna. Nobody is really interested in native ancient artifacts, of which there are few. The lure of gold and diamonds was stronger, and I succumbed."

"Been lucky?"

Kopke shrugged. "Can't complain. We'd be much richer, though, if it weren't for the Trading Commission."

"I know exactly what you mean. It seems to be a common complaint on Savanna." Collins agreed with the miner. "Do you know anyone who'll take me to that base?"

"Can you ride a horse?"

Collins grinned. "I raise horses."

"Give me an hour. I've got some things to take care of. I'll take you then. Dr. Sleaman is going to stay here. You can borrow his horse."

"I'd appreciate that. I don't want it for nothing. I'll pay you for it."

Kopke waved it off. "We don't want your money, but you can do me a favor. I'd like you to deliver a letter to my sister in Crystal City to let her know I'm okay. Everything else is explained in the letter. Would you be able to do that for me?"

"Gladly."

"Good. My place isn't far from here. I'll ride slowly to make it easier for you to follow me."

[17]

DANIELS LOOKED UP FROM THE FILES HE'D BEEN STUDYING WHEN Sheppard walked into his tent. "What's on your mind, Captain?"

"I was wondering what you're planning to do with those four miners. They're not happy."

Daniels chuckled, but it didn't sound friendly. "They're not happy? They should be glad I haven't put them in front of a firing squad."

Sheppard gave him a surprised stare. "I hope you're joking, colonel. You can't just execute them. They're civilians, for heaven's sake. Besides, they haven't done anything wrong."

"It's not a question of what they've done. They've stumbled into something of a highly secretive nature. They are in possession of information not intended for the general public. News of this discovery must not be spread. The balance of power in this galaxy is at stake, and we can't have civilians stand in the way."

"Stand in the way of what?"

"Of humans becoming the controlling species." Daniels glared at Sheppard. "This is too important to worry about a few miners. In any war there are casualties."

"I wasn't aware we're at war with anyone."

Daniels seemed annoyed. "You may not realize this, but we are at war, Captain Sheppard. The Spiders are our most dangerous enemy.

There are constant skirmishes with them. Most of the dragon races are hostile, especially the Mollard and the Sleevers. And don't discount the Accilla. With their ability to mimic any species, they can have their spies everywhere."

"That doesn't mean they're hostile. I think we should worry more about the enemy within our midst, like crime syndicates, pirates, and cartels. They're getting more powerful and dangerous. They've infiltrated governments everywhere. If you want my honest opinion, the Trading Commission is one of them."

"Be careful when voicing your opinions. You may be entering dangerous territory. The wrong people might hear you."

Sheppard laughed. "I really don't care. What are they going to do to me? Strip me of my rank? Transfer me away from here? I'm already at the end of the line. How much worse can it get?"

Daniels shook his head. "You disappoint me, Sheppard. I had such high hopes for you. What makes you so cynical?"

"Let's just say I've had firsthand experience with corrupt officials. How do you think I got to this forsaken piss-hole of an outpost? I have no illusions about my future."

Remembering his last trial, Sheppard had a bitter taste in his mouth. He forced himself not to dwell on the older memories rising from his subconscious mind.

"I don't believe that." Daniels regarded him silently for a while. "I've known from the first time I spoke to you on the ship that you're different from the usual lot they send to these dead-end outposts. I know you carry a grudge, and that makes you the perfect candidate for the position I need to fill."

Sheppard eyed him with narrow eyes. "What position?"

"I need a second-in-command once we have this post up and running. I want you to be that man."

"What would be my job? Execute civilians?"

"Don't be absurd. We haven't executed anyone, yet. If you're worried about those four miners, I can assure you they are in no danger."

"What is going to happen to them?"

"They will accompany us to Outpost Alpha where they will be kept under surveillance."

"In other words, they'll be incarcerated. For how long?"

Daniels shrugged. "Indefinitely, if necessary." The expression in his eyes became hard. "I will hold you personally responsible for them. Should any of them escape it will be on your head. Is that understood?"

Sheppard returned his stare. "I believe Colonel Wainwright will have the last word in that matter. After all, it's his outpost."

"Colonel Wainwright will do as I say. He is nothing but a figurehead with no real power. Dismissed!"

Sheppard saluted and turned away without a word. The longer he knew Colonel Daniels, the more he realized this was a dangerous man not to be crossed or trusted. He was about to go to the tent where the four miners were held when he happened to look east toward the mining town. A small cloud of swirling dust caught his attention. It seemed they were about to get visitors.

As he watched the dust cloud come closer, it became clear that it was caused by two riders. He was curious who it could be. It was too late in the day for any miner to want to enter the mountain.

The two riders had obviously seen him standing there and headed for him. One of the two men was big and bulky. The wide-brimmed, grey hat he wore declared him as a miner. Stopping their horses near Sheppard, the second man slid from his horse and stretched his legs. He was tall and muscular, but what made Sheppard scrutinize him closer was the laser pistol he had strapped to his hip and the protective suit visible underneath his open shirt collar. He certainly wasn't a miner. A miner would and should not be in possession of such a suit and a laser pistol, not here on Savanna.

The man took off his floppy hat and wiped off the dust. Then he ran a hand across his red hair. "I haven't gotten used to this damn heat yet," he complained. Holding out a hand, he said, "The name's Collins. I'm in need of a ride back to Crystal City."

"Why not use your horse?" Sheppard ignored the outstretched hand. He needed to know more about this man.

Collins dropped his hand and shook his head. "It's not mine. It belongs to someone else. I just borrowed it to get here."

"Get here from where?"

"From the mining town."

"How'd you get there in the first place?"

"A farmer dropped me off."

"Who are you?"

"I'm a rancher. I raise horses and cattle on my ranch a couple of day's ride from Crystal City." Collins smiled. "If you were a farmer or rancher, you'd have heard of me."

Sheppard studied the man with watchful eyes. "You don't look like a rancher, not in that armored suit you're wearing and armed with a modern laser. Civilians are not allowed to possess them."

"I'm aware of that. Before I came to Savanna, I was a lawman on Earth. Savanna is a savage planet, contrary to what we were told at immigrations, and I expected to find myself in situations where I would need modern weapons to protect myself and my family. Even though these are forbidden weapons on Savanna, I brought the suit and the laser with me anyway."

"You smuggled them and therefore broke the law."

"I'm glad I did. Without these weapons I would be dead now."

"How's that?"

"My son was murdered and my daughter kidnapped by a native renegade. I avenged my son's death, but I failed in rescuing my daughter from the clutches of the Snaar." Collins spoke harshly with a defiant tone. "I make no excuses for smuggling modern weapons to Savanna. From what I heard the military on this planet is doing a piss-poor job protecting human citizens. We have to take matters into our own hands."

"We're not here to police the inhabitants of Savanna," Sheppard stated, even though he knew his argument was weak.

"Then why are you here, and what's the purpose of setting up another outpost?" Collins glared at him.

Sheppard shrugged, remembering the words of Colonel Wainwright. *We're supposed to keep law and order on Savanna, but that is only a formality. The Trading Commission runs things here.* "We're here on the request of the Trading Commission."

Collins gave a barking laugh. "That's right, the Trading Commission. We could do without them. People would be much happier and wealthier. They're nothing but vampires."

The big man on the horse chuckled. "You've got that right. They pay us a pittance for our diamonds."

Sheppard looked up at the man and sighed, knowing this discussion wasn't going anywhere. "I can't argue with you, sir. What's your name?"

"Andreas Kopke."

"Pleased to meet you, Mr. Kopke." His gaze shifted back to Collins. "I have no beef with you, Mr. Collins, and what you've done isn't my business. I won't comment on the Trading Commission. I'm sure we can arrange for you to accompany us back to Crystal City. We'll be leaving here in a few days to get supplies. In the meantime, don't ask any questions, for your own good. The less you know the better. Remember, you're in a military compound."

"I'm not interested in learning any military secrets. I never did get your name."

"Captain Jeremy Sheppard, but I don't have the deciding word. I'll have to clear it with my superior, Colonel Daniels. I don't expect any problems." He turned to Kopke. "I assume you'll be riding back to town?"

"I am." He took the reins of the other horse from Collins' hand. Tipping his hat, he said, "Good luck, Collins. I have a feeling you'll need it. Perhaps we'll meet again."

"Perhaps." Collins reached up to shake the miner's hand. "Thanks for everything and don't worry about your letter. I will deliver it to your sister. Take care of yourself and say hello to Dr. Sleaman. Thank him for the use of his horse."

"Sure will." Kopke turned his horse and rode away with the second horse in tow.

Sheppard looked after the miner, wondering what it would be like to be a civilian. Free to do whatever he desired. Maybe even become a miner searching for treasures. He pushed the thoughts away. "Come, follow me and let's get this over with."

DANIELS GAVE HIM A QUESTIONING, ALMOST ANNOYED LOOK, when he and Collins walked into his tent. "What is it? Who is this civilian?"

"This is Mr. Collins. He's a rancher and wants to hitch a ride with us back to Crystal City. I told him it would be okay. I just want to confirm it with you, sir."

At first, it looked like Daniels would reject it, but then he nodded. "Permission granted. Just make sure he doesn't talk to any of the troopers. Remember, he's your responsibility, just like the other civilians."

"One more person in my care won't make any difference," Sheppard mumbled under his breath.

"What was that, Captain?"

"Nothing, sir. Just clearing my throat."

"I thought you said something." He made a dismissing motion with his hand. "Don't bother me again. I'm busy."

Sheppard glanced at Collins. "You heard. Come. Have you eaten?"

Collins shook his head. "Not since noon, and then only a sandwich and some water."

Sheppard chuckled. "I can't offer you a gourmet meal, but I think we can do better than plain sandwiches. We have a pretty good cook. First, we'll have to find you a place to sleep. You might want to get rid of your backpack and that shiny case you've been carrying. What's in it?"

"A rifle."

Sheppard didn't expect that answer. "What kind of rifle?"

"Not one of those that fires only one bullet. It's a bit more sophisticated and uncommon. Perhaps even you have never seen one like it."

"Can't say I'm surprised. I want to take a look at it later."

Collins gave him a sidelong glance. "As long as you don't get any ideas, Captain. I won't give it up. Neither do I want everyone to know about it being in my possession. There is none like it on this planet. I'm sure of that."

"I'm just curious, that's all. Your secret will be safe with me. I have enough problems of my own already. There is no reason for me to worry about a rancher with a sophisticated, prohibited weapon."

He took Collins to the tent with the four miners. As they passed the two troopers guarding the entrance, he gave them a curt nod.

Collins glanced at the troopers but kept quiet.

The miners sat on their cots. They didn't look happy. Sheppard couldn't blame them. They had discovered something they had not been searching for. Instead of keeping it a secret, they made the mistake of informing the military.

"When can we leave, Captain Sheppard?"

Sheppard shook his head, trying to avoid Buchanan's eyes. "I'm afraid the news isn't what you want to hear. Colonel Daniels decided it would be best if you went back to Outpost Alpha with us, all four of you."

"Reed and I will have to go back to get our horses, but Gardiner and Kohud don't need to. Why did you pick them up in the first place?"

"Because Kohud was with Gardiner when they made the discovery. Reed also knows about it."

"By now the military knows everything about the discovery," Gardiner said. "There is no reason for us to go to your outpost."

"It really is out of my hands." He spread his fingers. "Colonel Daniels outranks me, and it is his decision."

"What is going to happen to us? We trusted you, Sheppard." Buchanan's tone was clearly accusing. "We didn't want to talk to anyone but you, remember? You brought in this colonel."

"He didn't give me much choice. I had no idea it would be going down like this. If it were up to me, I'd let you go. I apologize."

"What is so important about those dusty old ruins in that cave, anyway?"

Sheppard's gaze rested on the little man with the goatee. "I am not allowed to tell you, Mr. Reed, but I can assure you the discovery is of great importance and must be treated with the utmost secrecy. Once we get back to Outpost Alpha, you will be briefed in detail, and then you can get back to your normal life."

He knew it would not be that simple, not with Daniels in charge, but there was nothing else he could tell these men. He indicated Collins. "This is Mr. Collins. He will be sharing these quarters with you."

"Who is this Mr. Collins? He doesn't look like a miner to me. Is he a spy or our watchdog?" It was obvious Reed was trying to be sarcastic.

"He's neither. He's a rancher and needs a ride to Crystal City."

Reed looked at Collins. "You'd better be careful, Mr. Collins. Don't put your trust in the military. Don't say anything and don't do anything they can use as an excuse to take you into their care. You will regret it. You may already have made a mistake by coming here. This could be your last day of freedom."

"Mr. Collins has nothing to fear from us." Sheppard, irritated and frustrated, turned to Collins. "There is an empty cot over there. It's yours. Unfortunately, I can't offer you a blanket."

"I'll be fine without it. The cot will do. Thank you."

"You're welcome. I'll let you know when supper is ready. It will be served in that large tent you must have seen." With one last look at the four miners, he left the tent.

He was looking forward to getting back to Outpost Alpha, but he knew life would never be the same again on Savanna. Daniels' team was scheduled to arrive in a couple of days to start organizing and planning the new military base. Things would be hectic from then on. He worried about the four miners, also. They had committed no crime, yet, they would be held prisoners. What harm could they really do? Even if they told others about the ruins they'd discovered, it wouldn't make any difference. Most colonists on Savanna had no interest in old ruins. They were too busy trying to survive. Chances were they wouldn't even know what the ruins represented. How many of them had even heard of star-portals and an ancient star-faring race? Probably none of them. Legends about lost civilizations existed on every planet, even on Earth. That didn't mean they were ever real or taken seriously.

He stood staring at the hole in the mountain. Inside that mountain lay the means to change the way the denizens of this galaxy traveled between the stars if they could find the coded key that opened the secret lock. Would it be a blessing or a curse? The ancient civilizations that created the portals vanished a long time ago, without a trace. What happened to them? The star-portals were the only proof they ever existed.

SHEPPARD WAS SURPRIZED WHEN HE SAW THE NUMBER OF MEN

arriving in two armored tanks and three military transport trucks. He counted a dozen troopers dressed in black and brown, tightfitting uniforms and armed to the teeth with modern weapons and fourteen men and women in civilian clothes. He doubted their status as civilians, at least not all of them.

Their first task was to erect tents for the troopers and the civilians. When he compared the troopers to the ones already at the camp, it was plain to see that the newcomers were of a completely different caliber. None of them seemed to ever smile. Their expressions were almost stoic, grim and serious.

Beside Sheppard, Sergeant Cahill wondered, "Where do these guys come from? They almost look and move like automatons. Nobody can be that serious."

"Perhaps they're pissed off to be stationed on this piss-hole," Benson ventured.

"They're not regular navy," Sheppard said. "Did anyone get a closer look at those insignia on their sleeves?"

"I did," said Linda Bouchard, the only female trooper in the group.

"What does it say?"

"It appears to be the symbol of the Atom inside a broken oval. I couldn't make out the letters below the oval."

"It's the emblem of a company called Glowstar Research, a division of Interstellar Sunburst Conglomerate," Sheppard said slowly. "This is not a good thing."

"Why would you say that?"

"Good question, Bouchard. Interstellar Sunburst appears to be controlled by of one of the giant cartels. Those are only rumors, nothing has ever been substantiated. These men are mercenaries."

Benson voiced his concerns. "If they are mercenaries, what are they doing here?"

"I don't know what the hell is going on. I would suggest you all tread carefully around these men. Don't get chummy with them."

Cahill snorted. "Fat chance of that going to happen. I don't remember ever seeing such a bunch of unfriendly faces."

"I'm not supposed to ask any questions, but I can't help wondering what all the activity is about." Sheppard gave Collins a warning look as he came up to the group. Collins kept on talking. "Are you planning to set up a new outpost at this location and why?"

"I suggest now, more so than before, that you keep your curiosity to yourself, Mr. Collins. It's in your best interest."

"Why? Will I be arrested or shot?"

"Of course not. We don't shoot innocent civilians."

"But you keep them in detention. In case you're wondering, I had an interesting talk with those four miners."

"What did they tell you?"

Collins shrugged. "That they discovered a bunch of ruins in one of the caves. Is that what this is all about?" He made a sweeping gesture. "I get the impression you're in the process of building some kind of fortress here. By the way, those emblems on the sleeves of those newcomers? They seem familiar, but I just don't remember where I saw them. I don't get good vibes when I look at them."

"Didn't you tell me you were a police officer back on Earth?"

Collins nodded. "I was. Perhaps that's how I ran across them." He wiped his forehead. "Somehow my memory of that period in my life is a bit hazy."

"Partial mind-swipe?"

Collins seemed startled by the question. "I don't recall a reason why I would have that done."

"You wouldn't remember. I've known troopers who experienced traumatic events and couldn't deal with it. They had those memories erased. Nothing to be ashamed of." He studied Collins with interest. "Whatever the miners told you, I advise you to keep it to yourself. They're just ruins. We don't want to spread rumors that may be blown out of proportion and have disastrous consequences."

"You said it yourself, they're only ruins. Is it possible there is more to those ruins than you're telling me?"

Sheppard had the strange sensation Collins was fishing for something. Who was this guy? Just a simple rancher as he claimed? It seemed strange for him to show up at this time. Then again, as a former cop, he possessed a natural curiosity. "Like I said, ruins. Let's keep it that way, for your own good. As a civilian, you're not privy to certain information. Remember, this is a military matter, and the security of this planet, possibly even Earth's is at stake anytime we stumble into unknown territory. Those ruins are unknown territory."

Collins chuckled softly. "Perhaps unknown only to humans."

"Somehow, I find that a strange remark."

"Why? There may be other races on Savanna. How do you know they haven't discovered similar ruins?" Collins gave Sheppard a challenging look.

"Is there something you know that we aren't aware of, Mr. Collins?" Sheppard spoke sharper than he intended.

"What would I know?" Collins lifted his shoulders and spread his arms a little. "I'm only a rancher and a civilian from Earth. Before I came to Savanna, I'd never even heard of most of the alien races that exist out there, but I've learned the majority of them are much older than mankind. Their knowledge about the Universe is most likely more extensive than what humans know. How do you know these are the only ruins in the tunnels below the surface of this planet? There might be dozens of them."

Sheppard relaxed. "Maybe there are, but these are the only ones of this kind we've found. It may be an important discovery or nothing at all. The scientists and researchers will determine that. Until then, this site will be off-limits to civilians, and the same goes for the discussion with anyone about the existence of the ruins. I hope that is clear, Mr. Collins."

"Crystal," Collins said with a little smile. "However, this is the thing, if I wonder about the sudden military activity here and the fortress you seem to be building, others will do the same. Something to think about."

"When you say *others* do you mean other races?"

"Those and civilians. How about the miners in that collection of huts back there?" Collins pointed over his shoulders. "I heard them discussing and already wondering what happened to the four men you're keeping prisoners in that tent."

"They're not prisoners. We only want to make sure the knowledge about the ruins stays with the military until such time as we decide it is safe to release the information." Sheppard looked at his watch. "I suggest you get your stuff ready. We'll be leaving first thing in the morning. I'm sure you want to get back to your ranch as soon as possible. See you for supper. Oh, one final word of advice. Don't discuss anything with the newcomers. I don't trust them, and neither should you."

Collins nodded. "I will heed your advice. Thanks, Captain Sheppard. I appreciate your help."

"Good." Sheppard almost said dismissed. He turned away and headed for Colonel Daniels' tent for last minutes instructions.

[18]

IT WAS HOT INSIDE THE TRUCK. COLLINS OPENED HIS COLLAR wider and unbuttoned the top of his shirt before he sat down. Traveling in the military truck could not be described as a pleasure trip. The dirt road was bumpy and covered with small rocks. He sat on one of the hard benches in the back with two troopers. Captain Sheppard was in the front with the driver. At least, they would sit on padded seats.

Collins didn't complain. He was happy to get a free ride back to Crystal City, even if it wasn't going to be an enjoyable one.

One of the troopers gave him a friendly nod and introduced himself. "I'm Stan Wolansky. This guy here is Leo Wong."

"Pleased to meet you. I'm Dennis Collins." He smiled. "A civilian."

"I wondered about that." Wolansky gave him a searching look. "Seeing you wearing that tightfitting outfit under your clothes and that shiny case you're carrying, I thought you might be a big-shot politician or some kind of secret undercover agent. What's in that case?"

"Nothing special. Just a rifle with a cut-off barrel." There was no reason to tell them the truth about his weapons. He had stashed his laser pistol in his backpack for fear it might be confiscated by those newly arrived troopers. No need to draw attention to his person and glad he hadn't. The not-so-subtle advice Sheppard gave him about the newcomers had been clear enough.

"What brought you to this cheerful corner of Savanna?"

Collins had to chuckle at Wolansky's question. "It's a long and boring story. Let's just say I ran into some trouble and got myself lost."

Wong watched him, curiosity clearly in his almond eyes. "Why would you wear a suit like that under your clothes? Don't you sweat wearing all those layers? You say you're a civilian. What exactly do you do?"

"I own a ranch." He lifted his shoulders. "I used to live on Earth where I was a cop. That's where I got the suit. I brought it with me when I came to Savanna, and I find it handy to wear. It keeps me cool. Nothing mysterious."

"Somehow, you don't fit the image of a simple rancher," Wong said.

Collins laughed. "What does a simple rancher look like?"

"I don't know. Certainly not wearing a tightfitting suit like that. At least your hat fits the image."

Collins shifted his body on the bench. "This bench certainly isn't comfortable. I'll take the back of a horse anytime."

"You have horses?"

"I raise horses and cattle."

"Do you own a large ranch?"

Collins nodded. "The largest in the area."

"That means you're rich?"

"Perhaps, I am, but living on Savanna is not an easy life. The days are long with spending many hours out in the pastures among the animals. Sometimes the weather isn't favorable. We have to deal with draughts and storms. Those aren't the only problems. We have to worry about gangs of indigenous renegades who demand protection money. We pay them with horses and cattle."

"Why would you do that?"

"Why indeed?" Collins stared grimly at his hands. "I decided to take a stand and not pay them anymore. I hope they got the message."

"What kind of message?"

Collins looked at Wolansky, not really seeing him. "I killed their leader and most of the members of his band."

"That doesn't sound good. What made you do that?"

"They murdered my son and abducted my daughter." His words came out slowly and hoarse.

"There must have been other men with you. What happened to them?"

"There was only my foreman and me."

"Wow! That's big." Wolansky stared at him. "When did this happen?"

"A couple of weeks ago. I seem to have lost track of time." Collins was still studying his fingernails, not caring one way or another if the troopers believed him. His insides were churning as he remembered the way Randolph died. Some people say talking about something that bothers you helps to deal with it. So far, he could not say that was true. It seemed to get worse every time he told his story.

"You're saying you went on a killing spree," Wong stated. "Out of revenge. Can't say I blame you. That's how you ended up here?"

"More or less." Collins tried to get his thoughts back under control. Nothing was gained from wallowing in self-pity. He looked up. "That place back there. All the activity. Do you have an idea what it's all about?"

"Well…" Wong started.

Wolansky interrupted Wong. "We're setting up another base."

Collins didn't miss the warning look Wolansky gave Wong.

"I'd say something big is brewing," Collins said. "Changes are coming to Savanna. I have a feeling your soft life is coming to an end. I saw those new guys. They're a different breed from you."

"Those aren't real troopers. They're guns for hire, men with no loyalty to anyone. They work for the highest bidder." The contempt was clear in Wong's voice.

"Why would the military bring in mercenaries?" Collins asked.

Wolansky shrugged. "They were brought in by Colonel Daniels, along with a group of scientists. Apparently, they've been stationed in Crystal City for quite some time, waiting for the colonel to give them the word."

"Hmm. Doesn't that cause you to wonder a bit? It seems to me your Colonel Daniels knew all along he was going to set up a new military base somewhere on Savanna. What was he waiting for to start this project?"

"Colonel Daniels isn't our colonel," Wong said.

"I don't understand."

"He showed up a few months ago. He called himself major at the time. Now suddenly he revealed himself as *Colonel* Daniels."

Collins gave Wong a questioning look. "I get the feeling you don't like him."

Before Wong could answer, Wolansky broke into the conversation. "You're asking far too many questions, Collins. Be careful. It could get you into trouble. Remember, you're getting a ride in a military vehicle."

Leaning back in his seat, Collins smiled. "It must be my background as a cop. I'm used to asking questions."

"By your own admission, you're not a cop anymore. Makes me wonder what's with all the questions and your real motive."

"I'm just curious. It makes the time go by faster."

"Perhaps it's a good idea not to ask any more questions. We're not even supposed to talk to civilians, especially not about the new base."

"I understand." Collins looked up at the canvas cover of the truck and said with a little smirk, "Somebody might just listen in on our conversation."

"Nobody does. You don't have to worry about that." Wolansky frowned. "Of course, now with Colonel Daniels in charge anything is possible."

Collins sat silent. This Colonel Daniels obviously didn't have a clue that the Accilla also were in possession of a portal. They may even have made some progress in deciphering part of the secrets locked up in that ancient installation. He smiled, actually feeling a bit smug. It seemed he, the civilian, knew more about the portal than the military, particularly this Colonel Daniels, who thought he was guarding a great secret. He wondered what Daniels would do if he became aware of how much Collins knew about the portal and that the Accilla had discovered one long before the humans did on this planet.

He decided not to mention anything about portals or the Accilla anymore, for his own protection. He didn't trust the military, especially not Colonel Daniels. He wondered what was going to happen to those four miners.

"What about Captain Sheppard? He seems like a likable guy?"

"I wish he'd be in charge instead of Colonel Daniels." Wong glanced at Wolansky. "He's all right. At least, that's my opinion."

"I think most of the troopers share your opinion," Wolansky agreed. "If I trust anyone in this whole outfit it's Captain Sheppard." He chuckled. "Then again, he's a relative newcomer. A few more years on this friggen planet will change him."

"How long has he been here?"

"He came with the last arrival of immigrants."

Something clicked in Collins' memory. "When was that?" he asked.

"A few months ago. He and Colonel Daniels." Wolansky snorted. "Of course, like Wong already said, at that time the colonel was only a major. It's obvious he hid his real identity from us. One wonders why and what else he's hiding."

"I thought they looked somehow familiar," Collins said. "The colonists were kept on a different level on the transport ship that brought us here. We didn't mix with the rest of the passengers, but I remember now seeing them after we landed."

Wong laughed softly. "Union troopers don't mix with civilians at the best of times." He yawned. "I think I'll try to get a little shuteye."

"Not a bad idea. I've haven't had much peaceful rest these last few days." Collins grimaced. "Of course, I may not get any with this uncomfortable ride."

"We troopers are used to discomfort," Wolansky said. "I think I'll follow Wong's idea." He leaned back and closed his eyes.

Collins did the same.

THE SOUND THE TIRES OF THE TRUCK PRODUCED CHANGED. Somehow, it seemed louder.

"I believe we've arrived in Crystal City," Wong announced. "We're traveling on cobblestones."

Even though the cobblestones didn't make the ride more comfortable, Collins was happy to see the journey come to an end.

Three hours sitting on a hard bench was enough for his back. He chuckled silently, thinking about the five hours he spent on a hard seat on the trip from the Accilla farmhouse to the mining town. He should be used to it by now. When the truck stopped, he got up and drew aside the flap in the back to look outside.

A few moments later Captain Sheppard appeared. "We'll drop you off here, Mr. Collins."

Collins jumped off the truck and looked around. "The office of the Trading Commission," he observed.

"I figure it's the best place to ask for help to get back to your ranch. Our destiny is a warehouse."

Collins held out a hand. "Thanks for your help. I appreciate it. Perhaps someday I can repay the favor."

Sheppard shook his hand with a smile. "You never know. Good luck."

"I wish you good luck also with your project. I hope everything works out with you, your colonel, and that secret project. Don't be surprised if it turns out not such a secret after all."

Sheppard looked at him strangely. "That has an ominous ring to it."

"I was told not so long ago that I'm a mysterious man." Collins chuckled. "I have a tendency to keep things to myself. Out of habit. Probably my years as a detective."

"Probably. Sometimes it's best to keep things to yourself." Sheppard stood silent for a minute, before he said, "I've been thinking about you and what you said when we first met about other races on this planet and that they may have discovered similar ruins. I have this nagging suspicion that you know more than you're telling."

"Perhaps I do, but I'm not sure I can trust you with what I know. I don't feel like spending my time in a military prison."

"This is just between you and me. Whatever you tell me stays with me. I promise."

Collins wasn't sure if he should trust the man. After all, he was a trooper. His loyalty lay with the military. Apparently, Sheppard was liked by the other troopers, and he had the distinct feeling Colonel Daniels was not on their list of popular men. "What about Colonel

Daniels? Won't there be repercussions if he finds out what I might tell you?"

With a shake of his head, Sheppard said, "I swear he won't find out whatever it is you know. I am not his puppet."

"Maybe not, but he is your superior. I know how that works. The military machinery is programmed a certain way. For it to work properly, each component must follow protocol. You are one of those components and not allowed to fall out of line."

Sheppard smiled thinly. "That may be so on other planets and other outposts, but things are a little different here. I shouldn't be telling you this, but discipline and normal order are not practiced on Savanna. Colonel Daniels may be my superior, but my relationship with him is complicated. Let's just say, I don't always do the things he asks me to do. If I tell you he won't find out, it will be so. You have my word."

Collins thought about it, and then he shrugged, "Okay. I know what those ruins represent. I won't go into details about how, but my information is solid. Before I came to your outpost, I spent a few days with the Accilla. They saved my life. When I was with them, they showed me a cavern filled with ruins and told me I was looking at a star-portal. They also know about the ruins you discovered and why you're building another outpost."

"The Accilla?" Sheppard looked dumbfounded. "Are you telling me they're on Savanna?"

Collins nodded. "They told me they've been here a long time."

"Interesting. The lower ranks are kept in the dark most of the time, but I wonder if the military upper brass is aware the Accilla have a base here. Also, how many humans on Savanna know about them? You say they're in possession of a star-portal? A working star-portal?"

"Not working, unlike the one on Salamander."

"You know about that one, also?"

Seeing the look on Sheppard's face, Collins chuckled. "I do. The Accilla told me. It seems what you believe to be a big secret isn't such a secret after all. Sorry to disappoint you, Captain Sheppard. I hope I can count on you keeping this to yourself? If for any reason you should be forced to tell someone, at least leave out my name."

"I gave you my word, Collins." He suddenly started laughing. "In a way, it's too bad I can't tell Colonel Daniels. It would be so satisfying to deflate his ego and watch him when he finds out he is guarding a secret known to the Accilla and probably other races." His mood shifted back to serious. "I think it's best, though, that you don't talk to others about it."

"I have no reason to do so. Actually, I'm already breaking a promise I made to the Accilla by telling you."

"It will stay with me." Sheppard held out his hand. "Take care of yourself."

Collins shook his hand and waited until the truck was out of sight before he walked across the street to the building that housed the Trading Commission. He noticed a second door that led into another office. Painted on the door was a sign for Glowstar Research Company, Division of Interstellar Sunburst, and below it was the symbol of the Atom inside a broken red oval.

A chill went down his back as he stared at the symbol. The new arrivals at the military base by the mountains sported those symbols on their sleeves. The symbol triggered something in his memory, but he couldn't recall anything substantial. Ghostlike fingers reached for him from deep inside his subconsciousness, making him shudder. Whatever it was, it was nothing pleasant, of that he was certain.

Shrugging it off, he opened the door to the Trades Commission. The woman behind the counter looked up as he walked into the front office and gave him a friendly nod. "Can I help you?"

"That office next door? How long have they been in there?"

"They've been there for a few months. They finally painted a sign on their door last week." She flashed him a conspiratorial smile. "You know, it's about time. People always walked into our office if they wanted them."

"What kind of people?"

She shrugged. "Military men dressed in black and brown outfits. They never smiled. In a way, they were kind of scary."

"I know what you mean. Listen, I wonder if you can help me. I need transportation back to my ranch."

"I'm sorry, but I wouldn't know anything about that. I can call one of the agents. He may be able to help you. Just give me a minute." She got up from her chair and walked through one of the doors in the back. She came back a few minutes later, accompanied by a man.

"Rosina tells me you're looking for transportation."

"I do. Back to my ranch. Do you think the Trading Commission can help me? Your vehicles are always traveling somewhere. Perhaps you've got one going in my direction."

The man shook his head. "We are not in the business of transporting people, Mister?"

"Collins," he said. "Dennis Collins. I've been here many times paying your ridiculously high taxes. You'll find me in your records, if they're up-to-date."

"Our records are in order, Mr. Collins. I don't really have to look you up, because we can't help you."

"It doesn't surprise me. You'll take our money, but you refuse assistance when someone is in trouble. Can you at least tell me where I might find help?"

"I suggest you look for a horse trader and buy a horse. You can ride, can't you?"

Collins laughed. "I can ride. I guess I'll have to go buy a horse. Seems kind of ridicules considering I'm usually the one selling them. Well, anyway, thanks for whatever." He smiled at the woman and walked out of the door.

Idiots.

It wasn't far to the place of the horse trader he knew, but far enough for him to get tired. The rifle and the backpack seemed to get heavier with every step. He wasn't used to walking for such long distances.

He greeted the stubby man behind the counter in the small office. "Hey, Jenkins, you're looking well."

Jenkins peered at him from behind his glasses. "Collins. What the hell are you doing here? The trading won't start for at least a couple of weeks."

"Actually, I'm not here to sell any horses. I want to buy one from you."

"I know my eyes aren't that good these days, but I sincerely hope my hearing isn't going. Did you say you want to *buy* a horse?"

Collins nodded. "You heard right. Don't ask me to explain. I got stranded here without a horse. Now I need one to get back home." He grinned. "I'll sell it back to you next month."

The stubby man scratched his head. "I don't have much in the corral, just a couple of mares. I could sell you one of them. She's still sturdy enough to carry your weight. She's not the fastest, but she'll get you home."

"As long as she doesn't drop dead before I get there, I don't care. Just don't try to rob me. I can always go to Praxton."

Jenkins put one finger under his eye. "Now you're hurting my feelings. I've never cheated anyone in my life."

Collins laughed. "I guess your memory is also going. I still remember quite clearly the first time I came to you with my horses. It may seem a long time ago, but it's only been a couple of months. Had I been uninformed, you would have charged me double the commission you charge others."

"Come on, Collins. I didn't know who you were. You were a stranger and should have told me right away that you took over Nelson Haggard's ranch. Once we had that sorted out, I charged you less commission than I charge other ranchers."

"You did, and I appreciate that, but you have to agree that I raise the finest horses in the region. I mean, Mr. Haggard did."

"That's true and that doesn't seem to have changed since you took over." He stroked his chin. "Tell you what. I wouldn't feel right taking your money. That mare is not the youngest. In fact, she's quite old, but she's still got spirit. I'll lend her to you."

"What's the catch?"

"No catch. Bring her back next month."

"What if she doesn't survive?"

Jenkins pulled up his shoulders, reminding Collins of a turtle pulling in its head. "I may have to charge you a small price. Or better yet—give me one of your horses."

Collins chuckled. "You always have a way to come out ahead, my friend, but you have a deal. I need to get home. It's too late today, but I'll be by early in the morning to pick up that mare. Now, can you recommend a place where I can rent a room for the night?"

"There is a hostel just down the road. You should find a place there. Give the old lady who runs it my name. That way she won't put you up with all the losers in there. Her name is Mrs. Stokker. If you pay her a little extra, she may even let you sleep in a private room." He winked. "I hear her daughter is quite pretty and not against making some extra money, if you know what I mean."

"No, thanks. Did you forget I'm a married man?"

"It's just a thought. Sometimes a man needs a change in his diet. Brings back the appetite."

Collins couldn't help but laugh when he looked into the little man's innocent looking face and those magnified eyes behind his thick lenses. "Like I said, I have a wife, and I'm quite happy with my diet. I'll be back in the morning."

The hostel was not far, like Jenkins had said. The old woman happened to have an empty room, and Collins was quite happy to pay the extra money.

He didn't sleep that well. He woke up in the middle of the night from a disturbing dream.

The more he tried to recall the dream, the more it faded away and only snippets remained. He seemed to be running through a small forest. Beside him ran a group of black-clad men, carrying rifles similar to the one he carried in his case. There had been an explosion. That's all he remembered of the dream. He didn't know what to make of it.

Mrs. Stokker made him breakfast in the morning and even packed him lunch.

When he saw the mare, it was clear to his practiced eye that she was no prizewinner, and he hoped she'd be strong enough to last the nearly two days on the road, carrying him and his gear. He could forget about traveling fast. However, he didn't have much choice. Jenkins supplied him with an old saddle that had seen better days, but, again, Collins didn't complain.

The morning was crisp. Fall was coming to an end soon, and he was anxious to get back to his ranch. There was still plenty of work to do before the first snow fell.

The mare turned out to be quite docile, and he wondered where she came from. He wasn't the only horse rancher in the region, but he was the biggest. It was obvious she came from good stock. Had she been younger, he might even have bred her with one of his finest stallions. It never hurt to bring fresh blood into the herd.

Before he left the city, he needed to fulfil a promise he made to Professor Kopke and deliver the letter to his sister. When he showed the address to the old lady, she knew where it was. He encountered no problem finding the place and hoped it wasn't too early for a short visit.

The woman who answered the door was younger than he expected. Rubbing the sleep from her eyes, she gave him an inquiring, somewhat suspicious look. "Can I help you?"

"Sorry to bother you this early in the morning, but I have a letter from your brother. He asked me to deliver it to you." With that, he handed her the envelope.

She took it with some reluctance. "Is my brother all right?"

"He is and told me you shouldn't worry." He groped around in his pocket, pulled out a tiny package wrapped in a piece of animal skin and gave it to her. "He wants you to have this."

"What is it?"

"A blue diamond. He said to tell you not to let the Trading Commission cheat you."

"That may be difficult to avoid," she said with a tiny smile. Looking him up and down, she asked, "Have you had breakfast?"

He nodded. "I have. If you're inviting me in, I must decline, but thank you. I have to get back to my ranch. By the way, my name is Dennis Collins. Perhaps someday we'll meet again." He tipped his hat. "Have a pleasant day."

HE STOPPED FOR LUNCH BESIDE A CREEK, WATERED THE HORSE and fed it from the bag of oats Jenkins gave him, for a price, of course.

It was late in the afternoon when he reached the Sanchez Farm and dropped in and, hopefully, would stay there overnight.

Herman was still out in the field, but his sister was home, preparing supper. She was delighted when she saw Collins standing in the doorway. "Dennis," she exclaimed and gave him a hug. "What a nice surprise to see you."

"Hi, Rosita. I hope I'm not intruding."

"Don't be silly. You're always welcome in our home. Come on in and sit down. You look tired."

Collins took off his hat and wiped his forehead. "I have to admit, I'm dead tired. These last few weeks have been grueling, and I think it's finally catching up with me."

Her dark eyes questioned him. "We haven't seen you since the funeral. I feel bad for you and Kristie. What about…?" She didn't finish sentence.

"Lisa?" Collins shook his head, unable to say more for his throat choked up. Things he had bottled up finally came to the surface.

"I'm really sorry, Dennis. So sorry." Her eyes filled with tears. "You and Kristie didn't deserve this." She turned to look at the door. "I believe Herman is here." She rushed to the door and opened it.

Sanchez walked in. When he saw Collins, his face lit up in a big, gap-toothed smile. "Hey, stranger. I didn't expect you here. That your mare out there?"

"It is." Collins nodded, trying to look cheerful. "I was getting tired of sitting on the back of those high-spirited stallions."

Sanchez grinned. "Fine story." He became serious. "What happened? I rode to your ranch shortly after the funeral. Kristie told me you'd gone seeking revenge."

"I did."

"And?"

"It's done. I killed the bastard who murdered my son. Him and most of his gang. They won't bother us anymore."

"How about Lisa?"

Collins shook his head again. "I almost had her. I'm afraid she's in the clutches of the Snaar now."

Sanchez looked at him, his expression grave. "That's not good news. If they have her…" He didn't finish the sentence.

"They might be gunning for me."

"What reason would they have to do that?"

"I killed a couple of them."

"You killed a couple Snaar? Wow! How'd you manage that? They got superior weapons."

"I do, too." Collins glanced at the case that held his rifle.

"You're one man against a ship full of them. That's a hell of a lotta trouble. A six-shooter, a shotgun, and a rifle aren't going to help you much."

"You're right. They won't, but this will." He opened the case and removed the rifle.

Sanchez stared at it. "What the heck is that? I've never seen anything like it. That doesn't look like any of the rifles we have."

Collins smiled thinly. "Not many people have ever seen or used one. Home-planet Security is keeping the existence of this rifle a secret. Apparently, only specially trained law-enforcement officers are provided one. They are used strictly to assassinate the most dangerous criminals, the ones the law can't touch."

"Where did you get this rifle?"

"I brought it with me from Earth."

"How?"

"I smuggled it."

Sanchez looked at him, curiosity clearly in his expression. "How is it that you got one of these highly secretive weapons? From what you told me, you were a cop, but you never mentioned anything about special training. What exactly did you do on Earth?"

Collins shook his head. "I was a detective, investigating crimes. Nothing special about that. I've been getting flashes of things I apparently did, but those memories are not clear and certainly not mine. Until a short time ago, I knew nothing about this rifle. Now, for some reason I know what it is used for. Don't ask me where this knowledge came from. I don't remember how the rifle ended up in my luggage. I just knew it was there when I needed it. Just like this suit I'm wearing underneath my shirt and pants. It makes me practically invincible."

"I've been wondering why you're wearing long underwear at this time of year. Another secret weapon?"

Collins nodded.

"You're aware if the wrong people find out you've smuggled forbidden weapons to Savanna, you'll be in big trouble. For one thing, they'll confiscate them, and you might end up in confinement." He glanced at his sister. "Not a word to anyone about what you just heard, Rosita."

Rosita looked hurt. "I'm not a blabber-mouth, big brother. I can keep a secret."

"I'm not saying you can't, but sometimes stuff slips out. We say it without thinking. I just want to make sure our friend's secret stays a secret with us." Sanchez slipped out of his jacket. "I hope you're staying for supper, Dennis."

"I was actually going to ask if I could spend the night. I'm kind of tired." Collins gave Rosita a hopeful look.

"You don't need to ask. You know you're always welcome here. Go with Herman and wash up while I finish supper. The boys will be delighted to see you. So, will the girls, especially Kalia." She winked. "I believe she has a crush on you, Dennis."

Collins grinned. "I think I'm safe. She's only 12 years old. I love her, too. She reminds me very much of Lisa when she was her age." He became serious. "Keep her safe. I failed my daughter."

"Don't say that, Dennis. There was no way you could have saved her from being taken. You were lucky those savages let you live." Rosita wiped her eyes. "We cared for her, too, you know. You'll find her again. Don't give up hope."

[19]

Rosita gave him a hug, holding him tight. "Tell Kristie we're thinking of her and tell her to stay strong. You take care of yourself, Dennis. Don't blame yourself for what happened. We'll come by next week for a short visit and bring you some of the newly harvested vegetables."

"That would be great. I'm sure Kristie will be delighted to see you again and the vegetables you'll bring."

Even though Collins was in a hurry to get back home, he dreaded it. He didn't know how to deliver the bad news about Lisa and at a loss as to what his next move might be. One thing was almost certain, there was the possibility she might be gone forever. How could he ever find her if she was on a Snaar ship? The thought of her being in the clutches of those terrible aliens, and her inevitable fate, was enough to make him want him lash out in anger at anything or anyone. It was clear to him that he couldn't expect any help from the Solar Union Space Navy.

His thoughts strayed to those newcomers at the new military base. Obviously, they were not regular union troopers. Seeing those emblems on their uniforms had triggered something, something disturbing. He couldn't shake the feeling the Accilla may have been right about the block in his mind. It seemed a door was opening, releasing fragments of memory. Were they his own or had they been planted?

Looking up into the gathering clouds, he wondered if they would get some rain. Even though the moisture would be welcome, it wasn't the best of time, not with the harvest in full swing. With still so much to do before winter, he needed to get the cattle to the market and possibly sell a few of the horses. It would be his first winter in this new world. Staring into the clouds, he wondered what the winter would be like.

The target was clear in the crosshairs of his scope. With cold detachment, he squeezed the trigger and watched the man collapse onto the marbled floor. There was no remorse inside him. The man deserved to die for the atrocities committed by the men he controlled. The only way to eliminate men like him was to assassinate them. No jury would ever dare to convict him, unless they had a death wish and unless they wanted to condemn their families and friends to certain death.

He opened his eyes and shook his head. He must have dozed off. What was happening to him? Those were not his memories. They couldn't be. He refused to believe that. He was not a man who would kill someone in cold blood. Or was he? He remembered his coldness when executing the members of Kiimzaan's gang. There had been no mercy inside him, yet, that was not the same as killing someone he didn't even know. They had stolen from him, murdered his son, and kidnapped his daughter. It had been personal.

It was noon by the time he saw the ranch, and he steeled himself for what he had to tell Kristie and Traverse.

Riding into the yard, he looked around and a lump formed in his throat. They had looked forward to a new life on a new world, on this world, a life filled with hope for a better future. Now his son was gone, and his daughter might never come home again. By now she may already be off-planet, possibly on her way to be sold as a slave on an alien planet.

He took his time tying the old mare to one of the posts. Shouldering his backpack, he took the long walk toward the main house.

Knocking on the door, he waited for someone to open it, not wanting to scare Kristie by just barging in. He heard footsteps approaching and took a step backward, anxious to see her again but worried how she would react when he told her the bad news.

The door opened. Kristie stared at him with large eyes. Her hands went up to her mouth and then she was in his arms. "You're alive," she sobbed and held him tight. "You're alive."

He held her to him, not wanting to let her go. "Yes, I'm alive," he said in a choked voice, "but I have nothing good to report."

She stepped back and looked at him with tear-filled eyes. "We thought we'd lost you. When Rhe-annur told us, you'd been shot by a poisoned dart and you didn't come back, we feared you were dead."

He managed to smile a little. "I am not easy to kill, but I didn't know myself if I would make it. I was fortunate to find refuge with some friendly people. They cured me of the poison." He looked toward the door when he heard someone coming. Then it was his turn to stare. "How is this possible?" he managed to blurt out before Lisa flung her arms around him.

"Dad," she shouted and broke into tears. "I am so happy to see you. You had all of us worried."

"Lisa?" he stammered, not believing his eyes.

"Yes, Dad, I'm alive and well." She laughed and hugged him again.

"I don't understand." He held her away from him, elated by the sight of her beautiful face and the happy sound of her laughter. All his anxiety washed away. His daughter was home and safe.

"It was Rhaam who rescued me."

"Kiimzaan's brother? Why would he do that?"

"He is really nice. He said he carries no grudge toward you. Kiimzaan was wrong for doing what he did. Many people in the village did not condone it, but they had no choice. He did feed them."

"Sure," Collins grumbled. "With our cattle."

"Don't stand out here like a stranger," Kristie said. "Let's go into the house. You look tired. I'm anxious to hear everything that happened to you."

"You will. What about Rhe-annur? Is he all right?"

"He's fine. He and Rhaam brought me home." Lisa hung onto his arm. "Everything will be okay now. I'm happy you're home."

"I'm happy to see you, sweetheart. I was going out of my mind when our rescue attempt failed."

"You didn't fail. Because of you, I'm here, Dad. You went after Kiimzaan and his gang."

"Yes, I did." He nodded grimly. "I did what had to be done, but I'm not proud of it." He walked over to a chair and sank into it. "I don't see Ernina, and where is Traverse?"

"Ernina is with Traverse. He and the ranch hands are rounding up the cattle to take to the market," Kristie explained. "I'm so proud of him. He's become a responsible man. He should be coming home tonight."

"That's good news. I'm anxious to see him." He sighed. "I'm going to sit here for a while, but then, I have to go outside and take care of our new addition to the stable." He smiled. "She's old but she carried me home safely without complaining. I'll have to find a special spot for her in the barn."

Kristie sat down in one of the other chairs. "There is something I need to tell you. A few days ago, two men from immigrations came by looking for a man by the name of Robert Hawkins. I told them nobody by that name lived here. They wanted to know how long ago we came to Savanna and what we did back on Earth. I told them we were working on a farm, preparing for life here."

"Did you tell them I was a cop before that?"

She shook her head. "I didn't think it was any of their business. I'm sure all the information about us is in their records. How could I even be sure they were who they claimed to be? Before they left, they said to tell you to come to immigrations. Something to do with some legal forms that need to be filled out."

"It sounds fishy to me. You did right by not saying too much." He studied her silently for a moment, deciding if he should tell her about his memory flashes. "Something odd has happened. My memory seems to be playing tricks with me. Do you remember ever going to see a psychiatrist after I quit the police force?"

"Not that I recall. What reason would I have had? Why do you ask?"

"I remember going to one to help me forget some of the things I witnessed as a cop."

"I remember that, also. Are those memories coming back?"

"I'm not sure what I remember." He looked at the case by the entrance to the living room, the case that contained an assassin's rifle he shouldn't even have. "You know what's in that case, don't you?"

"I know it's a special rifle, but that's all I know. You never told me anything about it."

"I smuggled it to Savanna. It's a forbidden weapon. If the Trading Commission finds it in my possession, they will confiscate it. If immigrations learns I brought it here illegally, I may be in hot water."

"Why did you bring it?"

He shrugged. "I don't really know. The strange part is I don't even remember buying it." He bent forward and glanced at Lisa. "I'm going to tell you something that neither of you should repeat to anyone. After I was shot by that dart, Rhe-annur took me to a healer. As it turned out, I ended up in an underground hospital where I was treated. The people who cured me belonged to an alien species known as the Accilla. They are shapeshifters and can take on any form they choose." He paused to let it sink in.

"Are you saying they weren't human?"

"That's what I'm saying. I had no idea people like them existed."

"Neither did I." Kristie looked uneasy. "Were they friendly? Why would they help you? What do they want from you?"

"They want nothing but to keep good relations with us humans. That's why they helped me. By the way, they can read minds?"

Lisa asked, "Doesn't that make them extremely dangerous?"

"One would assume so, but they assured me they don't snoop around in people's minds unless they get permission."

Kristie gave him a doubtful look. "You really believe that?"

"Actually, I do. They told me many things that opened my eyes. People on Earth are surely kept in the dark by our government, even here on Savanna. There are things going on that most of us are unaware of." He paused again, wondering how he could tell them what the Accilla told him. "There is something else I'd like to talk about, something that is disturbing. When I said, they don't snoop around in people's minds I wasn't quite truthful. They did with me, but only because they needed to find out who I was and if they could trust me. They discovered a barrier in my mind, a memory block. At first, I didn't quite believe them, but things have been happening to me that make me wonder. I've been having flashes of things I may have done but don't remember. According to what the Accilla told me, I am not who I think I am. Neither are you."

"You don't make any sense. I know my name is Kristie. I'm your wife. You are Dennis Collins, my husband, and that is our daughter Lisa. We had two sons, Traverse and Randolph. We came here from Earth to start a new life. Who else would we be?"

"I don't know."

He saw fear in her large eyes when she asked, "Remember, I told you about the two men from immigrations looking for a Robert Hawkins? Is it possible we changed our name?"

"Why would we? I can't see a reason we would do such a thing, and why wouldn't we remember that?"

"When you went to see the psychiatrist. He might have made you forget that you changed your name. That could be a possible explanation."

"For me, yes, but how do you explain that you can't remember. You said you never went to a psychiatrist." His gaze wandered to Lisa. "Do you remember anything odd about what may have happened to us back on Earth?"

Lisa shook her head. "Nothing out of the ordinary. I remember my school, my friends. I remember that you were barely home because of your job. That's all."

"Tell me about my job."

"I know very little. You were a policeman. Sometimes you were gone for days. You never talked about your job."

Kristie tilted her head the way she did when she was curious about something. "You said you've been having flashes of strange memories. What kind of memories?"

"It's all foggy. This morning, on my way here, I dozed off and had a daydream. Actually, it was more like a nightmare. It had to be. I saw myself killing a man with the same rifle that's in that case. I murdered him in cold blood. I felt nothing when I did it. No remorse. It was just another job that needed to be done. Why would I daydream about something like that? I never did that when I was a cop. I was a detective investigating murders, for heaven's sake, not an assassin."

"Did you ever shoot anyone, Dad?"

"Only in self-defense."

"There may be another explanation. You said those aliens discovered a memory block in your mind. They can read minds. Isn't it possible they planted those memories?"

"To what purpose?" He held up a hand. "I'm not saying it couldn't have happened, but they saved my life and helped me return home. They told me things about themselves and asked me not to broadcast my knowledge. Because of what they told me, I'm in possession of information only the military and certain government officials know. I saw with my own eyes what they were talking about, and it's mind-blowing."

"What sort of information?"

Shaking his head, he said, "Sorry, I can't tell you, for your own protection. The only thing I can tell you is that our military is setting up another outpost near the mountains."

"I assume there is a reason for that?" Kristie seemed to expect an answer, but he shook his head again.

"Don't probe. I'm not cracking." He gave her an apologizing smile. "As soon as we're ready, we'll take the cattle to Crystal City. I also want to sell a few horses. Then I'll go visit immigrations and find out what they want from me. Did those men leave their names?"

"Only one of them. He said to ask for Rod Stringer."

He got up from his chair. "I'd better go and rub down the old mare and then feed and water her."

"In the meantime, I'll prepare us something to eat." Kristie also got up. "You must be starved. For tonight, I'm making a nice roast. Traverse will be hungry. I was thinking we should invite Rhe-annur for supper. He'll be anxious to talk to you. By the way, Nelson and Angelica went to visit the Barkleys to celebrate Shirley's birthday. They won't be back for a couple of days."

"We don't really know the Barkleys that well. I've noticed at the funeral they're getting on in years, too."

"They are, but they've got their son, Alfred, to take over the farm. He is practically running it now already."

"Shirley told me that the younger son, Paul, owns a metal working shop in Crystal City, and their oldest daughter, Victoria, is married to a lawyer. Good to know, if we ever need one."

"I hope we never do. I wouldn't even know when we would need a lawyer." He looked at his watch. "I need to go to look after my horse. I won't be long." He picked up the case with the rifle. "I think I'll put this back where it belongs."

———

HE WAS IN THE PROCESS OF CHECKING OUT THE CATTLE IN THE corral, when he heard the sound coming from many hoofed animals. Looking in that direction, he saw a group of riders on alcks heading for the ranch.

Traverse, who just came out of the house, saw them also and joined Collins. "I wonder what they want," Traverse mused, touching the gun on his hip. "I hope it isn't trouble."

"Go get Rhe-annur and a couple of the men," Collins told Travers. "Tell them to arm themselves."

"Okay, Dad. Be careful." Traverse hurried to the big barn.

Collins watched the riders, anxious and apprehensive. As they came closer, her recognized Rhaam leading them and relaxed a little. He didn't think the young Suumir meant to cause trouble, but he had learned a long time ago, never to assume anything. That could turn out to be a fatal mistake.

The riders stopped a good distance away, only Rhaam rode closer. When he was nearly ten feet away from Collins, he jumped from his steed and stood waiting.

"Welcome to my ranch, Rhaam," Collins said.

"I am happy to see you in good health. Rhe-annur told me about your misfortune and possible death."

Collins smiled. "As you can see, I am still alive. I was told you rescued my daughter. For that I am grateful. How can I help you?"

"I came to get a few head of cattle."

Collins stiffened. "Are you taking over from your brother and start the whole thing all over again?"

Rhaam pushed out his chest. "My brother was evil. I am not my brother. I will give you gold in return for what I take. Will you trade with me?"

Collins removed his hand from his gun. "I see no problem with that, and I will give you a fair deal."

"Good." Rhaam nodded. His gaze wandered to Traverse and the three Suumir rushing out of the barn, carrying rifles. He looked mainly at Rhe-annur when he spoke. "We have a bond, you and I, Rhe-annur. I will never aim an arrow at you. There is no need for your weapons."

Rhe-annur looked at Collins who nodded, saying, "Rhaam is right. We have no need for weapons. He and his companions came in peace. They want to trade with us. I told him it would be no problem. From now on, the feud we had with his people is no more. We will live in peace and harmony with each other. Rhaam will always be welcome on our ranch, that I promise."

Rhaam gave his people a signal. They came closer but still kept their distance. Collins knew it would take time until there would be real trust between him and the Suumir, but this was a start. He was willing to forgive and forget. Nothing would be gained by carrying a grudge. He had punished the ones who had murdered his son, and it would end there.

"We have gathered a few of the cattle we want to sell at the market. Go and tell your companions to choose the ones you want," he told Rhaam. "Why don't you come into my house, and we can discuss terms."

Rhaam walked over to his companions and spoke to them, and then he came back to Collins. "We will take ten animals," he said. He touched a small leather bag hanging from a belt around his hips. "Let's go into your house and make the deal. This is a good day for my people."

"It's a good day for us also," Collins said.

[20]

To get the thirty head of cattle and the twelve horses to Crystal City, would normally take nearly five days. Collins knew there would be other ranchers there, and he was hoping to fetch a good price for two breeding stallions. They were of good stock, and he didn't expect any problem selling them.

He and Rhe-annur rode at the front of the herd, each with one of the two breeding stallions in tow, while five herders kept the cattle from straying. Two Suumir guarded the rest of the horses.

Rhe-annur turned his head to look over the herd. "We're making good time, Boss Collins. If we're lucky we may make it in four days."

Collins nodded. "It would be good to get there ahead of most of the other ranchers, but I don't want to rush. If it takes five days, so be it. This is my first-time trading cattle. Even though Mr. Haggard gave me a few pointers, I'm relying on your experience."

"I will be glad to advise you, Boss Collins. I've done this many times." He glanced at the darkening sky. "There is a small bluff ahead. I suggest we make camp there."

"Good idea."

It was a good place to spend the night. A large pond provided water for the cattle and the horses, and the trees gave the men protection for the night. They slept in the open under those trees.

Collins had a sleeping bag. The Suumir herders had only blankets, which they wrapped around their bodies. They preferred it that way.

They tied the horses to trees with ropes, but the cattle needed to be guarded. Sometimes a racc, one of the giant flying reptiles, strayed this far up north, and they were more dangerous than a droocor. It worried him a little after his first, and hopefully last, encounter with one of the droocor, those cousins of the extinct Sabretooth on Earth, had been nearly fatal. Only his rifle had saved him. He didn't have it with him now, but he did carry his laser pistol, hidden from view under his long leather coat.

A couple of the herders stood guard for the first part of the night until they were relieved by two of the others.

When they arrived in Crystal City, a few clouds had moved, and it looked as if they may even get some rain the next day. They drove the cattle into a corral at the edge of the city. The herders moved into one of the barracks near the corrals where they would stay until it was time to return home. There was also a stable for their horses. Collins and Rhe-annur took the horses destined for sale to another corral a few blocks away.

Rhe-annur rode back to join his men in the barracks. A few of the ranchers were already in town and most of the good available rooms were sold out. Collins decided to try his luck with Mrs. Stokker, hoping she'd have a free room. She was pleased to see him and rented him the room he'd stayed in before. When he asked if she would be able to prepare something for him to eat, for a fee, of course, she said she'd do it for free if he kept her company for supper.

He was tired from the trek and went to bed early, but his sleep was not peaceful. His dreams were haunted by running black-clad men, explosions, and faceless men in the crosshairs of a scope. He woke up disturbed and tired. Mrs. Stokker made him breakfast. When he paid her, he gave her more than she asked for. She was pleased and told him there'd always be a room waiting for him when he was in the city.

He went to check up on the herd and the men. Then he left again, leaving Rhe-annur in charge of the trading. He trusted him, aware his foreman was probably the better choice to deal with the buyers, anyway.

It was a different story with the horses. He wanted to make the deals himself. It would be a good opportunity to meet other ranchers and maybe get a few pointers from them. Jenkins, the trader and auctioneer, was already there, as well as a few sellers and buyers.

Jenkins was pleased with the horse Collins gave him. "She's a beautiful mare. You're a good man, Collins, and I'll make it up to you."

Collins smiled. "You didn't try to rip me off when I needed help, and I don't forget something like that."

"It's bad business to cheat customers. By the way, I may have a buyer for one of the stallions you brought in. He's not a horse-breeder, but he showed great interest in that black-coated one with the white spot. His name is Dr. Clark Evington. Perhaps you'd like to meet him?"

"I was hoping to sell that one to one of the ranchers, but, hey, if you can get me a good price, what does it matter?" He chuckled. "I'll have to apologize to the stallion. He'll have to stay celibate for the rest of his life."

Jenkins laughed. "Why should he have it better than me?"

Collins gave him a puzzled look. "Aren't you married?"

"Yeah, I'm married."

"Then what's the problem?"

"My wife has lost all interest in sex."

"And you?"

The stubby man shook his head, his smile sad. "There is plenty of juice left in me, if you know what I mean."

With a shrug, Collins said, "It happens. Usually when the wife is older than the man."

"That's not the case. She's younger and still quite attractive, which makes it even harder for me." He sighed. "I never thought I'd spend the final years of my life without the love of a woman."

"I'm sorry to hear your wife doesn't love you anymore. You could always divorce her and marry one who still likes sex."

"You misunderstand. I still love her, and she says she also loves me, just not the sex. I don't want to lose her. It's just one of those things life throws at us. So, I suffer."

Collins had to chuckle when he saw Jenkins' hangdog expression. "There are worse things than living without sex. You have children?"

"Two daughters. That's another reason why I cannot divorce my wife. It wouldn't be fair to the girls. Let's not waste time discussing my problems. Come, I'll introduce you to Dr. Evington."

Evington turned out to be a well-dressed man with a small goatee. The woman with him was tall and slim, and quite attractive.

"This is the man who is selling that stallion you're so interested in," Jenkins introduced Collins.

Evington shook Collins' hand. "I'm Clark Evington and this is my wife Nicol. May I inquire whom I'm dealing with?"

"Collins, Dennis Collins. Pleased to make you acquaintance, Dr. Evington." He nodded to the woman. "And yours, ma'am."

She laughed. "You're the second man to call me ma'am. I told him the same thing—don't call me ma'am. I'm Nicol." She pointed at Evington. "This is my husband."

"She's also a doctor," Jenkins injected.

"Actually, a psychiatrist." She smiled. "My husband is the physician."

Collins chuckled. "You treat crazy people."

"Don't say crazy, Mr. Collins. I prefer mentally unbalanced instead. I help them find their balance again."

"Can you ban bad dreams?"

She peered at him. "You have bad dreams?"

Collins shrugged. "I've been having them lately." He laughed, shrugging it off. "I can deal with it. Perhaps it's my subconscious telling me to take some time out. It hasn't been a good year."

"What happened?"

"I don't want to burden you with my problems, Dr. Evington. This is neither the time nor place for that. I came to trade horses not memories. Why don't we go have a look at the horse that caught your interest?"

"Sure, let's do that. By the way, I'm known as Dr. Savon. I'm using my maiden name to avoid confusion with my husband's last name."

"Sorry, Dr. Savon." Collins made a motion with his hand. "After you."

Evington walked beside Collins as they headed for the stable. "The horse is for my wife. I hope that stallion isn't too wild."

"He's high-spirited but good-natured. I wanted to keep him for my daughter, but she chose one of the mares. A sister to the stallion, incidentally. They come from good stock."

"Out of curiosity, why are you selling this stallion?"

"I breed horses, but I need only so many stallions. I still have the brother of this one." Collins smiled. "Not as friendly as Sunshine, though. That's his name, by the way."

"Sunshine? I like that name." He smiled. "It is fitting. My wife is the sunshine in my life. Without her I would live a life of despair on this forsaken planet."

Collins was surprised to hear that. "Why would that be? You seem to have a respected and prosperous practice if you can afford to buy a horse like Sunshine. I assume you were born on Savanna, or am I wrong?"

"My parents came to this planet when I was seven years old. I lost my older brother in a freak accident a couple of years later. My mother died of cancer, a disease easily treatable on Earth but not here. Even though my father was a doctor, he couldn't help her. We don't have the medicines needed to cure so many illnesses extinct on Earth and other, more advanced planets. We live under medieval conditions here, Mr. Collins, but you would know that, unless you're a newcomer."

"I know exactly what you're talking about," Collins said grimly. "Even though, I've been on Savanna only a few months, which makes me a newcomer, I've seen many things here in need of change to make life more comfortable."

"You arrived on that last immigration ship then," Evington observed. "The man my wife mentioned who called her ma'am was with the military. He was on that same ship. I still recall his name. Sheppard, Captain Jeremy Sheppard."

"Sheppard?" Collins looked startled. "I've met him. He seemed like an all right guy." He grinned. "As far as the military goes. They have their own way of doing things."

"Sheppard saved my and my wife's life. He came across as a trustworthy and honorable man."

They entered the stable. Dr. Savon and Jenkins were already standing in front of the stall holding the stallion. He walked up to the horse and touched the white spot on the broad forehead. The stallion snorted, its nostrils flaring gently.

"I hate to part with this one. He's got a bit of a temper, but basically, he's of a gentle disposition. My plan was to sell him to another breeder to spread his genes. I hope you're not expecting a bargain."

"Not a bargain but a fair deal," the woman said, putting her hand against the horse's neck and stroking it. "You're talking about this horse as if it were a person, almost like a member of your family. It doesn't take a psychiatrist like me to detect you're fond of it." Her grey eyes searched his face. "Name you price."

"I'm fond of all my horses, but I have to admit Sunshine stole my heart the first time I saw him, and yet, I've decided to sell him. Usually, he would be auctioned off. The highest bidder is the buyer. At the same time, I want him to go to a good home." Collins looked at Jenkins. "Mr. Jenkins is my agent. I must rely on his expertise and experience as to what price a horse like Sunshine would fetch."

Jenkins scratched his neck. "Every horse is different. The ultimate factor is, of course, the demand for an animal. This one comes from good stock, and there might be a higher interest in it than on some of the other horses. I'm not trying to push up the price, but good breeding stallions are in high demand."

Dr. Evington interrupted him with a little smile. "Don't keep us in suspense, man. No need to start a song and dance. Remember, my wife is a trained psychiatrist and knows when she's being played."

Jenkins lifted both hands in a defensive gesture. "I can assure you, I have no intentions of playing anyone. I just wanted you to be aware of what we're looking at here. Just to be fair, Mr. Collins deserves to get reasonable value for his horse. We could put it up for auction, and you can bid on it. That would be the proper way to go about it, or you can trust us that we offer you a deal we're all happy with. You decide what makes you comfortable."

"Okay, let us have it."

Jenkins glanced at Collins. "Usually, a stallion like this would start the bidding with six thousand credits. From experience, I know that we may get twelve, even fifteen thousand, but that is guessing. We have a good crowd out there today, which is a good sign. I'm thinking ten thousand credits would be fair. What do you think, Collins?"

Collins shrugged. "As I told you, I trust you completely." He turned to the woman. "Dr. Savon, I admit, I am new to this, but Mr. Jenkins isn't. Nelson Haggard, whose horse ranch I inherited, has been dealing with Mr. Jenkins for countless years, and he assured me that this man is probably the most honest trader on this planet. The ranchers trust him, and that's what makes him so successful in his business. I'm comfortable with this price, and I'm ready to seal the deal." He held out his hand.

The woman looked him in the eyes. "You have an honest face, Mr. Collins, and you seem sincere. It is easy to see your reluctance to sell this horse, and I can't blame you. He's a fine-looking specimen." She took his outstretched hand and shook it. "You've got a deal. I will give you ten thousand credits for Sunshine. I promise I will take good care of him." Her grey eyes sparkled with mischief. "I'll even keep his name."

"I'm happy to hear that, as will my daughter when I tell her."

"What's your daughter's name?"

"Lisa. She's nineteen."

"Does she have red hair like you?"

"She has," he said with a little chuckle. "And freckles."

"Just like the father." Dr. Savon smiled. "Perhaps someday I can meet your family. Is she the only child?"

"We have a son." His face darkened. "When we came to Savanna, we had two. Our youngest son, Randolph, was murdered not so long ago."

"I'm sorry to hear that. Losing a child is heartbreaking. How old was he?"

"Sixteen. He was a good boy. Full of life. He didn't deserve to die, not in such a violent way." Collins found himself slipping into a dark mood. Closing his eyes for a moment, he said, "If you don't mind, I'd rather not talk about it. There is still too much bitterness and hatred inside me. I don't want to get pulled back into the world I lived in those awful days after his death."

"I fully understand." She studied him from under half-lidded eyes. "Listen, if you ever feel like talking, come and see me in my practice. I'm a good listener."

"Thank you for the offer." He thought about the nightmares he'd been having. "There is a good chance I may take you up on your offer.

I'm trying to come to grips with a few things. Perhaps you can shed some light on them."

"Anytime, Mr. Collins. I'm looking forward to seeing you." She turned to Jenkins. "Shall we proceed to finalize the transaction?"

Jenkins addressed Collins. "The auction won't start for another hour. I'll look after the other horses if you want to check up on your cattle."

Collins nodded. "Thanks, Jenkins. I will stop by again later."

Knowing the cattle were in good hands with Rhe-annur, Collin took a ride to immigrations to find out what those two agents wanted.

The receptionist told him there was no Rod Stringer working for immigrations. When he gave her his name and the reason he was here, she said, "Let me have a look in my ledger to see if anyone with that name comes up." She flicked back the pages, suddenly stopped, and looked up. "You know, I remember now. A Rod Stringer was in here about two months ago wondering if we knew what had happened to the family of a man by the name of Robert Hawkins, who apparently came to Savanna in spring with the last shipment of immigrants. I checked out the roster and told him there was no record of a Robert Hawkins. When he described this so-called Robert Hawkins, I showed him the pictures of all the newcomers. He pointed at yours and said you were the man he was looking for. I gave him your address. Did he not find you?"

"He and another man came to my ranch, but I wasn't home. He told my wife I should come to immigrations. Did he say where he could be reached?"

"That I know. He's with Glowstar. They have an office in the Trades Commission building."

"I know where that is. Thanks for the information."

WHEN HE STOOD IN FRONT OF THE DOOR THAT LED INTO THE office of Glowstar and looked at the sign with the symbol of the atom inside a broken oval, a chill ran down his spine, just like the first time he saw it. He knew he had seen it before but couldn't remember where. Whatever it was connected to was ugly and dangerous. He was quite certain it played an important role in his past.

Opening the door, he walked in, apprehensive and curious at the same time. The woman behind the front desk gave him a questioning look and said, "If you're looking for the Trades Commission, you're in the wrong office."

"I'm in the right office. I'm looking for a Rod Stringer. I was told I'd find him here."

"I guess you're in the right place after all. Mr. Stringer is in his office. Who should I say is looking for him?"

"Tell him it's Dennis Collins. He was at my ranch a few weeks ago."

She got up and disappeared through a door in the back. She returned a short time later, accompanied by a tall man, wearing the same black and brown uniform some of the troopers at the new military camp had been wearing. "I wondered when you would show up, Mr. Hawkins," he said.

"Well, then I'm afraid you'll be wondering for a long time, Mr. Stringer. I'm not this Hawkins you're waiting for. My name is Collins. I was under the impression you are an agent for immigrations, but it seems I was misled."

"Would you have come had I told your wife I am an employee of Glowstar?"

"Probably not. What's this all about?"

"Come into my office and I'll show you."

Collins followed him through the door into another office. Sitting down in one of the chairs, he watched the other man walk behind his desk.

Stringer took some kind of gadget from a drawer and moved his fingers across its surface. The three-dimensional image of a man's head appeared above the desk. "This is a picture of Robert Hawkins. Isn't it eerie how much he resembles you, Mr. Collins?" Stringer remarked with a tiny smirk.

"How do I know it isn't a picture of me, and you're just making up that name? Who is this Hawkins guy you're so anxiously looking for?"

"He and a dozen other members of a secret death squad are responsible for the collapse of an arm of Interstellar Sunburst Conglomerate on Earth, Starbrite Enterprises and the assassination of its CEO."

Black-clad men ran into the forest, away from the flames that lit up the dark night as the explosion destroyed the huge glass building. The target had been eliminated.

Collins wiped his forehead to chase away the images. Where did they come from? Those memories were not his, couldn't be. He was Dennis Collins, a detective from the Metropolis Denverado. He investigated murders not committed them. He pointed a finger at Stringer. "I don't know what sick game you're playing here. If you're trying to pin a murder on me, tread carefully. I was a cop on Earth, a law-abiding citizen. You can find out all that information from immigrations. My job was to chase criminals and put them away. I can assure you, I was not part of a death squad assassinating people. I've never even heard of Starbrite Enterprises. Who the hell are you, anyway?"

Stringer leaned back in his chair. "I'm a special investigator and a trouble shooter among other things. Right now, I work for Glowstar, but my real employer is the Board of Directors of Interstellar Sunburst. They've hired me to track down a man by the name of Robert Hawkins, who destroyed their property and caused the demise of one of their subsidiaries. It didn't take a genius to deduct you may have left Earth where the atmosphere became a little bit too hot for you after that last job. The people at Interstellar Sunburst are powerful people. Getting access to data not available to the general public isn't difficult. Don't ask me to go into details, but my investigation led me to this planet." He bent forward. "You'd be surprised how little money it takes to get somebody to divulge supposedly secret information. The reach of Interstellar Sunburst Conglomerate is long, and it owns people everywhere, on Earth, and on every planet. Nobody can hide forever from its agents."

Collins let out a grim chuckle. "You must take me a fool if you want me to believe your imaginary story. You are correct in that it doesn't take much money to bribe people. Neither does it take much to pay someone to falsely accuse another man. I'm telling you once more, I've never heard of Starbrite Enterprises. I was a cop in Denverado, a city I never left. I wasn't aware of some secret death squad that assassinated people. My security clearance was not high enough to be privy to such information."

Stringer's expression challenged him. "Either you are a good actor or you really can't remember anything. Should that be the case, you may have undergone a brain swipe, but that doesn't absolve you from the crimes you committed. By the way, when did you get married?"

Surprised by the sudden switch in topic, Collins retorted, "How is that any concern of yours?"

"Just tell me."

"I got married twenty years ago. I remember it quite clearly."

"How old was your wife."

"She was eighteen."

"And you?"

"Twenty-three. Satisfied?"

Springer grunted. "You were both quite young."

"So, what? We met in high school."

"You were in the same class?" Springer sneered.

"Don't be a moron. Of course not. I won't go into details how my wife and I met. It's none of your business."

"Wow. I must admit you have all the right answers. They did a good job on you."

Collins wanted to hit the man and wipe that smirk off his face. "Enough of this farce," he growled, got up from his chair and took a step forward. "I don't give a crap who you are and who you work for. I'm not the man you're accusing me of being, and I have a clear conscience. Do you really believe immigrations would have let me leave Earth and go to another planet had I and my family not been upstanding citizens? We had to undergo a thorough security check before they even accepted our application. We came to Savanna to start a new, better life. I paid my taxes on Earth, and I'm paying my share of taxes here to the Trading Commission. Get off my back and stop this nonsense. Besides, you are not the law here and have absolutely no right to accuse me of anything."

"You'd be surprised what I can do, Mr. Hawkins. As I said, the Interstellar Sunburst Conglomerate has a long arm, and it controls the governments on many planets."

"My name is Collins not Hawkins!" Collins banged his fist on the desk. "Remember that, you stupid ass." Then he stalked out of the office.

[21]

Fox ran his fingers through his blond hair and glared at Sheppard across the table. "Don't you think it's time the rest of us get told what's going on in that new outpost near the mountains?"

Sheppard shrugged. "You don't have the clearance, Fox."

"I'm a lieutenant, Sheppard. Damn it! From what I heard, they're erecting permanent buildings there and enclosing everything with an electric fence. What makes those ruins inside that mountain so special they need protecting? What about that bunch of mercenaries strutting all over the place, displaying modern weapons? We're not even allowed weapons like that."

From the time when they left him stranded in Crystal City, Sheppard carried a grudge against Fox. "It's Captain Sheppard, Lieutenant Fox. Remember that."

"Yeah, yeah, *Captain* Sheppard. Start pulling rank on me. Nobody gives a fuck around here. Ever since you became Daniels' bosom-buddy, you've been acting like you were somebody special. You're still in Outpost Despair with nothing to look forward to but a slow death of boredom."

"I'm not his bosom-buddy. You should also be aware of the fact that it is *Colonel* Daniels."

Fox laughed loudly. "Like I said nobody gives a fuck. I have no respect for him. He comes here pretending he's just a major, then suddenly he reveals himself as a colonel? I don't trust him."

"He's a dangerous man, Fox. I suggest you tread lightly around him."

"You mean kiss his ass the way you do?"

Sheppard looked at him coldly. "Watch your mouth, lieutenant. You know nothing about me. I would have thought being a trooper taught you manners, discipline, and respect for rank. You have none of those. I can see why you ended up here on this forlorn outpost."

"If you're so bent on discipline and respect how come they sent you here?" Fox sneered. "You must have done something wrong."

Sheppard was about to retort but kept silent. Nothing was gained by trying to explain to Fox how he was falsely accused and railroaded. He was still bitter about it. He had dedicated his life to the Solar Union Space Navy, only to be discarded like a piece of useless rubbish. General Ortega, who he held responsible for the failure of his last mission and the death of all the members of his unit, had, apparently, been on the payroll of Interstellar Sunburst Conglomerate, which in turn was controlled by one of the giant drug cartels. Glowstar Research, a division of Interstellar Sunburst, had been hired to build and protect the new outpost. How did Colonel Daniels fit into the picture? What was his connection to Interstellar Sunburst? There was something wrong with having a private firm involved in a project that clearly fell under the jurisdiction of the Solar Military.

"Can't think of anything?"

Fox's mocking voice brought him out of his contemplation. "What?"

"Can't give me a reason for you being here?"

Sheppard shrugged. "It's not important. I don't want to talk about it. Besides, I don't owe anyone an explanation. Least of all you."

"I guess you don't. You're an odd one, anyway. I thought you might fit in with our little group, we'd become friends, but you disappointed me. Why do you resent me so much?"

"If you wanted us to become friend you certainly went about it the wrong way."

"Don't tell me you're still holding that against me when we left you behind that first time? You can't deny you had a good time with that half-breed woman. It was a gift from us. Call it an initiation into our circle. Don't you get it? Leaving you to fend for yourself was part of that initiation. You had no problem finding your way back to the outpost." Fox looked at the red-haired man sitting beside Sheppard, who had been listening quietly to the conversation. "We did the same thing to you, didn't we, Foster? You remember?"

"I remember. How can I forget waking up with a giant headache in the back lane behind the Night Star Club, wearing nothing but my underwear? Fortunately, whoever left me there let me have my pants as a pillow, but my pockets were empty. I couldn't even hire a carriage to take me back to the outpost. Yes, I remember it well." Foster gave Fox an accusing stare. "I don't blame Sheppard for being pissed off."

"Are you saying you're still pissed off at me, also?"

Foster showed his teeth in a forced smile. "Let's put it this way, forgiven but not forgotten. Know what I mean?"

"The trouble with you guys is you can't take a joke. None of you has a reason to complain. You all benefited from associating with me. Speaking of benefits, I'm planning another run into the city. Colonel Wainwright needs to replenish his stock. I talked with Sanders in the supply room. He found some stuff we could use for trading. It's been sitting in boxes for some time now. Nobody will miss it." He glanced at Sheppard. "You want in, captain? I'm making you a peace offering here."

"Is the colonel sanctioning this little outing?"

"He gave us his blessing. Like I said, he's running out of brandy."

Sheppard thought about it for a moment. Then he shrugged. "All right, I'm coming with you, but don't fool yourself into believing we're best buddies."

Fox laughed. "Just give it time, Sheppard. You'll come around."

"I doubt that." Sheppard rose. "If you men will excuse me, I have to check up on something." He said something but meant someone and walked to the infirmary where the four miners were being held. The guard at the door saluted sloppily when Sheppard walked in.

Every time he visited the miners, he felt guilty, even though it hadn't been his idea to incarcerate them. At least the men weren't kept behind bars. They had been given two rooms furnished with beds, chairs, and tables. They were even allowed to join the troopers in the canteen. During the day, though, they had to stay in the infirmary.

"When are you going to release us from this prison?" Reed demanded when Sheppard walked into the room.

"If it were up to me, you wouldn't even be here," Sheppard said. "However, there is nothing I can do."

"Then who can?"

"I'm afraid Colonel Daniels is the only one who has the authority to let you go home."

"What will it take to change his mind?" Buchanan inquired. "Gold, diamonds?"

Sheppard shook his head. "I don't think he can be bribed. Not with money anyway."

"I still don't understand what makes our discovery so important to keep it a secret. It's only a bunch of old ruins." Gardiner didn't look happy. "I was an idiot to report it to the military. I should have kept my mouth shut, and we wouldn't be in this situation now. I didn't even get a finder's fee."

"Isn't there anyone on this outpost who outranks this Daniels?" Kohud wondered. "I overheard from the troopers that there is another colonel here. He's supposed to be the original commander of this outpost. What about him?"

"That's true, but, apparently, Colonel Daniels outranks him, at least on this project."

"What this project's name?"

Sheppard gave Kohud an amused smile. "Nice try, but you know I can't divulge anything. Wish I could. Apparently, too much is at stake here. It could land me in hot water. I'm not even supposed to fraternize with you."

"But you are. Why?"

"I'm the one you contacted, and I feel you're here because of me. If we never would have met that night, Buchanan and Reed may not have come to the outpost. You trusted me, and your trust wasn't warranted. I'm sorry."

"No need to be sorry. It wasn't you who betrayed our trust," Buchanan assured him. "We are to blame, also. Our mistake was to trust that Daniels. I didn't like him from the beginning, and I should have gone with my first hunch. It usually keeps me out of trouble. This time I didn't listen."

"There is one thing I know for sure," Reed said in an angry tone. "When I'm get out of here, I'm going to complain to the Trading Commission. They're supposed to uphold the law on Savanna. It seems to me the military is overstepping its powers here."

Buchanan's laughter mocked him. "Good luck with that, Reed. The Trading Commission is not interested in your welfare. Both, the Trading Commission and the military, work for the Solar Union, and the Solar Union doesn't give a crap about us civilians. Keeping a low profile is the best thing you can do. Paying your tribute to the Trading Commission without complaining how they rob you blind and keeping your nose clean is how you survive."

Reed sighed. "I can't argue with that, but I'd like to add stay away as far as possible from the military."

Sheppard didn't want to sound bitter, but he knew he was only partially successful in hiding his self-pity. "I can't fault you for thinking that. I may even agree with you. Thinking back, I should have listened to my father who told me the same thing. He wanted me to become a miner."

"Why didn't you?" Buchanan seemed genuinely interested.

Sheppard gave his shoulders a slight lift. "I found mining boring. I wanted adventure and excitement. I wanted to travel to distant stars."

"Where were you born?"

"On Ceres."

"You're a Belter," Buchanan observed. "Nobody can blame you for leaving. I've never been on Ceres, but I know it's the largest asteroid in the Asteroid Belt. Your people live in artificial habitats." He smiled a little. "I know how that is. I was born on Ganymede, and I left. I was getting tired of living underground like a mole."

"Not much different from living inside a starship," Sheppard said. "It gets to you after a while. At first, when I came here to Savanna, I felt sorry for myself, but after spending a few months on the surface of a planet all the time, I don't hate it so much anymore. I'm even getting used to it." He studied Buchanan for a moment. "Since you were born on Ganymede, you shouldn't find it so daunting after spending your days digging for minerals inside a mountain tunnel, I assume."

233

"I admit it is easier for me than for others. Not all miners were born on an airless satellite or an asteroid, but they get used to living underground. They don't have much choice if they want to succeed." He pointed at Reed. "He was born on Earth, and he's got no problems."

"As long as I can come out of the tunnels every day and see the sky and the stars, I'm okay," the little man said, smiling.

Sheppard was about to sit down, when a trooper entered the room. With a questioning look, he said, "Is there a problem, trooper?"

"Colonel Wainwright wants to see you, Captain."

"Did he say what he wants?"

The trooper shook his head. "No, sir, he didn't. He just said he wants to see you immediately."

"All right. Dismissed."

The trooper gave him a sloppy salute, turned on his heels, and left. Sheppard looked after him with a little chuckle. Most of the troopers didn't bother saluting anyone anymore, and nobody cared. Discipline on Outpost Alpha was lax, to say the least. "I'd better go," he said. "I've been summoned."

"Perhaps you can bring up our problem?" Reed gave him a hopeful look.

"I can try, but don't get your hopes up." Sheppard left the room and made his way to Colonel Wainwright's office.

The colonel sat brooding behind his desk. When Sheppard walked in, he greeted him curtly. "I want some answers today, Captain Sheppard."

"Answers to what, Colonel?"

"Don't pretend you don't know what I'm talking about." Wainwright leaned forward and pointed a finger at Sheppard. "It seems to me you and Daniels have become close friends. Collaborators, I'd almost say."

Wainwright's accusation startled Sheppard. "To set the record straight, Colonel Daniels and I are not friends, never will be. As far as being collaborators, I don't know what makes you even suggest that. If you don't mind, I think you owe me an explanation."

"I really don't, captain. Last time I looked, I still outrank you. I could order you to spill everything, but I won't. The problem with forcing someone to talk is you only get the bare minimum of information, so I'm asking politely: What the hell is going on?"

"Going on where, sir?"

"At that new outpost Daniels is creating. I only hear rumors. What's behind those ruins some miners discovered in the tunnels of the mountain? I also heard that Daniels brought in a group of mercenaries and scientists. Why?"

"Do you mind if I sit down?"

Wainwright made a motion with his hand. "Sit down, sit down. Don't keep me in suspense."

Sheppard pulled the only chair in the room in front of Wainwright's desk and sank into it. "As I said, I am not fond of Colonel Daniels, and I don't agree with what he's doing. Besides, I don't owe him anything. I believe he is a dangerous man and is planning something that is not favorable to Savanna. I also believe it is not in the union's best interest. He needs to be stopped."

"Sounds ominous. What exactly are you talking about?"

"Colonel Daniels believes what the miners discovered is a star-portal."

Wainwright lifted an eyebrow. "A star-portal? You mean one of those mysterious doorways that allow you to travel from one planet to another in an instant?"

Sheppard nodded. "That's correct."

"Are you saying Daniels is guarding a star-portal? Have you seen it in action?"

"All I saw was a bunch of dusty screens, levers, buttons, and other electronic equipment. Everything is ancient and covered with a thick layer of dust."

"You're saying it is dead?"

"It's not functioning, but Daniels believes it's not dead. I have to admit, there is something strange about those ruins. Something is alive in that cavern. The room was ice cold, and I felt some kind of pulsing in my head when I entered the cavern. Everyone felt it. It is hard to explain. It's like some force is pulling and trying to twist your mind inside out." Sheppard paused, wondering if he had made the right choice in telling Wainwright this much.

Wainwright stared at him. Then he said, "I'll be damned. This means the legends about an ancient race that traveled among the stars long before we did are true. The ramifications of getting one of those portals to work are mind-blowing. Whoever controls the star-portals will possess power beyond anything in existence. You say Daniels wants to keep that secret for himself?"

Shaking his head, Sheppard said, "Not for himself. I believe he is working for some powerful people. Dangerous people. Remember the conversation you and I had after I arrived here? I have a strong suspicion that the gang of pirates my team and I were supposed to bring down was just another arm belonging to the giant drug cartel that owns Interstellar Sunburst. Glowstar Research, the company that finances Daniel's outpost, is a division of Interstellar Sunburst. It doesn't take a genius to put two and two together."

The colonel put his finger on his mustache, stroking it slowly. "I'll be damned," he said again. "I think I need a drink. How about you?"

"I won't say no, sir."

Wainwright walked to his cabinet and removed one of the bottles and two glasses. He filled them slowly, his expression thoughtful. When he handed one of the glasses to Collins, he said, "Do you think they'll be able to get the portal to work?"

"There is no way of knowing that. Daniels told me about a working portal on Salamander, which means there is a good chance they might crack the code on this one, but it is also possible they may not."

He sipped slowly from his drink, thinking, not sure if he should confide in Wainwright with the information Collins gave him. He already broke his promise to Daniels. Now he was ready to break another one. Putting the glass down, he watched the colonel drink. Although, he had never seen Wainwright in a drunken state, he wondered if the rumor was true that he was an alcoholic.

"There is something else I'd like to tell you, something you may be highly interested in."

"I'm interested in anything that relieves me from this boredom." Wainwright chuckled. "It seems to me I've been kept out of the loop on much that is happening these days. You're leading a far more interesting life than I."

"Then you'll like this one. When I was at the new outpost, I met an interesting man, a rancher. He came to Savanna the same time I did. I gave him my word I wouldn't disclose to anyone what he told me, which means I'm breaking my word right now. Apparently, he spent some time with the Accilla, here on Savanna. According to him, they are fully aware of the star-portal Daniels wants to keep secret. They have discovered their own portal. It isn't functioning, either, and they are working on it to decode the key that will open it."

"I wasn't aware the Accilla had a base here on Savanna. Did you know about that?'

"Not until Collins told me."

"I wish we would be made aware of that." Wainwright twirled the ends of his mustache, trying to suppress a chuckle. "Poor Colonel Daniels," he said. "The joke seems to be on him."

Sheppard smiled. "I had the same reaction to the news, but it doesn't diminish the danger this portal represents. What if he and his team of scientists manage to get it to work, even if only partially? The fact that the Accilla know about the portal is irrelevant. Whoever has a working portal has the upper hand, and I wouldn't want it to be Daniels and the people he represents."

"Neither do I. This is serious business, you know." Wainwright poured himself another drink. Lifting his glass, he asked, "Ready for another one?"

"Sure. Why not? I don't usually get the good stuff. In fact, we've run out of beer."

"That's why I ordered Fox to go into town to stock up again. Alcohol is usually forbidden on a military base, but I'm sure you've discovered by now this isn't your regular military outpost. Let's face it, the troopers are dying of boredom. I don't want to deprive them of the few pleasures available to them. That's why I don't enforce that law. By the way, how are those sex-droits working out?"

Sheppard shrugged. "I can't tell you. I personally never had the urge to find out. I prefer real women."

"I can't help you with that, unless you can persuade one of the enlisted female troopers to have a sexual relationship with you. Sorry."

"Isn't that against the rules?"

Wainwright emptied his glass and wiped his mustache. "Nobody cares about rules on Outpost Alpha, including me."

"Perhaps we should care about rules," Sheppard suggested.

"Too late for that, Captain. I admit it's partially my fault. I've let things slip when I realized what this outpost represented." Wainwright sighed. "Most of the troopers here don't fit into the mold. Men like you are out of place here and a rarity." He regarded Sheppard with a thoughtful expression. "Actually, you don't fit in at all. Ever since you arrived, I wondered about the real reason you're here."

"Why is that?"

"I've studied your file again. Everything looks fine on the surface, but when I looked closer, I discovered a few inconsistencies."

"Like what?"

"Like who you really are."

"You know who I am. I'm Captain Jeremy John Sheppard." He lifted his wrist and activated the ID-band to display his head and name. "You can't fake that."

"Anything can be forged. I don't doubt that you're a captain. The question is with which branch of the military. My curiosity aroused, I sent an inquiry to Military High Command about your assignments previous to the last one. Being so far away from the regular routes, it takes so long to get answers, but I finally did get one or what could be construed as an answer if nothing counts as such. I hit a road block. I was told my security clearance isn't high enough. There is no record of a Captain Jeremy John Sheppard, other than the one in the file you handed me."

"I'm afraid that's all you'll ever get. Until that last assignment, I was a ghost." Sheppard smiled thinly.

"A ghost? Are you telling me you are a member of the Solar Union Secret Service?"

Sheppard decided to tell Wainwright the truth. There was no reason to keep his past a secret from him. His career in the military had come to an end, and anything he told Wainwright would stay with him. He didn't have to worry about damaging consequences. Not here on Savanna or anywhere else. "Perhaps you should pour us one more drink, colonel," he suggested. "I am not a member of the SUSS. Of that, I can assure you, and what I told you about why I'm here is the truth, but there is more."

He paused and watched Wainwright fill the glasses. Reaching for his, he took a small sip. Putting down the glass carefully, he cleared his throat. "I have not shared with anyone what I'm going to tell you. My name is indeed Captain Jeremy John Sheppard, but I used to be a major with a special crimes unit. I investigated corruption in the upper ranks of the military, and I found plenty. I was responsible for the arrest and conviction of many, mostly in the lower ranks. I took my job seriously and pursued it diligently, perhaps with too much zest. I was young and ambitious and rose quickly to the rank of major. My brilliant career came to an abrupt halt when I went after bigger fish, like a couple of generals. One day, out of the blue, I was arrested on trumped-up charges and sent to a prison planet."

Wainwright looked startled. "Nobody ever returns from one of those. Are you by any chance an escaped prisoner?"

Sheppard chuckled, amused by the Colonel's statement. "No, I'm not. The time I spent on that planet was pure hell, I can tell you that. I got lucky. The man who ran the prison happened to be a decent human being. Somehow, he took a liking to me and let me do administrative chores. He wanted to know how I ended up in his prison, and I confided in him. For some reason, he believed me. He pulled some strings, and one year later I was exonerated of my alleged crimes. I got back my freedom but not my rank. My benefactors told me there was only so much they could do. However, I was allowed to join a black ops unit. They suggested the best thing for me would be to keep a low profile. I began my new career as a regular, and it took me years to become a captain again. Never made it to major, though." He sighed and emptied his glass. "My future looked promising, until that last assignment. You know the rest."

The colonel didn't say anything for a while, and then he nodded. "It seems you got railroaded twice. What rotten luck. I'm surprised you're still sticking to your principals. One would think you'd be so bitter you wanted to get back at the people who did this to you."

"Believe me, I'd like nothing better. When I became a trooper, my goal was to defend Earth's interests in a violent universe, to be honorable, and to be proud to wear the uniform, but my dream was shattered a long time ago. I found nothing but corruption and dishonor right up to the top level of the military and government officials. Yet, I still believe in my dream. I still believe there are men and women out there who are descent, and incorruptible, and willing to fight for those principles."

"I'm sure there are, but not here on Savanna. At least not on Outpost Alpha. All you'll find here are troopers who are as disillusioned as you are with no love for the Solar Union and its force."

"What about you, sir?"

"Me?" Wainwright turned to look out of the window. "I was once like you, young and eager to serve, to fight Earth's enemies, and to die for my home planet if necessary. My dream was to become a general, to command a thousand battleships and lead them into battle. I dreamed about Earth becoming a super player on the galactic stage. I wanted to defeat the Spiders and the Dragons and all those other alien races in a victorious war that would be remembered for eons to come. They would write songs about me and sing them on every planet."

He glanced back at Sheppard and smiled. "Yes, I was a dreamer, naïve, and starry-eyed. Not really a good model for the image a trooper is supposed to portray. My dream didn't last that long. I came down from the clouds quickly enough to realize there was no room for a dreamer in the Solar Space Navy. If I wanted to have a successful career, I had to fit in, become like a robot, a man who didn't display his emotions, formed no permanent friendships, and forget about family and former friends. My family was the navy, and nothing else mattered." He reached for the brandy bottle and poured himself another glass but didn't offer one to Sheppard. "I won't bore you with the details of my life. My reward for being a faithful servant to the union was this place. Ask me again if I'm disillusioned, Captain Sheppard."

Sheppard didn't comment, knowing Wainwright didn't expect him to respond.

[22]

THE COLD NORTH WIND PROMISED FRIGID TEMPERATURES FOR the next few days and even colder nights. Collins pulled up the collar of his long leather coat and squinted against the partially cloud-covered sun. "I have a feeling winter is not far away. I can taste the snow in the air."

Traverse nodded. "This will be our first winter," he said, turning his head to look at his father. "Uncle Nelson told me that we can expect some pretty nasty storms."

"He told me the same thing. Fortunately, temperatures don't usually drop much below minus two or so."

Traverse chuckled. "That's quite a bit colder than we used to get in Denverado."

"True, but further up north they get temperatures up to minus forty and lower. Now that's cold. I'm glad they didn't start the colony there. I don't know if any of us would be happy."

"You'll probably get used to that, Dad. Humans are quite adaptable. You just have to dress for it."

"It would be difficult to survive with temperatures like that here on this primitive planet. On Earth it can get very cold in some regions, but don't forget, the houses there are insulated and heated with solar energy. The vehicles people travel in are heated. You never have to go out into such frigid temperatures if you don't want to, because you can travel underground from one city to the next."

"I remember." Traverse laughed. "We've only been here for a little over half a year."

Collins let out a sigh. "Sometimes it seems as if we've been here forever already. Answer me this, Traverse, are you sorry we moved to this planet?"

"At odd time I am, but most of the time I'm quite happy here, even though we have to live under primitive conditions. I love the outdoors. The one thing I like most is that you spend more time with the family. On Earth, we barely saw you. You were so involved in your job, barely home. I don't miss that."

"Neither do I, son. I only wish Randolph could still be with us. I can't help but think had we stayed on Earth, he'd still be alive. It's something I will have to carry with me for the rest of my life."

"You can't blame yourself for Randolph's death, Dad. Ernina says her people believe it was his destiny to die on Savanna. His pure spirit will appease the gods to create a bond between the Suumir and the humans." Traverse slowed down his horse and peered into the distance. "I see a rider coming at high speed."

Collins pulled out his binoculars. "It's Ernina. I wonder why she is in such a hurry."

"Something is wrong, Dad. I have this sudden feeling of doom."

Collins didn't miss the tremor in his son's voice. "Don't jump to conclusions, Traverse. Perhaps she's missed you and can't wait to give you a hug." Collins tried to sound cheerful, but he shared his son's premonition.

When Ernina reached them, she jumped from her horse and ran toward Traverse. He also slid to the ground and took her in his arms. "What's wrong?"

She tried to slow down her breathing. "There is danger at the house." She spoke hurriedly, stumbling over her words. "Two men came in one of those carriages that moves without horses. They were dressed in black. I came out of the barn and saw them enter the house. They had weapons in their hands. When I looked through the window, I saw my parents tied to chairs. I did not see your mother, but I know she was there." She looked at Collins. "I didn't know what to do. I knew my father could not help them. He would have no chance against those Earth weapons, so I rode away hoping you'd be close to home. Only you can save them."

A sudden cold feeling washed through Collins. Would he ever be able to escape the violence he tried to leave behind when he left Earth? He was not afraid for himself, but the thought something bad could have happened to Kristie drove him crazy. He could not lose another person he loved.

"I must hurry," he said, his voice brittle. "I want you to stay behind," he told Traverse and Ernina.

"We'll come with you, Dad," Traverse protested.

"No!" He spoke harsher than intended. "This is something I must face alone. I will not put you in danger. When you arrive at the ranch go and hide in the barn until I tell you to come out. Understand?" Without waiting for Traverse to respond, he dug his heels into the horse's flanks and took off.

HIS HORSE WAS SLICK WITH PERSPIRATION, BUT HE WAS CALM, his mind cold and clear. He took the time to lead the horse into the barn, and then he went for his special suit. Sliding into it, he decided not to wear the tight skull cap. Instead, he put on his wide-brimmed hat. Then he pulled his regular pants over the suit. He knew his long leather coat would be a hindrance, so he put on one of the old shirts hanging from a hook on the wall. At first, he thought of leaving his colt behind, but then he strapped it around his waist anyway. The only effective weapon would be the laser gun, which he stuck into his belt in the back. He would have liked to take his rifle, but there was no advantage in having a rifle in a confined room. With a regretful look at the rifle, he left the shed and slowly walked across the yard, past the shuttle that was parked near the house, hoping he wouldn't be too late.

He saw Kristie standing in the kitchen when he entered the front entrance, and he breathed a sigh of relief. The two men were out of sight, but he knew their positions. The only place they could be would be the living room.

The fear in Kristie's eyes was plain to see, but when he nodded reassuringly, she relaxed visibly. He knew she understood. "You're home, dear." Her voice was surprisingly calm. "Where is Traverse?"

"Oh, he decided to spend the evening with Ernina," he said. "He probably won't be home for supper."

"That's good. I haven't started yet. Now I won't have to cook that much." She moved further into the kitchen to give him room to maneuver. "We have visitors."

"I know. I saw the vehicle." He stepped into the kitchen and turned to face the living room. One of the two men sat on the couch, while the other one stood in front of Haggard, who, as Ernina had said, was tied to one of the kitchen chairs. Angelica sat in the other chair, also tied. Both men held assault rifles in their hands. The one on the couch kept it casually across his knees. The other man aimed his at Collins.

"We've decided to pay you a little visit, Mister Hawkins. Good to see you."

Collins held his hands away from his body. "I wish I could say the same, Mister Stringer. Why are you insisting on calling me Hawkins? I told you in your office, my name is Dennis Collins."

"I know I know, you've said that, but you see I have trouble believing it. According to my information, you are Robert Hawkins, the same Robert Hawkins who is responsible for the death of one of Interstellar Sunburst's CEOs."

"I also told you your information is wrong. I am not that man." Seeing Stringer's amused smile, made him seethe inside, but he knew he could not lose his temper. He needed to control his anger and stay calm. "You know, you have some kind of nerve. You come into my home, armed with assault rifles, harass an old couple who have done nothing to you, scare my wife to death, and accuse me of a crime I have not committed. I want you to get out of my house—now. I will report you to the Trading Commission and the military."

Stringer grinned and broke into loud laughter. He turned to his companion and said, "Isn't this guy something? We were told, he's as cold as they come and quite dangerous. He doesn't look so dangerous to me. What do you think, Langley?"

The other man chuckled. "Dressed the way he is he actually does look like a rancher, but you know, looks can be deceiving. Personally, I believe he's just some poor snucker who attracted the attention of the wrong people. Maybe he pissed someone off." He shrugged. "Problem is we have to do our job. If he's innocent of the crime, well, that's just unfortunate. It happens. Let's get this over with."

"What are you planning to do?" Collins stood relaxed, watching the two men with cold detachment.

"Let's see, first I must ask you to remove that antique gun and put it on the floor. Do it slowly without any sudden movements. Then kick it over to me." The barrel of his rifle was aimed at Collins, his finger on the trigger.

Collins took the colt out of its holster with two fingers, dropped it to the floor, and kicked it away with his foot.

"Good man. Now I'm going to give you a taste of what you can expect, just so you know we mean business. It will hurt like hell, but you won't die." He laughed. "That's one nice thing about shooting someone with a laser. It's bloodless, so there never is a mess." He squeezed the trigger on his rifle.

Collins saw the flash of light and felt a dull thump on his lower left side. The acrid smell of burnt leather filled the air for a quick moment. He cried out and bent forward, clutching his side to pretend to be wounded and hurting.

"You have no honor. Shooting an unarmed man," he said, making his voice sound strained.

"Does it matter? Once you're dead, you're dead. What do you care if you were armed or not? We won't kill you yet, though. This is what's going to happen. Obviously, we can't leave any witnesses, you understand? We'll shoot the old couple first. After that, we'll have some fun with your wife while you watch. Once done with her, we'll cut her throat, watch her bleed out, and then we'll kill you. I promise you won't feel a thing." He laughed. "Except for the mental anguish of watching your parents die and your wife raped and killed, but that can't be helped."

"These two old people are innocent. They are not my parents. I beg you to let them live."

"We can't do that. They will be able to identify us."

"They won't. Both of them are suffering from a mental illness. They can't recognize faces and their memory is very short. That's why we took over their ranch. We're taking care of them. They are no danger to you, I swear."

Stringer glanced at Langley. "What do you think?"

Langley shrugged. "Maybe we should show them mercy. We might even earn some points with the Big Caretaker somewhere up there." He grinned and lifted his chin to point at the ceiling. "Heaven knows, we could use some."

"Maybe you're right. I feel a little charitable." Stringer chuckled and moved the rifle to aim it at Kristie. "I think I'll shoot the bitch in the arm, so she won't be able to scratch me when I fuck her."

"Please, don't," Collins said.

"Okay, okay, you win. I won't, but you know, I've changed my mind. I'm going to kill this useless old bag of bones first. Then I'll do the old bitch. I won't shoot them, though. I'll just cut their throats."

When he lowered the rifle to get his knife, Collins knew this was the opportunity he waited for. With one swift movement, he reached behind his back, drew his laser pistol, and shot Stringer in the head. Then he shot Langley.

It was almost anticlimactic. Stringer collapsed to the ground, his assault rifle crashing onto the wooden floor. Langley toppled forward. He slid off the couch in slow motion and fell onto his rifle.

Collins stared at the dead men and the small holes in their foreheads. His mind seemed to be detached from his body, a foreign object, a separate entity, and not a part of him. There was no feeling inside him. No remorse, no sympathy. Nothing but coldness. This was just another job he had been forced to do, and now, it was done.

Without consciously thinking about it, he bent to pry the knife from Stringer's dead hand and cut the ropes that held the old man prisoner to the chair. He walked over to Angelica and cut her bonds.

Haggard rose from his chair and patted Collins on the shoulder. "Thank you, Dennis," was all he said before he helped his wife out of the chair.

Collins turned to look at Kristie. She stood with her hands over her mouth, as if she wanted to stifle a scream. She seemed to shrink away from him when she looked into his eyes.

"You killed them," she finally said with barely a whisper. He could see her shiver. "Who are you, Dennis? As long as we've been married,

I've never seen that look in your eyes and face. So cold and without any emotion. You're suddenly a stranger to me. You scare me."

He could feel his face soften and the coldness leave him. Now there was nothing but relief inside him. "I'm the man who loves you," he said softly. "I'm the man who would do anything to protect you and keep you safe. I don't know who this Robert Hawkins was or is. All I know is I'm Dennis Collins, a rancher. I'm a man who wants to live in peace and make a life for me and my family on this planet. Nothing more and nothing less." He walked over to her and took her in his arms. "I love you, and I'm sorry I put you in such danger. These men are dead. They can't harm us anymore."

She clung to him, sobbing. "What if they send others?"

"Let's not worry about that now. I'll find a way to keep us safe, I promise."

"I do worry. Why do these people want you dead, want us dead?"

He shrugged. "You must have heard what Stringer said. Apparently, this Robert Hawkins is responsible for the demise of one of Interstellar Sunburst's CEOs."

"I heard." She took his face between her hands and looked at him. "Dennis, remember what you told me about those aliens that healed you? You said they discovered a memory block in your mind. Is there no way you could find out what that block is supposed to hide? Perhaps recover those suppressed memories?"

"I've been thinking about it. When I was in Crystal City, I sold a horse to a Dr. Savon. She is a psychiatrist. She said if I ever need to talk to come and see her."

"It may be a good idea to do that. We need to get at the truth, Dennis. We'll go together, you and me." She took his hand and pulled him toward the living room. "My knees are threatening to give away. I have to sit down." Her gaze took in Haggard and Angelica. The old couple had been watching silently. "I'm sorry we brought this on you. This would never have happened to you had we not come to your ranch."

Angelica came and put her arms around her. "Don't talk nonsense. It isn't your fault. You've been looking after us until now. We couldn't have asked for a better family to take over our ranch. Besides, we're still alive, thanks to Dennis. He's a real hero."

Haggard gave the corpse at his feet a vicious kick. "This son-of-a-bitch called me an old bag of bones. Now look who's nothing but a bag of bones. He was going to cut our throats. In my younger days, he would never have managed to tie me to a chair." He looked at Collins. "You sure took care of them. They deserved what they got. I have to agree with Kristie, though. The man who killed these two wasn't the Dennis Collins I know, but I won't question it. It may be something we should discuss at a more convenient time. Right now, we'll have to get rid of their bodies."

"I'll get Rhe-annur to remove them and bury them somewhere far away from the ranch."

"Burying is too good for them. We'll take them into the woods and feed them to the carrion eaters," Haggard said fiercely.

"That's barbaric," Angelica protested. "We don't want to stoop to their level. We're churchgoing people, and we will act accordingly. They'll get a decent burial."

"I agree with Nelson," Kristie said with a voice as fierce as the old man's. "They deserve nothing but having their bodies ripped apart by wild animals."

Angelica shrugged. "It looks like I'm outvoted. I just don't feel right about it." She looked at the blackened hole in Collins' pants. "You're injured. Aren't you in pain?"

"I'm fine. My leather pants are ruined, that's all."

"Are you sure?" Haggard gave the hole a closer inspection. "I'm not quite familiar with these modern weapons, but it looks to me as if that bolt of energy should have gone right through your body. There is no way it could have missed you. Besides, it would have burnt some object behind you."

Collins sighed. "I'm wearing a special suit underneath these pants. A burst from a laser or even a bullet will not penetrate the tough material." He smiled thinly. "When I wear this suit, I'm practically invincible."

"Where did you get it?"

"I brought it with me, but let's not discuss this subject. To get rid of the bodies is the least of our problems. We also have to hide the fact that these men came to us in a modern vehicle. Nobody must know they were here, especially not the Trading Commission.

I'm in violation of the law being in possession of this suit and a laser gun."

"Anyone seeing those tiny holes in their foreheads will wonder how these two died. That's why we have to leave them to the carrion eaters. They won't leave any evidence behind," Haggard insisted.

"I agree." Collins nodded, thinking. "I'll have to drive their vehicle back to the main road. Remember the lake after you passed the Sanchez farm? I'll sink it into the lake. Nobody will ever find it."

"It's a good idea," Haggard agreed, "as long as nobody sees you."

"We'll do it at night. Traverse can accompany me with the horses, so I can get back home."

"Where is Traverse?" Kristie wondered.

"I told him to stay behind with Ernina. She's the one who warned us about the assassins. I suggested they hide in the barn. I'd better go and tell them it's over, and we're safe."

"I'll come with you," Kristie said. "You should go and tell Rheannur about what happened and ask him to remove these two bodies before they begin to stink up the place. At least, we don't have to worry about cleaning up any blood."

Haggard picked up one of the assault rifles. "What about their rifles? I've never seen anything like them before. They might come in handy."

"It is tempting, but we can't keep them. Too dangerous. I'll sink them with their vehicle in the lake. If someone ever should find the vehicle or the weapons, there will be no linking them to us. It would have been different on Earth. Anyone ever touching anything leaves evidence behind that can be traced but not here. Not on Savanna. There is actually an advantage to living on a primitive planet. You can get away with a crime."

"I don't consider killing these two a crime," Kristie argued. "You acted in self-defense."

"I did, but there would be many questions as to why they were after me and many more. Questions I wouldn't be able to answer satisfactorily. It is best we keep this whole incident a secret."

"Agreed." Kristie said it.

Haggard and Angelica just nodded solemnly. "It will be a secret I'll take to my grave. I promise," the old man said and winked. "Even though a certain person who shall remain nameless stated that my memory is gone, I shall remember how you took out these two for the rest of my life, with every tiny detail."

"I'm afraid so will I," Collins said with a little smile. "Except for me it will be more like a nightmare. I wish this would never have happened. I do not cherish or condone violence."

"I didn't get that impression when I saw you shoot these two men," Haggard noted. "You are not a stranger to violence. Why did they call you Hawkins?"

Collins shrugged. "A case of mistaken identity, I'm sure."

"I don't think I'll be sleeping soundly for a long time," Kristie said. "Something else occurred to me. Somebody will be missing these two men. What if they come looking for them?"

"They were paid assassins. I doubt they advertised their plan to kill some people today. If anyone comes looking for them, they won't come here. That's why it is important we get rid of their vehicle and their bodies to avoid a connection between them and us. I will do it tonight."

[23]

"BEFORE WE BEGIN, MR. COLLINS, I WANT YOU TO BE AWARE that there is no guarantee you will get your memory back."

Dr. Savon's expression was solemn as she looked at him over the top of her black-rimmed glasses. It reminded him, again, painfully that they were on a low-tech planet. On Earth, a simple operation would have given her perfect vision.

"Not even a little?"

"I'm hoping for more than just a little." She smiled. "I'm curious. What makes you suspect you have a memory block?"

"I've had flashes of things I apparently did but don't remember. They've become more frequent lately. Most of my memories are of a violent nature. You see, I was a cop before I came to Savanna. I might have had those memories suppressed by my own choice, to either keep myself from going crazy or to prevent me from divulging certain information not meant for private citizens. You know how secretive governments are."

"I've never been involved with the government, at least not one like you have on Earth or other more advanced planets, but I can imagine how government agencies operate. They probably have no choice, especially when it comes to police work."

"Secrecy is most important when working a case," he agreed. "If we would broadcast every move we make, we would never catch any criminals."

"I suppose that is true. Another thing I should mention. Tampering with the mind and memories can change a person's personality. If we are successful in restoring your lost memory, there may be the danger your old personality is going to be the dominant one."

Collins looked at Kristie. "We've discussed that, and we're willing to take the chance. We both feel it is important I remember what happened before we came to Savanna."

Kristie nodded in agreement. "We suspect that I had some of my memories erased, also. I would like you to find out if that is the case."

"Is there a chance you both may have had all of your real memories replaced with false ones?"

Remembering what the Accilla told him, Collins said, "We suspect that may be the case. We want to find out if it's true and why."

"Okay. May I suggest you make yourself comfortable in the waiting room, Mrs. Collins? The process takes all my concentration and the subject, your husband in this case, needs to be able to relax completely without any distraction. Help yourself to some cookies from the jar on the table and have some fruit juice. I'll need about an hour, hopefully less. If you get lonely or impatient, you can always take a nap," Dr. Savon said with a little laugh.

"Thank you. I think I'll be fine. I brought some wool and knitting needles. I'm knitting scarves for everyone."

"I never learned to knit. It's a useful skill, especially now with winter coming."

Dr. Savon waited until Kristie was out of the room to turn to Collins. "Please, lie down on this couch, close your eyes, and relax."

He did as asked. Closing his eyes, he tried to calm his mind and body, but it wasn't easy. Too much stuff was floating around in his head. A cool hand touched his forehead, and Dr. Savon's soothing voice suggested he think of a pleasant place and an enjoyable activity.

He found himself sitting on his horse, overlooking the valley where the cattle were kept. He watched a team of horses galloping across the prairie, long manes flying in the wind. He could hear Dr. Savon's voice droning in the background, but it slowly faded away.

•   •   •

252

He opened his eyes. The first thing he became aware of was a white ceiling above him. When he turned his head, he expected to see screens and gently flashing light. Instead, he looked at white walls, adorned with paintings and a woman in a white coat sitting in a chair near the couch he lay on.

"Who are you?" he asked and sat up.

"I'm Dr. Savon. How are you feeling?"

"How should I be feeling?"

She smiled. "I don't know. You tell me."

"What happened to Dr. Sullivan?"

She shrugged. "I have no idea. Who is Dr. Sullivan?"

Getting impatient, he said, "He's the man who was supposed to suppress my memory and turn me into someone I'm not really fond of becoming, but it needs to be done. I assume it didn't work. Why are you here instead of Dr. Sullivan? Are you a member of Global Security?"

"I'm here to bring back your memory as you instructed me to do. Don't you remember?"

He closed his eyes for a moment, a wave of confusion rushing through him. Something like that had never happened to him. He was never confused.

"What is your name?" the woman asked.

"My name is Robert Hawkins. Before I give you more information, I need to know if you're a member of Earth Global Security, your badge number, and your security clearance. I also need to know why you are here instead of Dr. Sullivan. Where am I, anyway? This room does not look like it's in EGS Headquarters."

The woman leaned back in her chair. "It seems whatever I feared most happened. Give me a moment to explain. The procedure to suppress your memory was a success, even though it doesn't seem to you right now." She held up a notebook made from paper. "Your story is on these pages. I wrote everything down, so you could read it yourself. If you want, I can give you a shortened version verbally. You told me everything about yourself when you were under. By this, I mean I put you into a deep trance to enable me to extract your memory. First, I want you to close your eyes again and relax."

"I won't be doing any such thing before I get some answers. How did I get here, and where is this place?"

She sighed. "Let me show you something. Get up and come with me." She didn't wait for him and walked to the window where she pulled apart the curtain.

Looking outside, he saw a dirt street lined with small houses. Most of the houses were clad with what looked like wooden boards. There were no skyscrapers or any tall building anywhere as far as he looked. A wagon with wheels pulled by a horse came down the street.

Brushing his hand over his forehead, he found it damp with perspiration. What he saw couldn't be real. Nobody used horses to pull an antique wagon manufactured from wood. Notwithstanding the fact that horses only existed on animal reserves. Streets were paved not packed with dirt.

"I don't understand. Where am I?"

"Let's put it this way, you're not on Earth anymore. You're on a planet we call Savanna, and you've been here for many months. Your name isn't Robert Hawkins. It's Dennis Collins. Your wife is in the other room."

"My wife? I'm not married. Never have been. My line of work didn't allow me to get married."

"You are married. The memory of the man you were before you came to Savanna had been suppressed and, as was evident, quite successfully. Apparently, it was done for your own protection. You came to me and asked me to bring back that memory, which I did. It seems, your old personality took over again and is suppressing the consciousness of Dennis Collins, the man you've become. I need to put you under again to get you to remember the last two years of your life to balance your two personalities."

He hesitated, becoming suspicious. "How can I trust you? Perhaps this is all just a trick." He stepped away from her. How he could get out of this room? He didn't want to kill her unless it was necessary. She didn't give the impression of someone who meant him harm but looking harmless could be one of her covers. How could he be sure what he saw on the other side of the window was real? It could be nothing more than a hologram.

Looking out of the window again, he asked, "Can you take me

outside, so I can smell the air?"

"Sure, we can go outside. There is one thing, though. We have to go through the next room where your wife is waiting for you."

"I told you, I don't have a wife."

"You don't, but the man you became does. Let me go first and talk to her, okay?"

"No tricks. I warn you."

She heaved that sigh again. "No tricks. It is clear you were a suspicious man in your old life, not trusting anyone and not loving anyone. You should be happy you finally left it all behind." She pointed at him with one hand. "Stay here until I call you."

She walked toward the only door in the room and opened it. He went to the window again and looked out, contemplating breaking it and escaping, but if it was only an illusion, there may be nothing waiting beyond the glass to get him to safety. He turned when he heard the door opening.

The woman waived and said, "Let's go."

Entering the other room, a blond woman sat at a table. He estimated her to be in her late thirties. He also noted her quiet beauty. She looked at him with wide, blue eyes. He had the feeling she wanted to say something, but she kept silent. A vague sense of recognition flashed inside him, but then the feeling was gone.

He followed the woman who had introduced herself as Dr. Savon through the door that led outside, ready to bolt away.

What awaited him outside was not what he expected. Taking a deep breath, he felt a rush of euphoria. He had never smelled air this fresh and good. There was no smog, no strange odors. When he looked up, he saw blue sky that went higher than he had ever seen before. It was strangely silent everywhere. He actually heard birds singing instead of the sound of airborne vehicles that should clutter the sky above him and the humming noise that is the beating heart of the large cities on Earth.

"Convinced?"

He looked at the woman. "It seems you told me the truth, even though I can't remember anything. The last thing I remember is lying under a bright lite and hearing Dr. Sullivan's voice."

"What you remember happened two and a half years ago, back on

Earth. Much has happened to you since then. I can bring those memories back again, if you let me."

He contemplated his next move but realized he didn't have much choice. Obviously, he wasn't on Earth anymore. He had to trust this woman. "You said when I wake up, I will still remember what I know now?"

She nodded. "That and the memory of your new personality. However, you must know that only the last couple of years are real, the rest are the memories of another man. You will understand when you wake up again."

Resigned to his fate, he lay down on the couch. "Okay, let's do it."

WHEN HE REGAINED CONSCIOUSNESS AGAIN, HE FELT DIFFERENT. He was still Robert Hawkins, but he was also Dennis Collins.

Sitting up, he held his head for a moment, trying to sort out things. At first, the memories of both personalities seemed to be all jumbled. He couldn't tell the difference between which ones were real and which ones were not, but clarity snapped in. He looked at Dr. Savon. "I don't know how this works, but I can actually separate my two personalities. In a way, I wish it wouldn't have been necessary to bring back those old memories, but now more than ever do I know it was important." He gave her a little smile. "Somehow I don't like this Robert Hawkins. He was not a good man. Cold and violent with no conscience. I don't ever want to become him again."

"You don't have to unless you want to. It is up to you. There may be times in your future where you need to become Robert Hawkins to protect yourself and your family."

He nodded. "Yes, my family. I don't know what I should tell Kristie, but she needs to know the truth. She'll want to know."

"We can go to her now. She's anxiously waiting. When she saw you before, she became scared, worried you may never again be the man she knows as Dennis Collins." She got up from her chair. "Come, let's go and talk to her."

When Kristie saw him, she said, "Dennis?"

He walked up to her and took her in his arms. "I'm back. Before I say anything else, I just want to say I love you."

"I love you, too. You scared the hell out of me when you walked into the room. You looked different. You were not my husband but a stranger. Your eyes and your face were cold and distant."

"The man you saw was Robert Hawkins, an assassin, a cold-blooded killer who would have killed you without blinking an eye had he found it necessary." He stroked her hair. "I'm not that man anymore, sweetheart. I have his memories, but now I'm Dennis Collins, your husband."

She looked at him with questions in her eyes. "There is much I don't understand. How is it possible that I remember us getting married twenty years ago? I was sixteen years old when we met. You were this older, dashing, red-headed rookie cop. I fell in love with you, and we got married two years later. I married Dennis Collins not Robert Hawkins. Are my memories wrong?"

He shook his head. "No, they are not wrong, but it wasn't me you married. It was the real Dennis Collins. He was a detective in Denverado. He died in an accident."

Her hands flew to her face. Taking a step back from him, she said, "That means you're an imposter."

"In a way I am, but you agreed to marry me a few months after Dennis passed away."

She sat down, her face colorless. "I don't remember any of that. Why would I agree to marry you and keep on believing you are my husband, pretending he never died? It seems our life together has been a lie."

"Part of it has, but not the last couple of years. I wouldn't want to trade them in for anything else. I love you, and I love the children. It's been the best part of my life."

"How can you love us? Lisa and Traverse are not your children. How are we going to explain this to them?"

"We don't have to explain anything to them. It's best for all of us if they don't know the truth."

"Of course, they need to know," she said vehemently. "It wouldn't be right to keep this from them. They should remember their real father, the way he was. They need real memories not artificial ones."

"Their memories of their father are real. The only thing they don't know is the part that I took his place after he died. In a way they were spared to deal with their father's death." He spoke soothingly, almost desperate to convince her that everything was all right, but he knew the bond between them had been shattered. "I wish I had left things alone," he said softly.

"So, do I." She looked at him with a tearful face. "You know, looking at you, I still love you. I still see you as Dennis, my husband, and not the man you say you are. Who is or was Robert Hawkins?"

"I, as Robert Hawkins, was a member of a squad of assassins, a secret branch of Earth Global Security. We took care of things that needed to be done, things outside the law. My team and I went on a mission to bring down one of the drug cartels, Starbrite Enterprises. We killed all the executive members of that company. I'm the one who shot and killed the CEO. We were responsible for the demise of Starbrite Enterprises on Earth. It brought down on us the wrath of Interstellar Sunburst Conglomerate, the company that really owned Starbrite.

"Even though it was a highly secret mission, a spy in our department divulged the list of names of my team. After two of the members were murdered, it was decided to dissolve the team. None of us was safe anymore. My superiors suggested it would be in my best interest and for my protection if I changed my identity and immigrated to another planet."

"That explains why you are here, but what about me? How and why would you take on my husband's identity?"

Dr. Savon injected. "The only way to find out is if you let me put you under hypnosis, the way I did with your husband," She gave them an apologetic smile. "I mean Mr. Hawkins. Sorry."

"You don't have to apologize. I'm not this Hawkins any longer. I am Dennis Collins, a rancher, who is married to a beautiful woman, and I have a son and a daughter. They are my family, and I love them with all my heart. I will do anything to protect them from harm. That's the reason I needed to know about my past, so I could use that knowledge to make sure they stay safe." He looked at Kristie. "Perhaps you should take up Dr. Savon's suggestion to find out what really happened. I think you will understand everything much better."

Kristie nodded slowly and looked at Dr. Savon. "Okay. Let's do it.

I need to know."

———

"THIS JOB OF YOURS IS TEARING US APART, DENNIS. WE BARELY SEE you anymore. I get no help from you, and I know it's taking its toll on you as well."

Dennis smiled. "I'll be home for a while, at least for a couple of weeks."

"Sure. Much help you'll be with that bullet in your arm."

"Come on, Kristie, I don't have a bullet in my arm. The bullet just grazed me. I'll be good as new in a short time." He reached for her with his good arm, but she evaded him.

"What about the next time you get shot?"

"There won't be a next time."

"How can you be so sure?"

"I wasn't going to tell you until it was official, because I wanted it to be a surprise. What would you say if I told you I put in my request for retirement?"

She gave him a surprised look. "You don't qualify for retirement. You haven't been with the police department long enough."

"Seventeen years. I won't get a full pension, and it won't be enough to live on, but I can get another job." He hesitated. "We've always talked about how wonderful it would be to have our own piece of land, a nice house by a lake. The kids and I could go fishing and hunting. A place where the air is pure and clean and the noise level bearable, where you can see a blue sky with fluffy, white clouds lazily floating above."

"Where on Earth can you find that? I don't believe a place like that exists, and if it did, you and I won't be able to afford it."

"Exactly, but I wasn't thinking about Earth. I was thinking we could migrate to one of the frontier planets. I talked to a guy at work. He told me about someone he knows who is moving with his family to a planet called Savanna. They are taking applications now. Savanna is an Earth-like planet with ideal conditions, pure air, and clean water everywhere. Just imagine, we could have our own farm, grow our own vegetables, free of hormones and pesticides. We could raise our own livestock. Wouldn't that be great?"

"It would be if we knew how to farm."

"That's the beauty about all of this. Before the immigrants leave, they have to go to orientation meetings where they find out about their new home. They know exactly what to expect. They also have to work on a state farm where they are taught everything they need to know about farming. I'm not saying it would be easy, but we would be free from all the pollution, the noise, the crowded cities, all the restrictive laws. Everything. We'd finally have our own place with room to breathe. Best of all, I would be with you and the kids all the time."

She sighed. "It sounds wonderful, but it would be a huge step. Life changing for sure, especially for the kids."

"They are young and adaptable, more so than you and I. Can you imagine raising horses, for instance? I mean real horses. The boys would love it."

She shook her head. "How about Lisa? She's at that age where she wants to go out with boys. I was sixteen when I met you and look what happened."

He grinned and put an arm around her. "You were mature. Lisa is still a child."

"She's fifteen."

"Like I said, a child." He became serious. "I'm not kidding about migrating. I've been thinking about it for quite a while now. I want you to give it some thought. There is not much of a future for us here on Earth. The crime rate is high, politicians are corrupt, the cartels and gangs are practically running the cities. It would be great to start fresh on some virgin planet."

"There was an accident, Mrs. Collins. It happened so fast. One of the corn harvesters toppled over. It fell on your husband and crushed him. I'm afraid your husband won't survive the accident."

"I am sorry to inform you that the commission has not renewed your application to migrate to Savanna. Only whole families or single men and women are eligible, but no single women with children. Since the death of your husband, you no longer qualify, but don't give up yet. If you should remarry the commission would certainly look at your application again."

"Someone from Earth Global Security wants to talk to you, Mrs. Collins."

"Who is this Robert Hawkins, and why does he want to marry me?"

"He's a former agent of EGS. I won't go into details, but circumstances force him to leave Earth. He is not married, but he needs to be married to complete his cover. Computer Central has determined that your husband and Mr. Hawkins are a close fit in appearance and manners. Also, they are of the same age. That's why it was decided to keep the death of your husband a secret and have Mr. Hawkins take his place. He saw your picture, and he is willing to marry you."

"I can't just marry a stranger, especially since it's been only a month since my husband passed away."

"You won't be strangers, Mrs. Collins. Mr. Hawkins, you, and your children will have to undergo a special procedure. Neither of you will remember your real husband's death. Mr. Hawkins will become Dennis Collins. For you and your children, it will be quite a simple procedure, but for Mr. Hawkins it will be a major change. His memories will be of your husband's life. He won't remember his own former life. For him, Robert Hawkins will cease to exist. He is aware of it and has agreed to become Dennis Collins, if you are willing. It is up to you."

———

SHE OPENED HER EYES, MOMENTARILY CONFUSED. SITTING UP, she wiped her hand across her forehead, trying to hang on to the strange visions.

"Are you feeling all right?" a woman's voice inquired.

She nodded. "I'm fine, Dr. Savon." She looked at the man standing not far from the couch. "I remember everything." She slid from the couch and walked toward him. Looking into his anxious face, she said with a quiet voice, "The people from Global Security brainwashed me to believe you are my husband, Dennis. I, also, know that you had to undergo the same conditioning to make you believe I was your wife. Now I know the kind of man you were before, but I also know who you are now. You may not be the same man I married twenty years ago, but during these last two years we've spent together, I've grown to love you more than I ever loved the real Dennis Collins. You are my husband now, and I want nothing more than spending the rest of my life with you...Dennis."

He took her face between his hands and kissed her gently. "I want the same. Remembering the truth has not changed my feelings for you and the children. I love you, and I love them as if they were my own. As far as I'm concerned, Lisa is my daughter, and Traverse is my son."

She clung to him, overwhelmed by an outburst of sudden tears. "You are right. We cannot tell them," she sobbed. "This will be our secret. Telling them would serve no purpose."

[24]

DANIELS WAS FURIOUS WHEN HE FOUND OUT THAT COLONEL Wainwright gave those four miners their freedom. "It wasn't your place to release them. They were under my protection."

"Your protection?" Wainwright found Daniels' words amusing. "Protection from what? The way I saw it, they were four innocent men held against their will on my outpost. You understand, *Colonel?* My outpost, not yours. I'm still the commanding officer, and I won't have civilians kept as prisoners behind these walls, unless they've committed a hostile act against this outpost or any of the troopers. If, for some reason, they are guilty of a crime, we don't have the authority to judge and punish them. That is the job of the Trading Commission."

Daniels glared at him. "You may be the commanding officer of Outpost Alpha, for whatever it's worth, but the way things are developing on Savanna, it's only a question of time until that will change. You are meddling in affairs you don't understand, and you have no idea the damage you may have caused by letting those miners back into the community. It could have far-reaching consequences."

Shaking his head, Wainwright chuckled. "Are you really so naïve to think I don't know what is going on? That little outpost you are creating has not escaped my attention. The troopers here may not be role models of how a trooper of the union behaves and acts, but they are not ignorant idiots. They hear and see things, and what they hear gets back to me. I know about the private army you've hired, and I'm aware that your so-called outpost is financed by Glowstar Research, a division of Interstellar Sunburst. You are trying to create your little empire with the help of a criminal organization, and I am certain that is something not sanctioned by the military. I'm not your superior officer, and therefore cannot order you to stop what you're planning, but perhaps the Trading Commission will be interested in your little undertaking."

With a contemptuous laugh, Daniels said, "The Trading Commission? It has no jurisdiction over the military. We both know it's not even an arm of the Solar Union. It is controlled by another giant cartel, and I don't have to tell you what that means. As far as my *little undertaking* goes, I have the backing of influential people in high places, in the military and in the government. While you're dying here on this backwater planet, the universe is not standing still. Things are happening, things you don't understand."

"Things I don't understand? Hmm, let me guess. You wouldn't by any chance be talking about the star-portal now, would you?"

Daniels' eyes narrowed. "I have no idea what you're talking about."

"Really?" It was Wainwright's turn to laugh. "Don't take me for a fool, Daniels. I know that the star-portal the miners discovered is the whole reason for you even being on Savanna in the first place. You mistakenly believe it is a secret only you and your cronies know about." He bent forward. Dropping his voice, he said, "I'll let you in on a little secret of my own. I'm not the only one who knows about it. The Accilla are fully aware of the portal you think you discovered, and they are keeping an eye on you." He leaned back, watching Daniels react to the news.

As expected, Daniels was not happy. "How do you know this?"

"You don't really expect me to tell you? Let's put it this way, I have my sources."

"I can guess how you found out. I should never have brought those miners here. I was a fool to believe they would keep their mouths shut. However, I'm curious about the Accilla. I didn't know they had a base on Savanna."

"Apparently, they've been here for years, watching us humans and keeping track of our activities. With their ability to become anything or anyone they want, they could be hiding anywhere." Wainwright smiled. "How do you know I'm not one of them?"

"I believe we can rule that one out. Before coming here, I made it a point to study each and every man and woman on Outpost Alpha. That includes you. I know where you were born, where you grew up, how many brothers and sisters you have, and more. If you weren't a true blooded human, I'd know. I don't take chances."

"Neither do I. I was curious about you, so I made some inquiries. I still have certain connections, you know. I found out you were born on Earth. You started your career as a peacekeeper at age twenty. At age twenty-four you joined the Solar Space Force. You studied to become an engineer, specializing in artificial intelligence and spatial sciences. At age thirty-two, you became a member of the Solar Union Secret Service. Unfortunately, that's all the information I could get, but it was enough to tell me you're not regular Navy. You came here under false pretenses, pretending to be a major and a bridge builder. I knew you couldn't be trusted."

"There are many levels of trust. When it comes to important issues, I can be trusted, but there are also many circumstances where trust is unimportant and not warranted." Daniels made a dismissing gesture. "It doesn't matter if you trust me or not. You're not an important element in my world, just an inconvenient obstacle." He gave Wainwright a calculating look. "If you have delusions of undermining my work here, let me warn you. I have powerful allies, and your feeble attempts at disrupting my work will have dire consequences. Accept it, there is nothing you or anyone can do to stop me. The new outpost will be built, and once we get the portal working, many changes will come to Savanna. It is inevitable."

"It seems to me I don't really have to worry much about those changes, unless you can overcome that huge stumbling block—getting the portal to work."

"It'll happen. It's just a matter of time."

"Yes, time. That is the unknown factor in your equation." Wainwright allowed himself a cheerful chuckle. "If only you had a thousand years or more."

"I won't need a thousand years. I have the best brains I could find, including myself, working on the problem. We will crack it. Don't worry."

Wainwright got out of his chair and walked over to the window. The few clouds in the sky looked like it might snow soon. Even though it was warm in the room, he felt a chill running through his body. He had spent ten winters on this planet. Some had been colder than others, but most of the time they were boring with nothing to do on Outpost Alpha. He had no interest in visiting Crystal City, especially after the snow covered the ground. His bottle was his consolation and companion. Maybe change would do him good, but at the moment, he needed a drink.

When he turned around, Daniels was gone. He wasn't sorry. He was just about to get out a bottle from the cabinet, when someone knocked on the door to his office.

"Come in," he called, wondering who it could be.

Sheppard stepped into the room "Sorry to barge in on you like this."

He brought another man with him. Tall and athletic looking, his face tanned from spending time outdoors. Though he was dressed like a farmer, Wainwright somehow had the feeling it was not his true profession. When he walked in, he scanned the room with watchful eyes, as if expecting danger.

He tipped his wide-brimmed hat and gave Wainwright a courteous nod.

Sheppard introduced the man. "This is Dennis Collins. He's one of the colonists that came on the same ship as I."

"Does that mean you know each other?" Wainwright pretended this was the first he heard of Collins.

"We are acquaintances," Sheppard acknowledged, "but we didn't meet on the ship."

Wainwright looked at Collins. "I assume you have something important to tell me. Otherwise you wouldn't be here."

Collins nodded. "What I have to tell you was actually only meant for Captain Sheppard's ears. He convinced me to talk to you. He says you can be trusted." He glanced at one of the chairs. "May I sit down? I've been on the back of my horse for hours. I'm a bit tired."

Wainwright indicated the chair. "Please, sit. I'm anxious to hear your story."

Collins chuckled. "I'm playing only a small part in it. Mostly it's about the star-portal."

Wainwright sat up straight and stared at the man. "How do you even know about the portal? You're a civilian."

"I've been talking to the Accilla."

"Where?"

"At their outpost here on Savanna."

"Not many people know the Accilla have an outpost here, especially not civilians."

"Well, I do."

"What's your connection with the Accilla?"

"They saved me from certain death, after I had been shot by a poisoned dart."

Wainwright suddenly felt like an interrogator. "Who shot you?"

With a little smile, Collins said, "One of the Snaar shot me after I shot and killed a few of them."

Wainwright held up a hand. "I'm a little confused. First the Accilla, now the Snaar. I'm curious to find out what connection you have with the Snaar. For a simple farmer, you seem to be getting around. Perhaps you should start at the beginning, but before you do, I need to have a drink."

He got up and picked a full bottle, having the distinct feeling it wouldn't stay with one drink. After a moment's hesitation, he took out three glasses. "You drink, Mr. Collins?"

"I do, but most of what I've been drinking lately has been homebrew."

"Then you will enjoy this. Brandy from one of the distillers in Crystal City. It's almost as good as the imported stuff, only much cheaper. I can't afford anything imported from Earth, not on the money the military pays." He filled the glasses, offered one to Collins and another one to Sheppard.

Collins sniffed on his glass and then took a small sip. "Good," he said, nodding approvingly. Then he downed it and wiped his mouth. "It's been awhile since I tasted something this good."

"Glad to hear." Wainwright emptied his glass. "Now, go ahead."

"What I'm going to tell you is strictly confidential. I've had one attempt on my and my family's life, and I don't want to go through that again." He paused and took a deep breath. "I won't bore you with any details. I'll tell you only what's important. Here on Savanna, I am a rancher. I raise horses and cattle. On Earth, I worked for a secret branch of the government. I was a member of a special death squad—an assassin. After being responsible for the demise of one of the drug cartels on Earth, I had to go into hiding. I changed my name, got married, and migrated to Savanna. The name of the cartel we took out was Starbrite Enterprises, which was owned by Interstellar Sunburst, the same company that owns Glowstar Research. I've seen their private army on that new outpost your Colonel Daniels is building. If they manage to get that Star-portal working, it will be in the private hands of a criminal organization that already has too much power. It will have catastrophic consequences. Colonel Daniels must be stopped and Glowstar Research shut down on Savanna, before they become too powerful."

He held out his glass. "If you don't mind, Colonel Wainwright, I'll have another one."

"Me, too." Wainwright filled the glasses. Looking at Sheppard, he noticed he hadn't touched his glass, yet. Putting down the bottle, he said, "You are in possession of dangerous information, Mr. Collins, information a civilian should not have."

"I may be a civilian now, but on Earth I worked for the government. In a way, I still do. Once you have reached a certain level, you have knowledge of issues the average citizen never hears about. Before I came here, I underwent a complete memory swipe, but I had that reversed and am again in full knowledge of what I learned while an employer of the Earth government. It is my duty, to stop what is happening here on Savanna."

"This is an alien planet, Mr. Collins. You have no powers here and nobody to back you up."

"I'm aware of that, but that won't stop me from taking certain action."

Wainwright shrugged. "It sounds very noble, even heroic, but I don't see what you can do. If you were hoping for help from the military, I must disappoint you. My hands are tied, and we are powerless. The Trading Commission runs things on Savanna. They are the law and good luck to getting help from them. The Trading Commission is as corrupt as Glowstar Research."

"That is something I also know. Don't you think it's time to change that?"

With a laugh, Wainwright said, "I'm sure every citizen on Savanna will agree with you there, but I'm afraid it will remain a pipedream. The Commission built up Savanna from the beginning. It invested a lot of money without being reimbursed from Earth or any other government. The stockholders will want their investment back with a pile of interest. Sure, it is a long-term investment, but they will not allow anyone to interfere with their plans."

"Which are?"

"To make more money, what else?"

"In the meantime, everyone pays exuberant taxes to the Trading Commission. The investors get even richer on the backs and the labor of every miner, farmer, rancher, and any other hardworking, honest citizen."

"Hasn't it always been that way? On Earth and on any planet humans decide to make their own? By the way, you never did tell me what your association is with the Snaar."

"None." Collins looked past Wainwright and gazed out of the window, his eyes unfocused. "One of my sons was murdered by the Suumir. They also kidnapped my daughter. I hunted and killed the ones responsible, but my daughter almost ended up on one of the Snaar slave ships. While trying to rescue her, I shot three of the slavers, but one of them managed to put a poisoned dart into my neck. Had it not been for the Accilla, that poison would have killed me. That's how I met the Accilla."

"Well, that was short and swift. It sounds like a simple story. Perhaps someday you will have to explain to me how you, one man, were able to kill a number of Suumir and three Snaar and get away. The Snaar have superior weapons."

Collins smiled grimly. "Yes, the Snaar do have them. You forget I'm a trained hunter of men and a killer. That's what I did on Earth."

"On Earth but not on Savanna. There you had advanced weapons and equipment at your disposal." Wainwright looked expectantly at Collins, waiting for an explanation.

The man only shrugged, saying, "If you don't mind, I don't want to go into any details on how I managed it."

"I won't press you. I hope you're aware that you are a marked man with the Snaar. They will hunt and find you to take revenge. The Snaar are ruthless killers and relentless when chasing their quarry. Be on guard, Mr. Collins." He looked at Sheppard who had been silent all this time. "Did you know any of this?"

Sheppard nodded. "Most of it. Before we came to you, we had a long and intimate conversation. I feel a certain kinship with Mr. Collins. Our careers seem to have run along the same lines and both of us received a raw deal in the end."

Wainwright studied Collins silently for a moment, wondering what he could tell him. "Like I said, I would really like to help you, but it isn't possible. I'm sorry."

"In other words, this Colonel Daniels is going to get away with what he's doing. I actually expected more from you." He got up from his chair and tipped his hat again. "Thanks for the drink. I'm sorry to have wasted your and my time."

Wainwright also rose. "To be honest, Mr. Collins, I don't know who I can trust in the military and in the government. The corruption reaches right up to the highest levels. Captain Sheppard and I have experienced it firsthand. How do you think we ended up here on this forsaken planet?"

"May I suggest something?" Sheppard broke into the conversation.

"Go ahead." Wainwright wondered what Sheppard would come up with.

"You could always go to the scouts."

"The scouts? Who are they?" Collins seemed perplexed. It was obvious he had never heard of them.

"The scouts are a huge organization. They are almost like another branch of the military, except they are independent and have nothing to do with the military." Sheppard smiled. "Scouts and troopers don't play well together. In the eyes of a trooper, the scouts have no discipline. The scouts don't think much of us, either. They think we are just a bunch of robots with no feelings and interests other than playing with guns and military hardware."

"What do the scouts actually do?"

"The scouts are usually the first ones to explore and map a newly discovered planet. They might even set up a base before the military does. The scouts are also trouble-shooters sent to fix problems, perhaps negotiate between settlers and the indigenous population. Things like that. I don't know that much about them, either, but from what I'm told they are incorruptible."

"This is the first I even hear of them. Do they have a base on Savanna?"

"Not a real base, but they do have a small office in Crystal City."

"What can the scouts do, though? It doesn't seem they have any actual power."

"About twenty years ago, I was on a planet called Epsilon. I was under the command of a Scout Master by the name of Stonewall. He was as tough as any trooper. He took a stand against the Trading Commission, and he got my full respect. Colonel Daniels mentioned his name, and it seems to me he is somewhat afraid of Stonewall. He told me that Stonewall and his team were successful in operating a star-portal on Salamander. According to Daniels, Stonewall has powerful friends. I think the scouts are your best bet."

"I appreciate the information. It will certainly be worthwhile looking into it. I have nothing to lose." Collins turned to leave. "I guess I'll be going then. It's a long ride home." His gaze fell on Sheppard. "Perhaps you'll be so kind as to have someone bring my gun belt. I'll feel safer out there with my colt strapped to my hip."

"You're not really thinking of leaving today?" Sheppard looked at Wainwright. "Colonel, we can't let the man ride off like this. It's nearly evening. He'll never make it back to Crystal City before dark."

"It's no problem," Collins said. "I brought a small tent I can sleep in."

"Nonsense. The nights are getting cold, and I heard someone spotted a family of droocor roaming the area."

Wainwright agreed. "Captain Sheppard is right. We won't let you leave tonight. How about joining me for dinner this evening in my private quarters?" His glance moved to Sheppard. "I'd like you to be there, also, Captain, but for now, show our guest one of the rooms where he can spend the night in a comfortable bed." He allowed himself a chuckle. "As comfortable as army cots can be."

"I appreciate your invitation, and I will accept. As for the army cot, believe me, nothing can be worse than sleeping on hard rocky ground during a downpour. As a rancher, I'm used to sleeping outdoors. A cot will be a luxury."

[25]

IT DIDN'T MATTER HOW MANY TIMES A MAN STEPPED ONTO THE alien soil of a new planet and breathed the air for the first time. It was always an exhilarating feeling, and it brought back memories of first visits to other alien planets.

This time it wasn't much different.

Stonewall looked across the tarmac. In the near distance, he saw the outskirts of Crystal City, the only large city belonging to the humans on Savanna. He had done his research and knew there were other human settlements on this planet, but they were small and insignificant. Apparently, before Crystal City began to flourish, a few settlers tried to establish a city further south, but conditions there had not been favorable. Now the only evidence that humans had tried and failed were crumbling ruins, covered by dirt and vegetation.

Taking a deep breath, he turned to look at the scout ship that brought him and his team to Savanna. His team of specialists was waiting inside the ship for him to give the okay to disembark. There were only twelve, but each one was handpicked by him. He could rely on each member to obey his orders without questions.

Perhaps not all twelve of them, because three weren't human, in addition to being females.

As he studied the big ship, a slim figure appeared in the doorway and climbed down the short staircase. He knew it was Gorana. She was a captain in the Anorian Space Force. They had met on Salamander, where she joined his team. At first, he had not been enthused about her presence, but she had proven herself to be a valuable ally.

In the Anorian race, the females were the dominant gender. Anyone not familiar with their species might only see a beautiful and seductive alien woman, by all appearances soft and cuddly, especially since they had the habit of not wearing any clothes and freely displaying their curvy bodies. Stonewall knew different. Anorian females were aggressive and formidable warriors. Fortunately, since joining his team, she had not insisted in parading around naked. Instead, she wore the scout's uniform like the other members.

"It seems the humans have managed to add another planet of great value to their empire," she said as she came closer.

He gave her a friendly smile. "I'm sure the Anorians were not unaware of the existence of Savanna."

"We weren't, but we had no interest in this planet. Of course, that will change after this." She took a breath and held it for a moment before exhaling it sharply. "The air is a bit too much on the dry side for me," she observed.

He chuckled. "Perhaps I should be relieved about that, otherwise you might challenge our presence here, the way you did on Salamander."

"Salamander was different. The air was more to our liking. I can't see us having much interest in Savanna, at least not for colonizing."

"I am happy to hear that. One worry off my mind."

He smiled as he said it. He and Gorana had become good friends in the short time they knew each other. She would never go behind his back and betray him, not even to her own people.

"Weren't we supposed to be met by one of the local scouts?" She scanned the area. "I don't see anyone." She hunched up her shoulders. "I find the temperature cool. A good thing I started wearing clothes."

"As I understand it, it is still winter in this hemisphere. Actually, I was expecting snow." Stonewall squinted against the bright burning disk in the sky. "The primary of this star system is almost a twin of the sun in the human solar system, as is this planet. I believe it is time we bring some order to this place."

He spied a moving object heading for them from the direction of the city. "Someone is coming," he said.

As the object came closer, it turned out to be a wooden carriage drawn by a couple of large animals. "Horses," he exclaimed loudly. "This definitely is a backward planet."

"I've never seen horses," Gorana admitted.

The carriage came to a halt, and the two men sitting on a seat in front of the carriage, climbed down. One man wore the scout's uniform and the other man was clearly a trooper. He was tall, with short-cropped black hair. A laser pistol hung from the wide belt that circled his narrow hips.

The scout stopped in front of Stonewall and laid his flat hand against his chest. "Welcome to Savanna, Master Scout," he greeted him. "I'm Scout Linklatter." Pointing at the trooper, he said, "This is Captain Sheppard from Outpost Alpha."

Stonewall scrutinized the trooper. "I wasn't expecting a military man to come and meet me here."

"May I inquire why not?"

"Because one of my jobs here is to investigate the military."

"I'm aware of that." Sheppard smiled. "It was my idea to bring you here, Master Scout Stonewall."

Stonewall peered at him. "You look familiar. Have we met?"

"Yes, we have, sir. On Epsilon. I was one of the troopers stationed there."

"Epsilon, that's over twenty years ago."

"That's right, but I remember it quite clearly, especially how you dealt with that gang of terrorists in Epsilon City."

That incident had been on Stonewall's mind many times. "The Tunnel Rats. It isn't something I'm proud of, but Commander Chelzic put me into that position by making me Chief of Security. He left me no choice."

"I know, sir. All the troopers there were in agreement that you did the right thing. You gained a lot of respect that day."

"That's comforting to hear." He gave the trooper a closer look. "I must apologize, Captain Sheppard. Even though you look familiar, I don't really recall you."

"That's okay, sir. I was just a rookie then and used to being ignored."

Stonewall held out a hand and smiled. "I won't ignore you again. How would you like to become my special advisor here on Savanna?"

"I would be honored, but I'll have to clear that with Colonel Wainwright. He's the commander at Outpost Alpha and my superior."

"I'll handle that. I'll have to visit Outpost Alpha, anyway, to get more information about the situation on Savanna. What about this Colonel Daniels? He's the main reason I'm here. I had him investigated, and what I discovered is disturbing, to say the least. I will go into more details when I meet with Colonel Wainwright. By the way, I also checked him out."

"I don't know what you found out about him, but he's a good man. He didn't deserve to be shipped to this godforsaken place."

"I can't promise that I can do anything about that, but one thing I can promise, things will change on Savanna. For one thing, you will have a governor. The rule of the Trading Commission has come to an end."

"People will be happy to hear that. How long will we have to wait for that to happen?"

Stonewall chuckled. "No time it all. As it happens, Governor Armstrong is part of a group of people that has accompanied me and my team to Savanna. As soon as he is settled in, he will begin his duties as governor of this planet."

"How will he enforce his position? Does he have a large staff with him? What about security guards? Where will he stay?"

"Many and good questions. To answer your last question first, I trust accommodations for the governor have been arranged by Scout Linklatter and his office." When he looked at Linklatter, the scout nodded. Stonewall continued, "They will be temporary. A Builder-Ship is going to arrive within a few days. It will erect a governor's mansion, befitting for the residence of the most powerful and important man on Savanna. Governor Armstrong's family and his staff will join him as soon as everything is ready. Security? You will provide that." Stonewall smiled. "I'm certain Outpost Alpha can spare a few troopers."

Sheppard returned Stonewall's smile, but Stonewall could see he was doubtful.

"It all sounds so easy and simple, but how are you going to deal with Colonel Daniels, his private army, and the Trading Commission? They will laugh in your face when you tell them their game is over. They will not transfer their rule to a scout. I hope you brought a large army with you. Those mercenaries guarding Daniels' new fortress are tough."

"My men are tougher. Also, I'm not worried about what Colonel Daniels and the Trading Commission will or won't do. The High Senate has decided to give Savanna special status because of its unique location and the presence of the star-portals. Savanna will not be a colony of Earth but an independent planet with its own representative in the senate. Those are the details that will be worked out as things develop."

Sheppard regarded Stonewall with a strange expression on his face. "I don't envy you. I can see difficult times ahead. It may be impossible to achieve those plans."

Stonewall nodded. "Difficult, yes. Impossible? No. It will happen, and I want you to be a part of it."

"I'm intrigued by the challenge. It's been awhile since I was part of something big."

"Then it's settled. Like I said, I will handle Colonel Wainwright." Stonewall touched his ear piece to contact his team on board the ship. "Begin debarking."

A large portal opened on one side of the ship, and one after the other a dozen shiny spheres floated into the open, like a swarm of giant insects. They settled on the ground not far from the ship. A gift from the Spiders or Kraach, as they called their species. Actually, not really a gift. The payment had been the key to the star-portal on Salamander. Salabet, one of his team members, had negotiated the deal with the Spiders.

Stonewall spied her among the other eleven members of his team as they followed the spheres out of the ship. Salabet was another non-human. Her body had been grown artificially in a vat to make her human in appearance, but her mind was that of a Spider. Kraach scientists transplanted her brain into the human-like body after her real body had been destroyed in an accident.

The third female in the group was Red, also not human. A female Accilla. She had chosen to appear in the form of a redheaded woman with deep-green eyes and a body designed to attract a healthy human male as surely as a magnet attracts a piece of metal.

His gaze shifted to the male members of the group. Five of them had been with him on Salamander. Robert Lee, Marvin Denchuk, Michael Delrosi, Raymond McLaughlin, and Randhir Sandhu. Five men he trusted with his life. The other four, just as trustworthy, had joined him after the events on Salamander.

"That's my team," Stonewall pointed out.

"I assume these are your closest associates, each one designated for a specific task," Sheppard said. "Quite a large and impressive group. How many soldiers did you bring?"

"This is it. There are no others." Stonewall chuckled, amused by Sheppard's expression. Having expected the question about the number of soldiers, he hadn't been surprised when Sheppard asked. "Don't let the fact they are scouts fool you. They are highly trained and as capable as any union trooper. Actually, I can safely say any one of them will defeat any trooper when it comes to skills with weapons and hand-to-hand combat."

Shephard looked skeptical. "I don't doubt their abilities, but come on, Master Scout, to compare them with troopers that think and breathe mental and physical discipline? Men and women with minds manipulated to the point of being brainwashed by living in a constant state of readiness for conflict? I find that hard to swallow."

"I don't blame you for thinking that. However, you will soon get the chance to see my team in action. It will change the way you think about scouts."

"They will have to be superior fighters if you want to go up against Daniels' mercenaries. They are a tough lot with no allegiance to anyone but Glowstar Research and now Colonel Daniels. They don't care about the law, only about the money they get paid."

"They will discover that this time they made the wrong choice. The only compensation they will receive for the work they're performing is either a quick death or spending the rest of their lives on a prison planet."

"What about Glowstar Research?"

"It will be shut down, the executives arrested."

Shephard still seemed unconvinced. "You're making is sound so matter-of-factly. I wish I had your confidence. I'm still saying it won't be easy. There will be bloodshed."

Stonewall let out a sigh. "Unfortunately, no conflict is ever easily resolved. There are always fatalities."

"I'm curious about those spheres?" Sheppard wondered. "I don't recognize them. What are they?"

"Warcraft. Sealed units piloted by an artificial mind. Ancient technology given to us by the Spiders. They have been reprogrammed to obey their new commander, me."

With a nod of sudden comprehension, Sheppard said, "Now I understand your confidence. I assume there is no defense against those warcraft?"

Stonewall shook his head. "There isn't. They cannot be destroyed. We are fortunate to have established a good relationship with certain factions of the Spider race. Weapons like this are just a small sample of what they possess. I've always warned against starting a war with the Spiders. It would be a war we can't win. They have weapons far superior to ours. I tried to convey this to Commander Chelzic, but he was convinced the Solar Union Space Navy could match anything the Spiders might throw at us."

"I remember Commander Chelzic, quite well." Sheppard chuckled. "He was a bit of a pompous ass."

Stonewall made a snorting sound through his nose. "That's an understatement. He was a pompous ass through and through. An arrogant son of a bitch, to be blunt. He would have started a war with the Spiders without thinking of the consequences."

"I apologize for interrupting, sir," Gorana said beside him. "We should get started." She glanced at Sheppard. "I am Gorana. I'm looking forward to working with you."

Sheppard peered at her closely. "You're not human," he observed.

She gave him a silvery laugh. Her split tongue played for a quick moment across her full lips. "You've noticed."

"How can I not? Just looking into your golden reptilian eyes told me enough. You're an Anorian. I'm surprised to see you wearing clothes," he said with a little smile.

She laughed again. "Master Scout does not permit going naked, at least not while I'm under his command." She approached him and said with a lowered voice, "I could always make an exception should we find each other alone somewhere. You're a handsome specimen of a human."

Sheppard chuckled. "Thanks for the compliment. I don't believe Master Scout Stonewall would approve as long as you're under his command."

Stonewall shook his head, though not because he disapproved of Gorana's behavior. She was free to do anything she wanted. He didn't control her. Being a member of his team was strictly voluntarily, but he didn't want Sheppard to get the wrong impression about the discipline or lack of discipline in his team.

Anorians couldn't read minds, usually, but they were sensitive empaths. He wasn't surprised when Gorana turned around to look at him. "Sorry, Colonel. I got carried away, as usual."

He didn't miss Sheppard raising his eyebrows. "Colonel? I had no idea there are ranks like that in the scouts' organization?"

"It's not common knowledge. Neither is the fact that we have a secret security branch. I'm actually a colonel with Scouts Security."

"This is getting more and more interesting. What else will I find out about the scouts?"

Stonewall smiled. "That most of us, including me, are not really much into making small talk. This is the longest conversation I've had with someone other than a scout. I don't know what you have planned for the rest of the day, but why don't you get to know the members of my team while we are planning strategy? Scout Linklatter, how many passengers fit into that carriage of yours?"

"There is room for six people inside."

"Good. Perhaps you could take Governor Armstrong and his advisor with you to Crystal City and show them their temporary quarters. I'm almost positive Dr. Spinelly and his wife would also be interested in traveling inside one of these antique vehicles. They'll get a kick out of it."

"Is that the scientist couple?"

"Dr. Spinelly and his wife were part of the team working at the portal on Salamander. I assume you have arranged accommodations for them also?"

"I have."

"Then it's settled. Gorana, be so kind and get them. Take Captain Sheppard with you. He's probably anxious to take a look at our ship."

———

SHEPPARD HADN'T BEEN AT THE NEW OUTPOST FOR QUITE SOME time. He was surprised to find how fast it had grown. The tents were all gone. Instead, he saw wooden structures with clay tiles covering the roofs. The windows were sheets of transparent plastic, and the doors had locks on them.

The whole outpost was surrounded by a high electric fence. It left no doubt that Daniels believed in security and wasn't taking any chances.

Stonewall and his team arrived in the early morning hours. They had traveled in two armored vehicles floating on magnetic fields.

Sheppard accompanied Stonewall as he walked to the gate. The two armed guards blocked their way as he and Stonewall tried to enter the compound.

"Step aside, you fools!" Sheppard said with an authoritative voice. "Don't you recognize me? I'm Captain Sheppard, and I want to speak to Colonel Daniels."

"We recognize you," one of the guards said coldly. "We have strict orders from the colonel not to let you enter. He doesn't trust you."

"He doesn't trust me? What kind of crap is that? I'm giving you a direct order. Move or I'll have you arrested for disobeying an order from a superior."

The guard put his hand on his sidearm. "You have no authority here. We are not troopers of the Solar Union. We have only one commander, and that is Colonel Daniels. Turn around and walk away before I shoot you!"

Sheppard looked at Stonewall. "Did you hear that? He's going to shoot us. Imagine that."

"I heard. He threatened us. We can't let that pass, now can we?" As he spoke, he punched the guard in the stomach, doubling him over. Next, he pushed the barrel of his laser against the guard's jaw.

Sheppard acted at the same time. Kneeing the other guard in the groin with full force, he brought his balled fist down hard in his neck when he folded. The guard collapsed without a sound and lay unmoving in the dirt.

Stonewall gave his laser another push. "One false move and it'll be your last one," he said with a hard voice. He reached around and removed the man's weapon. "You won't need this anymore. Walk slowly toward that first vehicle and don't even think about running away. My men will be watching your every move. If they don't like what they see, you'll never reach that vehicle alive. Understand?"

The guard grunted something and sneered. "A scout? How far do you two clowns think you'll get? There are twenty trained and heavily armed soldiers on this outpost. If anyone dies, it'll be you."

"I don't believe so." Stonewall gave him a smug smile. "Why don't you look up and tell me what you see."

The guard looked. Sheppard knew what he would see without checking it out, but he looked anyway. He didn't have to count. There were twelve shiny spheres floating about a hundred feet above them, waiting for Stonewall's orders. They would burn the outpost down until nothing but ashes remained should he order them to, but that was not the plan. Stonewall needed the buildings. They would be the foundation of their new base on Savanna.

"What are those?" the guard asked.

"That's my persuasion unit, my enforcers if you want. Indestructible war machines like you've never seen. Those twenty trained mercenaries will be dead before they realize what they're up against if they resist. I've changed my mind. I want you to go into the mess hall and interrupt everyone's breakfast with the good news that's coming their way. Make sure you tell them what the situation is out here. Can you do that?"

The guard glared at him. "I'm not an imbecile or a child. I hope you don't shoot me in the back when I walk away."

"I won't. Scout's honors." Stonewall grinned. "I've never broken that principle, but..." He shrugged. "There is always a first time for everything. Now go!"

As they watched the guard hurrying toward the mess hall, Sheppard asked, "Do you think they'll give us trouble?"

"Mercenaries are unpredictable. Anything can happen."

A few moments later the door to the mess hall opened and a couple of men in black and brown tightfitting outfits appeared, holding long-barreled rifles. Both men aimed them at the spheres in the sky and fired. Two bundles of raw energy spewed from their rifles and blue, fiery glow momentarily bathed two of the spheres. When the fire died, the spheres floated unharmed above them.

"I believe a lesson is needed." Stonewall spoke in a cold tone. A pencil-thin beam of light shot from the nearest sphere. It hit one of the two men in the head. He collapsed with his rifle still aimed at the sphere. The other one turned and disappeared inside the mess hall.

"I don't like bloodshed, but sometimes it cannot be avoided," Stonewall remarked. "I hope he can persuade his comrades to give up, but I'll kill each one of them should it become necessary." He turned and looked back at the two parked vehicles. "Perhaps it's time the others join us. I need to convince Colonel Daniels that his time on Savanna is up."

With the rest of the team behind him, Stonewall walked through the gate. Half of them entered the mess hall to take care of the mercenaries inside. They others accompanied Stonewall and Sheppard.

One of the buildings was larger than the others. It wasn't difficult to guess it was Colonel Daniels' office and quarters.

Their presence was challenged by a guard inside the building, but before he could sound the alarm, Robert Lee shot him with one quick burst of his laser.

Colonels Daniels sat behind a wide desk built from real wood. He looked up, obviously annoyed, when the group rushed into his room. "What the Hell?" he bellowed. Then he spied Sheppard. "I hope you have a good explanation for barging into my office unannounced. How did you even get past my guards?"

Sheppard grinned. "One is asleep, and we convinced the other one it would be in his best interest to cooperate."

Daniels glared at Stonewall. "A scout," he said, sarcasm dripping in his voice. "What's so important you would bring a scout onto my outpost? Who is this guy anyway?"

"I'm Terrex Stonewall, Colonel Daniels. You may have heard of me." Stonewall spoke in a quiet tone, as if ready for a friendly chat.

Daniels gaped. "You're Stonewall? The famous Master Scout Terrex Stonewall?"

"Actually, I am Colonel Stonewall of Scouts Security."

"Colonel Stonewall of Scouts Security," Daniels repeated with a chuckle. "Are you telling me the scouts are playing at being soldiers now? That's absurd. Scouts are not trooper material, otherwise they wouldn't be scouts."

"I never claimed to be a trooper. I'm still a scout, but my rank is Colonel. Scouts Security is just another branch of Scouts Investigations, except we are a highly trained unit. The government sends us into situations where others can't go. We fix things. We prevent things from happening."

"Sounds interesting, but what do you want here? What do you think you'll fix on Savanna?"

"Everything." Stonewall stepped closer to Daniels' desk. "Colonel Daniels, I hereby place you under arrest. You are charged with collaborating with a criminal organization and conspiracy to commit crimes against the Solar Union. Please rise and step around your desk. Do not try to resist or take any hostile action against us. My men have orders to shoot and kill should you refuse to cooperate. Whatever you chose to do it doesn't really matter to me."

Daniels stared at Stonewall, a stunned expression on his face. He closed his eyes for a moment and shook his head, giving the distinct impression of a man who wished he were somewhere else. When he opened his eyes again, he broke into loud laughter. "I didn't know what to expect when you waltzed in. Anything but this, though. How many times did you have to rehearse that speech? Quite impressive, I admit. What is going on in that tiny scout's brain of yours, Stonewall? Do you know who you are dealing with, you idiot? I have connections to people so powerful they'll chop you and your little group here into pieces so small nobody will ever know you existed. Now, get the hell out of my office before I call my men. You'll never leave this compound alive."

"If anyone has a good chance of not leaving here alive, it's you, Daniels. Don't count on any help from your soldiers for hire. By now they'll all be disarmed and shackled. You didn't think I came here with only these men? All right, let's make this quick."

Stonewall gave the two nearest to Daniels a sign. One was Robert Lee and the other one, the Anorian female. Gorana. Sheppard remembered her name.

"An Anorian," Daniels sneered. "It seems you have joined forces with an alien species. This smells a lot like treason to me. If anyone needs to be arrested it is you, Scout Stonewall!" He pointed an accusing finger. "You have no right to be here, and you certainly don't have any powers on Savanna. I can have an army here in a short time, and I have the power to command a battle cruiser to protect my investors' and my own interests on this planet. Do you understand?" He fairly shouted his last words.

"Don't be melodramatic. For your information, I have absolute power, backed by the authority of the High Senate, and I outrank anyone, regardless of the position they hold. Right now, I'm the highest-ranking Government representative on Savanna. I even outrank the Governor until further notice."

"We have no governor."

"You have now. His name is Phillip Armstrong, Governor Phillip William Armstrong. He's already in Crystal City. Yesterday, we've arrested everyone in the office of Glowstar Research, and the place has been shut down. Just for your information. Now I'm asking you one last time to come peacefully and resign to the fact that your scheme has failed. Resist and your career and life will end here."

Daniels made one last effort. "You're making a big mistake. I could be of great help and a powerful ally. Do you have any idea what is going on here? What we are working on?"

"We do. It isn't such a big mystery. You're trying to unlock the secrets of the star-portal." He looked at Gorana and Lee. "Cuff him and take him away."

EPILOGUE

"It's hard to believe that a year has passed since Randolph was murdered. So much has happened since then." Traverse scanned the sky and pointed. "Look, Dad, this is the third one I've seen today. Do you have any idea what is actually going on?"

Collins was pleased to hear him say Dad. Then again, why shouldn't he? Only Kristie and he knew the truth. There had been no reason to tell Traverse and Lisa that he was not their real father but an imposter. He loved them both as if they were his own children. Nothing had changed his feelings for them. The loss of Randolph was still painful, even though he hadn't been his son.

"You know when it comes to the government, us private citizens are never fully informed about things. It's called politics, son. My friendship with Captain Sheppard helps to get a few tidbits once-in-awhile, but he doesn't tell me everything."

"You must know something. Come on, this is your son you're talking to. Don't keep secrets from me." Traverse laughed when Collins frowned. "Tell me what you know. I can keep my mouth shut."

"There are really no secrets to tell. I've heard rumors that they are making progress with the star-portal, and I'm inclined to believe them. Apparently, ever since Governor Armstrong was sworn in, the status of Savanna has changed. No longer are we considered a Class

Five planet where modern machinery and weapons are forbidden. You'll be seeing more and more aircraft. Most of them are military, but not all belong to us humans. The Accilla and the Anorians aren't keeping their presence here a secret any longer. Perhaps that's a good thing. At least we don't have to worry about the Snaar anymore."

"Do you really think they would have come after you?"

Collins shrugged. "I was told to be vigilant all the time. Once the Snaar mark you, they won't give up until they find you."

"They might still be a threat. Maybe they're just biding their time. I would still be careful."

"Don't worry, I will. By the way, how are things with you and Ernina?"

"You know how they are. I love her, and nothing will ever change that. She's beautiful, intelligent, and good-hearted. She loves me, too, and I want to be with her all the time. It doesn't matter to me that she isn't human. Why do you ask?"

"Your mother and I want to make sure you're happy. Should you marry Ernina, the road ahead won't be easy for both of you. There are plenty of people out there that don't approve of such unions. Should you have children, they will face hardship. They will be neither human nor Suumir."

"Ernina and I have discussed that. We don't care what people think. We may never have any children, anyway. From what I heard, chances of mixed couples having offspring are low, and that's just fine with us. We can be happy without children, as long as we love each other." He gave Collins a questioning look. "I know we've never really talked about this, but tell me honestly, do you and Mom approve of Ernina?"

"We have no ill feelings toward her. She is a lovely girl, and as far as Mom and I are concerned, we have no objections should you want to choose her as your life's partner. You're old enough to make your own decisions. You must realize, though, you can never get married legally, not even in church."

"We don't care, Dad. It's only a piece of paper." Traverse smiled. "As far as the church goes, I'm not a church-goer, anyways."

"Neither am I, but your mother is. We have to respect that. Going to church has helped her tremendously to cope with Randolph's death."

"Can we change the subject, Dad?"

"Of course. What's on your mind?"

"I talked to Roberto Sanchez. He told me that Governor Armstrong is creating a militia, and they are recruiting right now. He's thinking about joining." He hesitated. "I've been throwing it around in my mind, also. It wouldn't be a permanent position, you know. I could still help out on the ranch. It isn't as if you really need me. I mean, there are plenty of ranch-hands around. You wouldn't even miss me."

Collins shook his head. "Perhaps I wouldn't miss you in the field, but your mother and I would surely miss having you around. You're our son, Traverse. You're family. Nobody can ever replace you. We've lost one son. We don't want to lose another one."

"You wouldn't lose me. I'd still be here, except not every day. I'm not joining the military. This is a civilian army to keep law and order if the need should ever arise. Once the initial training period is over, I'd be in the Reserves and free to pursue my regular activities. You'll have to face it, someday I will have to move out."

"It's not that simple. You're supposed to take over the ranch one day."

"What about Lisa? She and her future husband could run the ranch."

"They could if she ever finds a husband."

"She seems to like Roberto. They'd make a fine couple."

Collins nodded. "They would, except he doesn't have any interest in farming. You say he wants to join the militia. His father told me that Roberto wants to become a blacksmith and move into the city." He chuckled. "Nothing wrong with that, except there goes the prospect of him being a candidate for running our ranch someday."

"Winter is coming. I'm not really needed on the ranch. The ranch-hands are quite capably of looking after the horses and the cattle without me. I'd be back in spring." He looked at Collins with a pleading look. "Savanna will be playing a vital role on the galactic stage. I want to be part of this new Savanna. I want to be involved in things that make me feel I'm doing something important. I want people to remember me as someone who helped shape the future of this planet. You understand what I'm saying, Dad?"

"I understand, more than you know. You have high ambitions, and I'm beginning to realize your place in this new world is not on this ranch, and I can't really blame you." He looked up at the sky. "You know, when we came to Savanna, I wanted nothing more than get away from the past, start a new life. I was elated when I inherited this ranch, the horses, the cattle, and this huge tract of land surrounding it. All this suddenly belonged to me, the land, the forests, the lakes, and the streams. It was like a dream, almost unreal. Of course, reality has set in since then. Don't get me wrong. I still love it all, and I'm grateful for having been given the chance to start all over, but at the same time, I recognize how much hard work and dedication it takes to keep it all going. Sometimes, it's overwhelming. That is one of the reasons I would like to have you by my side, but I don't want to hold you back. You must choose your own destiny, and I would never want to trap you into doing something you don't want to do."

He turned to look at Traverse and saw the agony in his eyes.

"I would never want to hurt you, Dad. I love you too much for that. If you need me by your side, I will stay."

Collins pulled Traverse to him and held him for a moment. Traverse patted his back. "We're family, Dad," he said softly. "We must stick together."

Collins let go of him and smiled. "Because we are family, we must not be slaves to each other's needs. You follow your heart, and I will support you in anything you choose to do. Perhaps, someday you'll be an important politician on Savanna. I would be proud of you."

A bright flash and the sound of an explosion made them both face the sky.

"It seems a Crow ship has just dropped out of Over-Space. This is the second one this month," Collins said.

"Why do they have to come out this close to the surface of the planet? One of these days they'll miscalculate and materialize inside," Traverse mused.

"I doubt that. The Crows are an ancient race, and their technology is far superior to that of most of the other races. Nobody has the ability to travel as fast as they do in Over-Space, and they will never share that secret. A month ago, I never even heard of the Crows. Now they're just another of the many different species populating our galaxy."

Traverse nodded. "Also, another one showing interest in our planet. There'll be more. We have to make sure we don't lose our right to live here. Savanna is our home now."

THE END

——

Don't miss out on your next favorite book!

Join the Melange Books mailing list at
www.melange-books.com/mail.html

THANK YOU FOR READING

Did you enjoy this book?

We invite you to leave a review at the website of your choice, such as Goodreads, Amazon, Barnes & Noble, etc.

DID YOU KNOW THAT LEAVING A REVIEW...

- Helps other readers find books they may enjoy.
- Gives you a chance to let your voice be heard.
- Gives authors recognition for their hard work.
- Doesn't have to be long. A sentence or two about why you liked the book will do.

ABOUT THE AUTHOR

Herbert lives near Winnipeg, Canada. He spends his free time spinning tales about imaginary worlds and the strange creatures inhabiting them. His first published story 'The Anniversary Gift' appeared in 'Sweet Revenge' published by Midnight Showcase. Even though he writes in other genres, his love is Science Fiction. He enjoys building alien worlds and societies. Most of his stories contain an element of Erotica. All of his books are available from Melange Books.

Website: www.fictitioustales.weebly.com
Blog: hegro.blogspot.com
Blog: hergros.blogspot.com
Email: hegro@shaw.ca

ALSO BY HERBERT GROSSHANS

Novels
Bullet of Revenge

A Matter of Justice

Mark of the Cobra

Orola

Orion

Rhodar Series
Clouds Over Maridaan

Operation Stargate Series
Codename Salamander

Seeds of Chaos Duology
Eden's Gate

Hell's Gate

Stardogs Duology
Return to Redsky

Redemption

Stars in Chains Duology
Slave

Liberator

A Stonewall Chronicles Novel
Outpost Epsilon

A New Dawn